Praise for *The Nightmare Affair*

"*The Nightmare Affair* is brimming with wit and charm, along with plenty of mysteries that kept me guessing to the very end. Mindee Arnett has created a brand-new school of magic to delight and enthrall us, and I'm sure I won't be the only reader impatiently awaiting the next adventure at Arkwell Academy."

—Marissa Meyer, *New York Times* bestselling author of *Cinder*

"Arnett offers quick pacing and plenty of plot twists."

—*School Library Journal*

"The scrappy first-person narration and integration of frightening dreamscapes make Arnett's debut a fun paranormal mystery."   —*Publishers Weekly*

"A half-muggle teenager acquires new powers, meets hunky boys, and saves the world."   —*Booklist*

"Mindee Arnett has a knack for magic. The world of Nightmares, Sirens, Wizards, and Demons at Arkwell Academy is wondrous and strange, yet so human and well-drawn that you get the feeling you might stumble into it by accident if you go out wandering too late. *The Nightmare Affair* is whimsical and wild. I read it too fast. What's next, Arnett?"

—Kendare Blake, author of *Anna Dressed in Blood*

~The~
Nightmare Affair

MINDEE ARNETT

TOR
TEEN

A Tom Doherty Associates Book

NEW YORK

THE NIGHTMARE AFFAIR

A Tor Teen Book
Published by Tom Doherty Associates, LLC
175 Fifth Avenue
New York, NY 10010

www.tor-forge.com

Tor® is a registered trademark of Tom Doherty Associates, LLC.

The Library of Congress has cataloged the hardcover edition as follows:

Arnett, Mindee.
    The Nightmare affair / Mindee Arnett.—1st ed.
        p. cm.
    ISBN 978-0-7653-3333-9 (hardcover)
    ISBN 978-1-4668-0067-0 (e-book)
  1. Magic—Fiction.   2. Supernatural—Fiction.   3. Dreams—Fiction.
4. Boarding schools—Fiction.   5. Schools—Fiction.   I. Title
    PZ7.A7343 Ni 2013
    [Fic]—dc23

                                                    2012038823

ISBN 978-0-7653-3336-0 (trade paperback)

Tor Teen books may be purchased for educational, business, or promotional use. For information on bulk purchases, please contact Macmillan Corporate and Premium Sales Department at 1-800-221-7945, extension 5442, or write specialmarkets@macmillan.com.

First Edition: March 2013
First Trade Paperback Edition: February 2014

Printed in the United States of America

0 9 8 7 6 5 4 3 2 1

To Adam, Inara, and Tanner, for being my foundation,
my purpose, and my heart

Acknowledgments

Dusty and Eli aren't the only ones whose dreams come true. Mine did. You're holding it in your hands right now. But it's one that never would've happened without the support of a lot of people.

Firstly, thanks to God and his Son from whom all good things come.

Thanks also to Suzie Townsend, my rock-star agent and the book's first champion. I will be forever grateful; your support and guidance have changed my life. To Sarah Goldberg for pulling me out of the slush pile, and to the entire team of New Leaf Literary and Media—you all are the best.

To my wonderful editor, Whitney Ross. Thank you for first loving this book and then for making it better. The experience has been magical. To Kate Forester for my beautiful cover art. Also thanks to the entire team at Tor Teen for taking my little Pinocchio of a story and turning it into a real book—Lisa Davis, my production editor; Seth Lerner, the art director; Jane Liddle, the copy editor; Sally Feller, my publicist; and John Morrone, the proofreader. And, of course, to Tom Doherty and Kathleen Doherty for giving my book and so many others such a fabulous home.

To my amazing critique partner, Lori M. Lee, who is not only a fine writer, but also the absolute best at providing insightful feedback and infectious enthusiasm. You made the dark days bright. To Cat York for making the world of my book come to life through her gorgeous art. And to my awesome beta readers: Mallory Hayes, Leigh Menninger, Ashley Aynes, Katherine Hazen, and Jamie Stryker.

To Barb Ryan, my sixth-grade teacher, who opened my eyes to the possibility of writing my own stories. And to Sharon Rab, my first creative-writing teacher, who showed me the beauty of language and character.

To my parents, Betty and Phil Garybush, for your love and encouragement. Thank you, Mom, for bestowing on me your love of reading and for teaching me to be strong and independent. To my dad, Jim Gaver, for exposing me to the wonders of all things fantasy and sci-fi. To my brother-in-law, Jay Sharritt, for your enthusiastic reads and awesome analytical feedback. And also the biggest of thanks to my sister, Amanda Sharritt—you are my first reader, my ideal reader. I write them all for you, Sis.

To my children, Inara and Tanner, for giving my life purpose and filling it with laughter and joy like I've never known before. And last, but never least, to my husband, Adam. Thank you for your constant love and support and for always keeping my feet grounded. You are my rock.

And finally, to you, dear reader. You give stories life, and that makes you the only real magickind I know.

The
Nightmare Affair

❧ 1 ❧

Scene of the Crime

Breaking and entering wasn't as easy as it looked in the movies. Especially not from the second story of a house in the suburbs. Yet there I was, perched on the ledge by my tippy toes and tugging on the stupid window that refused to budge even though I could see it wasn't locked. My feet were starting to cramp.

I gave the window another hard tug, and it came free at once, smacking the top of the frame with a loud thump. The force of it knocked me off balance, and I tumbled inside, landing on my face.

Way to go, Dusty, I thought.

But it could've been worse. Might've gone the other way.

Panicked by the noise I was making, I sat up, certain the bedroom's occupant would be coming at me with a baseball bat any second. My heart felt like a jackhammer trying to break its way through my chest. I froze, listening for movement but heard only the soft sounds of someone sleeping.

I looked up and saw a huge bed towering over me. A repugnant smell, like the inside of a gym locker, filled my nose. I glanced down and realized I was sitting on a pile of clothes, including what appeared to be several pairs of dirty boxer shorts. *Gross.*

I stood and tugged the bottom of my fitted black tee down around my hips, taking a deep breath. I could smell the person's dreams from here. Those dreams were the reason I'd broken in. I wasn't some criminal or weirdo who liked watching people sleep or anything. I was just an average sixteen-year-old girl who happened to be the offspring of a normal human father and a mother who was a Nightmare.

Literally.

She was one of those mythic creatures who sat on your chest while you were asleep and gave you bad dreams, the kind where you woke up struggling to breathe. Some stories said that Nightmares were demons (not true), while others said they were "hags," as in scary old women who lived in the forest and abducted lost kids to cook for supper (more true, although I didn't recommend saying so to my mother).

Only kidding. Moira Nimue-Everhart didn't eat children, but she did eat the stuff dreams were made of—*fictus.* Nightmares had to dream-feed to live, including me.

I approached the side of the bed. The occupant was lying on his stomach. Go figure. The subject—I refused to think of him as a victim—was almost always on his stomach. At least this guy didn't sleep in the buff, too. Not that the red boxers hid much. The sight of his naked back stunned me. It was so *perfect*. Even in the darkness, I could see the muscles outlining the backside of his ribs. More muscles bulged in his arms.

He was by far the sexiest dream-subject I'd encountered, and I fought off an urge to run away. Not that I preferred my subjects to be ugly or anything, but something in the middle would've been all right.

Trying to ignore the more interesting bits of that naked body, I reached over and gently took hold of the guy's arm. One soft tug and he rolled over. When I saw his face, I almost cried out in alarm.

Eli Booker.

A sensation of weightlessness came over me from the shock of recognition, as if I were on a roller coaster that had just plunged over the first hill.

Then I really did try to run away, even though I knew it was pointless. I made it as far as the window before something that felt like invisible tentacles grabbed hold of my body and pulled me back to the bedside. I sagged against it in defeat, knowing better than to fight The Will. It was too powerful a spell. No, not just a spell, more a *law*, like gravity. The magickind government created The Will to prevent magical misbehavior. It kept fairies from stealing babies, witches from turning people into toads, and for a Nightmare like me, it determined whose dreams I fed on, when, and how much.

Basically The Will says, "Jump," and Dusty says, "You got it."

The invisible grip on my body eased, and I shook off the unpleasant feeling of being manhandled by a magical spell. Trying to ignore the trembling in my knees, I looked down at that familiar face once again.

Eli Booker was the hottest guy at my old high school, maybe in all of Chickery, Ohio, itself. He was a sophomore like me, but his hair was black and his eyes cornflower blue. Tall and with a face so handsome even old ladies swooned at the sight of it, he was the guy every girl crushed on. Didn't hurt that he had a bit of a bad-boy, daredevil reputation, either. My eyes dropped to the scorpion tattoo on the left side of his chest. I'd heard rumors that he had one but this was the first time I'd seen proof. I wondered how he'd gotten it.

I forced my eyes away, aware of how quickly my heart was beating. So, yeah, even I had wasted a daydream or two fantasizing about him, and now I had to kneel on his chest and enter his dream.

Great. Who knew The Will had such a sense of humor?

Still, I wasn't about to sit on him half-naked like that. I grabbed the sheet lying rumpled at the foot of the bed and swung it over him. Eli sighed as the sheet touched him, and my heart leaped into my throat. I held my breath, expecting the worst.

When he didn't wake, I screwed up my courage and climbed onto the bed. If I didn't, The Will would start nagging me to get on with it. If I resisted too long, the spell would get physical again. I planted my feet on either side of Eli's arms and squatted down until the majority of my body weight rested on his muscular chest. Trust me, it *was* as strange as it sounded and even stranger being the person doing it. Once I was in position, an ache burned inside me like a terrible, desperate thirst. My body craved the fictus it needed to replenish my magic.

A soft moan escaped Eli's throat, but this time I didn't panic. Once a Nightmare was in place around a victim . . . er . . . subject, the magic kicked in, rendering the person powerless, even to wake. Which was why a girl like me, five foot four and 115 pounds, could sit on top of a sleeping boy without his knowing. *Thank goodness for the little things.*

I closed my eyes and exhaled, placing my fingers against his forehead. Bright light burst inside my mind like professional-grade fireworks as my consciousness left my body and entered the dream world of Eli Booker.

I knew at once something was different. I might be new to the Nightmare gig, not having come into my powers until a couple of months ago, but I'd done this enough to worry at the strange intensity of the colors swirling around me as the dream world came into focus. Most dreams were gray and foggy, old black-and-white horror movies, the kind with wide-angled shots of the rickety castle. This one was in full Technicolor. I felt like Dorothy first stepping out of her house into the Land of Oz.

I stood in the middle of a cemetery, surrounded by crumbling headstones and mausoleums thick with ivy. It was nighttime, but the full moon overhead shone bright enough that I could see the dark green of the ivy and the way its leaves stirred in the faint breeze. The murmur of voices echoed eerily around me, and for a moment I thought they might be ghosts. Then I turned and saw a bunch of police officers milling about with flashlights in hand. The presence of cops didn't surprise me; Eli's dad was a detective.

I looked around, trying to find Eli. With so many people, tombs, and trees scattered about the place, he could be anywhere. But I had to find him quick. Rule *número uno* in dream-walking: always know the subject's location. It was absolutely essential not to have any physical contact with the dreamer. Touching them would break all the enchantments holding them in the dream and make them wake up. It was a lesson I'd learned the painful way.

Not seeing Eli anywhere, I flew into the air to get a bird's-eye view. I spotted him at last on the other side of a supersized mausoleum, the kind reserved for an entire family's worth of dead bodies. He looked strange, dressed up in a fancy gray suit with an obnoxious orange-and-blue necktie. It was the kind of thing his father wore when he gave statements to the local news channels about cases, and I guessed Eli was dreaming that he was a detective. I grinned. The whole thing was sort of sweet, like a kid playing dress-up. And totally out of character for someone like Eli, a guy who I imagined thought of himself as way too cool and rebellious to want to grow up and be like his dad. Or at least a guy too cool to admit it.

I lowered myself to the ground, a safe distance away

from Eli. One of the best things about dream-walking was that reality was flexible. I could fly, change my appearance, you name it. Usually the first thing I did when arriving in a dream was to replace my frizzy red hair with sleek, straight platinum. Not this time though. I was too distracted by the dream's strangeness for vanity.

My gaze fell on the name etched in the stone above the doorway of the nearest mausoleum—KIRKWOOD. This wasn't any old graveyard Eli was dreaming about, but Coleville Cemetery, the local burial place for magickind. Only that was impossible. Coleville was located on the grounds of Arkwell Academy—*my* high school. It was a school for magickind, with twelve-foot-high, magically enforced fences and security-guarded gates, and completely inaccessible to ordinaries. Eli *couldn't* have been here before.

Yet somehow he must've been. The details were too good. The place looked exactly like it did in real life, right down to the bell tower in the distance and the odd placement of statues and stone benches among the grave markers. Coleville wasn't just a cemetery, but a local recreational spot for Arkwell students and teachers, sort of like the campus green, only with dead people.

The heady scent of lilac bushes and jasmine tickled my nose. Even the smells were right on. They were so real, for a moment I almost forgot I was in a dream.

That was impossible, too. Dreams were never so close to reality. Most were like trips through the funhouse, complete with distorted images, naked people—usually the dreamer himself—and disturbing settings like public rest rooms that resembled torture chambers.

I focused on Eli, trying to ignore my growing unease. He was talking to some of the uniformed officers, a serious look on his face. He kept gesturing behind him to where some more cops stood circled around something. Curiosity got the better of me, and I walked over.

Sprawled on the ground lay a pale-faced girl with bright blond hair, the kind I would've killed for in real life. Only, it looked as if someone *had* killed her. She was perfectly still, her eyes open but staring at nothing. Dark, purplish bruises rimmed her throat like a grotesque tattoo.

A thrill of fear went through me, and I covered my mouth to muffle a scream. It was Rosemary Vanholt, one of the fairies who attended Arkwell Academy. And she wasn't just any fairy; she was the daughter of Consul Vanholt, the head of the Magi Senate. A lot of the politicians' kids went to Arkwell. The magickind capital city of the United States was located nearby on a hidden island somewhere in the middle of Lake Erie. The lake itself was one of the most magical places in America.

She's like the president's daughter. And someone had *murdered* her.

"It's just a dream," I whispered. It was possible Eli had seen Rosemary around town or that he knew her. Seniors like her were required to hang around ordinaries for practice sometimes. That was the whole point of a place like Arkwell, to teach magickind how to live undetected in the human world.

Sure, that made sense, but it didn't explain the Coleville setting. There wasn't one for that.

On the verge of a freak-out, I turned around, trying to put more distance between me and Rosemary's body.

In my horror I hadn't realized that Eli had moved. He now stood less than a yard away from me, so tall and physically imposing he might as well have been a brick wall in the path.

"Crap," I whispered, sidestepping to avoid him. My foot caught on a tombstone, and I stumbled but managed to swerve my momentum left, barely missing a collision. Too close for comfort, I hurried past Eli, heading for a safe distance.

Something touched my arm, and I shrieked as a jolt of pain went through my entire existence. I turned to see Eli's gaze fixed on my face, his hand gripping my arm. The world around me began to slip away, the colors melting like fresh paint in the rain. Then my consciousness was hurled out of the dream back into my body hard enough that I screamed again—for real this time. I let go of Eli's forehead and grabbed my own, trying to stop my brains from rolling around like marbles inside my skull.

The pressure helped for a moment, but then Eli sat up and shoved me. I tumbled off the bed, landing on my back. I tried to take a breath, found I couldn't, and panicked, arms and legs thrashing. Eli's bewildered face appeared over me. He grabbed me by the shoulders and hauled me to my feet as easily as if I weighed nothing at all.

As soon as I was upright, my wind came back. So did my senses, and I cast the corrector spell like I'd been taught to do in moments like this. "Aphairein!"

The spell struck Eli, then *bounced,* hitting me instead. The corrector spell worked like an undo button on a computer, but it wasn't meant to be self-administered. Instead of undoing my actions, it slammed into me with the force of a battering ram. Eli still had hold of my shoulders, and both of us went crashing to the ground this time. He landed on top of me so hard I felt like I'd been sat on by an elephant.

"Get off," I said, struggling to breathe. I cast another spell at him, but it bounced, too. *What the—?*

Eli rolled off me and stood up. When I realized he'd been lying on top of me in only his red boxers, I blushed from head to toe. My skin was so hot I thought I'd turn to ash any second.

"Who the hell are you?" Eli pointed at me, his chest muscles flexing in a way that made me want to giggle.

I resisted the urge and leaped to my feet. We were close enough to the window that the moonlight shone full on my face.

Eli made a choking sound. "I know *you.* What are you doing here? And what's wrong with your eyes? They're . . . *glowing?*"

I groaned inwardly, ashamed that this hot boy who'd probably never noticed me before was now seeing the worst of me, and there was nothing I could do to stop it. *Stupid, stupid, unreliable magic.* In the daytime, Nightmares looked as human as anybody else, our unusually pale eyes strange but not alarming. At night, our eyes glowed white. The glamour I usually wore to hide the glow must've come undone.

"What kind of *freak* are you?" Eli said.

I glared at him, ignoring the sting of his words. "At least I'm not the freak dreaming about dead girls."

He gaped. "How do you know that?"

Uh . . . More embarrassed than any one person should ever have to be, I decided it was time to make a break for it. I could hear loud footsteps outside his door and knew I had about two seconds to escape. His dad was a cop; I was certain he would shoot me first and regret later.

I ran to the open window. Rule number two in dream-feeding: always have an escape route. I climbed over the edge, grabbed hold of the ivy-covered drainpipe, and slid down as quickly as I dared. Thank goodness for all those gymnastic lessons when I was younger. Normally, I would've used a glider spell to get down, but with my magic misfiring, I couldn't risk it.

As my feet touched the ground, I looked up to see Eli staring down at me, mouth open. I stuck my tongue out at him. Then I turned and sprinted up the sidewalk.

A few minutes later, I slowed to an easier pace. I had a few blocks to go until I reached McCloud Park, where I'd stowed my bicycle in some bushes. Would've been nice to have a car or motorcycle for these late-night dream-feeding adventures—hell, I wouldn't have turned down a moped— but my chances of getting any kind of motorized vehicle were slim to zero. Arkwell was a boarding school with a strict no-student-vehicles policy.

I spotted my bicycle sitting between some bushes where I'd left it and dropped down to a walk. If Eli or his dad hadn't caught up to me by now, they probably weren't going to.

Should've known better than to trust my luck.

An enormous black sedan rounded the corner into the parking lot, and I froze as the beam of headlights struck me. It came to a stop, and all the doors opened in unison. Four hairy-looking men in matching gray suits stepped out.

Four *werewolves,* to be precise. Local law enforcement for magickind.

2

Dream Come True

They put me in the back of the sedan, a werewolf on each side. The guy on my right was Hispanic and the guy on my left black. Not that it meant anything. Most magickind didn't come from any one ethnic group. We had enough trouble getting along without adding racial divisions. Our divisions came from our magical classifications. Think Carl Linnaeus, although instead of class, genus, species, we had "kinds."

There were three main kinds with loads of sub-kinds, all under the generic umbrella of magickind. The divisions were based on how we get our magic. There was witchkind, like wizards, witches, and psychics, whose magic was self-fueled. Naturekind, like fairies, dryads, and mermaids, who derived power from nature and the elements. And darkkind, like demons, werewolves, and Nightmares, of course, whose power came from other living creatures. I was part-ordinary, considered halfkind, which put me one step above reject in the social hierarchy.

I cleared my throat. "Um, where are we going, guys?"

All four ignored me. Werewolves tended to be surly that way. They also tended to be big, even when in human form, as they were now. I kept my arms tight against my sides to keep from bumping into the two beside me as the car turned corners.

I wasn't going to get anywhere with this conversation.

I leaned back on the seat, trying to ignore the smell of wet dog so prominent in the confines of the sedan I might as well have been locked in a kennel. My hair was so poofy from the late summer humidity that I had to pull the ponytail over my shoulder to rest my head. I spotted a leaf tangled in it and plucked it out. I was too far from the window to toss it, and I didn't think throwing it on the floor was a very good idea, so I closed my hand around the leaf and whispered, "Cine-aphan."

There was a loud crack, and all four werewolves jumped.

"Oops, sorry." I opened my now empty hand and freed a puff of smoke from where I'd just disintegrated the leaf. I'd meant to vanish the darn thing, but after my dream-feed with Eli, my temperamental magic was on supercharge. Well, that and I wasn't very good at spells in general. Most halfkinds couldn't work magic at all, but were born magically sterile.

I tried to ignore the wolfish glowers fixed on me and zone out for a bit, but I couldn't stop thinking about what had happened with Eli. Temperamental or not, my magic *should've* worked on him. The Will was the gatekeeper for all magic usage, and its prime directive was to keep the existence of magickind a secret. The disaster at Eli's house had to be the reason this werewolf police force picked me up. The Will spell must've alerted them about my magic misfiring. But it wasn't my fault. It was as if Eli was made out of magic rubber. I didn't doubt that this apparent immunity was why he detected my presence in his dream in the first place. *He* touched *me*. Surely somebody would believe the truth when they heard it.

But in my heart I knew that wasn't likely. When you were Moira Nimue-Everhart's only daughter, everybody was keen on you living up to the bad reputation. My mother was, after all, the girl who in her senior year set fire to the Alchemy building at Arkwell, an act she claimed was an accident, but which everybody else suspected had been revenge against a teacher who dared to give her a failing grade. Nobody could prove it though. Getting away with things was Mom's special talent.

Too bad I didn't inherit it.

After a while, the car slowed, then came to a stop. The driver lowered his window and spoke briefly to someone outside before moving on. When we came to a stop again a few moments later, the driver killed the engine and all four werewolves got out. I figured they wanted me to follow, so I scooted over and stood up, taking a big gulp of dog-free air.

I recognized our location at once. We were at Arkwell, on the northeast side of campus, parked next to one of the entrances into Coleville Cemetery. The stone archway leading into the cemetery looked three times larger than usual set against the backdrop of the night sky. Through it, I could just make out the first row of headstones.

My stomach did a nosedive as goose bumps blossomed on my arms and legs. If there was one thing I'd learned about the magical world, there was no such thing as coincidence.

"Follow," said the werewolf who'd been driving.

"Where're we going?"

He gave me a stern look then turned and strode off toward the archway. I fell into place behind him, the other three following suit. I tried not to panic, surrounded as I was by four creatures capable of turning me into Kibbles 'n Bits in about 2.3 seconds. I knew The Will prevented werewolves from attacking anyone without due cause, but given my current criminal status, I wasn't sure that included me.

We followed a winding path in and around mausoleums, benches, statues, trees, and flowerbeds. The place was beautiful in a creepy, gothic kind of way. It was scary, too, full of shadows and odd noises.

Eventually the lead werewolf came to a stop out front of a gigantic mausoleum I recognized at once as the Kirkwoods'. A sudden sensation of déjà vu made me shiver with dread.

The werewolf pointed at a bench next to the door into the Kirkwoods' tomb. "Sit. Wait."

Did I mention werewolves were chatty?

I sat and waited.

He walked around the building, leaving me alone with

the other three. They continued ignoring me and I them. We had a mutual understanding.

I focused my attention on the murmur of voices on the other side of the tomb. Lights flashed here and there above my head, reflecting off leaves and structures, but I couldn't see anything from where I sat.

"Who found her?" a male voice said. To my surprise, I recognized one of my teachers, a wizard named Mr. Marrow. Knowing there was somebody I knew here made me a little less nervous. I liked Marrow, mostly because he taught history, a subject that didn't require us to use a lot of magic, thereby lowering my chances for making a fool of myself.

The voice that answered him, however, I'd never heard before and hoped never to again, it was so horrible. Female and ancient, it sounded like the grinding of old gears in desperate need of oil. "The maintenance man found her. Mr. Culpepper was on his way home from fixing a plumbing problem at Flint Hall when he heard a disturbance."

"This late? I've never known him to be so willing to repair something in the *student* dormitories after hours."

"Yes, well, he says he was worried about structural damage if he didn't fix it right away."

"I see." There was a long pause, then Mr. Marrow said, "I suppose, given the missing hand, she was one of the Keepers?"

Missing hand? Keeper? I didn't like the sound of that at all.

"Yes. I've been telling the senate for years they shouldn't allow Keepers so young, but the families have started to treat it like a rite of passage, mere ceremony. They've grown complacent about the threat."

"Well, now I imagine they'll realize none of the Keepers are safe."

The old woman took a deep breath. "Ambrose, I didn't see this coming."

"No sign at all?"

"No. It's as if something's blocked my visions. I can't begin to fathom the kind of magic necessary to do that."

"Yes, but best to focus on what we can for now."

"You're right. I'll know more once I speak to the girl."

Sheriff Brackenberry appeared from around the side of the mausoleum. He stopped beside the bench and stared down at me, so big he blocked the moon from sight. He looked like an NFL linebacker with some extra paunch and body hair. Not only was he head of the magickind police force in Chickery, he was also the alpha werewolf.

"Listening in, were you?" said Brackenberry.

I swallowed.

The sheriff shook his head. "I would think someone who's been up to as much trouble this evening as you, Miss Everhart, would know better than to press her luck by eavesdropping." He paused and smiled, his mouth all long teeth and snarl. "Then again, I guess it's not that surprising after all."

His condescension was a little undeserved, I thought.

Aside from the night last March when I first came into my Nightmare powers and went on an unauthorized dream-feed on the neighbor boy, I'd never been in serious trouble. Nothing worse than a couple of detentions and a D on my alchemy final last year. Well, there *was* that incident in spell-casting class when I turned Katarina Marcel into a snake, but it had been an accident.

He must be judging me by my mother. Made sense, given he was a cop. He'd probably arrested her a couple of times before he became sheriff. Mom had been a social activist in her twenties, leading protests on magickind issues, such as when she tried to get the ban on romantic relationships with ordinaries lifted. She'd gone to all that trouble just to be with my dad, only to divorce him a few years later. Typical that her self-serving behavior would be causing me trouble now.

"I didn't do anything wrong. I swear."

He grunted. "Like I've never heard that before. Funny, but I expected a little more originality from Moira's daughter."

"Yeah, well, the dog ate my notebook with all my good excuses."

Okay, so mouthing off to the sheriff wasn't my smartest decision of the night, but I couldn't help it. Smartassitis might not be a clinically defined disease, but it should be.

Brackenberry growled at me. Seriously! He *growled*. I closed my eyes and pretended to be invisible. A small part of me half-expected it to work. There were spells for stuff like that. Not that I knew any.

"I think that's enough intimidation for now, Sheriff," Mr. Marrow said, appearing behind him.

Relief bloomed inside me, and I beamed up at Marrow. He didn't smile back, but I detected a friendly twinkle in his eyes.

"Come with me, Dusty."

I stood up like someone had lit a stove burner beneath my butt and hurried past Brackenberry. Marrow led me around the Kirkwood mausoleum, then came to a stop. He faced me, resting his hands on top of his cane. He didn't need the cane to walk, even though he was kind of old. Silver threaded his storm-cloud gray hair and neatly trimmed beard, and his skin resembled aged leather. The cane was Marrow's wizard staff disguised by glamour. All wizards and witches needed a magical object in order to use magic, sort of like needing a mouse to use a computer. I was glad Nightmares didn't need wands and stuff. I would've just ended up losing mine—or breaking it.

"I must say, Dusty, one of these days your tongue is going to dig its way right into your grave," said Marrow.

I sighed. "I know. I don't mean to. My mouth just works independent of my brain sometimes."

"Obviously. Though I'm glad you're wise enough to admit your shortcomings. That's the first step to overcoming them. However, I suggest you make every attempt to control yourself now. There's someone waiting to talk to you who won't be as tolerant as the sheriff. Lady Elaine is an oracle. Do you know what that means?"

I nodded. I paid enough attention in his classes to

know that an oracle was a witchkind born with the rare ability to see far into the future. They were prophets whose predictions almost always came true.

"Good," Marrow said. "Show her the utmost respect and be completely honest about everything she asks you. Understand?"

"Yep. Will do."

He turned and walked on. Ahead of us, a woman stood in between a row of headstones. She was staring at me as if I were a science experiment starting to bubble over the side of the beaker. Behind her, I saw some kind of magical shield, like a wall of woven light, hiding the area beyond.

As we drew closer to the woman, I slowed down. She looked about four feet tall and seventy-five pounds, but I knew enough about the power of oracles to be afraid of her. Her arms, visible beneath the tight black turtleneck she wore, resembled broom handles, the bones the same width from shoulder to wrist. I reckoned it wouldn't take much to break one, but I doubted very many people would try to harm her. She had a look in her pale, almost milky eyes that made me think of dragons and other creatures that favored teenage girls for dinner. Besides, she'd probably see an attack coming.

Marrow came to a stop a few feet away from the oracle. "Lady Elaine, this is Destiny Everhart."

I cringed at the use of my real name. It was so important sounding, like somebody with, well, a *destiny*. Not me. That was why I went by Dusty—it fit better. Plus, my mom *hated* it.

Lady Elaine looked me up and down with a dire expression, her lips compressed into a tight line. "You were dream-walking earlier?"

"Uh-huh."

"Did something go wrong?"

I started to fidget with my hair. "Oh, you could say that, yeah. The guy woke up and then my magic wouldn't work on him."

"Yes, I see. Good." She nodded to herself. "This confirms it."

"Um, confirms what?"

But the old lady wasn't listening. "Tell me what happened. *Everything.*"

Now, I knew the definition of everything meant, well, everything, but I didn't see any reason why this old woman needed to know how distractingly hot I thought Eli was in his red boxer shorts. So I censored the more embarrassing details and spilled the rest—the setting at Coleville, Rosemary, even the way Eli had touched me, and kicked me out of the dream. If Lady Elaine was surprised by any part of my tale, I couldn't tell. The expression on her face, grave with a side of crankiness, didn't change.

Not that I looked at her much. My gaze kept drifting to the wall behind her. It didn't take someone with less of an imagination than mine to guess it might be hiding a pale-haired fairy girl. But I didn't want it to be Rosemary Vanholt. Not just because the idea of someone so young being murdered, especially someone I knew, was so horrible, but because if it was her, then that meant there'd been something *special* about my dream-walk. I didn't want to be a part of anything special. Bad things happened to special people. Usually failure followed by an early death.

When I finished recounting the story, Lady Elaine asked, "Was Rosemary's body intact in the dream?"

"Um, yeah," I said, trying not to remember the missing hand business.

"Was she wearing a ring?"

I gulped, certain the ring in question was no doubt magical and probably dangerous. There was no shortage of magical artifacts hanging around. If it weren't for The Will keeping stuff in check, a lot of those things could kill you just by touching them, like a cursed sweater designed to shrink the moment you put it on and not stop until it squeezed the life right out of you. Magickind was pretty civilized nowadays, but it didn't used to be.

"Well?" Lady Elaine said.

"Um . . . I don't know. Looking at dead people's not really my thing."

"I see." She sounded disappointed. "What about this boy, Eli Booker? You knew him already?"

I forced my hands away from my hair and the knots I'd managed to put in the ends of it. "Not really. I only know who he is because we were in the same grade at my old high school."

"But do you have . . ." She broke off as a terrible noise sounded behind us. A loud, piercing shriek. I glanced back, expecting to see a banshee or maybe a harpy, but it was far worse. A woman with the same bright blond hair as Rosemary was stumbling toward us.

"Tell me it's not true." She stopped when she reached Lady Elaine and grabbed the old crone by her bony arms. "Tell me it's not!"

Lady Elaine didn't respond, but I guessed that was response enough from an oracle. The woman let go and continued her stumbling walk toward the magical shield. I knew who she was, of course. Mrs. Vanholt, Rosemary's mother.

I fought back tears, struggling to breathe as the woman's grief filled the air around us. I watched as Mrs. Vanholt approached the shield. She stopped before it, raising her hands. The shield vibrated a moment like a plucked harp string, then vanished.

I caught only a glimpse of what was behind it before Marrow took hold of my arm and turned me around, but it was enough to confirm my worst fear. Lying on the ground in the same position as I'd seen her in the dream was Rosemary. Her right hand was missing, cut off at the wrist.

"Let's go," said Marrow.

He didn't have to tell me twice. I hurried back the way we'd come, wishing I could run and fighting the urge to be sick. When we reached the other side of the Kirkwood mausoleum, Marrow said, "That's far enough."

I disagreed. A hundred miles wouldn't be far enough, but I halted and faced him.

He touched my shoulder, squeezing it gently. "Are you all right?"

I started to nod, thought better of it, and shook my head. "What's going on? Is that really Rosemary? Why's her hand gone? And how did I see it in Eli's dream, and . . ."

"Shhh," he said in his soothing, gravelly voice. "Take a deep breath. There, that's better." He smiled, the gesture creating deep caverns on his face. "I know you have a lot of questions, and I'm certain the oracle will address them as soon as she's able. But now is not the right time. Agreed?"

"Agreed," I said through a throat tight with the thought of Mrs. Vanholt's grief.

"Good." Marrow waved at Sheriff Brackenberry, who was standing with a couple of the other werewolves a few yards away. The alpha approached us alone.

Marrow said to the sheriff, "Would you mind escorting Miss Everhart to her dormitory? I think it best, given the circumstances."

The expression on Brackenberry's face suggested he definitely minded, but he said, "Yes, sir. Of course."

"Thank you." Marrow looked back at me. "Try to put everything out of your mind for now."

Yeah sure, no problem.

"Come on," said Brackenberry as Marrow walked away.

The sheriff made me sit in the back of the car like some kind of jailbird, but I didn't complain. My dorm, Riker Hall, was on the opposite side of campus, a good ten-minute walk that I didn't feel like making in the middle of the night with a killer on the loose.

I sat back and tried to think about nice things, like my dad making French toast on Sunday mornings or how I'd kicked the winning goal at the soccer play-offs last year, back when I'd still been an ordinary. Back when dreams were only dreams.

But all I could see was Rosemary's dead body.

The car pulled to a stop a few minutes later. Brackenberry got out and opened my door. "Hurry up. I've got things to do."

I climbed out and looked around at the familiar buildings, a mix of stone cathedrals and mini-castles, complete with looming towers, a lot of pointed arches, and walls as thick as bank vault doors. Riker Hall stood to my right, looking like a squat fortress. I didn't want to go in there and back to my dorm room. What if I dreamed about Rosemary? I didn't have nearly the amount of power in my own dreams as I did in everybody else's.

In a pathetic attempt to stall, I asked, "What about my bike? It's still at McCloud Park."

"I'll have one of my boys drop it off later."

"Oh. Um, thanks."

"Something wrong?"

I bit my lip. "Well, I guess I'm just surprised I'm not in trouble. I mean, I exposed myself to an ordinary."

Brackenberry snorted. "Would you prefer I haul you to jail? I can do that if you'd like." He opened the door again and waved.

"No thanks." I wasn't entirely certain he was joking.

"I guess it's just a lucky break or something. That's kind of unusual for me."

A wide, unpleasant grin stretched across his wolfish face. "Well, maybe your luck's changing."

He couldn't have been more wrong.

～ 3 ～

Dream Duty

News about Rosemary's death spread through the student body the next day faster than a Facebook chain post. It didn't help that there were now werewolf police officers walking the hallways and patrolling the grounds. The atmosphere in the underclassmen's cafeteria at breakfast hummed with voices, the sound a mixture of fear and excitement. I tried not to listen, but it was impossible.

"She died?"

"Someone *murdered* her. On campus."

"I thought The Will stopped stuff like that from happening?"

"First time in who knows how long."

"I heard that her body was found by that Nightmare girl. You know, Dusty, or whatever."

Great, so my participation in last night's events had made it into the rumor mill, too. I didn't bother correcting the boy even though he was sitting just one table over from me. He'd probably just ignore me anyway. I wasn't exactly popular at Arkwell, more like the unintentional loner. I'd tried making friends, but most people acted like I was mentally deficient or something. Magically deficient, more likely. Most weren't outright mean, but it seemed I would be the new girl forever.

My luck from the night before finally went bust in English class. Typical of Monday mornings, our teacher, Miss Norton, was hungover. She was a squat fairy with curly, auburn hair and a broad face. Today her large eyes looked red and puffy behind her wire rim glasses. I suspected she might have done some crying last night along with the usual drinking and I tried not to think what about.

School gossip claimed Miss Norton had a serious Coke addiction. And by Coke, I mean the sugary, caffeinated beverage. Fairies were immune to the effects of drugs and alcohol, but they had a serious sugar weakness. This meant sugar was a banned substance at Arkwell. The vending machines contained only diet, caffeine-free sodas and sugar-free candy and snacks, most of which tasted like cardboard. There were mornings I would kill to get my hands on a Mountain Dew and a powdered doughnut.

"All right, kids," said Miss Norton after the bell rang. "Let's form the talking circle."

Relieved chatter broke out at her announcement, mixed with the scrape of chair legs against the stone floor as we pushed our desks around until they were lined up in some vague circular fashion. I ended up with my back facing the wide, arched windows and my gaze pointed toward the dry erase board in the front of the room. Arkwell might look like a large medieval town on the outside, but the insides were full of modern classroom amenities.

Miss Norton clapped her hands, and the noise quieted down. Then she produced the "talking stick," pulling it out of one of the huge pockets of the flowery housedress she wore. The stick was roughly the size of a school ruler and as crooked as an arthritic finger. Its surface was made of some kind of pale wood, smooth like glass, and whenever I held it, it seemed to radiate warmth.

"Given the tragic events of last night," said Miss Norton, "I think instead of discussing the reading assignment, we should take this time to share our thoughts and feelings about what happened."

Now the class gave a collective groan, myself included. Actually, I was probably the loudest. What was the deal? The talking circle was normally an excuse for Miss Norton to get out of teaching. The free-form, rambling discussions, usually more goofing off than serious introspection, gave her time to nurse her hangover headache. I couldn't understand why she was making today's topic about our feelings over Rosemary's death. Maybe she wanted to make sure everybody left her class feeling as miserable as she did. Wouldn't surprise me. Fairies were a vindictive lot.

I felt an elbow in my side and glanced at its owner. My roommate, Selene, was looking at me with a worried expression, the same one that had been there ever since I told her about what happened while we were getting ready this morning.

"You don't have to talk, you know," she said. "When the stick gets to you, just pass it on."

I smiled weakly back at her, appreciating the suggestion but doubting its chances of success.

Miss Norton lifted the talking stick into the air. "Who would like to go first?"

No one answered, and I held my breath, hoping Norton would see how reluctant we were and return the discussion to *Macbeth* and the prejudicial vilifying of witches during the seventeenth century.

Katarina Marcel raised her hand. "I'll go."

I braced for the worst as Katarina's icy gaze flashed on me for a second. She had hated me ever since I turned her into that snake. The spell had lasted less than a minute before the teacher turned her back, but not in time to prevent Katarina from falling victim to snake instinct and swallowing a couple of the earthworms we'd been using for spell practice. Nobody believed me when I said it was an accident, especially not Katarina. Didn't help when I suggested maybe she was part shape-shifter and had discovered her true form at last.

Yeah, not my smartest moment, given her popular status. Since then Katarina never passed on an opportunity to expose me to public humiliation. To make matters worse, she and Rosemary had been friends.

Miss Norton let go of the talking stick. It levitated in the air for a second then flew across the circle into Katarina's outstretched hand. Most of my classmates believed that Miss Norton used her magic to make the stick fly around like that, but I always doubted it. The stick some-times gave me the impression that it was alive, or at least that it could hear and react on its own.

Katarina took a shaky breath. "I just can't imagine it. I mean, how can Rosemary be dead? Why would someone hurt her?" Katarina's voice grew thick with emotion, and her eyes glistened with unshed tears. I knew her well enough to be suspicious of such a theatrical display of grief, even if the feeling behind it was genuine. Katarina was a siren, which meant that the ability to manipulate people's emotions came as easy to her as breathing. Across the room, Miss Norton was eating up Katarina's words like they were M&M's. She might start sobbing any second.

Katarina looked at me again. "And I just can't imagine how anyone could have seen something like that and *not* be devastated. Only the most terrible, heartless person could be so uncaring."

All of the other students looked at me, and my face went red. Everybody knew I'd been there. What they didn't know was that I *had* cried. Into my pillow, in private. I fought the urge to defend myself, to not play into her game. I bit down on my tongue hard enough it hurt. I *would* stay quiet for once in my life.

A loud voice came over the PA system: "Destiny Everhart, please report to the main office at once."

The red in my face drained away. A few students snickered, and a couple said, "Ohhhhhhh."

I scowled at the worst of the noisemakers. "What, are we in second grade still?" I stood, feeling faint.

"Well," said Katarina, her voice mocking. "You *are* less than a year old, magically speaking. So it's only appropriate we treat you like a child."

I rolled my eyes. "Aw, did you come up with that all by yourself? Aren't you clever."

Katarina's expression turned smug. She brushed her long, velvety brown hair over her shoulder. All the boys present let out a collective sigh. That was the problem with sirens. They were so physically beautiful they could get away with anything. That beauty was a key part of their manipulative, seductive magic.

"Yes, I am," Katarina said. "But you forgot to add beautiful, talented. Oh, and *not* magically deficient."

Only a siren could say something that conceited and not be ridiculed. I searched for a scathing reply, but nothing good came to me. Trouble was, she hadn't said anything that wasn't true.

Selene snorted, coming to my rescue. "You forgot the part about how you're a stuck-up twit, too. Wouldn't want to forget that."

Even more of our classmates *ohhhh*ed this time, shifting their stares from me to Katarina. That was Selene's doing. She was a siren as well and just as good at manipulation. She was as beautiful as Katarina, too, but spent most of her time trying to hide it. Her hair was silky black like wet ink and her eyes the color of amethysts, but she dressed like a tomboy in baseball caps, baggy T-shirts, and no makeup. The tomboy persona was a recent development, a form of social protest against the objectification of sirens.

Katarina's eyes narrowed to pinpricks as she glared at Selene. She opened her mouth to say something back, but Miss Norton, who'd been busy rubbing her temples and pretending not to hear, finally decided to play teacher.

She smacked her desk with the palm of her hand, drawing everyone's attention. "That's enough, girls." Miss Norton fixed her gaze on me. Her pointy ears made her look like a hissing cat. "Dusty, go to the office."

I cast Selene a grateful glance as I shoved my battered copy of the *Collected Works of William Shakespeare* into my backpack. She winked back at me. Then I strode from the room, my heart pounding from the confrontation with Katarina. You'd think I'd be used to it by now.

Fear replaced anger as I reached the main office in Jefferson Tower. I had a sinking feeling I was finally going to get in trouble for last night. Or worse, find out what it all meant. The secretary gave me a friendly smile that I immediately found suspicious.

She paged Dr. Hendershaw, and a moment later I entered the head principal's office. Hendershaw was sitting behind her desk, typing away on a keyboard with her eyes fixed on the monitor. The keyboard made odd sound effects reminiscent of the Three Stooges as she struck the keys, but Hendershaw didn't pay it any mind. A lot of inanimate objects on campus tended to become a little wonky after a while from a phenomenon known as animation. It was a side effect of being exposed to both magic and the electromagnetic fields generated by elec-

tricity. Any object could be affected given enough expo-
sure, but electronics were doomed from the start.

Hendershaw motioned for me to sit without looking
up. I did so, trying hard not to fidget, and failing. The
principal was a short, plump witch with toady eyes behind her Coke-bottle glasses. Unfortunately, I was pretty
certain she was a member of the "judge me by my mother"
party. Rumor had it Hendershaw had been the alchemy
teacher when my mom was a student here, the one who'd
given her the bad grade. Whenever I saw Hendershaw, she
kept her gaze locked on me as if I were a hellhound she
thought might bite her the moment she wasn't looking.

She finished typing and addressed me at last. "Do you
know why I've called you down here?"

"I've been elected class president?"

Hendershaw's eyes flashed dangerously. "You're *here*
because the Magi Senate has decided to make a change in
your magical status."

"Come again?"

"You're no longer going to be required to dream-feed
every other week."

"I'm being cut off?"

"Of course not. You will now be required to feed *more*
often."

"What? Why?"

Hendershaw took off her glasses for a moment and
rubbed the bridge of her nose. "We'll get to that. First let
me caution you about the risk you'll be undertaking.

Since the ratification of The Will Act, there has been a tight restriction on the amount of magic a person is allowed to channel, hence the limitation to your dream-feeding."

I cut her off, impatient to get to the point. "Yeah, I learned that in orientation. It's also why witches like you are only permitted to own two magical instruments at once."

She glowered at me, but not before her eyes flicked to the fountain pen sitting in a holder next to her keyboard. Must be her wand in disguise.

"Yes, well, I'm glad to hear you listened so well *then*," said Hendershaw. "Let's see if you can do so again *now*. Shall we?" Her expression dared me to respond.

I kept my mouth shut.

Hendershaw continued. "As I was saying, the restrictions are even greater for underage magickind. Everything is always so much more exaggerated to a child. The smallest slight from a peer seems like the end of the world. Before The Will it wasn't uncommon for serious injury to occur on a weekly basis, sometimes even death. But you children are so much safer now."

I gritted my teeth, in actual pain from the effort of holding back a wiseass remark. I didn't appreciate being referred to as a child.

"Now, however, the senate has decided to increase the frequency of your dream-feeding to three times per week."

I sat up, my stomach lurching. "Seriously? Why so much?" Sitting on sleeping strangers once every two weeks was bad enough. The last thing I wanted was to do it more often. Unlike a lot of my peers, I didn't give a crap about making my magic more powerful. I had a hard enough time handling what I already had, thank you very much.

"Because," said Hendershaw, "Lady Elaine believes you are a dream-seer."

"A what?"

"Dream-see-*er*," a raspy voice enunciated from behind me.

I jumped even as I recognized that unpleasant sound from the night before. I turned to see Lady Elaine standing in the doorway. She looked the same as she had yesterday, old and skeletal. She seemed to favor dark, snug-fitting clothes, but the purse slung over her shoulder was bright pink and as big as a pillowcase.

"You have the ability to see the future through *dreams*," she said.

"Ah, Lady Elaine, so glad you made it." Hendershaw stood up and motioned the other woman to take her seat. Lady Elaine came forward and assumed the position behind the principal's desk.

I sat and stared, feeling as if I'd swallowed a jar full of spiders, hundreds of little hairy legs scurrying around in my tummy.

"Now, young lady," said the oracle, "the gift of dream-seeing is very rare, and very *important*. You should feel honored."

"Oh, I'm thrilled." I felt like throwing up. "But how can you be sure I'm a . . . a dream-seer?"

"The signs are unmistakable. The moment The Will spell detected your magic failing, there was little doubt it could be from anything else." Lady Elaine set her massive purse on the table, bumping the pen holder.

"Yes," said Hendershaw, rescuing the pen—most definitely her wand—before it fell to the floor. She spoke in a hurried tone that gave me the impression she was trying hard not to be excluded. "However, the ability only works with the appropriate partner. In your case, Elijah Booker."

I grabbed the arms of my chair to keep from falling out of it. My eyes darted between the two women as I prayed one of them would smile and admit this was some cruel joke. They looked back at me with matching serious expressions.

I cleared my throat. "Are you saying what I *think* you're saying?"

Lady Elaine said, "From this day forward and until such time as circumstances change, you will only be permitted to dream-feed with Eli."

I shot to my feet. "No way. I can't! My magic doesn't work on him. What if he wakes up again and his dad shoots me? What if he—"

"Sit *down*." Lady Elaine whacked the desk with the palm of her hand.

I sat.

As if it was scolding, the keyboard made a couple more Stooges sound effects.

Lady Elaine gave the keyboard a shove, an annoyed look on her face. "Your fears are understandable, but unnecessary. Eli has been made aware of the situation and is being enrolled as a student here as we speak."

My jaw dropped onto my chest, and I glanced at Hendershaw. "You've got to be kidding."

The principal smirked, folding her arms. "Not at all, my dear."

"Somebody kill me now," I muttered, leaning back in the chair and placing a hand over my eyes.

Lady Elaine's voice was harsh as she said, "You shouldn't make such jokes, not after what you witnessed last night."

I swallowed and let my hand fall into my lap as I looked back at her. "I'm sorry."

She let out a humph.

"But how does this work, exactly? I mean, Eli's an ordinary."

"We have protocols for dealing with a situation such as this one, even though it's extremely rare," Lady Elaine said. "Eli's father has been informed of the existence of magickind, and his name has been added to The Will registry to ensure he will be unable to tell any other ordinaries the truth about his son."

"Not that he would try in the first place," Hendershaw added.

"Oh," I said, thinking about my dad. Things had been much the same for him when he hooked up with Mom.

Lady Elaine tapped the desktop with her index finger. "I cannot stress enough how important it is that you take this seriously. You must dedicate yourself to developing your dream-seer abilities."

I shifted in my seat. "But why? I mean . . . it doesn't seem all that useful."

Lady Elaine ignored my question and addressed Hendershaw. "Would you mind giving us a couple of minutes?"

The principal frowned, but she left the room without argument.

As soon as we were alone, Lady Elaine said, "*You* were able to see what happened last night while *I* was not. For some reason, you and Eli are more attuned to unfolding events."

I shook my head. "By the time I saw the dream, Rosemary must've already been dead. If I'd seen it a week ago, maybe I could've saved her, but it's just torture when it's too late to stop it."

"Ah, but last night was the first time you ever dreamwalked with Eli. If you had been visiting his dreams regularly you most likely *would've* seen it far enough in advance to prevent it."

All the air in my lungs evaporated. Talk about laying a load of guilt on a person. Tears stung my eyes.

Something of my horror must've shown on my face because Lady Elaine said, "Now, I don't want you to feel responsible for what happened, because you most definitely are not. It's not as if you have any choice when it comes to your dream-feeders. Missed opportunities are one of the drawbacks of The Will, I'm afraid."

"*Drawback?* That's putting it mildly." Rosemary had died, and I might've been able to stop it.

Lady Elaine pursed her lips. "Moving forward, I'm sure your gifts will prove more useful. With practice, it's even possible you'll be able to revisit Elijah's dreams from before the attack and identify Rosemary's killer."

Her little speech about not feeling guilty didn't help much, but I nodded, pretending it did. At least I might have an opportunity to make some kind of amends. It was better than nothing.

Lady Elaine flashed a yellow-toothed smile at me then reached into her big pink purse and withdrew something slim and rectangular. She handed it to me, and I realized it was an eTab, the magickind version of a tablet computer.

"What's this for?" I said, turning it over in my hands. The advertisements for this sucker said it was animation resistant. I'd wanted one for a while now, but they were pretty expensive.

"It's an eTab."

"No kidding."

Lady Elaine yanked the zipper on her purse closed a little harder than was necessary. "You will use this device to record the content of Eli's dreams. *Every* dream. As soon as you have completed a dream-walk, you will fill out an entry in the dream journal application already installed. You must do it as soon as possible so you don't forget anything important. I expect something so small should be easy to carry with you at all times."

She was right about that. The thing was so light it felt like nothing at all. I ran my fingers over the touch screen, admiring the smooth, shiny surface. Surrounding the screen were thin, barely discernible engravings, rune marks designed to dampen the animation effect.

"Your entries should be as specific as possible. Pay special attention to recurring images or patterns. All dreams are symbolic at their basic level, even the ones that predict the future."

I forced my attention back on Lady Elaine, trying to make sense of what she'd said. Symbols, reoccurring images, or patterns. That didn't sound very easy. "But what I saw about Rosemary was almost exactly what happened. How's that symbolic?"

"Sometimes the closer to the event, the clearer the vision."

I thought about it a moment. "You mean it sort of comes into focus? I guess that makes sense."

"Indeed. Here is your username and password." She handed me a slip of paper. "The device is connected to the school's wireless system, but you will be expected to obey classroom rules about its usage. There is also an instant message application. Make sure you check it regularly. I may sometimes contact you in that manner."

"Okay." The wireless stuff was pretty cool, but I was still hung up on the bit about symbols.

"You'll start your new dream-feeding schedule on Wednesday."

"Right. But is there anything specific I should look for? I mean, aside from the obvious. What about the ring you asked me about?"

Lady Elaine hesitated. "No. There's nothing . . . specific."

I could tell she was lying. "Okay. Then what's a Keeper and why do you think Rosemary was one?"

She stared at me, at first thunderstruck then angry. "Where did you hear about Keepers?"

I gulped, but it was too late to worry about the consequences. "I heard you and Mr. Marrow talking."

"You should be careful about eavesdropping. You're liable to hear more than you want to."

I wasn't about to argue with her on that one, but I couldn't just unremember what I'd heard. Besides, this was a life-and-death matter, in a very literal sense. "So what's a Keeper?"

To my surprise, the old oracle smiled, the gesture something other than condescending. It looked almost like affection. "You're certainly Moira's daughter. But no, I'm not going to tell you what the Keepers are or what they're guarding."

She paused, and I knew she'd intentionally let slip the guarding reference. It was a clue.

She continued. "It's a forbidden subject. I *can't* tell you anything more."

"Who forbids it?"

"The senate, of course." Lady Elaine stood. "Well then. I think we're finished here. Oh, I almost forgot. I would like you to attend some additional lessons in dreamwalking with Ms. Grey. She'll be able to teach you how to extend your abilities and to recognize potential signs."

Great. I'd taken a couple lessons with Ms. Grey, or Bethany as she preferred to be called, before, and she was about as much fun as a Marine drill sergeant the first day of boot camp. She *hated* my mother, too, a fact she loved to go on about whenever the mood struck her. Which was pretty much all the time.

"You'll meet her tomorrow after classes in room three-fourteen of Jupiter Hall," said Lady Elaine.

I repeated the room number, committing it to memory.

"Do you have any questions?"

I hesitated. "Why didn't my magic work on Eli?"

Lady Elaine looked relieved, as if she'd been expecting something else. "You and Eli are a dream-seer pair. As I said before, that is one of the indicators. Dream-seers are fated to work together as if they are one person, like magnets of opposite charge. It's a bond almost impossible to break. You can't use any magic on him that you can't use on yourself."

Awesome. More good news. "So are all dream-seer pairs between a Nightmare and an ordinary?"

"No. The dreamer is usually magickind. The fact that Eli is an ordinary might have something to do with your heritage, although no one can say for sure."

"Oh."

Lady Elaine picked up her giant purse and slung it over her shoulder. "Any more questions?"

Just one, but I was almost too afraid to ask. "The way the senate is going on about this and the business with the

Keepers and ring, I sorta get the feeling you're expecting more bad stuff to happen."

Lady Elaine nodded, a grim look in her eyes. "What happened to Rosemary Vanholt is only the beginning."

~4~

Daytime Nightmare

"Cheer up, Dusty. It won't be so bad."

I stifled a yawn as I glanced at Selene sitting across the table. Around us the cafeteria was in full breakfast-time swing, the noise level at a dull roar from so many voices and clanging dishes. I'd been up all night worrying about everything—the dream-seer stuff, facing Eli again, and worst of all, the fear of failure. It was a hard thing to live with, knowing that if I didn't discover the killer's identity, someone else might die.

"You should be excited," Selene continued, doing her best to lighten my spirits. "Just think of all the cool things you'll be able to do with that much extra magic."

I rolled my eyes. "That's half the problem. I have a hard enough time handling what I do have. Anything more and I'll probably blow myself up."

"You don't give yourself enough credit. For as little time as you've had to learn, you're doing great."

"Yeah, sure. Tell that to your hair, why don't you."

"Don't even try that." Selene reached behind her head and slid her long black braid over her shoulder. She picked up the end and examined it. "See. You can't even tell it was ever singed."

I tapped my fork on my plate. "That's because you're a siren, and your magic corrects imperfections quickly."

Selene frowned. I had her there. At the end of gym class last Thursday, the tip of her braid looked like the top of a burnt candlewick. I hadn't meant to set her hair on fire, but we'd been studying combative magic that day. Well, we studied it most days. Sure, we did the usual stuff like sit-ups and dodgeball, but our classes more often resembled paintball games or laser tag, only with spells instead of toy guns. Before The Will, people learned combative magic to survive, given all the magickind-on-magickind violence. Now we learned it for sport.

Selene tossed her braid back behind her shoulder. "Accidents happen. Besides, that capture the flag game was intense. I saw loads of people come out of it beat up."

"Sure. Only how many of them were injured by their own teammates?"

Selene shrugged as if this didn't matter. Then a grin spread across her face. Even without makeup she was stunningly beautiful. "It's not *always* so bad when your magic goes awry. I think we can count the Katarina snake incident as a total win."

I couldn't help it. I grinned, too.

"See, your day's getting brighter already," said Selene.

"Yep. Somebody get me some shades." I shoved a forkful of eggs into my mouth, still nervous but trying to put a good face on it for my friend's sake.

Selene took a dainty sip of her hot chocolate, the action so at odds with her tough-girl, tomboy appearance. She sported the combat-boot-and-army-pants ensemble today. She looked tired and her violet eyes were thoughtful. It seemed she was now falling victim to her own bad mood. I knew she hadn't slept well, either. Some of it was no doubt my restlessness in the bed opposite hers, but I suspected most of it had to do with Rosemary. Selene used to hang with the same "in" crowd as the consul's daughter before she launched her sirens-are-more-than-sex-objects social protest. I didn't think they'd been close friends or anything, but friendly enough.

"You know," whispered Selene, "you should ask Melanie about Rosemary's ring."

"Who?"

"Melanie Remillard. She and Rose were best friends." Selene dropped her voice even lower. "I bet if Rose told anybody about this Keeper business, it was her."

"Sure, okay. Do you see her anywhere?" I scanned the crowd, which was kind of pointless since I had no idea what Melanie looked like, and she was most likely an upperclassman and wouldn't be eating in this cafeteria in the first place.

"She hasn't been in school since it happened."

"Oh," I said, unsurprised. If someone killed my best

friend, I'd probably go into social hibernation as well. I'd be devastated to lose Selene.

"But how did they *do* it?" Selene rapped her knuckles on the table. "How'd they get around The Will?"

I prodded an apple slice on my plate with the tines of my fork. "Maybe it's not as hard as they say."

"I dunno. I've tried before and never had any luck. Only, hasn't your Mom done it?"

"All the time," I said. This, more than any other reason, was why my mother had such a bad reputation. She made a regular—and miraculous—habit of breaking The Will.

"Any idea how she does it?" asked Selene.

I opened my mouth to respond but the cafeteria suddenly went silent. I peered around, wondering what had gotten into everybody. Didn't take long to figure out.

Eli stood just inside the main entrance, surveying the crowd. He looked as hot as ever with his short black hair and eyes so bright a blue you could almost see the color from a distance. His dark gray T-shirt with some band logo on the front fit snug across his chest, and his frayed jeans hung low on his hips. Things would've been a lot less uncomfortable if I didn't find him quite so appealing. *Stupid male magnetism.*

He wore his usual tough-guy expression, but I detected shock and a little fear in the rigid way he stood there. I sympathized. The students had reacted with the same judgmental silence when I made my first appearance. I was sure it didn't help that Eli was so new to the whole concept of magickind. The faces staring back at him weren't all *that* weird, not with Arkwell's ninety percent Human-oid Resemblance Requirement for admission, but plenty were weird enough.

That remaining ten percent could be a doozy if the kids weren't wearing their glamour charms that day: some had pointed ears or oddly colored skin, even horns and tails. Selene and the other sirens had wings. Not that I'd ever seen them. Sirens were like birds in that way; their wings were visible only when they were using them. But The Will prevented people from flying, which meant sirens rarely had a reason to unfurl them.

Still, Eli was the true weirdo here. He was one hun-dred percent ordinary. Talk about being a disadvantaged student.

Eli gazed at me, his eyes narrowing into something like a glare. A spark of fear went through me, and my nerve end-ings tingled. I wanted to look away, but couldn't. Silly as it sounded, we were connected now. For better or for worse.

It was definitely going to be worse.

For one terrible, nauseating moment I thought he was going to come over to me right then and give me a telling-off for getting him involved in this mess, but he marched down the main aisle through the row of tables until he reached the one farthest from the cafeteria monitor's station. Not just any table, of course, but *the* table. The popular kids' table. Mr. Popularity himself, Lance Rathbone, im-mediately started introducing him to the other cool kids. Lance was a wizard whose father was a big-shot senator.

Eli's easy acceptance surprised me. The amount of magic a person could wield—at least in theory—mattered a lot when it came to the social ladder around here, and Eli had none. Katarina bestowed one of her dazzling smiles on Eli and gestured for him to sit beside her. Eli's eyes widened, and he practically fell into the chair. Apparently, I'd underestimated the importance of good looks even among magickind.

"Geez," I said, looking back at Selene. "Is being at the top of the social food chain like a universal birthright or something?"

She grimaced. "I think there's a national registry. It's online at eat-crap-dot-com."

I forced another smile.

"So I guess he was popular at your old school?"

"Um, yeah, you could say that." Back at Chickery High, I'd been fairly popular, too. I didn't inhabit the inner circles Eli did, but I had plenty of friends, most of them my teammates from soccer.

"Well, he *is* pretty cute," Selene said, looking him up and down. "Not that *I* care one bit about that. Looks shouldn't matter when it comes to judging a person."

I snorted. "Yeah, right."

She grinned. "So you think he's hot, too."

I shrugged, feeling suddenly warmer than before.

"He must be Lance's new roommate."

"Looks like it." I glanced over my shoulder. It was weird to see Eli looking nervous. He was usually so cool, almost to the point of being aloof, but right now he appeared on the verge of bolting for the door. No wonder he'd glared at me. Two days ago he'd been a normal high school boy in a normal human world. Now he wasn't.

And it was my fault.

I turned back to my breakfast, contemplated another bite, then stood and approached the nearest trash deposit area. I sorted out the recyclables into the appropriate bins and dumped the rest into a large rectangular trash can nearby. At once the plastic lining the bin started to rustle, but I paid it no mind. That was just the trash troll, a small, ugly creature that lived inside the bin and fed on the waste. Nearly all the trash cans at Arkwell contained trash trolls. They were mostly harmless, unlike their giant-sized kin that lived in the more remote areas of the world. Even still, it was a bad idea to try and fetch something out of a trash can once you tossed it in. At least one student in my year had lost a finger that way.

"Geez, Dusty," said Selene as I returned to the table. "Why do you look like someone just broke your favorite spell?"

"Well, I'm not exactly excited about Lance and his cronies getting a firsthand account every time I screw up dream-walking." Lance was the school jokester, the king of pranks and rumors. I could hear it now—jokes about how much I weighed, jokes about my lack of sex appeal, because let's face it, even though there was nothing sexual about dream-feeding, the mechanics of it *were* a little kinky.

Selene shook her head. "You don't know that'll happen. Eli might not tell those guys anything."

"Sure, and Lance is going to ask me to homecoming."

"What's homecoming?"

I sighed, hating it when I mixed up magickind traditions with ordinary ones. "It's like the Samhain dance."

"Oh, that's right. I knew that." Selene wrinkled her nose. "Well, who cares what he says one way or another? You shouldn't worry so much about what people think. If you want my advice you should sit back and enjoy the ride."

This painted far too vivid—and accurate—an image in my mind. "Ugh, I think I'm going to be sick." I gathered up my things, ignoring Selene's bemused stare. There was nothing I could say that would make her understand. I wasn't like her. I couldn't just bat my eyes and pout my lips and make Eli adore me. She hadn't heard the way he'd called me a freak. She couldn't understand how much he intimidated me on a purely physical level.

Selene patted my arm. "If it bothers you that much, why don't you try really hard to get good at this dream-seer stuff. Maybe once you catch the killer, the senate will let up and you can go back to normal."

"Yeah, sure. Because my life used to be so *normal*."

I slung my backpack over my shoulder and hurried for the door, doing my best not to glance at Eli. I felt better once I was out of the cafeteria. I shouldn't have to worry about seeing Eli again anytime soon. Arkwell was big enough that chances were good he wouldn't be in any of my classes.

Except three minutes before the homeroom bell rang, Eli walked in. I froze in my chair, braced for another glare from him, but he didn't even look at me as he walked past and took an empty seat in the far corner. Knowing he was there made my skin prickle. For a second I contemplated moving to the other side of the room, but I didn't want to look like a coward. Plus, I was too chicken to move.

When the class started a few minutes later, I decided to pretend he didn't exist. It was just homeroom, after all. I could handle twenty minutes. I lingered after the bell, making sure he left the classroom before I did. As soon as he was gone, I took a deep breath. No more Eli.

But when I walked into Miss Norton's classroom, there he was sitting next to Katarina. I told myself this wasn't a pattern, just coincidence. No matter my principal belief that there was no such thing as coincidence in the magical world.

Sometimes I really hate being right.

Eli followed me to spell casting and then to history afterward. I would've seen him at lunch, too, except I decided to skip it and head to the library to do some research on Keepers. The place was practically deserted at this time of day, giving me my pick of computer terminals. I sat down at one in the corner and woke up the screen with a push of the mouse. A pop-up box with a smiley face and the words "Hello, student!" immediately displayed on the screen. The animation phenomenon was particularly prevalent in the library.

I gritted my teeth and contemplated switching to another terminal in the hopes that it would be less lively than this one, but decided it wasn't worth the time. None of the computers in here were new.

In the text box below the greeting I typed "hi thanks" and pressed enter.

The pop-up disappeared, giving me access to the library's custom search engine. I typed "keeper" and "ring" in the box and pressed the search button.

Another pop-up appeared on the screen: "Are you sure you want to search for that?"

"Yes," I typed.

"Lots of people aren't, you know, sure." The smile on the smiley face widened.

"I'm sure."

"Sure, sure?"

"YES!!!" I pounded on the keys, trying to get the point across.

The smiley face frowned. "Okay, but don't say I didn't warn you."

At last, the stupid thing displayed the results, and I sighed in relief. There were three sets, one from the library archives, one from the ordinary Internet, and one from the e-net, which was magickind's version of the Internet. The "e" stood for enchantment, naturally.

I scanned the library results and selected one that looked like an encyclopedia entry:

A Keeper is a generic term reserved for a living being whose life force or force of will has been used as a key component in a magical spell. The binding of such a force makes the spell unbreakable for as long as the being in question remains alive, or in the case of the latter, remains committed to holding the spell. Death is usually the only effective means of breaking a Keeper spell.

Oftentimes, magical objects such as a ring, necklace, bracelet, or in rare cases, tattoos were used as the primary lynchpin of the spell. Generally, the lynchpins would seal themselves to the Keeper's body, requiring force to be removed. These lynchpins were virtually undetectable and impervious to many spells and charms, including those to locate, vanish, break, etc. Widely considered to be a form of black magic, the practice of using Keepers was banned by the Black Magic Purge Act of 1349.

A chill went through me as I finished reading. So Rosemary had been the Keeper of some kind of spell that the killer wanted to break. Well, that explained Lady Elaine's comment about Rosemary's age. Eighteen seemed awfully young to commit to a spell where the only way out of it was dying.

I skimmed through the rest of the library results, hoping for something more detailed, but found nothing. Next I tried the e-net results, but they contained only more simple definitions. Not that this was a big surprise, considering the practice of Keeper spells was illegal. The magickind government blocked any questionable material on the e-net.

With zero expectations, I clicked on the Internet results.

The first few were advertisements for rings designed to keep other rings in place. One was for a romance novel for sale on Amazon. A couple more had to do with World of Warcraft.

The title of the last entry on the page stopped me cold:

Death at Coleville, First Seal Broken

What was something like that doing on the Internet? I clicked the Web link, taking in the name of the website as I did. Reckthaworlde.com didn't exactly give me a warm fuzzy.

Another pop-up message from the computer appeared on the screen, the smiley face frowning again. "Sorry, Charlie. No can do."

"Why?" I typed.

"That site is restricted. No social media access in the library."

I frowned. Was Reckthaworlde.com some kind of anti-social Facebook? Seemed a little contradictory.

I closed the search engine on the library terminal, then pulled the eTab out of my bag. Social networking sites were perfectly allowable on personal devices. I performed the same search and clicked on the link again, appreciating how fast and normal the eTab responded. I wondered if it would ever show symptoms of animation. If it did, I bet it would have a cool personality. That would be nice. My desktop computer back in my dorm had already been two years past warranty when I moved in last spring, which meant it now had the personality of a crotchety old man, constantly complaining about how tired and over-worked it was and always going to sleep on me the second I stopped using it.

This time the screen popped up with a log-in box asking me to either enter my username and password or register as a new user. I clicked the latter and typed in my throwaway e-mail address. Another message appeared on the screen:

Welcome, dusty3125@gmail.com. In order to complete your registration, please enter the name of your initiator.

Say what? I'd never heard of such a thing. Was this some kind of online secret society?

Frustrated, I set the eTab down on the table harder than I meant to, almost dropping it.

"You might want to be more careful with that," someone said from behind me. "Those things can be pretty fragile."

Both startled and annoyed at the interruption, I said, "Really? And here I thought it was made out of rubber."

"Yeah, people make that mistake all the time."

I looked over my shoulder and did a mental stutter. The speaker was a seriously good-looking guy, maybe seventeen or eighteen, a senior probably. He was standing in front of a cart loaded down with library books ready to be shelved. He was tall and on the thin side, but still muscled. He wore his blond hair in a short ponytail at the base of his neck, but some of the strands had worked loose and now hung in his eyes. *Cute.* I realized I was staring and blushed.

He didn't seem to notice. "Did you just get it? The eTab, I mean."

"Yeah." *Okay, Dusty. You've got to do better than the one-word sentence.*

"Mind if I take a look? I've been thinking of getting one."

"Sure." I picked up the eTab, pressed the home button, and handed it to him.

He took it, an eager expression on his face. I watched as his adept fingers moved across the touch screen, opening apps, closing them again. He clearly knew his way around electronic devices. He handed it back to me a moment later. "Thanks."

"No problem." A two-word response. Fifty percent improvement, but still a long way from where I wanted to be. I tried to think of what Selene would say and decided to go for honesty. "I'm surprised you know so much about using it."

"Sure. I guess I'm a geek that way."

I smiled. "*You* are definitely not a geek."

He grinned. "Hel-lo," he said, pointing at himself. "Student *library* aide."

I laughed, half-tempted to point out that at least he was a *hot* library aide. And he definitely didn't get those bulging muscles in his forearms by shelving books. "Could be worse. You could be a hall monitor."

His grin broadened. "I'm Paul."

"Dusty."

"Yeah, I know."

"You do?"

He brushed the hair back from his eyes. "Sure. Who doesn't?"

"Oh, I get it. Your parents went to school with my mom, right? And they've warned you that any daughter of hers must be a real *nightmare*."

Paul chuckled. "Well, you don't look scary to me. Just the opposite."

A warm flutter passed through my stomach. The air felt charged with electricity, like in those rare moments when you know the person looking at you thinks you're attractive, and the even rarer moments when the feeling is mutual. Now at a complete loss for what to say, I was both saved and foiled by the warning bell.

"I guess you'd better go," Paul said, putting his hands on the library cart.

I smiled. "Yeah, I guess so."

"See you around." He walked away, disappearing behind a row of books.

I took a moment to catch my breath, then headed off for my psionics class. In the excitement of my brief interlude with Paul, I'd almost forgotten about Eli until I spotted him sitting in the top right-hand row beside Lance. The classroom had an auditorium setup that was more common in colleges than high schools. I took my usual seat in the left-hand side of the second row, determined not to let his presence unnerve me.

Our teacher, Mr. Ankil, arrived a few minutes late as usual, announcing a pop quiz as he came through the door. The whole class groaned.

Ankil put his hands on his hips and pretended to be disappointed. "Come on, guys. We have a new addition to our illustrious ranks, and the last thing we want to do is make Elijah think we don't have a blast in here. Am I right?"

"You're right," Lance said, giving him the finger-gun salute and doing a perfect imitation of Ankil's flamboyant, over-the-top style.

Mr. Ankil grinned. He was one of those teachers always trying to act like your friend rather than an authority figure. For the most part, he pulled it off. It didn't hurt that he wore his hair long and unkempt and favored the jeans-and-sandals look. He also sported multiple piercings in both ears, and he wore rings on all his fingers, including his thumbs.

Most of his success, though, could be attributed to his ability to influence our emotions with his empathic abilities. Ankil was a psychic, extremely gifted in all types of mind-magic—telepathy, telekinesis, and so on. Perfect for psionics, the study of mind-magic.

I wasn't very happy about the quiz. Psionics was my best magic-based subject, but it required a calm, focused state of being, something I sorely lacked today.

"Now, all you have to do is place your tennis balls inside the basket with *no hands*." Ankil motioned toward the storage closet on the other side of the room, and the door opened at once. At least twenty bright yellow Wilson balls flew out from it and began distributing themselves to all the students. Then Mr. Ankil summoned his wastebasket from beside his desk and placed it in the center of the room in front of us.

As pop quizzes went, this one was absurdly easy and well below even *my* skill level, but it was typical Ankil. He liked any excuse to give everybody a passing grade.

Easy or not, I still managed to bomb it.

I started off okay, lifting the ball into the air just by thinking about it, but then I heard Lance whisper loudly, "Be careful, Eli. There's no telling *where* this thing might go."

"Oh, I'm sure you're right," Eli said. "I've seen her in action."

Mortified, my concentration broke as memories of my disastrous encounter with him two nights ago flashed in my brain. I lost control of the ball, spiking it upward. It zoomed across the room like a yellow missile and smacked Lance in the forehead. I sunk down in my seat as several people laughed at my unintentional bull's eye.

His face flushed in anger, Lance picked up his tennis ball and winged it at me. There wasn't time to catch it, but I managed to swat it away with the back of my hand. It went flying again, and this time struck Mr. Ankil square in the chest.

Mr. Ankil shrugged it off like it was no big deal, but he summoned Lance's ball with his telekinesis and sent it sailing across the room where he set it on the desk in front of Lance.

"Since you seem so keen on throwing the ball," Mr. Ankil said, "why don't you try and make it into the basket using just your hands and *no* mind-magic."

Everybody recognized the challenge in the task and the chatter of voices from my classmates reacting to the scene died away, leaving an almost breathless silence. For me, I couldn't help but feel a swell of affection for Mr. Ankil. I knew as well as he did that Lance would miss. Magickind—wizards and witches in particular—weren't very skilled at hand-eye coordination.

Lance flubbed it. I mean, that sucker wasn't even in the same hemisphere as the wastebasket. I grinned in triumph at Lance.

Beside him, Eli picked up another tennis ball, and then with a casual gesture sent it soaring across the room and right into the basket as easily as if he *had* used magic.

Show-off. Go figure that the new guy, the I-can't-even-do-magic guy, would pass the quiz when I didn't.

After class, Mr. Ankil asked me to stay behind. I waited near his desk while the other students left, trying not to look nervous about whatever I must've done to warrant an after-class lecture.

Mr. Ankil said, "Lance picks on you a lot, doesn't he?"

I blinked at him, surprised. "Well, yeah, but Lance picks on everybody."

"So I've noticed. I went to school with guys like him. Wizards have a tendency to be full of themselves, arrogant to the point of stupid."

I grinned in total agreement.

Ankil grinned back. "How 'bout I show you a little trick you can use on the trickster?"

"Okay."

He turned and walked to the closet, pulling out one of the head-and-hand dummies. The dummy was a mannequin of a man's head and upper body that we sometimes used to practice more difficult skills. Ankil set the dummy on his desk and wedged a pencil into one of its hands.

"I was picked on a lot when I was a kid," Ankil said. "Shocking, I know, considering how *cool* I am now." He winked. "But seriously, psychics are often regarded as lower on the food chain than other witchkind."

I nodded. There were all kinds of tiers and levels among magickind based on their obsession with perceived power.

Ankil said, "The attitude stems from the belief that because mind-magic must obey the laws of physics, it is somehow weaker than spells that only obey the laws of the spell itself and nothing else."

"That's stupid."

"Yep, and utter nonsense. Mind-magic simply requires more practice, and a basic understanding of physics. When you've got that, you can do lots of things with it that spells can't. For example, you can use what I like to call the 'snatch-and-smack.'"

He faced the dummy then flicked his wrist. The pencil flew out of its hand, spun like a boomerang, and hit the dummy in the forehead.

"Did you see what I did there?" Ankil asked.

"Not really."

"Aha, but that's why it's so effective. As you well know, The Will wouldn't let you use magic to perform any act of violence against someone else. The Will can anticipate nearly all of our actions, both physical and magical. But if you break up the action, The Will can't guess your next move or prevent the laws of physics from doing their part. What I did was yank the pencil out but not hold on to it. As soon as it started to fall, I struck the tip of it, causing it to spin and then *wham!*"

He demonstrated the move again.

I watched more closely this time, catching on. "So it's like serving the ball in tennis or volleyball."

"A little, I suppose. But it's very tricky. You have to learn the right amount of force to get the object to move how you want it to when you hit it. Very effective if done right. Especially if the object in question is, say, a wizard's *wand.*"

"Oh," I said, brightening. "Are you're saying I can use this on Lance the next time he does something crappy?"

Ankil smiled. "I'm not giving you permission to do anything. I'm simply pointing out that it *can* be done. And trust me, nothing unnerves a wizard more than losing his wand. Or being attacked by it."

I laughed at the mental image of Lance being chased

down the hallway with his wand pelting him repeatedly from behind.

"So," Mr. Ankil said, "I want you to practice this technique for me as extra credit. Master it and you'll have a guaranteed B minimum for the quarter. Deal?"

"Deal."

I left Ankil's class a moment later. He was the coolest teacher ever.

But once again, my joy was only temporary as Eli was in my math class and then in alchemy after that. I was going to have to see him every day, all day long. Not to mention the thrice-weekly dream-sessions.

By the time I reached the girls' locker room before gym, I was feeling completely dejected. "Why are they doing this to me?" I asked Selene as we changed into our gym clothes.

"Who?"

"The school administrators, the Magi Senate, the powers that be." I threw up my hands. "Everyone."

Selene sighed sympathetically. "Maybe it has something to do with the way the dream-seer stuff works. Maybe you've got to spend a lot of time with the person to get a feel for it."

"Sure, like spending my nights with the guy won't be enough." That sounded dirtier than I intended, and Selene grinned as she pulled her blue-and-gray Arkwell T-shirt over her head. The image of our school mascot, Hank the Hydra, smiled at me with all seven heads from the emblem on the center of the shirt.

"You could always ask your Nightmare trainer," Selene said.

"I suppose so."

Not that it would change anything.

I finished tying the knot on my sneaker and stood up. "What I don't get is why they have him taking magic-based courses. He's not capable of doing any magic, right?"

Selene tugged on the front of her T-shirt, making sure it wasn't too tight. "Well, it's not that uncommon. There are halfkinds at this school that can't do magic, either, but they're still required to take the same courses. They just have to do a lot more textbook work and written exams than the rest of us, and all practical examinations are simulated. I think the idea is there's some value in learning the theory of magic even if you'll never use it."

"Huh," I said, seeing her point. The only reason I hadn't been forced to go here from day one was because my dad was an ordinary. Everybody figured I was completely ordinary, too, until I came into my powers. Just why they'd shown up so late, nobody knew. Or at least they hadn't told me. Halfkinds were rare, and a part-ordinary halfkind even rarer. I was probably the only one of my generation.

For once, gym was uneventful. Instead of war games, we played basketball, which gave me the chance not to look like an idiot. With the class as large as it was, Coach Fritz split us up into four random teams, and we played two half-court games at the same time. I got a double shot of luck as Eli ended up on a different team and a different court altogether.

After class, I had just enough time to take a shower before heading off to Jupiter Hall to meet Bethany Grey. Only when I came through the door into the classroom, it wasn't Bethany waiting for me but my *mother*.

The sight of her made my legs feel as if someone had replaced the muscles with jelly and the bones with wet noodles. What was she doing here? Not once in my life had her unexpected appearance signified anything good. I glanced around, half-expecting a police force to come bursting in to arrest us.

Moira was pacing back and forth across the room, her eyes fixed on the floor in front of her. For a moment, she didn't know I was there. *Run away now while you still can!* a voice shouted in my head.

I would've, too, except Mom was muttering to herself, "How can they do this? She's just a child. They've no idea what they're asking. The sheer arrogance."

She spotted me and stopped. "Destiny." From her, my name sounded like a curse.

"Hi, Mom."

Moira strode over, the spiked heels of her tall black boots striking the tiled floor like tiny hammers. She was wearing a fitted black jacket over a short skirt—she must've been at the office earlier. Mom owned a highly successful therapy practice, famous across the region for its unique, ahem, *dream* therapy techniques.

She grabbed me by the shoulders. "Finally. We've no time to lose. We need to get you packed."

I blinked at her, a bit alarmed at her panicked state. My mom was usually the definition of calm and cool, like a female James Bond. "What for?"

"You and I are running away. *Now.*"

5

Basic Training

S ay what?"

"We're running away," Moira repeated.

"Come again?"

She rolled her eyes. "Honestly, you'd think I never taught you English. What part of running away don't you understand? You, me, Mexico." She nodded to herself, as if this plan was news to her, too. "Yes, that's it. We'll wait it out with sun and cocktails until this thing with Rosemary is over."

I glared at her, furious at her audacity in thinking she could swoop into my life whenever she felt like it and start dictating. She gave up that parental right when she abandoned me and Dad a long time ago. Sure, she'd been coming around more often now that I'd inherited my Nightmare powers, but fair-weather mothering didn't count. And we weren't "girlfriends" or BFFs, either. *Cocktails indeed.*

"I'm not going anywhere," I said. "Besides, I'm not old enough to drink."

Moira put her hands on her hips, assuming her "I'm the boss" stance. "You *are* coming with me. You're not getting involved in this murder business. It's too dangerous, and you're too young."

My mom, a study in contradictions.

I decided it was time for a subject change. "Where's Bethany?"

Mom scowled. "Don't worry about it. I took care of her."

"Geez, Mom, what did you do now?" I looked around for cops again.

"She'll be fine. You don't want to learn from her anyway. She's a horrible woman."

"But where *is* she?"

"Taking a little nap. Long enough for you and me to get out of here."

I groaned, certain she had used a sleeping spell. I kept hoping Mom would give up her habit of breaking The Will, but apparently, it was never going to happen. Just how she got away with it was a mystery, although most of the rumors suggested she was friendly with a lot of high-ranking Will-Workers, those weirdo magickind whose job it was to keep The Will running smoothly, and who made sure the spell knew who it needed to keep in check by maintaining the registry.

"I can't believe you! You're going to get us both in trouble," I said.

"Don't be ridiculous. We'll be fine."

"Yeah, sure."

"Come on. Let's go." She reached for my arm.

I pulled away. "No."

Moira frowned, a look of momentary surprise in her pale, almost white eyes. She wasn't used to people defying her. Shame. If she'd stuck around more often, I'd have given her loads of practice.

"You've got to come away with me, Destiny."

"Not until you tell me why."

She blanched. "I can't tell you."

I rolled my eyes. "I'm not five anymore, Mom. You can't just make demands and expect me to obey without question."

"Fine. Because it's dangerous, and I don't want you to get hurt."

Well, *there* was a satisfying response. Common sense told me I should be afraid of anything that provoked this much anxiety in my mother, but as usual I felt the opposite. My curiosity skyrocketed, and for the first time, I envisioned myself solving the mystery, saving the day. Being the hero.

"Well," I said, "that's too bad, because I'm *not* running away with you, and I *am* going to do what the senate wants and be the best dream-seer *ever*."

"You are so stubborn." Moira shook her head.

Encouraged by her frustration, I added, "You forgot rebellious and a smart aleck."

She glowered at me for a second, then grinned. "I know. I'd expect nothing less from *my* daughter."

Crap. I hated when she turned the tables on a perfectly good argument. Why did she have to get all proud about my misbehavior? Why couldn't she stay angry and maybe ground me like a normal parent? I supposed I could turn the tables back on her if I started behaving like the perfect kid, always doing what I was told, never back talking, but I just didn't think I had it in me.

"All right," Mom said. "I suppose running away really isn't an option."

I stared, speechless at her sudden reversal, and a little suspicious, too.

"Don't look so shocked. Contrary to what your father says, I *can* be reasonable. But I'm not happy about this. You've no idea the danger."

"I'll be fine, Mom."

"Of course you will, until the killer finds out you're a dream-seer. When he does, what do you think he'll do next?"

I gulped as horrible visions of the killer coming after me flashed in my brain.

Moira smirked. "That's what I thought. You *haven't* thought about it."

"Wait a minute. If that's true, why hasn't the senate kept me and Eli a secret? Far as I can tell, everybody knows about us."

"That's because the discovery of a new dream-seer pair is too *prestigious* for the senate to keep it quiet."

"How do you mean?"

"It's about status, Destiny. A dream-seer is a powerful

tool, a *weapon,* and the Magi Senate is now the only governing body in the magical world to currently have one. The Magi Parliament in Britain had the last pair years ago, and it helped them gain the power they have now. The senate will seek to do the same with you. They'll want everybody to know."

I frowned, less than thrilled at the idea of being the government's shiny new gun. "So you're saying I might predict more than just stuff about the killer?"

"Yes. In the past, dream-seers have identified spies, uncovered assassination attempts, all sorts of things."

So much for hoping this would be a one-time gig. I bit my lip. "So we're like the psychic CIA."

Moira tapped her foot. "Don't be ridiculous."

"But why are dream-seers so important? It seems a lot like being an oracle to me."

"Not at all. Oracles only see what they are able to see. They have little control in directing the subject of their visions. Dream-seers don't."

I started to nod then stopped. "Hang on. How do *you* know so much about dream-seers? Until yesterday I'd never heard of such a thing."

A somber look crossed Moira's face. "Because you're not the first in our family to be one. Our ancestor was one over a thousand years ago."

I frowned. "Well, if I really am so important to the senate, they must be doing something to keep me safe."

"Are you *sure?*"

Well, no, but I refused to admit it. "The killer's not just some random psycho. He's looking for something specific. Rosemary was guarding something, or at least the Keeper spell on her was."

"How do you know that?" Mom sounded breathless with shock.

I thought about placing the blame on Elaine, but I wouldn't put it past my mother to take vengeance on the old lady. "I put two and two together."

Moira crossed her arms. "I know you don't *really* expect me to believe that."

I closed my mouth and refused to say more.

She sighed. "Well, I guess it's too late to pull you out of this. I suppose I'll just have to keep an eye on you myself."

I tried not to laugh. "You're going to be my bodyguard?"

"Either that or I'm going to kidnap you."

I put my hands on my hips. "You could help me instead. The sooner they catch the killer, the more likely I'll live to see junior year."

"That's not funny, Destiny."

"I'm serious. Nobody will tell me anything. I don't even know what it is I'm supposed to be looking for other than the obvious. But I doubt this guy's just gonna show up in Eli's dreams."

Moira nodded, her short, pixie-cut blond hair fluttering around the sides of her face like butterfly wings. "You're right. But nobody can tell you what to look for. There's no way to know. Every minuscule aspect of a dream could be brimming with signs of impending doom. Or it could mean nothing at all."

"That's helpful."

"But I *can* teach you a few tricks about dream-walking. Come on. Let's get to it now while we've got a chance." She strode toward the door.

"Where are we going?" I said as I followed after her.

"The janitor's closet."

"Mind telling me why?"

"That's where I put Bethany. She'll make an ideal candidate to practice on."

You know how they say nurses make the worst patients? Well, the same was true of Nightmares and dream subjects. Bethany detected us almost at once. Her dream was taking place in a vast room that bore a strong resemblance to the pictures I'd seen of Senate Hall where Consul Vanholt and the rest of the Magi held their meetings. Bethany appeared to be occupying the consul's chair.

She stood up at once and pointed at my mother. "*You.* What are *you* doing here?"

Moira gave her a little wave, almost like a salute. "Hello, Beth. Long time no see."

"Get out," Bethany sneered. Then she charged us, which would've been scary enough in the real world given her resemblance to a gorilla—she was thick and stout, with black bushy eyebrows—but she was twice as scary in her own dream. The black-and-white world around me began to melt as Bethany's mind neared consciousness. Any moment now and I would be kicked out. I closed my eyes, bracing for the inevitable pain.

Bang!

I opened them again to see Bethany lying on the ground a few feet away, moaning. *What the—?*

"Never do learn, do you, Beth?" Moira said. She took hold of my arm and hauled me toward the two huge doors at the hall's entrance.

"What did you do to her?" I said to my mother.

"Glass wall." Moira pushed open one of the doors and stepped through. I followed her into the middle of a shopping mall. It wasn't unusual for the scenery in a dream to change without warning, but I knew at once this was different. For one, the scene was solid again, all the melting and slippage now gone. For another, I was pretty sure this was the Macy's department store in New York City, one of my mom's favorite places in the whole world. Every summer she took me on a five-day shopping spree in New York as part of her annual attempt to buy my affection. I found it pretty unlikely Bethany would be dreaming about Macy's of all places. From the looks of her, she hadn't bought new clothes since 1989.

"Did you do this?" I asked.

Mom grinned, her bright eyes flashing as she faced the door we'd just come through. It was now normal sized and labeled JANITOR. She waved her hand over the door-knob, and the lock clicked into place.

From the other side of the door Bethany screamed, "Stop manipulating my dream, you bitch!"

I just stared. "How are you doing it?"

Moira grabbed my hand and pulled me down the aisle at a run. "Any Nightmare can change the content of a dream. If you've got enough power, that is." She stopped and ducked behind a shoe rack display, yanking me beside her. She whispered, "That's one of the reasons why the Magi only want you to feed every other week. A fully charged Nightmare can do whatever they want inside a dream. Here, we're like gods."

A chill went through me at her words. It all sounded a bit too much like *A Nightmare on Elm Street* for my tastes. I understood the danger of that much power, having experienced enough bad dreams in my lifetime to know how scary and *real* they could be.

Moira continued. "Now that you're allowed to feed more often, you can do this, too."

"But why would I want to manipulate someone like that?"

"Lots of reasons. A dream-seer is two people, Destiny, not one. As the Nightmare, you read the dream's content, but Eli is the channel for the contents. It flows *through* him. If you're not getting anywhere, you can always help the flow by setting the scene."

"You mean I could re-create what he saw about Rose-mary?"

"Maybe. At the very least you can simulate the locale."

I shook my head, but before I could ask any questions, Bethany burst through the door and came running down the aisle toward us. Moira stood up and faced her.

She glanced at me, and said. "You can also do *this*." Moira raised her hands, and this time I saw the glass appear in front of Bethany, boxing her in.

Bethany slid to a stop and pounded on the glass with both fists. "Let me out. This is *my* dream."

"All in good time, sweetheart." Mom faced me. "Now I want you to create something. It should be small, inanimate, and familiar."

"Don't teach her that!" Bethany shouted.

Moira waved her hand again, and this time all the noise Bethany was making vanished. Mom turned back to me. "Go on."

I hesitated, glancing at Bethany's rage-twisted face. "Are you sure about this?"

"Quite. Beth's just being paranoid. There's nothing to worry about. Now go ahead. Try and create something you know well."

Silly, I know, but the first thing to come to mind was a Milky Way Midnight bar. It was my favorite candy, and I was starved from skipping lunch. Plus, I'd always liked the wrapping with its purple-and-black galaxy background. No sooner had I pictured the thing than it appeared on the display table in front of me.

Moira spotted it at once and beamed. "Good job."

I wasn't used to her complimenting me, and I flushed

as I picked it up. The candy was solid in my hand, and when I peeled off the wrapping, the smell of the dark chocolate made my mouth water.

I glanced at my mother. "I don't know how I did it."

She waved off my doubt. "Just try again."

I did, but this time nothing happened.

Moira said, "Changing a dream works like mind-magic, but instead of using your mind, you use your imagination."

"What's the difference?"

"More than you'll ever know. Now try again."

I closed my eyes and did as she asked. Instead of visualizing the candy bar, I sort of day-dreamed about it. It took a long time, but I eventually managed to create a second Milky Way. The effort left me feeling like I'd run a marathon.

Mom patted me on the back. "Don't worry. It'll get easier the more you practice and the more you feed."

She probably meant this as encouragement, but being reminded of my feeding duties only made me want to quit. "Can we go now?"

"You first. I need to let Miss Grouchy Pants out of her cage."

I figured Bethany had a right to be grouchy, but saw no point in arguing. I slipped out of the dream into my body. To my astonishment the Milky Way I'd created was still in my hand. I tightened my fingers around it, testing its solidity. It vanished.

My mother came back to her body a moment later. She

stood and pushed me toward the door. "Go on. Get out of here before Beth wakes up. I'll smooth things over."

Somehow, I doubted that. I wanted to ask her about the candy bar, but Bethany's eyes opened and now obviously wasn't a good time. I backed out of the janitor's closet and closed the door. A second later I heard loud bangs and muffled shouts, but I refused to worry as I headed down the hallway out of earshot. Physical violence was restricted by The Will, so whatever they were doing to each other couldn't be too bad. Besides, with my dream-feeding session with Eli quickly approaching, I had my own battles to worry about.

6

The Black Phoenix

I had every intention of using my newfound knowledge when I went to Eli's dorm room the following night, but things didn't exactly work out that way.

We'd spent another long, awkward day ignoring each other. When the time came for the session, I headed downstairs to the foyer only to find the security guards blocking the way out—two medieval knights I'd nicknamed Frank and Igor. They weren't actual people but rather animated suits of armor as hollow on the inside as a chocolate Easter bunny. They turned their masked faces toward me, swords pointed.

"Whoa, hey guys," I said, coming to a stop. "I've got a dream-feeding session. Um . . . may I pass?" This wasn't something I normally had to ask.

They kept staring for a moment. It was a little creepy to sense they *were* staring even though they didn't have eyes, just black slits in their helmets. Finally, they moved aside, and I hurried past them with a friendly wave. I always tried to be as nice to the knights as possible. As a Nightmare, I thought it a good idea to make sure they liked me so as to avoid any accidental maiming when I came and went for dream-feeding sessions. Of course, I was working under the assumption that empty suits of armor were capable of such feelings as liking.

I passed at least half a dozen werewolf police officers on my walk to Eli's dorm, all of them eyeing me suspiciously but not saying anything. I went through the same drill with the knights guarding Eli's dorm, the tightened security a result of Rosemary's murder.

I expected Eli to be asleep when I arrived, but he was wide awake, sitting in a chair by the window. The dorms at Arkwell were sectioned into two rooms, one side for the beds and the other side for living space, with only a flimsy divider between them. Lance's father was a rich senator, so the dorm room was tricked out like a movie star bachelor pad, complete with a massive flat screen TV and a sound system powerful enough to vibrate the stone walls.

Eli stared at me as I came in, looking wary.

I hated how uncomfortable he made me. "Hi," I said, running a hand through my hair. The curls were so thick, my fingers got stuck halfway. *Smooth.*

"Hey."

"What are you doing awake?" He was also fully dressed in jeans and a T-shirt. I wore my usual dream-feeding outfit of black stretchy pants, black fitted tee, and soft black leather moccasins. It served the purpose of being concealing and flexible. His outfit served the purpose of sending me a clear message: he had no intention of playing along. *Great.*

Eli stood up, and I resisted the urge to step back. *Get over it already, Dusty,* a voice that sounded an awful lot like Selene's said in my mind. *He's just a guy with a hot body. Big deal. Who cares?*

"I'm not going to let you do this," said Eli.

I refused to be intimidated. "You can't stop it."

"Sure I can. I saw what happened last time. Your *magic* didn't work on me." He made the word sound like something dirty.

"Didn't you pay attention in orientation? It's not my magic you've got to worry about but The Will's."

He folded his arms across his chest. I tried not to stare at the muscles. The guy was like a roller coaster, all bumpy and stuff. I glanced at the entrance into the bedroom part of the dorm where I could hear the sound of steady breathing. Lance Rathbone, no doubt. What a comfort.

Eli said, "I don't believe there's any such thing as The Will."

I turned back, feeling a little smug. "You'll find out soon enough."

"I'll never fall asleep with you in here."

"Sure you will. I'll just wait." I sat down on the sofa across from him and waved at the TV. "Any chance I can get a remote?"

Eli looked at me as if I'd just sprouted a second head. I shrugged and picked up a magazine off the end table.

Guns and Ammo wasn't exactly my favorite, but it was better than nothing. I rifled through the pages.

"Are you really just going to sit there?" said Eli.

"Would you prefer me to hit you over the head with a frying pain?"

He didn't reply, but sat down in the chair again. I stole a glance at him. His silence was unnerving. I always knew he was the brooding type, but this was like being locked in a cage with a panther. Everything from the slant of his dark eyebrows to the way he slouched in the chair exuded danger. The thought made my skin burn.

I glanced back at the magazine, playing it cool. I would wait him out.

After a while, he said, "So you're a *Nightmare*?"

"In the flesh." I looked over at him.

He smirked. "Lance told me to be careful of you."

The admission stung, but I managed not to react. It was totally unfair. Lance had never been the victim of one of my magical mishaps. "He's a jackass."

Eli's chuckle took me by surprise, the sound deep and throaty, very *male*. "Yeah, sometimes. But he's pretty cool to me, which I didn't expect. You know, considering somebody like me has no business attending a school like this."

I flinched at the sound of his bitterness, trying not to feel guilty.

"This place doesn't even have a football or baseball team."

I didn't say anything. I knew all too well how he felt. It had been the same for me, as if I'd been transported to an alien world full of different rules and expectations. But at least I could do magic, unlike Eli. I wanted to say something commiserating, except I remembered what a jackass *he'd* been in psionics yesterday.

Eli's behavior still surprised me. He might be a bit of a troublemaker and too arrogant for his own good, and he went through girlfriends about as often as he got a haircut, but I'd never seen him be an outright bully. Just the opposite. More than once I had watched him stand up for the little guy, like that time our freshman year when he told off a senior during a pep rally after the guy started making fun of one of the freshman cheerleaders for being bigger than the other girls on the squad. I thought the senior was going to kill him, but Eli didn't back down. He hadn't cared that the guy was older and bigger. All he had seemed to care about was that the girl had run out of the gym crying.

Apparently he was a different person here. Just as well. I'd rather dislike him than secretly pine for him or something equally as stupid. Of course that would be a lot easier if somebody would hit him with the ugly stick. I wondered if there was a spell for something like that.

"Well, I'm not dangerous, no matter what Lance says," I said.

Eli opened his mouth to respond, but ended up yawning instead.

I returned my attention to the magazine, knowing he would be asleep soon. I could feel The Will at work, those invisible tentacles tugging at me to complete my task. He felt it, too.

It took the better part of five minutes, but eventually I heard the sound of his head hitting the back of the chair. I stood and walked to him, happy to get this over with.

The happiness was short-lived. I'd never dream-fed on someone sitting up in a chair, and I quickly learned why—it was a pain in the ass and awkward as hell. It was also perilous. With my feet perched on the arms, I'd go tumbling off the moment Eli decided to move at all. At least the chair let me keep the direct body-to-body contact at a minimum. That was something.

Given that I'd dream-fed twice since Sunday, I wasn't feeling particularly hungry. Not that it mattered to The Will—it grew insistent the moment I was in position. I sighed and placed my fingers against Eli's temples and entered his dreams.

I half-expected to be back at Coleville, but no such luck. Eli was dreaming about football. I was standing on the bleachers at Chickery High stadium, shoulder to shoulder with students. Some of them had the distinctive faces of people I knew, and some were just blank. The blank ones were creepy, like walking, talking mannequins. The dude in front of me was one. He turned around and looked at me with his shapeless eyes, nothing more than divots on his peach-colored skull. Then he pumped his hands in the air as if expressing his enthusiasm for the game.

A little freaked, I flew up and away from the stadium crowd. I spotted Eli on the field among his teammates, who all had distinctive features, thank goodness. Going off what my mom told me about Eli being the channel for the important stuff, I decided to stick close to him.

I alighted onto the field behind a hulking player I recognized as Brian Johnson. Seeing him brought back memories of the first time I ever dream-walked. Not particularly good ones. Nobody thought I'd inherited any Nightmare powers until I woke up one night feeling a hunger no Snickers bar could satisfy. Half-dazed, half-terrified, I broke into Brian's house, climbed on top of him, and found myself in a dream-world populated by naked girls with big boobs. One of them had been a friend of mine. When I caught Brian trying to grope her, I kicked him, not knowing any better.

Yeah, it didn't end well.

I contemplated giving Brian another kick now for old times' sake, but I needed him for cover. I couldn't trust that Eli wouldn't spot me again. I peered around his baby-elephant-sized frame and oriented my gaze to match Eli's. He was staring at something near the stadium, and it took only a second to figure out what. A handful of cheerleaders stood with their backs to the field while they jumped and shouted at the folks in the stands. All save one. Katarina Marcel, wearing the red-and-white short-skirt, short-top ensemble of the CHS varsity cheerleading squad, was facing the field and staring right back at Eli.

"Yeah, this blows," I muttered.

Talking was a mistake. Eli's body went rigid, and he spun toward me. "What are *you* doing here?"

"Whoa, big guy. Hands off." I raised my arms like a shield, but he kept advancing. I flew up out of his reach.

Eli stopped and stared up at me, wide-eyed. "How are you doing that?"

"I'm a Nightmare, remember? Or did nobody explain it to you?"

He thought about it a moment then his shoulders relaxed. "This is a dream?"

"Yeppers. *Your* dream."

"Why can't I fly?"

"Dunno. Have you tried?"

A moment later he was hovering in the air in front of me, looking pretty silly as he did floating pirouettes in his football uniform. I backed away from him, leery of such close proximity.

"Cool," he said, doing a flip this time.

Across the field, Katarina was still smiling at him, completely unfazed by his sudden ability to fly. I couldn't help but glare at her. Why did Eli have to dream about *her* of all people? It was bad enough I had to see her during the school day. Maybe I could turn her into another snake.

"What are you looking at?" Eli glanced over his shoulder.

"Nothing," I said, more sharply than I intended. "I mean, everything. That's why I'm here, remember? We're supposed to be solving a murder."

He grinned. "Okay, Nancy Drew. But I got the idea we're supposed to be predicting the next one."

"Same difference."

"No, it's not."

"Yes, it is."

"No, it's not."

If I'd been on the ground I would've stomped my foot at him. Instead I let myself float down until I was standing again. He plopped down beside me.

I glared at him, considered pursuing the argument further, then decided I'd wasted enough time already. Regardless of what you called it, we did have a job to do here. An important one.

I looked around, trying to spy anything significant. As before, Eli's dream was surprisingly undreamlike. Aside from a couple of little things like the faceless people in the grandstands, everything was exactly as you'd find it on any Friday night in the fall. Even the school band was its usual state of bad.

"Booker!" a gruff male voice shouted from the sidelines. Eli and I both turned to see the head football coach waggling a finger at him. "Get your butt out there."

I grinned. "Yeah, Booker, why don't you run along and play while I see if there's anything useful around here?"

"No way. I'm not letting you poke around my dream by yourself."

I wasn't listening. Something strange had caught my eye. Perched on the rail that separated the field from the grandstand was a huge bird, nearly the size of a human. Slick black feathers covered its head and body while the feathers in its tail were a brilliant scarlet and gold. It looked a bit like a heron with its long neck and legs and narrow beak, but I didn't think it was. There was something almost dragonish about it with its weirdly intelligent eyes, so bright a yellow against the black they seemed to glow. It was looking at me as if it had something to say, a bone to pick, maybe. A thrill of fear shot through me at the sight of it. It looked so real, and so very capable of snapping off one of my appendages in a single bite.

I stepped toward it for a closer look. Nothing in a dream could hurt me, no matter how scary.

The bird disappeared.

I glanced at Eli. "Did *you* do that?"

"Do what?"

"Never mind." I marched past him toward the grandstand to investigate. I thought I could see some dark marks on the metal railing where the bird's talons had gripped it.

Eli grabbed my arm. I had a second to think, *not again*. Then the dream world disappeared, and I crashed back into my body. Disoriented and in pain, I lost my balance and tumbled backward off the chair. My flailing arm struck the table as I went down, knocking it over. A can of diet, caffeine-free Mountain Dew hit the floor, and yellow soda sprayed out, covering me in warm liquid.

"You okay?" Eli took hold of my arms and lifted me as if I were a toddler. But then his foot slipped on the wet floor, and we went down again. I landed on top of him, my face pressed against his stomach. Nobody's abs should be that hard.

He grunted. "Are you always this klutzy or is it just because of me?"

I jumped up, shoving him in the chest as I did so. "You're an idiot." I waved my hand over the mess of soda and said the incantation for the only cleaning spell I knew, "Drasi-neo."

The lightbulb in a nearby lamp exploded.

"Nice one."

I scowled at Eli. It was his fault my magic was on super-charge again and that I was too dizzy to obtain the proper level of concentration required for the spell. "Didn't any-body tell you not to touch me when I'm dream-walking?"

"Well, yes, but they didn't say why."

I rolled my eyes. "Typical. Leave it to you to break the rules."

He stood up. "What's that supposed to mean?" Before I could answer, he started grinning. "You can't stay in the dream if I touch you, can you?"

Too furious to speak, I turned around, only to crash into Lance standing just beyond the doorway to the bed-room. I grabbed my nose, which had struck his ridicu-lously hard shoulder, my eyes watering.

"That was quite a show," Lance said. "Do you straddle all your victims even after they're awake, or is it some-thing special you reserve for Eli?"

Heat burst over my body, turning my skin as red as my hair. I pushed Lance out of the way and made a beeline for the door. I sprinted down the hallway and didn't stop running until I reached my dorm room and locked the door behind me.

Then I slumped onto the sofa, taking a moment to wallow in misery as visions of the ridicule I would face tomorrow played out in my brain.

When I finally got tired of feeling sorry for myself, I stood and tried to shrug off the worry. I wanted to go to bed, but I remembered Lady Elaine's insistence that I complete a dream entry as soon as a session ended. Considering how badly the rest of the night had gone, I didn't want to piss off the old woman. Lance and Eli might be able to make my social life hell, but I had a feeling Lady Elaine could do a lot worse.

Sighing, I walked over to the desk where the eTab sat in its docking station beside my desktop computer. I opened it to the dream journal, typed a quick entry, and hit send. Then I pressed the home button and was about to put the eTab to sleep when I noticed the instant message app blinking at me. Only one person would IM here.

I opened a message from a user called OracleGirl: "Did the bird look like this?"

Below the message was a drawing of a bird that bore a striking resemblance to what I'd seen.

"Yes," I typed back. "But the one in the dream had black feathers instead of red. What kind of bird is it?"

Lady Elaine took a long time responding. "Phoenix."

Huh. I'd heard of them before, but I'd never seen one. They were as rare as unicorns and usually lived in the most remote places, far away from the eyes of ordinaries and magickind alike. Lady Elaine's interest in the bird made me uneasy. I was on the verge of asking the oracle what it meant when her next message derailed me.

"Why did your dream-session end so early?"

I groaned. I hadn't planned on telling anybody about Eli booting me from the dream. The last thing I wanted was to get a reputation for being a narc. But I didn't see a way out of it short of lying—not such a good idea with an oracle—so I told her what happened.

"I see," Lady Elaine responded when I finished. "Don't worry. I'll have a talk with Eli in the morning."

Awesome. Couldn't wait to see the results of that one.

7

The Diary

Eli wasn't at breakfast the next day. I got to enjoy that fact for all of two seconds. Then I made the mistake of walking by Lance's table with my tray in my hand and saw him reenacting my fall from last night.

I heard him say, "Yeah, she totally wrecked our room. Spilt soda all over the place. The girl's psycho, I'm telling you."

I took a step toward him, planning to knock him out of his chair, then pour milk on him for good measure.

Selene put a hand on my shoulder. "Don't bother."

She was right, and I knew it. The Will wouldn't let me hit him. I contemplated using Mr. Ankil's snatch-and-smack trick, but I hadn't practiced it yet, and Lance wasn't carrying his wand, just the stupid joker playing card he liked to fiddle with whenever he was bored, weaving it in between his fingers like he was some kind of card shark.

I'd once asked Selene what the deal was with the card, and she explained that Lance was obsessed with the Joker from Batman. In an ordinary high school, he would've been ridiculed for this behavior, but not at Arkwell. Most magickind teenagers were fanatics about ordinary pop culture. Almost everybody was a Comic-Con–attending, play-dress-up fan boy. And he had the nerve to make fun of *me*. Go figure.

I spent the rest of breakfast doing my best to ignore the laughs coming from behind me. I decided this was how I would live my life from here on out—pretending like the bad stuff wasn't happening.

But I found out later that you couldn't pretend something didn't exist when it was staring you in the face. Or in my case, when it came up behind me in the hallway and closed my locker door while I wasn't looking. I supposed I was lucky Lance hadn't shut it on my fingers.

"Thanks, you jackass," I said, glaring.

He grinned at me like a cat that knows it's got the mouse cornered. He had bright green eyes, light brown hair, and a wide mouth, a bit like the Joker's, actually. Still, he was handsome enough I had no trouble understanding why Selene had once dated him. "Anytime, sweetheart." He leaned against the adjacent locker, arms crossed, head cocked sideways, and reeking of attitude.

"Don't you have something better to do?" I said, reentering the combination. "Like, entertaining your little friends some more? I know. You could do something *really* spectacular this time like pat your head and rub your tummy. Or walk and chew gum. That is, if you think you can manage it."

"No thanks. I'd rather sit here and look at you. It gives me so much *pleasure*."

"Yep, I get that *all* the time." I wrenched my locker door open, trying to whack him in the face with it. That would've given *me* loads of pleasure. The Will might restrict direct physical violence, but accidents happened.

Lance dodged the strike easily, and before I could stop him, he closed the door again.

"Would you quit it? Seriously, I've known cockroaches more mature than you."

He leaned toward me close enough I could smell the musky scent of his shampoo. It was a surprisingly pleasant smell from such a rotten guy. "You could always report me like you did Eli. Then maybe I could spend the morning in the principal's office and get an awesome lecture on proper dream etiquette, too."

So that was what this was about. I should've known. I almost apologized, then remembered who I was talking to. I felt bad I'd gotten Eli in trouble, but he deserved the apology more than this creep. "Go away. You're not worth the effort."

"Oh, baby, you have no idea what effort I'm worth." Lance made a rude gesture with his hips.

I ignored him and opened my locker a third time, keeping my hand on it so he couldn't shut it again.

"Leave her alone, Lance," Selene said, coming up behind him. Her expression was cool, and her voice held a sharp edge.

Lance flashed a mischievous smile at her. "Or what? You'll break up with me and go sit at the losers' table again? Put on a ball cap and act like a guy? Right. Because that was such an effective punishment last time."

If sarcasm were butter, you could've spread him over toast. I could tell his words had hurt Selene. The sparkle in her eyes wasn't from an overabundance of happy.

Lance made a kissing gesture at her then turned and strode away. I was so furious I wanted to hit him. I wanted it so badly, I almost saw myself doing it.

Then Lance flinched as if struck. He cupped the back of his head and spun around. "What the hell? Who did that?"

When no one answered him, he glowered at me before stalking off. The back of his neck was as bright as a cherry lollipop. I focused on it, this time actively engaging my telekinesis to try and do it again. I felt the magic leave me and then . . . nothing. The force of the spell simply evaporated, absorbed into The Will like always.

Selene looked at me, her violet eyes wide. "Did *you* do that?"

I frowned. "I'm not sure." Only that wasn't entirely true. It felt sort of like how I'd made that Milky Way appear in Bethany Grey's dream, imagination instead of thought. But I'd had such vengeful thoughts hundreds of times before without any results. Somebody else must've done it.

I looked around, half-expecting to see my mother. She said she was going to play bodyguard, but she was nowhere in sight.

I noticed Mr. Marrow standing in the doorway to the teacher's lounge, staring at me with a peculiar expression on his face. He must've seen what happened. My stomach sank as I recognized that look, shame washing over me. It lasted only a second before his usual, kind smile came to his face, but I knew that a moment before he'd been afraid. Of me. I'd seen others give similar looks to my mom whenever she did something she shouldn't be able to do.

I smiled back, then turned around, trying not to think about it anymore. Since the day she'd left me and Dad, I'd promised myself I wouldn't grow up to be like my mother.

Maybe that was easier said than done.

When I arrived at history class a few hours later, Mr. Marrow acted normal toward me, which was a relief. I wanted to ask him about Keepers, and I figured it wouldn't hurt to ask him about phoenixes, too. The brief time I'd spent researching them this morning before school hadn't told me much. Most of the articles seemed fixated on the immortality of the phoenix, the way they died and rose again from the ashes. Legend said that if a magickind was able to make a phoenix their familiar it would transfer some of its immortal powers to them. I didn't know much about familiars other than that it was a magical bond between a magickind and an animal where the animal became a sort of magical servant. But I understood why people would want a phoenix as one. Lots of famous magickind had gone on quests to capture one for that very reason, although none had ever succeeded as far as I could tell.

I didn't have a clue what the phoenix meant in Eli's dream. The most obvious interpretation was that something or someone was going to be reborn, only I couldn't see how that fit with Rosemary's murder. Maybe the phoenix represented an upcoming event unrelated to her death. Or maybe it meant nothing at all. The whole thing was beyond frustrating, like trying to put together a jigsaw puzzle in a pitch-black room.

I didn't get a chance to talk to Marrow. When class ended, he disappeared out the door ahead of everybody else. I hoped it was because he had an important lunch date and not that he was avoiding me.

When school ended for the day, I came back to his classroom. The door stood ajar, but I knocked anyway.

"Come in," Marrow called.

Trying not to be nervous, I marched straight to his desk.

"Oh, hello, Dusty," said Marrow. "You weren't who I was expecting."

"Sorry, I was just hoping to talk to you."

"Oh? What about?"

I adjusted the strap of my backpack. "I thought you might be able to help me with this dream-seer stuff."

"I see."

"I've got all sorts of questions."

"Such as?"

"I heard you and Lady Elaine talking about Keepers,

and she told me that the spell was guarding something, but she didn't say what. I was hoping you could tell me."

Marrow leaned back in his chair and tented his fingers in front of him. "Why do you *need* to know what the spell is guarding?"

The question took me off guard. I supposed I *wanted* to know mostly out of curiosity, but I sensed that wouldn't be a good enough answer. Then the reason for why I *needed* to know came to me. "I think it will help me identify the killer."

"How so?"

"Because the type of object it is might point to the type of person who'd want it."

Marrow smiled, a pleased glint in his eyes. "Very good. But I'm not sure I'm the one who should tell you. It's a sensitive subject."

I grimaced, unsurprised by his hesitation. "So Lady Elaine said."

Marrow chuckled. "Yes, she can be quite a stickler for rules. She—" He broke off as someone entered the classroom. I looked toward the door and saw it was the boy I'd met in the library on Monday.

"Hey," I said. "What are you doing here?"

Paul grinned as he walked toward us. "Mr. Marrow is helping me with my college admission essay."

"Oh, yeah? Where to?"

He looked a little embarrassed. "MIT."

"For real?" I couldn't keep the surprise from my voice. A lot of magickind decided to attend an ordinary college after graduating rather than go to one of the four international magickind universities, but I knew there weren't many of us smart enough in ordinary classes to make it into a college as prestigious as MIT.

"It's only an application. No guarantee of admission," said Paul.

"He's being modest." Marrow stood and came around the desk. "Our Mr. Kirkwood here is quite brilliant with computers and other ordinary technologies."

Well, that explained his fascination with my eTab, but I was surprised to learn his last name was Kirkwood. They were one of the most prominent witchkind families around, on par with the Rathbones. He hadn't struck me as the politician's-kid type.

"That's fantastic," I said. "I'm impressed."

"Yes," said Marrow. "But I'm afraid we do have a meeting now. Perhaps you and I can finish our conversation later. I'll consider your request and get back to you."

"Oh. Sure. Thanks." I glanced at Paul. "Well, I guess I'll see you around."

"Definitely."

I left the classroom as quickly as I could, absurdly happy at his friendliness and that I'd managed a whole conversation with a cute boy without being a klutz. It was a nice change.

I hurried across campus toward my dorm. The clouds hung low overhead, bloated and gray with the promise of rain. Thunder rumbled nearby.

By the time I reached Riker Hall ten minutes later, I

was soaking wet and wishing I'd taken the tunnels. But I hadn't wanted to be down there by myself this late in the day, not with a killer on the loose. The tunnels at Arkwell weren't like those on other campuses. Sure, they served the same purpose of allowing people to get from any of the more than twenty buildings on campus without going outside, but they weren't well-lit underground hallways. They were actual caves, dark and damp and with jagged walls and uneven floors. There were even canals running parallel to the walkways for merkind and naiads and other water types to use. In other words, there were lots of ways for a killer to do his business—drowning, head-bashing—and a lot of dark corners to do it in.

I trotted up the steps to the third floor, eager to strip out of my wet clothes. I thought I might even try to take a nap before dinner.

But when I came through the door into the living quarters, a girl I didn't recognize was sitting on the couch across from Selene at her desk. The girl was tall with broad shoulders that sloped down from her neck, giving her a stooped appearance. In sharp contrast to her sturdy body, her face seemed made of porcelain, the features smooth and delicate. She was very pretty. Especially her eyes. They were so big and bright they looked like a pair of Christmas bulbs. Her small, pointed ears told me she was a fairy.

"Hi, Dusty," Selene said, waving me in. "This is Melanie Remillard."

It took me a moment to place the name. "Oh, you're Rosemary's best friend."

"*Was* her friend," Melanie corrected me.

I swallowed guiltily. "I'm sorry. I didn't mean to . . ."

Melanie shook her head. "No, it's my fault. I'm still getting used to the idea that she's gone. The past tense helps."

"I understand."

An awkward silence descended, and I wondered what to do with myself. A puddle of water had formed on the floor around my sneakers, and I was beginning to shiver from the cold.

Selene stood up. "Here, let me help." She waved her hand over me and at the same time sang a couple of notes, invoking her siren magic. A burst of hot air swept over me, making me shiver harder. But a moment later, I was perfectly dry and warm.

"Thanks," I said. I couldn't help being envious—Selene made everything about magic look easy.

She waved me off. "Melanie's here to talk to you, Dusty."

"Oh, right." I crossed the room to my desk chair and sat down. Even though it was against my nature to be patient, I managed to sit quietly, waiting for Melanie to begin.

"Go on," Selene prodded. "Tell her."

Melanie bent forward and picked up her shoulder bag from the floor beside the chair. The bag was covered in bright sunflowers, so at odds with its owner's glum mood. Melanie reached inside and pulled out a small, tan-colored book. She handed it to me.

"What's this?"

"Rosemary's diary. I thought it might help."

"With what?"

"Finding her killer." Melanie's voice trembled as she spoke, her anger coming off her in hot waves.

Selene said, "Melanie thinks there're clues in there."

"Then why give it to me? I mean, the police are investigating, right? You should give it to them."

"Rose wouldn't have wanted them to have it," said Melanie. "There are personal things in there nobody should know about. Especially her parents."

I nodded, having a pretty good idea of the sort of stuff she meant. I'd kept a diary myself until two years ago when a girl from our rival soccer team stole it from my backpack and posted an entry I'd written about my first kiss online. Lesson learned: writing about personal experiences in the Information Age—not such a good idea.

"She was seeing somebody," Melanie continued. "In secret."

I sat forward on the edge of my chair. "Who?"

"I don't know. She wouldn't tell me. But she talks about him a lot in there. She calls him by the initial *F*. I don't know what it stands for."

"But you two were best friends, right? So why wouldn't she tell you who it was?" I said.

Melanie grimaced. "She couldn't risk anybody finding out even by accident. Whoever this guy is, she would've gotten in a lot of trouble for dating him."

A forbidden love affair? I suddenly felt like the guest star in a cheesy police procedural TV show. "Was it a teacher?"

"I don't know. Maybe."

I frowned. "Well, who else could it be?"

"A nonfairy," said Selene.

"Huh?"

"That's right," said Melanie. "Her parents would've disowned her if they found out she got involved with a darkkind or witchkind."

"But why? I mean, I know interkind dating is a bit of a no-no, but lots of people still do it."

"The rules are more rigid when you're the *consul*'s daughter," said Melanie.

"When you're *any* politician's daughter," Selene added with a note of bitterness in her voice. "Or *son* for that matter."

Melanie sighed. "You would know."

I looked between them, not understanding.

"Lance's dad's objection to his son dating a siren was just one of *many* reasons why we broke up," Selene said. "The rest were all because he's a jackass."

I snorted.

"Anyway," Melanie said. "Rosie was pretty serious about this F guy. You'll see it for yourself in there."

I opened the diary and scanned the first couple of pages. Thankfully, Rosemary's writing was big and neat, easy to read. I looked up at Melanie. "So what makes you think this secret boyfriend is the one who killed her?"

"She had a habit of sneaking out of the dorm to see him. It was what she was doing that night, according to the last entry."

Well, that put a different spin on things. It didn't seem likely a secret boyfriend would be connected to a Keeper spell. Maybe it was a case of bad timing. She might have been on the way to meet the boyfriend when the killer attacked. If so, it was possible the guy had seen or heard something.

"Did you tell the police about the boyfriend?"

A guilty expression crossed Melanie's face. "Only that she might have been meeting someone."

I debated whether or not I should hand the diary over to Sheriff Brackenberry. In the ordinary world, this would be considered evidence and not handing it over could get me in big trouble. But this was the magical world. All the rules were different here.

"Please," Melanie said, her voice trembling again. "You've got to help. The police are just going to screw up like they always do."

"What makes you think *I* won't screw up?"

"You're Moira Nimue's daughter. She can do things nobody can."

Melanie's attitude toward my mother was so different from the norm, I was taken aback, unable to respond.

She went on. "And you're a dream-seer. That gives us a better chance than the police. I want to find the killer and make sure he gets what he deserves."

I shivered at the menace in her tone. It reminded me why The Will restricted the use of combative magic. Melanie Remillard would kill the guy if she got a chance, no question.

"So will you look into it?" Melanie asked.

I considered the question. Since I was already looking

for the killer, I didn't see how taking a more hands-on, detective-like approach would hurt. Besides, the idea was sort of appealing. I might actually get somewhere. It would certainly be easier than trying to muddle my way through Eli's dreams.

"I'll try," I said. "But I've got a couple of questions."

Melanie sat up, looking eager. "Ask me anything."

"Do you know if Rosemary was wearing a ring on her right hand that night?"

"Yes, of course."

"Why are you so sure?" asked Selene.

"Because she only had one ring and she never took it off, not since her father gave it to her last summer for her eighteenth birthday. She loved that thing—don't know why. It was pretty enough, but it was made of *iron*, of all things."

Iron had lots of magical properties, including the ability to repel ghosts and other spirit-based creatures. "Hang on. I thought iron was poisonous to fairies."

Melanie shook her head, a slight grin on her face. "Nope. That's just a rumor fairykind started back in medieval times to trick ordinaries into believing we're less dangerous than we really are."

"Oh." I should've guessed that. Magickind started rumors about themselves in the ordinary world all the time, the latest example being the ordinary pop culture obsession with vampires as misunderstood victims who'd rather kiss a human than kill one. *So* not true.

Melanie said, "But it's not completely false. We're not

fond of iron, in general. Especially as jewelry. It has a way of messing with our magic. It doesn't block it exactly, but it can sometimes make a spell go awry. Nobody wants to set the sofa on fire when you're trying to light the lamp, you know?"

I understood the dilemma all too well. Shame I couldn't blame my magic going awry on something as simple as an unfortunate piece of jewelry.

"What did the ring look like?" asked Selene.

"Just a band with a couple of imbedded diamonds, and a silver coating on it so you wouldn't know it was iron."

If Rosemary had only gotten the ring last summer, then she hadn't been a Keeper for very long. Did that mean the Keeper spell was new, too? I tried to think of the most current events among magickind, but nothing struck me as significant. Not that I paid a lot of attention to that sort of thing. Then again, it was possible the spell wasn't new at all. She might have been made part of a preexisting spell through a transference ritual. Given what Lady Elaine had said about the Keeper ring being a rite of passage, that seemed more likely.

"Do you think the ring has something to do with her murder?" said Melanie.

"Maybe."

A loud crack of lightning made us all jump.

Melanie glanced at her watch and blanched. "I've got to go." She stood up. "If you have any more questions, let me know."

"Okay."

She picked up her bag and slid it over her shoulder. She looked back at me, her expression deadly serious. "Promise me something. I want to know who it is. I want to be the *first*."

Not hardly, I thought as I gave her an unenthusiastic nod. Maybe this wasn't such a good idea after all.

But I had a sinking feeling it was too late to back out now.

~ 8 ~

Wannabe

I didn't read any entries in the diary during school the next day since I was too afraid of getting caught with it. The day went by quickly and smoothly all the way until sixth-period alchemy, by far my worst subject. Alchemy was basically chemistry, but with magic ingredients. I just didn't have the right temperament for it, unlike my lab partner, Britney Shell.

Britney was a mermaid with curly strawberry blond hair and eyes the color of aquamarine set in between a rather large, bulbous nose. Like all mermaids, her pale, almost translucent skin held a natural sheen that made her glisten in strong sunlight as if she was wet. And also like a lot of mermaids, she was painfully shy, almost socially comatose. It was this same shyness that made her so good at alchemy. She had no trouble ignoring distractions while she carefully counted the number of stirs and added the right ingredient at the right time.

If our teacher, Ms. Ashbury, would only allow Britney to do all the hands-on stuff for us all the time, my grade would've been a lot higher. But Ashbury was an equal opportunity teacher, which meant today was my turn to do the mixing while Britney read the instructions for the cooling draught we were tasked with making.

"Add this on stir twenty-one," Britney said, holding out to me a vial of pureed bladderwrack leaves. I took it from her when I reached nineteen, trying not to be distracted by the odd webbing of skin in between her fingers. She never bothered to hide it with a glamour. You'd think I'd get used to stuff like that, but it seemed I never did.

Still, I managed to dump the bladderwrack into the beaker at the right time, turning the bubbling liquid from gray to dark green.

"Good job," Britney said in her tiny, musical voice.

I beamed at her, delighted with how well I was doing. But then my gaze fell on Eli at the next table. He was watching me with an expression that sent jitters bouncing along my nerve endings. It wasn't hostile, exactly, but inscrutable and full of that intense vibe I usually got from him, as if he were more physically present than everybody else in the room. All day yesterday and today he hadn't said a word to me about getting him in trouble with Lady Elaine, but he just might be thinking about it now.

I ripped my gaze off him, running a nervous hand through my hair. When I dropped the hand to my side, I hit the ragwort jar on the table, knocking it to the floor.

"Crap," I said.

"We need to add that next!" Britney sounded close to panic as she stooped, trying in vain to gather up the minced leaves strewn among broken pieces of clay. "Don't lose count," she added.

"Twenty . . . seven, twenty-eight."

"Here, use ours." It was Lance. He set a jar full of dark leaves on the table in front of me.

Without thinking, I picked up the measuring cup, dipped it into the jar, and then dumped the contents into the beaker just as I reached thirty.

Boom.

A streak of lightning exploded from the beaker, shattering it. Hot liquid splattered my hair and forearms, which I had managed to raise in front of my face just in time. I yelped in pain, and ran to the sink, quickly rinsing off the liquid before it could burn my skin.

"What's going on here?" Ms. Ashbury stomped over to us, her face livid with anger, and her dark eyes blazing in between her hooked nose. I'd never seen a witch look more like a witch in my life. Even her dyed-purple hair looked menacing. "Are you all right? What happened?"

"Uh . . ." I sputtered. "I have no idea. I just added the ragwort, and it exploded."

"*What* ragwort? Show it to me."

I looked at the jar Lance had brought over, realizing my stupidity.

Ms. Ashbury picked it up and smelled it, her nose wrinkling. "This is mountain ash, not ragwort. What were you thinking?"

"It wasn't her," Britney said. "Lance gave it to us. He did it on purpose."

I smiled at her. It took a lot of courage for someone like Britney to call out Lance on one of his tricks.

Ms. Ashbury glanced at Lance, who was barely holding back a grin. She pointed a long, crooked finger at him. "You know better, Mr. Rathbone. Detention. Monday morning. My office." She looked back at me. "Be more careful next time, Dusty. Now you and Britney clean this up."

The bell rang a few minutes later, and Britney and I were only halfway through sweeping up the mess. Eli came over, carrying a dustbin. I glared at him, convinced he'd played a part in what happened.

"They don't need your help, Mr. Booker," Ashbury said from the front of the classroom.

Eli frowned, looking ready to argue, but he set the dustbin on the table beside me and left.

Good riddance.

When I arrived at Eli's room that night for our next dream-session, I was still angry and determined to ignore him. At least I'd brought my own reading material. As I expected, Eli was awake again, sitting at the desk and doing work in a textbook while he listened to music. The song issuing from the stereo on the desk beside him was a familiar one.

I froze, my mouth open in surprise. "You're listening to Black Noise?"

Eli looked up, his eyebrows raised. "Sure, they're the best."

"I know."

He tilted his head as if in disbelief. "You like them?"

"No, of course not," I said with an exaggerated eye-roll. "I just know all their songs by heart because I hate them so much." I paused. "They're only my favorite band in the whole world."

Eli folded his arms and leaned back in his chair. "Mine too. Cool."

A flutter went through my stomach—he and I actually had something in common. Other than the dream-seer thing.

"Nobody here's heard of them," Eli said. "I guess they're not big enough yet. It kind of—" He broke off as a horrible sound, like a cross between a foghorn and a car accident, burst out of the speakers. Scowling, Eli slapped the top of the stereo. "Stupid thing. It keeps doing that."

I stifled a grin. "Have you tried being nice to it?"

"What do you mean?" Eli said, turning down the volume.

I stepped forward and gave the stereo a little pat. "It's just forming its animation personality. If you're nice, it might be nice back." That was one of the theories, at least.

"Okay," Eli said, a note of disbelief in his voice. "What's that?" He pointed at Rosemary's diary tucked under my arm.

"Nothing. Just a diary," I said, remembering that I was

supposed to be mad at him. I sat on the sofa across from his desk and opened the book to the last entry.

"Cute hair," Eli said, his voice amused. "Were you going for a punk rocker look or something?"

I screwed up my face at him, visualizing my appearance. My hair was covered in pale pink polka dots from where the cooling draught had landed, bleaching it. "You like it? It's your handiwork after all. Awesome dirty trick by the way. I *really* appreciate it."

"What? I didn't do that to you. Lance did."

"Oh, sure. You were just an innocent bystander."

He slammed the book on the desk closed, then folded his arms, assuming his most menacing posture. "I had no idea that was mountain ash *or* that it would shoot off lightning. Why would I know? I'm *new* here, remember? Oh, and I'm the only person who can't do magic in an all-magic school."

"You're not the *only* one," I said.

"What?"

"Never mind." I didn't feel like explaining the halfkinds-are-usually-sterile thing to him.

My gaze fell on the spine of the book he'd been working in—*Alchemy Projects for the Non-Magical*. Geez, the administration might as well give him a scarlet letter to wear on his chest. A big, red "O" for ordinary. Or zero. Take your pick.

No wonder the guy hated me.

Unsure what to say, caught between lingering anger and something like regret, I returned my attention to the diary, hoping he would fall asleep quickly. The final entry in the diary was dated Sunday, the day Rosemary died:

I'm going to see F again tonight in Coleville. I've decided to end things. He used to make me feel so great, but lately when he kisses me he seems cold. Then there're his strange questions about my parents. He's hunting for something. I think I know what, but the idea of him being after it is so unbelievable. I'm going to confront him tonight, if only for my own peace of mind.

"So whose diary is it?" Eli said.

"Rosemary Vanholt's," I answered automatically.

"Really?" To my surprise he sounded interested. "Any clues about who killed her?"

I closed the diary and stared at him, leery, but could see no reason not to tell him. "Maybe. She was supposed to meet somebody that night. A secret boyfriend."

"Yeah, I heard she was dating someone in secret. I've asked around trying to figure out who, but no luck so far."

"You've been investigating Rosemary's murder?"

"My dad is a detective." He hesitated, cracking his knuckles. "And it's sort of what I want to do. Be a cop. Maybe even join the FBI."

I snorted.

"What's so funny?"

"You always struck me as more of the criminal type."

He grinned. "How would you know?"

Uh . . . my brain stuttered. "Everybody knows that you

were the guy who spray-painted Mr. Patrick's car last year."
He'd been rumored to have done a lot of other things, too,
but that was the only one he'd gotten in trouble for that I
knew of. Like my mom, he seemed capable of charming
his way out of a tight spot. *Must be nice to be so good-looking.*

Eli sighed. "I guess you would believe that."

I raised my eyebrows at him. Was that a denial? "What
do you mean?"

"Nothing." He gestured toward the diary. "So are you
investigating, too?"

"Sorta. But I'm not exactly getting anywhere."

"I've got something that might help." He pulled out a
piece of paper from the desk drawer, yawning hugely. He
drew something on the page, then stood and handed it to
me. Goose bumps went up my arm when our fingers
touched for the briefest moment.

I ignored the sensation and stared at the paper. He'd
drawn a grid with labeled columns across the top: Name,
Motive, Method, Opportunity. In the Name column he'd
written Frank Rizzo. Frank was a senior and a Mors demon, one of the more heinous of the kinds. Mors magic
was fueled by death. Before The Will, they were known to
start wars in order to generate feeding grounds. Now their
magic was fueled by special potions whose primary ingredient was collected at ordinary hospitals. The idea turned
my stomach.

"The person who fits in all those categories is most likely
the killer," said Eli, taking a seat on the chair he'd occupied
during our last dream-session.

"Why Frank?" I didn't know him personally, just rumors about his bad reputation.

"It's probably nothing, but he told me *he* was the secret boyfriend. Pretty sure he was lying, but you never know."

"Right," I said, my body tensing. Frank's first initial was quite a coincidence, and he definitely wasn't appropriate boyfriend material for the consul's daughter, either.

"Hey, you didn't tell Katarina about my dreams, did you?" Eli sounded half-drunk with sleepiness.

I grimaced. "Not hardly. Why do you ask?"

"She's just been *really* friendly to me the last couple of days. It's weird, but I never used to remember my dreams before you came along." His eyes drifted closed, and I stood, setting the diary and paper on the sofa before coming over to him. I waited for his breathing to deepen.

"I'm sorry," he said, surprising me, "that Lance did that to you. Do you think the pink will fade?"

"I hope so."

Eli smiled, his eyes still closed. "You should get back at him. I think he might even respect you for it. He's a heavy sleeper, you know."

Revenge against Lance was an intriguing thought. I opened my mouth to ask him if he had any suggestions on what I could do, but he'd fallen asleep. I sighed, and then joined him on the chair and in his dreams.

Eli's dream that night proved to be a bust. It was about ice fishing on Lake Erie with his dad and Katarina. Boring, cold, and pointless, although at least I made it through the entire session without getting booted, intentionally or otherwise. Progress.

Best part of the night by far was after the dream ended. With Eli still asleep in the chair, I rummaged in Lance's desk, found the perfect ink pen for the job, and then snuck into the bedroom portion of the dorm. The pen was a come-and-go pen, the kind you could only buy in a magickind novelty store for a lot of money. Like the name suggested, anything written with it would sometimes be present and sometimes not. A little lever on the side of the pen controlled the charm that designated when the ink would appear. I set it eight hours ahead, about the time I figured Lance would be eating breakfast.

Eli was right about him being a heavy sleeper. Lance didn't wake once.

It worked better than I could've hoped. The words appeared right as Lance crossed the cafeteria with his tray the next morning, "jackass" written across his forehead. A wave of laughter and finger-pointing followed him. Sitting next to me, Selene was beside herself with glee, her body wracked by huge guffaws. I'd never seen her so happy. As soon as Lance realized what people were laughing about, he immediately looked for me.

I gave him the finger.

An evil smile crossed Lance's face, and I watched his lips form the words "Game on."

Despite the chill that swept down my back, I knew this had totally been worth it.

The rest of Saturday wasn't nearly so exciting. I spent a good part of it reading through the diary, but Rosemary's emotional ramblings didn't provide a lot of clues. All I knew about F was that he was good-looking and liked to go for midnight strolls in secluded places on campus, such as the cemetery and the tunnels. There was nothing to indicate how old he was or which magickind. He could be anybody.

By the time Sunday rolled around, I was so depressed from reading about Rosemary's dreams and knowing they would never be fulfilled, I was determined to start filling in some of Eli's suspect graph. I figured I'd read through the diary again and make a time line of when things happened. Maybe there was a pattern to the meetings.

After breakfast, which proved to be much quieter than the day before with no Lance present, I went to the library to find a quiet place to work. Selene did her musmancy homework in the dorm on Sundays, which required her to both sing and play various instruments while she practiced her music magic. I liked listening, but it was impossible to concentrate on anything. The music was too mesmerizing to ignore.

It was the weekend, so I expected to find the library deserted except for the librarian on duty, but when I walked by the row of computer terminals on my way to the study desks in the back, I heard someone typing. I could see the guy's sneakers underneath the desk but nothing of his face hidden behind the divider in front of the terminal. At least, I assumed it was a guy, given the size of those feet, although you never could tell with magickind.

I spent the next forty minutes drawing up my time line. I started with the day Rosemary's father had given her the ring—June 30. She'd written:

I can't believe it's finally here. I've waited so long. I'm finally old enough to bear the responsibility of my heritage as my mother did before me and hers before that. Mother says I'm too young to wear the ring, but Father thinks differently. He knows how important it is that I prove myself to the Magi. I know where my future lies.

From this, I finally accepted that the Keeper spell wasn't new. Shame. It would've been easier to identify the item if it had been recent, and the regular use of black magic raised some troubling doubts about the magickind leader and his family.

Rosemary started dating F sometime between the eleventh and nineteenth of July, and they met regularly after that, always on campus. So the guy had either been living on campus through the summer or somewhere nearby. This meant I could eliminate any of the students who went home to other cities for the break.

When I finished the time line, I pulled out the suspect graph and placed it beside the list of dates. I stared at them, willing the answers to jump out at me. On the graph, I'd written *F* in the Name column below Frank Rizzo. I'd also placed a check in the Opportunity column since Rosemary had been on her way to meet F in Coleville that night. The rest were a complete blank.

For Motive, it was possible F had killed her in a fit of rage over the breakup, and then somebody else had come along and cut off her hand, but I doubted it. Too coincidental. It was more likely that F's reasons for being in the relationship had been fake, judging from Rosemary's reasons for breaking up with him. But who could it have been? What was he after? My head began to ache.

"Ugh," I muttered, dropping my pen. It rolled and fell off the desk. "Too many questions I don't have the answer to."

"Do you always talk to yourself?"

I jumped so hard I almost fell out of my chair. I looked up and saw it was Paul Kirkwood. My pulse increased. Glancing at his shoes, I knew he'd been the person typing earlier.

I smiled at him, glad I'd worn a ball cap this morning to cover my polka-dot hair. "All the time, actually."

"Hmmm. I imagine it makes for good conversation."

"Do you *live* here or something?" I asked.

"Yep. I've got a cot in the librarian's lounge. They let me use old newspapers for blankets and books for pillows." He pulled out the chair next to mine and sat down. "Seriously, I'm just working on my senior thesis paper. Wanted to get an early start."

I nodded, in awe of his devotion to schoolwork. I waved my hand toward my pen on the floor, summoning it with my telekinesis. To my surprise it flew up at once and into my outstretched fingers without a hitch. *See, I can do magic without screwing it up,* I thought. Too bad Eli wasn't around to see it.

"So what are you doing?" Paul said, tapping the diary.

"Oh, um. Studying."

His gaze took in the suspect graph and time line, and he raised his eyebrows. "For what?"

I blinked, at a loss for a response. I didn't want to lie, but I couldn't see telling him the truth. I'd been sitting here trying to visualize myself as Veronica Mars, all smart and badass. But in reality, I felt more like Inspector Gadget with my go-go button stuck in neutral.

"This is about Rosemary, isn't it?"

"How'd you guess?"

"It was either that or homework for a criminology class. Only Arkwell doesn't offer any." He brushed hair out of his face. I wished he wouldn't do that. I liked the way it hung in his eyes. "Are you trying to figure out who killed her?"

"Trying being the operative word. I'm not having much success." I said. Here was a guy smart enough for MIT, and here was me playing cops and robbers.

"Would it help if I told you the police have a suspect?"

"Really? I've been keeping an eye on the news but I haven't heard anything."

Paul leaned forward, resting his arms on the desk. "Well,

it's not like magickind are big on the virtues of freedom of the press."

"No kidding. So who is it?"

He grinned mischievously, and I was momentarily stunned by how attractive he was. His high, prominent cheekbones looked almost exotic combined with his crooked nose and blond hair. Sexy combination. "Now, hang on a minute. This is top-secret information. I could get in trouble for telling you."

It took me a second to realize he was joking. I leaned into him, lowering my voice to conspiratorial level. "I promise I won't tell anybody. Cross my heart."

Paul shook his head. "Not good enough. You've got to give me something in equal trade."

"Like what?"

He seemed to consider the question seriously. "How about a date?" He grinned again, only there was something a bit shy and insecure about it.

My stomach flipped over, but I managed a smile. "Hmmm . . . well, that's a pretty high price, but I guess I can do it."

He winked. "You won't regret it. How about next Saturday?"

"Okay." I ripped off a piece of paper from the time line, jotted down my cell and dorm numbers, and handed it over. "Now spill," I said, anxious to move on. I was afraid if we didn't, he might admit he'd been joking after all. Or he might remember that he was a Kirkwood, and I was the daughter of Moira Nimue-Everhart.

Paul slid the paper into the front pocket of his jeans, and said, "Mr. Culpepper."

I chuckled. "You're kidding, right? Blaming the maintenance man—I mean you might as well say the butler did it."

"You know he's a Metus demon?"

I rolled my eyes. "That's my point. He's too easy a scapegoat. Just because Metus demons get their power by feeding off others' fears doesn't make him the killer." I knew I was being a bit defensive, but I couldn't help it. Most darkkinds got a bad rap because of the parasitic way their magic worked. I might be a halfkind, but my magic came from my darkkind side.

"Yes," said Paul, "except there's the small matter of Culpepper lying about his alibi."

I raised my eyebrows. "I thought he was fixing a problem in Flint Hall?"

"He was. Except the Flint students have him leaving around midnight, and he didn't report finding Rosemary's body until after one. Claims he stopped by the maintenance garage to drop off some tools, but nobody believes it would've taken him that long, and it's way out of the way. So what was he up to?"

"Good question." I chewed on the inside of my cheek, thinking it over. Was it possible the *F* in Rosemary's diary referred to Culpepper? I wondered what his first name was. Only, I couldn't imagine him being the secret lover. Culpepper had to be at least thirty or older. He wasn't necessarily bad-looking when he kept the demonish parts of his anatomy hidden behind a glamour, but he'd never struck me as attractive. Still, he did work for the school, making it a good bet he'd been on campus this summer. And attraction was subjective. Maybe Rosemary had a thing for scary-looking older dudes.

"Not only that," Paul continued, waving a hand through the air, "but the coroner put her time of death somewhere in that time frame."

"Hang on. How do you know so much about it?"

"My uncle's a magistrate. All of the Magi are getting updated on it. I pay attention."

"Oh. Right." Maybe I should reconsider going out with him. Magistrate was one rank beneath consul—too much potential for my life to become a *West Side Story* parody. Then again, how often was I going to get a chance to date a guy who was both good-looking *and* smart? Not to mention, extremely easy to talk to. I was surprised at how relaxed I felt around him. It had been awhile since any boy had shown an interest in me. Thoughts of Eli tried to force their way into my brain, but I pushed them out.

Paul said, "And did you know Culpepper was a sniper in the Marines?"

"You mean like United States military?"

"Uh-huh."

"No, but that's not surprising. A lot of magickind enlist." The Magi Senate encouraged enlistment, especially to demonkind. It was an easy way for some of them to fulfill their magical needs without doing anything illegal. No doubt that had been the reason Culpepper had signed up.

Paul leaned back, folding his arms across his chest. "Well, yeah, but my point is he's sort of a trained killer."

"Maybe when he was fighting ordinaries. But Rosemary was magickind. How could he have done it?"

Paul shrugged. "I don't know. But somebody did. The Will or no."

"True." I glanced down at the suspect graph, reading the column names for at least the hundredth time. I looked back at Paul. "So have the cops found anything on him?"

"Not yet. They searched his house and office but came back with nothing."

I rolled the pen between my fingers, my thoughts churning. "Hey, you wouldn't happen to know anything about Keeper spells, would you?"

"What's that?"

Well, it had been worth a shot. "Never mind." I wrote "Culpepper" in the Name column beneath F, then put a check mark under Opportunity. I set the pen down, feeling a thrill of both excitement and trepidation at my progress. Maybe I had a knack for this detective business after all.

Then again, maybe not.

～ 9 ～

Stakeout

Tailing somebody was a lot trickier in real life than in TV shows and movies. What with classes, homework, and a regular dream-feeding schedule, I could only spy on Mr. Culpepper in short bursts. Monday, I spotted him on the way to some repair job on campus and followed along behind him, hoping to catch him doing something suspicious. Just what exactly, I had no idea, but I figured I would instinctively recognize this suspicious behavior when I saw it. The next day, I walked by his office in the maintenance garage and saw him sitting behind the desk writing in the leather-bound notebook he'd been carrying the day before. Wednesday, I didn't find him at all. Thursday, he was in the office writing again.

The notebook interested me. Why carry it around everywhere? It wasn't like he could use it to fix a leaky faucet. But if Culpepper was involved in a secret love affair with a student, he might have chronicled it in a diary, too. And his first name was Faustus.

Finding out wasn't too hard. The school's directory listed the first and last name of all the faculty and staff, and I amused myself for nearly twenty minutes looking up the names of my teachers. Some of them were pretty funny, like Wilhelmina Norton and Ignatius Fritz, even Arturo Ankil.

I knew I needed to get a peek at that notebook, but didn't have a clue how to do it. By Thursday night I came to the conclusion that I needed to devote a whole day to following him. I was tempted to ditch Friday's classes, but Selene reasoned me out of it.

"Not worth the risk," she said when I mentioned it during dinner.

"You don't know that. If he *is* the killer, it's totally worth it."

Selene shook her head. "There haven't been any signs about Culpepper in Eli's dreams, right?"

"Well, no. Just more football playing, ice fishing, and Katarina." I made a face.

"Then it's definitely not worth it. I get you want to find the guy. I do, too, but those dreams are your best shot. And way less risky."

"What risk? Worst-case scenario, I get caught ditching and end up in detention."

"I dunno, Dusty." Selene shuddered. "Culpepper gives me the creeps. People say he's crazy. What if he hurts you?"

"How? He's magickind. I'm magickind. Never the two shall meet."

"Tell that to Rosemary."

Ouch. Maybe I should have been spending as much time trying to figure out *how* she was murdered as why.

I let the subject drop as I caught sight of Lance holding up a piece of paper in my direction from across the room. Written across it in big black letters was *Dusty 1, Lance 2*. I sighed, catching the warning at once. A whole week had gone by without him retaliating, and I'd half-hoped he would be happy keeping things equal between us. But apparently he had another prank in the works.

"Better watch your back." Selene obviously had come to the same conclusion.

I glanced at her, startled by her dark tone. "You don't think he'd do anything really bad, do you?"

She took a drink from her water goblet, considering the question. "Depends on your definition of bad. I mean, he wouldn't do anything to hurt you physically. He's too much of a coward for that. But he's not particularly concerned about hurting people emotionally."

"I guess you would know?" I said, making the statement a question. Selene might be my best friend, but she was also the most private person I knew. She'd much rather talk about my troubles than hers. I'd never learned the real reason why she'd ditched the in crowd, although I'd gathered it had a lot to do with Lance.

"Yes," Selene said, surprising me with that admission. I pressed her for more, but she refused to elaborate.

Still, I took her advice, and was extra cautious the rest of the night and all through breakfast the next morning. But Lance didn't strike until psionics class. Distracted by

Mr. Ankil asking me how the snatch-and-smack practice was going, I failed to check my seat before sitting down. A huge fart sound erupted from beneath my butt, followed by a smell so realistic it might as well have been the real thing. I leaped up, red-faced. I looked down at my seat and watched in horror as a whoopee cushion, one bewitched with an invisibility glamour, came into view.

Humiliation was too inadequate a word for what I felt as a couple of people laughed and even more snickered. I noticed Eli wasn't laughing, though. He stood up and came over to me. He picked up the whoopee cushion and tossed it in the wastebasket, the action effortless.

"You all right?" he said, touching my shoulder. His hand was impossibly warm through my shirt. I shivered, the sensation far more pleasurable than it should be, considering how mortified I was.

With a feeble shrug, I brushed him off. "I'm fine."

Later, it was my lingering humiliation, and the prospect of seeing Lance's triumphant expression again, that prompted me to ditch gym class and tail after Mr. Culpepper. Or so I told myself.

I spotted Culpepper walking across the Commons, looking suspicious. He usually shuffled along with a slight hitch to his step as if he had an old injury, but today he moved quickly, looking over his shoulder as if he expected something to attack him any moment.

I kept a fair distance between us as I trailed after him, staying hidden behind trees and buildings. After a while, he made a right down the path around Jupiter Hall, and my certainty that he was up to something increased. If he'd been heading for the maintenance garage, he would've turned left at Jupiter. But the faculty and staff town houses were this way—maybe he was going home.

Culpepper didn't continue down the path toward the faculty housing, but made a left at the Lady of the Lake statue. A couple of turns later, we arrived at one of the side entrances into Coleville cemetery. I hid behind a building, and poked my head around to watch him. I wondered whether this was some kind of sociopathic behavior. Maybe he was returning to the scene of the crime to gloat over it. He didn't have any work reason to be in there. There wasn't a single mechanical thing in the entire place that might need fixing. Electricity was forbidden in the cemetery because of the animation effect—nobody wanted a bunch of corpses and skeletons milling around the gardens.

I followed after him, finding easy cover behind the trees, mausoleums, and statues. I had no idea how large Coleville was in terms of acreage, but Culpepper traveled so far into it the place began to feel as vast as Yellowstone Park. We were well off the main paths, but Culpepper moved with a certainty that suggested he came this way often.

Finally, he slowed down, and I ducked behind a headstone, crouching low and peering carefully around the side. I could just see Culpepper in the distance, standing in front of the door of a small, ancient-looking mausoleum. Whatever name used to be engraved above the doorway had long since faded. The edges on the building were chipped and crumbling in places. I wouldn't have been surprised if the thing were haunted, but Selene had assured me time and again that ghosts weren't very common. That was a good thing, because real ghosts were supposed to be far scarier and more dangerous than those reality TV shows made them seem.

Culpepper stood there a moment, and I heard the sound of keys jangling. A second later, the door swung open, and he disappeared inside.

What the—?

I struggled to recall everything I knew about Metus demons and their power. Was it possible Culpepper was some kind of necromancer? Necromancy had been banned by the Black Magic Purge, but given what I knew about Keeper spells, I didn't think that meant a whole lot. Only, I was sure Metus fed off the fears of living victims, not dead ones. So what business did he have inside a crypt?

I had no way to tell from outside, so I sat down to wait for him to emerge. The minutes turned into an hour, then two. Eventually, I got bored enough to risk coming out of hiding. I spent some time practicing the snatch-and-smack on a nearby statue using twigs and branches of various sizes. By the time the sun hung low on the horizon, filling the cemetery with shadows, I was getting pretty good at it.

I was also getting tired. Not to mention hungry and cold. Culpepper had to come out soon. He *had* to. The mausoleum couldn't have been more than ten feet long and five feet wide. There was only so much a person could do in an area so small.

When my teeth started chattering, I gave up. Either Culpepper wasn't going to come out again this evening or he couldn't. Regardless, I knew for sure I didn't want to be in this cemetery when night arrived. The twilight surrounding me now was disturbing enough. I started to go, but then on a reckless impulse turned and approached the mausoleum.

I stared at the door, debating whether or not to go inside. There wasn't a handle to speak of, just a keyhole, so I put my hands flat against the stone and pushed. The door didn't move. Culpepper must've locked himself in. I considered knocking, but had no idea what I would say if he answered. No, I had to be patient and smart about this. Something was definitely going on here. I couldn't say for sure it was related to Rosemary's death, but it might be. Either way, I was determined to find out.

But not tonight. Too cold, too dark, and too dangerous.

I turned around, hoping I could remember the way back on my own. A little panicked at the possibility of being lost, I hurried down the way I'd come in.

Someone grabbed me from behind.

~ 10 ~

Background Check

I shrieked and spun around, lashing out with the first spell that came to mind. "Hypno-soma."

It was a stupid decision; the dazing curse was combative magic and restricted by The Will. Yet, purple sparks flew out from my fingers and struck the attacker square on the chest. He gasped then stumbled backward, landing hard against the ground.

It was Culpepper. I stared down at him, thunderstruck. My shock turned to panic—no time for questions. Culpepper was already stirring as the spell's effects retreated. In a moment, he would be on his feet again. He didn't look so big or scary lying on the ground, but standing up he would loom over me. His eyes flicked open. I started to turn but froze when I spotted the notebook lying beside him. On impulse, I willed it into my hands, then I bolted.

I stumbled along, unsure of the way, trampling flowers and bumping into headstones and statues. I soon heard the loud noise of Culpepper running after me, spurring me onward. It was like being chased by a semitruck.

"Stop! That's mine!" he bellowed.

I made the mistake of looking over my shoulder and saw he was even closer than he'd sounded. My terror quadrupled at the sight of him. The physical aspects of his demon heritage, usually hidden behind a glamour, were fully visible now, making him look even scarier. His eyes glowed electric green, and his horns looked like two curved daggers growing out from his skull. Any doubts I'd had that Culpepper was capable of murder vanished in an instant.

I swallowed a scream and looked forward again, running faster than ever.

Think, Dusty, think! But it was so hard with fear clouding my brain. My breath came in short, painful gasps. I knew if I didn't get a grip soon, he was going to catch up with me—and then what? I wanted to believe The Will would protect me, but I wasn't about to test the theory. Besides, my dazing curse had worked even though it shouldn't have. What if there was something wrong with The Will? Maybe Culpepper could attack *me* with magic.

The thought scared the fear right out of me. I ceased my pell-mell trek through the cemetery and started weaving in and around obstacles on purpose. I knew I needed to keep out of his direct line of sight if I had any hope of dodging an incoming spell. I flinched at every sound coming from behind me, the smallest twig snapping as loud as gunfire.

"Stop! Thief!"

At the sound of desperation in Culpepper's voice, I

clutched the notebook tighter, convinced it held the answers. I was getting tired, my breath coming in short, side-wrenching gasps and my strides faltering from legs that felt strained to the point of breaking. I needed to find help soon. But I was completely lost. No part of the cemetery looked familiar. I might even be running in circles.

Then at last, growing desperate myself, I turned and cast a befuddlement jinx over my shoulder. "*Ceno-crani!*"

The magic leaped out from my fingers in a streak of purple and struck Culpepper on the forehead. He blinked in surprise and stumbled sideways. He tried to right himself, but his legs weren't working properly. He looked like a drunk person trying to walk the line for a sobriety test. I didn't stick around to see how long it would last. I sped up again, already thinking of what spell to cast at him next. For the first time in my life, I was grateful gym was a required subject.

I pushed my way through a row of bushes, and my feet hit pavement. I looked up and spotted the familiar sloping spire of Monmouth Tower. I veered right down the sidewalk toward the Commons, hoping to find some police officers on patrol.

A dark figure appeared in the path in front of me, and I instinctively cast the dazing spell. A part of me knew this couldn't possibly be Culpepper, but I couldn't help it. The instinct to defend myself was too far in control now. He'd gotten the jump on me once before, after all.

The spell left my fingers and hit the mark. The figure grunted and fell. As I ran past, I glanced down at the person's upturned face. When I realized it was Mr. Marrow, I skidded to a stop and spun around, heart in throat.

I knelt beside him, panting. "Oh, I'm so sorry. Are you all right? I didn't mean to, I was scared and—"

"Be quiet," said Marrow.

I shut up, my stomach doing backflips. I'd been in trouble before, but never like this. I attacked a *teacher*! I stood and stepped away from him, deciding distance was best here.

But the anger I heard in Marrow's voice was gone when he sat up a moment later and said, "That was some impressive spell work, Dusty, if a little uncalled for." He rubbed his chest where the spell had struck.

"I didn't mean to hit you. I don't know why but The Will—"

"Doesn't work as effectively on Nightmares as it does on other kinds," interrupted Marrow as he pushed himself to his feet. He ran his hands over the back of his brown slacks, wiping away the dirt.

I gaped at him, trying to decide if he was serious. "But . . . why?"

He shook his head. "Not now and not here." Marrow's gaze took in my disheveled appearance. "Where have you been the last few hours? Half the school is out looking for you."

"They are?" I finally remembered the notebook in my hands. I glanced down at it. The word *ledger* was written across the front in raised letters. That was odd. I opened it and saw the pages were full of numbers and abbreviations.

This wasn't a secret diary at all. It was probably some official record of maintenance parts.

And I'd *stolen* it.

"Indeed," Marrow said, drawing my attention back to him. "Selene in particular was most distraught when you didn't show up for class."

I looked up at my teacher, tongue-tied and smarting with guilt. I hadn't considered how Selene would react to my disappearance. This whole thing was nothing but a stupid, selfish, *pointless* stunt. Somebody get me the dunce cap.

The sound of footsteps pounding pavement distracted me from my self-berating. Marrow and I both turned to see Culpepper running toward us. The Metus demon slowed when he spotted Mr. Marrow, but the teacher's presence did nothing to quell his anger. His eyes, still glowing that livid green, were fixed on the ledger in my hands.

He stopped a few feet away and said between pants, "This girl stole from me, sir. That book is *mine*. I want it back."

Marrow raised a hand, silencing him. Then he addressed me. "Let me see it, Dusty."

I handed it over. Marrow opened to some random section and examined the numbers filling the lined page. I took a second look myself, trying not to be obvious about it. Now that my initial shock at my blunder was wearing off, I wondered why Culpepper would be so upset about the theft of a ledger—assuming it was being used for legitimate reasons. What if it wasn't? What if Culpepper was cooking the books, as they say? Or maybe he was running some kind of business on the side.

Marrow closed the ledger and looked at Culpepper.

"She's been spying on me, sir," Culpepper said, now sounding more sullen than angry. He had a broad face with a pointy nose. He wore his hair too short to determine the color, but his eyebrows were blond.

"I see," said Marrow.

"And she used *spells* on me. *Illegal ones.*"

Marrow raised an eyebrow at him. "Illegal, you say?"

"Yes, sir. And I mean to press charges."

Marrow's brow rose even higher then fell. "Are you *sure* you want to do that given your recent trouble? I'm certain Sheriff Brackenberry will be most curious as to why you were chasing a student in the first place."

Culpepper paled and shook his head. "No, sir, I don't want that."

"Yes, I thought so."

Culpepper pointed a finger at me. "I won't press charges, but you need to mind your own business and leave me alone."

Like hell I will. If anything, I was even more interested in what he was up to. Innocent people didn't behave so shadily.

"I'm sure that won't be a problem," said Marrow, handing the ledger back to Culpepper. "I suggest you move along quickly. The sheriff is on campus tonight."

Culpepper didn't need any more encouragement. With a final glare at me, he stalked off the way he'd come.

"I think it's past time we talked, Dusty," said Marrow. "Would you mind coming to my office?"

"Okay." I tried not to sound reluctant, but probably failed. I was sweaty and exhausted and well aware that I was still in trouble.

I followed him into Monmouth Tower and up the winding staircase to his office on the third floor. He unlocked it and led me inside. A large desk occupied most of the room, its surface cluttered with books, sheets of paper, and various writing instruments. Shelves lined the walls from floor to ceiling, filled with more books and an odd assortment of objects. An antique spyglass stood atop a wooden stand with a compass set beside it. The needle on the compass was spinning around as fast as a plane propeller. I wondered what it was supposed to point to, guessing it wasn't north. One entire column of shelves was devoted to jars full of the herbs and chemicals used in alchemy.

Marrow walked around to the back of the desk and picked up the receiver on the rotary phone sitting among the clutter. "Have a seat." He motioned to the chair across from him. I sat down, and listened to the odd whirring sound as Marrow dialed.

A moment later he said into the receiver, "This is Marrow. I've found her . . . yes, she's fine. She'll be home in a bit . . . okay . . . thank you." He hung up.

"I'm really sorry," I said. "I didn't know that ditching would be such a big deal."

Marrow sat in the desk chair and looked at me, his expression thoughtful. "It's a big deal, as you say, because *you* are a big deal now."

I swallowed. "Because I'm a dream-seer?"

He nodded. "You'll want to be more careful in the future. That is, if you value what little freedom you still possess. Any more strange disappearances and the senate will assign you a full-time bodyguard."

I grimaced. So my mom hadn't been exaggerating after all. "I understand."

"Good. Now, why don't you tell me what you were doing?"

I sighed and wondered if it was possible to blush so much your face stayed red permanently. "I saw Mr. Culpepper go into Coleville, and I wanted to see what he was doing. I heard he's a suspect in Rosemary's murder and thought he might be headed back to the scene of the crime or something."

"Did he?"

"No." I gave him a quick summary of what happened. When I finished, I asked the question most pressing on my mind. "How is it I was able to cast those spells?"

"You're a Nightmare," Marrow said as if this explained everything. "Your magic works differently from other magickind. You're the exception to The Will's rule. You just never had occasion to discover it before now."

Marrow hesitated a moment, the age lines on his face deepening. "The things I'm about to tell you are not common knowledge. However, I'm a firm believer that people ought to know the truth. But you must promise you'll keep the information to yourself as much as possible."

"I promise."

He took a deep breath. "Despite the senate's attitude to the contrary, The Will is far from perfect. It has its chinks and weaknesses same as any spell. The Will-Workers who maintain and administer the spell are just as flawed as the rest of us and more than capable of mistakes. But The Will's greatest weakness, its *blind spot,* you could say, concerns Nightmares. The reason The Will fails to control your kind is because of the fictus that feeds your magic. Fictus is the very essence of imagination. It is the one magical force that resides inside all sentient beings, enabling them to create, imagine, dream, and other such activities. Imagination cannot be controlled or predicted by a spell. It is one of the few powers in the world that is truly wild."

"But I thought fictus was just a form of mind-magic?"

"That's a misnomer." Marrow rested his arms on the desk. "True mind-magic comes from thoughts generated by all those electrical impulses in the brain. Fictus comes from something more on the level of instinct than consciousness. It's why a dreamer usually has no control over the subject of their dreams or why artists can rarely identify the source of their inspiration. Understand?"

I began to fidget with the zipper on my jacket. "I think so. But . . . if that's true, how come this is the first time

I've ever been able to do something restricted by The Will? I mean, it usually stops me the same as anybody."

"Ah," he said, his dark eyes twinkling. "There are two reasons for that. The first is you're consuming a lot more magic than you used to. The second is that fictus-fed magic must be used on the level of imagination and not mere thought. Simply muttering the incantation and aiming for your target the way you've learned in school won't work. You must wield the magic the same as you do inside a dream."

"But I don't use magic in dreams, normally."

Marrow tilted his head. "Do you ever bend the laws of reality? Walk on the ceiling or manipulate your appearance?"

"Sure. All the time."

He smiled. "Then you have used magic inside dreams. You just didn't know it."

"But there's nothing to that. I picture myself with blond hair, and it happens." I snapped my fingers in emphasis.

"My point exactly. You use your *imagination* to affect the dream. Imagination *is* magic. You see?"

I thought of the Milky Way I'd conjured. Was it really the same as using magic in the real world?

Marrow must've sensed my uncertainty for he said, "Why don't you let me see if I can demonstrate. Stand up, please."

I did as he asked and waited as he came around the desk, stopping a few feet away from me.

"Now," he said, "I want you to cast the same dazing spell you used on me earlier."

I gaped at him. "Are you sure?"

"Yes. Now go ahead."

"Okay," I said, still uncertain. But *he* was the teacher after all. "Hypno-soma!" The magic left my body but faded at once, absorbed as always into that unseen force. "See. That's what usually happens all the time, but it didn't earlier."

"Earlier you weren't *thinking* about casting the spell as you are now. When you cast it against Mr. Culpepper, you did it purely on instinct. And a Nightmare's instinct works on the level of imagination. It's simply how you're designed. Now, try again, only this time pretend we're in a dream."

I closed my eyes a moment, trying to picture the spell working.

"Hypno-soma." A minuscule jet of purple light shot from my fingers. The spell was so weak it faded long before it reached Marrow, but it definitely wasn't stopped by that invisible force field. I stared at my fingers, possibilities expanding in my mind like balloons. Was this how my mother did it? Had she simply learned to use her magic like she was in a dream all the time whenever she wanted? No wonder nobody liked her. Lots of people would kill to be able to do whatever they liked without The Will's interference.

Marrow clapped. "Well done. Weak now, of course, but it'll get better the more you practice."

"Why would I want to? My mom disobeys The Will all the time, and people hate her for it. I don't want them to hate me, too."

Marrow came back to the desk and sat down. "Yes, I understand. And you're right. You shouldn't go around flaunting the ability the way Moira does. I've often wondered about her reasons for doing so, especially given the tragic history of your kind."

"What tragic history?" I asked, sitting down, too.

"Haven't you ever wondered why there are so few Nightmares around? Counting you and your mother, there is only one other living in Chickery."

"Bethany Grey," I murmured.

"Yes, Bethany."

"I . . . I didn't know there were only three of us. I mean, I know I'm the only Nightmare in school, but I thought that was just some kind of fluke."

"I'm afraid not." Marrow folded his hands in his lap, leaning back. "While there *are* other Nightmares in the world, their numbers are very small. They were once heavily hunted by other magickind, almost to the point of extinction. Your kind is still recovering."

I gripped the arms of my chair. "Why?"

"Fear, mostly, and hatred. As I've already explained, Nightmares are very powerful because of the nature of their magic. So powerful, in fact, that a Nightmare can drain a person of all the fictus inside them, leaving them in a soulless state, neither alive nor dead but stuck forever in between. It's a fate far worse than death. The risk of doing this to one of your dream-subjects is why there is a time limit on your sessions. Unfortunately, before The Will, Nightmares got a reputation for destroying their victims so often, it resulted in their persecution."

I thought I might be sick. "But . . . are you saying Nightmares are *evil*?" Was I some kind of *monster*?

Marrow shook his head. "No. Concepts such as good and evil aren't so definite as the stories would like you to believe. Your kind simply did what they had to do. Before the Magi came to be, the various kinds were at war, each group trying to gain dominance over the other. The nature-kinds hated witchkinds for their desecration of the natural world, and both groups hated darkkinds for their parasitic magic. But all the kinds employed Nightmares for their cause, usually to work as assassins. But the Nightmares didn't kill their targets. They drained them of fictus. They were so good at this that when the wars finally ended, the newly formed Magi determined they were too dangerous to exist in such numbers and sanctioned the hunting of Nightmares until they no longer proved so great a threat."

My stomach clenched. The idea of an entire group of magickind being hunted like animals was horrible. But on the other hand, it might've been deserved. "Wait." I paused, my confusion growing. "I thought the Magi have always been made up of representatives from all three kinds."

Marrow smiled, a pleased glint in his eye. "I'm glad to learn you pay such good attention in my classes. Yes, all three kinds have always been involved in *all* Magi business."

I blinked. "But then that means that the darkkind Magi had to agree to it, too. Only, how could they do that when Nightmares are darkkind as well?"

Marrow sighed and ran a hand over his beard. "I'm afraid that's just another example of the argument that the good of the many outweighs the good of the few. And I doubt if it was a difficult decision for the darkkind Magi of the time. Nightmares have always been regarded as outsiders."

I crossed my arms over my chest, shivering from something other than the cold air in Marrow's office. This must be the reason I had such a hard time making friends at Arkwell. What if the fear and hatred of Nightmares had been handed down to my classmates from generations of magickind who still remembered what my kind had done?

Marrow leaned toward me, his voice earnest. "I didn't tell you about these things to distress you, Dusty, but I believe it's important you know the truth of what you are, where you come from, and more importantly, what you're capable of. You must learn to control your abilities."

"But why?" I knew his answer already, but I thought I would rather avoid all negative situations from here on out instead. Maybe I should become a nun.

"To protect yourself from persecution," said Marrow. "The Will's ineffectiveness on Nightmares isn't common knowledge. You don't want word to spread that you're casting illegal spells, and the best way to do that is by learning to control your magic. That way, you don't accidentally do something you shouldn't."

Like suck Eli's soul out through his dreams? I swallowed. Yeah, the whole nun thing was looking better and better. I couldn't possibly go full-out evil if I were a nun, could I?

"And also," said Marrow, his expression deadly serious, "you don't want the killer finding out that you've learned the trick of thwarting The Will."

I blinked, not understanding. "It's not like I'm going to start helping the guy."

"Ah," Marrow said, wagging a finger at me. "That's the rub, isn't it? The killer, whoever it might be, is clever. Clever enough to trick you into helping him"—he paused—"or her, without you even being aware you're doing it. And a Nightmare's ability could prove quite useful, no doubt."

Nausea twisted my belly into knots as I thought about Rosemary. It was likely that she'd been lured into Coleville by the killer. Was it possible the same could happen to me?

Some questions were better left unanswered.

Cold Case

By the time I left Mr. Marrow's office, I realized I was in over my head. How could I have been so stupid? If Culpepper was involved then the killer already knew what I could do. Or would find out soon enough. That was it. No more of this wannabe Nancy Drew sleuthing. Selene was right. I should stick to the dream stuff. That was safe. That was simple.

Coward.

But I was just a teenager. I couldn't vote or join the army. I didn't even have my own car. I had no business taking on a killer. Besides, the whole of magickind thought I was evil. Not even vampires had been hunted to near extinction and most of them *were* evil. Best to keep a low profile.

By the time I reached the dorm, I'd successfully forced my thoughts onto the more pleasant subject of my upcoming date with Paul. In truth, I'd thought about him a lot since last Sunday.

I wondered if I'd missed any calls and pulled out my

cell from the front pocket of my jeans only to find it was off. *Grrrr.* The stupid thing had developed a surly personality from the animation effect, which meant it shut down whenever it wanted to. Usually when I was expecting important phone calls.

I switched it on and was immediately rewarded with twenty text messages, all from Selene. No wonder she'd been so worried. I didn't have any voice mails though, and disappointment that Paul still hadn't called struck me like a sudden cramp. He was cutting it a bit close—we were supposed to go out tomorrow night, and I didn't know when or where.

Naturally, Selene was still up when I came in. She spent ten minutes lecturing me on how I should never do something so stupid again. I didn't argue with her. She was totally right.

I couldn't shake the certainty building inside me that Paul *wasn't* going to call, and by the time I headed off for my dream-session with Eli, I was ready for this day to be over. But things went from bad to worse when I saw Eli standing out front of Flint Hall with Katarina.

They were kissing.

I ducked behind a tree, going red from head to toe. Could this night get any worse? It was bad enough Eli had already been dreaming about Katarina in skimpy cheerleading outfits. Now that they had progressed to the making-out stage in real life, I could only imagine what the dreams would be like as a result. *Naked* Katarina, no doubt.

Hot, angry tears stung my eyes. It was too much after the day I'd had—the humiliation in psionics, finding out I was a monster who could kill people in their dreams, the likelihood that I was going to get stood up by the first boy at Arkwell ever to show interest in me, and now this.

I took a deep breath and told myself I didn't care about Eli kissing somebody. Still, he and I did have a dream-feeding session, which was a perfectly good reason to interrupt them. But then I glanced at my watch and realized I was five minutes early. Of all the luck.

At least Eli said good-bye a few moments later, after one of the werewolf policemen on patrol told them to break it up and gave them a warning for being out after curfew. I waited until Katarina was out of sight before going in.

"Hey," Eli said as I came through the door. "What happened to you today?" He eyed me up and down.

I crossed my arms over my chest, wishing I'd taken the time to change into my usual dream-feeding outfit. I felt oddly vulnerable in my V-neck tee and low-rise jeans. "What do you mean?" *God, I hope he doesn't smell like her.*

Eli closed the space between us, stopping an arm's length from me. He was so tall I had to look up at him even from that distance. "You disappeared before gym. Everybody's been out looking for you."

I took a step back. "So I've heard."

He frowned. "You okay?"

"Never better." I uncrossed my arms and motioned toward the chair. "Can we get on with this?"

His frown deepened. "Did something happen?"

"No."

He put his hands on his hips. "You're lying."

I glowered at him. "Like you know me well enough to know when I'm lying."

His expression turned menacing again. "What's *that* supposed to mean?"

"Nothing. Just don't bother acting like you care what happens to me. It's really not necessary."

He didn't say anything, just kept staring at me with that pantherlike expression. After a moment he turned and sat in his usual chair, his mouth opening into a huge yawn.

I sat down across from him, arms folded over my chest again and eyes fixed on the posters on the wall. It was easy to tell which ones belonged to Lance and which were Eli's. More than a dozen incarnations of the Joker grinned back at me. Eli's contributions to the décor included several posters of rock bands, Black Noise among them, along with a Cincinnati Bengals decal, and a recruitment poster for the FBI. I guess he hadn't been kidding about his life's ambition.

"So where were you?" Eli asked in a much softer tone than before. "I was worried you'd disappeared."

I sighed, unable to hold on to my bitchy attitude in the face of his concern. "I was doing something stupid."

A grin teased the edges of his lips. "Like what?"

I focused my gaze on his ear to avoid looking in his eyes. "I thought I had a lead on the killer, but it didn't pan out."

He yawned again. "Yeah, I'm not having any luck, either.

But just keep using the graph I gave you." He leaned back in the chair, his eyes already slipping closed.

I moved into position as his breathing deepened. The dream was another one about ice fishing, cold and miserable. When I spotted Katarina, an irrational urge to do her harm came over me. It was as if all the emotions I'd been struggling with on the outside had followed me into the dream—and been intensified by ten.

I scowled at her, resentment for every time she'd mocked me, for that kiss with Eli, burning inside me like wildfire. The dream-Katarina let out a scream. The flesh on her face began to bubble like melting wax. Her hair blackened as if burned, then fell out. A sudden burst of fear inside me loosened the anger's tight grip over my mind. What was going on?

Eli rushed over to her, a look of utter terror on his face. "What's happening?" he yelled. He took hold of her arms, but the skin there had started to fester and flake off, revealing the bones beneath. Her face looked like a mummy's.

What are you doing, Dusty?

Horrified, I realized *I* was responsible for this. My thoughts, my actions, my *magic*. Even worse, I knew Eli's fear was genuine. For the first time he didn't know this was a dream—a *nightmare*.

I closed my eyes, disgust at myself leaching away the last of my anger. I pictured being somewhere else. No Katarina, no ice fishing. I imagined the wind soft and warm instead of sharp as razor blades against my skin. The sun hot and low in the sky, like in Hawaii.

I opened my eyes and gasped at the change I'd wrought. Eli and I were alone, standing on the sundeck of a yacht.

He looked at me, dazed. "What happened? I saw Katarina . . ." He gulped. "Did *you* do that to her?"

I didn't answer. Couldn't. Something huge and dark was flying in the distance over an endless stretch of blue-green water. The black phoenix. Something dead hung from its talons.

I tried not to think about what I'd done in Eli's dream as I waited by the phone for Paul to call the next day. But I did think about it. A lot.

And Paul didn't call. I figured he wouldn't, but that didn't make it hurt any less. By six o'clock I gave up.

"Maybe something happened," Selene said. "He might've lost your number."

"He could've looked it up in the directory."

"Maybe there was an illness in the family."

I slumped down onto the sofa in our dorm room. "He's a Kirkwood. We would've heard about it on the news."

Selene sighed. "Well, if he doesn't have a good explanation then screw him. He doesn't deserve you anyway. He's just a mu—" She hesitated. "Loser."

I stared at her, shocked by what she had been about to say. "He's a mule?"

Selene frowned. "That's a nasty word, Dusty."

"You're the one who said it."

"*Almost* said it."

"Same difference." A mule was a derogatory word for someone who couldn't do magic. The term was normally directed at halfkinds, whose magical sterility was the result of their parents being different kinds, similar to how most real mules couldn't reproduce because of the whole horse-donkey chromosome thing. "Wait, so Paul's a halfkind?"

Selene shifted uncomfortably in her seat across from me. "His mother is Eliza Kirkwood, Magistrate Kirkwood's younger sister. Nobody knows who his dad is, but he definitely wasn't witchkind. My mom says it was a big scandal when it happened. People still talk about it every now and again."

"Why didn't you tell me?"

Selene pulled her ponytail over her shoulder and began finger-combing her hair. "I didn't think it would matter to you."

She was wrong. It did matter, but only because I realized he and I had a lot more in common than I thought. Not that it counted much. He'd still blown me off.

And after what I did in Eli's dream last night, I wasn't sure I blamed him. *Evil, evil, evil,* a nasty voice kept whispering inside my head.

"Are you okay?" Selene asked.

I nodded, but tears burned my eyes.

Selene came over and sat beside me on the sofa. She put an arm around my shoulder, hugging me. "Seriously, he's not worth getting upset about. No boy is."

I hugged her back and then stood up. I hadn't told her

the horrible things I'd learned from Marrow or what I'd done in Eli's dream. She was my only true friend, and I didn't want to risk having her opinion about me change.

"I'm going for a run," I said, disappearing into the bedroom. I changed into my running clothes, then headed for the door.

"Be careful," Selene said, worry in her voice.

I didn't answer and closed the door behind me. I took off at a jog down the hallway and broke into a run as soon as I was outside. I ran as fast and hard as my body would let me, allowing the physical demand of it to siphon away all the bad feelings inside. When tears dampened my cheeks, I told myself it was from the wind.

I didn't pay attention to where I was going, up one sidewalk and down another, lapping the entire campus as the minutes ticked by. After a while, my legs began to feel like they were made of lead instead of muscle. My lungs ached from exertion, and I knew as soon as I stopped I would have a coughing fit.

But I didn't stop. I pressed on and on. In the rare moments when I allowed myself to think, I knew that what I really wanted was to go home to my dad. To run back to my old life. To be normal again, an ordinary. Not some kind of monster that could kill you in your sleep.

It was impossible. Even if I woke up tomorrow as magically sterile as most other halfkinds, I couldn't just step back into my old life as if I was only pulling on a pair of comfortable shoes. It didn't fit anymore. Too many holes, too much damage.

Sometime later, long after the sun had set, I slowed to a walk and made my way back to Riker Hall. I took a long, hot shower, grateful to have the community bath to myself for once. By the time I returned to the dorm room, Selene was asleep. I didn't bother checking to see if I'd missed any calls. I knew I hadn't.

I went to bed and fell asleep in minutes, physically and emotionally exhausted. And I, the Nightmare, slept without dreaming.

～ 12 ～

Cop Out

The next two weeks passed with little incident. For the first time in my life I was maintaining a low profile, keeping my head down and my nose out of trouble. Mostly, I didn't want to risk bumping into Paul or even spotting him from afar. I was avoiding Eli, too. I managed to show up a half hour late to all our dream-sessions, ensuring he was asleep by the time I got there. He tried to talk to me inside the dreams, but I was able to disguise myself more often than not.

Avoiding him during school wasn't too hard, either. Katarina was taking care of it for me. Every time he tried to talk to me or even when he looked at me, Katarina was there, forcing his attention back to her.

Even Lance had been quiet. I suspected he was waiting for me to pull the next prank, but I wasn't interested in playing that game anymore. No trouble for me from now on, thanks.

The Friday before the Samhain dance, Selene and I lined up outside the gymnasium with the rest of the student body waiting to be let in for the school assembly about the significance of Samhain. Selene warned me it was dull stuff, but I was looking forward to the early dismissal afterward. Not that I had any reason to be excited about the weekend. The dance was tomorrow night, and I didn't have a date.

A few feet ahead of us, Katarina stood talking to one of her snooty friends, a witch named Carla Petermeier. Didn't take long for me to realize they were talking about me. I wanted to ignore them but couldn't.

"Did she *really* try to seduce him?" said Carla, flashing me a dirty look.

"Oh, yes. You know how Nightmares are," said Katarina. "Think they're succubi, don't they? She came to their last dream-session wearing lingerie. As if Eli would *ever* look at her when he has me."

Selene punched me in the shoulder, and whispered, "Don't listen to them. Kat's just jealous and insecure."

"You *think* so?" I whispered back in my most sarcastic tone.

"Yes, I do. You share a connection with Eli that she can never have."

I wrinkled my nose. "The only thing we share is an hour's worth of boring, pointless dreams." This wasn't precisely true, but I'd decided it was up to Lady Elaine and the senate to judge the significance of Eli's dreams. I was just the observer. "Eli doesn't even talk to me or anything."

"That's just because you're avoiding him." Selene made

a face. "Oh, don't pretend it's not true. Eli's attracted to you. I can tell. He stares at you when he doesn't think you're looking. I've caught him doing it a bunch, and I'm sure Katarina has, too."

My stomach did a little flip at the idea, but I ignored it. It couldn't possibly be true. Selene was just trying to make me feel better.

"And it doesn't matter anyway," Selene said, shaking her head. "She would hate you regardless."

I huffed. "What did I ever do to deserve that? I mean, besides the stupid snake incident."

"That's just it." Selene poked me in the shoulder with her index finger. "You did the worst thing possible to a siren. You made her unattractive in the eyes of others. I mean, she ate *worms*."

I couldn't resist a smile. It had been pretty gross.

"And you might find this hard to believe, but Katarina really is insecure. She can't help it. A lot of us—sirens, that is—are insecure. It's kind of our Achilles' heel." Selene tucked a piece of black hair that had come loose from her braid behind her ear. "We can't help being attractive, but it's not really us but our magic. You know? Makes it hard to be certain that the people around us like us for who we are and not because of what we look like or how we make them feel."

I blinked, completely surprised by her speech. It was so unlike her to be so open. And even though she was talking about Katarina, I knew she was talking about herself, too.

"Besides," Selene went on, a slight flush in her cheeks.

"You're really pretty and smart and funny and it's all you. Not magic. Katarina can't help but be jealous about that. And she knows sooner or later that Eli will figure out the difference, too. It's inevitable."

I rolled my eyes, embarrassed by the compliment.

Katarina was looking directly at me now and speaking even louder than before. "I mean how many times does Eli have to say no before she gets it?"

"I think you should seriously consider the snake thing again," said Selene, equally as loud.

"Would if I could, but—" I broke off, remembering the truth about my magic.

"Beats me," said Carla. "Then again, Nightmares aren't known for being smart, right?"

Selene flashed them the double finger.

Katarina grinned so maliciously, I contemplated casting a jinx at her, maybe the silencer so nobody could hear her talk or the jab aimed at her nose, see if I could break it. I'd had enough of being docile. Ever since what I'd done to her in Eli's dream I'd been trying to be nice, but enough was enough.

I flipped her the finger instead.

"Put it down." Selene grabbed my hand and forced me to lower it. Too late, I realized Mr. Ankil had seen me.

He came over, an uncharacteristic frown on his face. He looked oddly pale and tired. His long hair appeared as if he hadn't washed it in days. I wondered if he were sick or something. "I think that's quite enough of that, Dusty."

"Okay," I said, somewhat stunned by the reprimand.

Ankil rarely played the part of disciplinarian. I thought he of all people would understand, given what he'd shared with me about his own picked-on childhood.

He nodded absently in my direction, his mind and attention already elsewhere. He looked around, unconsciously wringing his hands over and over again.

"Is something wrong, Mr. Ankil?" I asked.

"What?" He looked sharply back at me as if he'd forgotten about me already. His voice trembled as he answered, "Oh. Not at all. Just behave yourself, Dusty." He walked away.

"That was weird," I said, ignoring the victorious grin on Katarina's face.

"Yeah, I know. But he's been acting strange lately," said Selene.

I thought about it for a moment and realized she was right. The last couple of days his classes had been oddly subdued, less hands-on and more time spent reading the textbook or answering essay questions. "I wonder— Oh, *crap*."

"What?" Selene said.

"It's him," I whispered, ducking behind her. "Hide me." Paul was walking down the hallway toward us. I pressed my shoulder against the wall and pushed Selene farther out for coverage. Not that her slender personage was nearly big enough to accomplish the task.

Paul stopped when he reached us. I couldn't help it. I stepped beside Selene to see him more clearly. I ran my fingers over my hair, trying to make it lay flat. At least the pink polka dots were finally gone.

"Hey, Dusty," he said.

"I don't think she wants to talk to you." Selene crossed her arms in front of her, fixing him with her sternest glare. She looked more tomboy than ever.

"I know. I don't blame her." Paul shifted his gaze from Selene to me. "But please let me explain."

"Humph," said Selene.

I knew I ought to tell him to take a hike, but I wanted to hear what he had to say. He looked every bit as pale and tired as Mr. Ankil. The telltale yellow color of a half-healed bruise rimmed his right cheek, and his nose appeared even more crooked than I remembered. I wondered if he'd taken up boxing or something.

When his rich brown eyes locked on mine, I couldn't pretend I wasn't still attracted to him. "You have two minutes."

Paul glanced at Selene and shifted the backpack on his shoulder, clearly uncomfortable with talking in front of her. A muscle ticked in his jaw as he clenched his teeth. "I was sick."

Selene snorted. "Too sick to call?"

Paul ignored her, keeping his gaze on me. "I got hurt the Saturday morning before we were supposed to go out and ended up at Vejovis for a while."

My eyes widened. Vejovis was the local magickind hospital, but students rarely went there. Most ailments and injuries could be treated by the nurses who worked in Arkwell's infirmary. Only serious injuries ever required the level of magic the doctors at Vejovis provided. It must've been bad if Paul had ended up there.

"What happened?" I asked, taking a closer look at him. Besides the old bruise on his face, I couldn't spot anything else wrong.

"I . . . went home Friday night and fell down some stairs. Broke a couple of bones." He purposefully turned to Selene, pointing to the yellow spot beneath his eye. "Including my cheekbone. Talking hurt." He looked back at me. "By the time I *could* talk, I didn't know what to say. I knew you'd think I stood you up. I just got back to school today, and I wanted to explain what happened in person."

I swallowed, thinking about all the times the past two weeks I'd wished something bad would happen to him. "I'm sorry you were hurt. But you're okay now?" It was a stupid question, but I couldn't think of anything better.

"Yeah, I'm fine—better now."

Selene frowned. "You fell down the stairs and broke your *cheekbone*?"

I winced at the skepticism in her voice, even as a part of me agreed with her. It did seem an unlikely thing to happen.

Paul shifted his backpack again. "It was a bad fall. There were lots of steps. I broke my wrist, too, and sprained an ankle."

"Ouch," I said.

Paul opened his mouth to reply, but the loud creak of the gym doors opening stopped him. We all turned to look as the first in line finally started moving inside.

"Let the fun begin," Paul said, stepping in beside me. It seemed his level of enthusiasm for the assembly was on par with Selene's. He moved in close to me, our bodies nearly touching.

Most of the talking stopped as everybody filed in and sat down. The three of us ended up in the top row of the bleachers, which was nice. If this thing really was as boring as Selene claimed, at least I could lean my back against the wall and nod off. Well, I could if I'd wanted to, but with Paul present, I didn't think I would be so inclined.

It took more than twenty minutes to get everybody seated. Fortunately, Katarina and her friends were in the next section, adding enough distance that I wouldn't have to listen to any more taunts. I wondered where Eli was, and I looked around, hoping to find him sitting elsewhere, a sure indicator that the relationship was in trouble.

No such luck.

Eli jogged up the stairs in between the two sections a few minutes later. His eyes met mine, his expression dark and intense like always. My heart seemed to seize in my chest. He looked away first, shifting his gaze to Paul. A disapproving frown curved his lips. Was Selene right? *No, don't be silly,* I told myself as Eli turned and sat down beside Katarina.

Dr. Hendershaw appeared on the makeshift stage set in the center of the gym floor. She gave us the usual welcome stuff, then handed the microphone over to the show choir director, Mrs. Hovick. Hovick, along with all the show choir performers, male and female, was a siren. Selene couldn't stand her, but I found her entertaining in a ditzy, over-the-top kind of way.

She introduced the choir, who then performed. Chickery High School had a show choir, too, but it was nothing like this. When the sirens began to dance and sing everybody in the gymnasium went quiet, completely mesmerized. A pleasant, tingly warmth swept over my body as my thoughts turned fuzzy. I was vaguely aware of Selene muttering beside me something about how wrong it was for sirens to be made into sexual objects in front of the whole school and how there was so much more to sirens than being beautiful. I didn't pay her any mind, my eardrums too enchanted to listen.

When they finished, I stood and cheered same as everybody. As the sirens exited the stage, the force of their magic slowly faded. I once again became aware of myself, where I was, and what I was doing—sitting in a darkened gym next to Paul Kirkwood. We sat so close, his leg and shoulder touched mine. I couldn't resist tilting my head toward him. My heartbeat quickened as he did the same.

Before us, a movie started, displayed in the area over the stage. Well, it was more of a hologram than an actual movie, the 3-D images created by magic rather than any type of electronic equipment. The voice-over began to narrate the history and significance of Samhain while images flashed, documentary style. The narrator explained that Samhain was a time when the wild magic that dwelled between the realm of the living and the dead was allowed to run free and renew all the magic reservoirs in the world, like the one that supposedly resided beneath the grounds of Arkwell itself.

I did my best to focus on the presentation, but I didn't catch more than a sentence or two. I was too preoccupied with the sound of Paul's breathing, the way he shifted in his seat, and especially how good he smelled, the scent somehow intensified in the darkness.

"So, speaking of Samhain," Paul said, leaning close. His breath tickled my ear, sending shivers over my skin. "Any chance you'd go to the dance with me tomorrow?"

I held my breath, unsure of what to say. I wanted to so badly. But I was afraid of getting hurt again.

"That is, if you don't already have a date."

I almost laughed. Me? The Nightmare? I shook my head. "How do I know you'll come through this time?" I turned toward him so that our eyes met.

A stricken expression crossed his face, and I almost regretted doubting him. His story about the fall down the stairs might not be true, but there was no denying he'd gotten hurt somehow. Paul reached over and took my hand in his. A pleasant thrill slid up my arm into my chest.

"I will," he said. And then he held my hand through the entire assembly. His touch was all the promise I needed.

That night, I decided to go to my dream-session with Eli on time for once, confident and unafraid of facing him for the first time in days. Only that confidence vanished completely when I stepped into the dorm room and saw a shirtless Eli emerge from the bedroom. His bare chest was even more stunning than I remembered, that black scorpion tattoo and rock-hard abs.

Realizing too late I was gaping at him, I forced my mouth shut. Eli smirked as he slid a T-shirt over his head.

"Long time no see," he said, pulling the shirt down around his hips.

I shrugged, trying to play it cool even though my face felt like it was on fire. *Just remember Paul,* I thought. *Just remember Paul.* To my relief, it helped.

Eli turned and sat down on the sofa in the place I normally occupied while I waited for him to fall asleep. "Why have you been avoiding me?"

I rolled my eyes. "Don't be ridiculous. I haven't been avoiding you."

Eli arched an eyebrow at me. "Uh-huh. Right. That's why I haven't talked to you since the night you ditched gym."

Since the night I terrified you with my evil, Nightmare powers, I silently added for him. "It's not like we hang with the same crowd."

He didn't answer, but stared at me for a couple of moments, his face expressionless. I contemplated sitting in the chair he normally occupied, but I didn't feel like walking past him just now. I hadn't managed to get the sight of him half-naked out of my head, and it was making me jumpy. With my luck, I'd probably trip and break something.

"So who was that guy you were sitting with during the assembly?"

I blinked, surprised by Eli's tone. He didn't sound annoyed exactly, but I could tell it wasn't just a casual question, either. "Nobody to you."

Eli grunted. "Is he your boyfriend or something?"

"Nah, I just like to randomly hold hands with strangers."

"Is that so?" He turned sideways and stretched out, laying his head on one arm of the sofa with his feet dangling over the side of the other. "I guess that's why you've never held—" He broke off, yawning hugely. Then he fell asleep.

I stared at him for a long time, wondering what he'd been about to say. Then I walked over and climbed on top of him, grateful he'd chosen the sofa this time. It made my job a lot easier.

I entered his dream, wanting to get this over quickly. When the dream world solidified around me, I saw the familiar setting of Chickery High School's gymnasium as it normally looked for the homecoming dance. Red and white streamers hung from the walls and across the ceiling. More streamers rimmed the tables set around the edges of the dance floor. Loud pop music blared from the speakers, providing some sense of beat to the chaos of writhing bodies.

I saw Eli nearby, dancing with Katarina. I considered switching into my old-lady disguise to hide from him again, but I never got the chance as a strange, horrible sight drew my attention. In the center of the dance floor, towering over the heads of the students, was a Minotaur. It was dancing along with the music, having a good time, just one of the crowd. A huge iron ring hung from its snout. Blood dripped from it, splattering the creature's bare chest with crimson.

I took a step toward it, trying to make sense of its presence in Eli's dream. A loud shriek rang out above the music, and I froze in place. I looked up, my head pounding with a sudden surge of adrenaline as I saw the black phoenix swoop down at the dancing crowd, claws outstretched, beak opened. Before I could react, it grabbed the Minotaur by the neck and ripped its head from its body with a sickening crack. The students began to scream as the creature's huge body fell to the floor, blood spurting from its neck.

The next thing I knew, Eli was standing beside me, his face slack with shock as people swarmed past us in a frenzied panic. Seeing his fear only increased my own. I didn't want to deal with this. Not now. Not ever. I'd seen enough and didn't want to see anymore. I pulled back from the dream and fled before Eli woke up. I went to bed as soon as I finished typing my dream journal. But I didn't sleep. Not for a long, long time.

～ 13 ～

Samhain

Paul picked me up at my dorm room before the dance. Selene and her date, a siren by the name of Justin Damico, had already left. I spent a whole ten minutes by myself, utterly convinced I would be stood up again. But Paul's knock sounded promptly at seven-thirty, and I hurried to answer, almost breathless with relief.

"Hello," he said, taking in the sight of my dress, an off-the-shoulder ball gown made of gold silk overlaid with cream-colored lace. "Wow. You look great."

A flutter rose in my chest at the way he looked at me, his mouth half-opened, his eyes wide. I didn't consider myself very pretty, but his expression made me feel like I was. I'd borrowed the gown from Selene. It was beautiful, though there was no helping my unfortunate red hair, which even now was starting to frizz despite the liberal amounts of hair products I applied.

Paul, of course, was a knockout in his black suit and black tie offset by a red waistcoat. "So do you," I said.

"Where's your mask?" He glanced behind me at all the mess in the dorm room.

"One sec." I retrieved the matching gold-colored mask from beside my computer. The Samhain dance was a masquerade ball, the first I'd ever attended. I felt a little silly as I slid the mask on, but it was sort of fun, too. The mask was a Columbina, according to Selene, which meant it only covered the top half of my face. Bedecked in feathers and sequins, I looked a bit like a golden peacock.

I came back to the door. "What about yours?"

Paul reached up and pulled his mask down from the top of his head, where he'd been wearing it like a pair of sunglasses. It was a Columbina, too, but just a simple unadorned black. Combined with his blond hair pulled back in a ponytail, he looked like he could grace the cover of a romance novel.

"Let's go." Paul extended his arm, and I slid mine beneath his. He pulled me close to him, our sides brushing as we moved along. Walking arm in arm with him felt as natural as breathing. Heat radiated off his body, keeping me warm as we headed across campus to Vatticut Hall.

The front lawn was packed with students and the occasional faculty member. They congregated around the bonfires lit here and there, passing the time until the feast began. A couple of werewolf policemen were patrolling around, their presence so commonplace since Rosemary's death as to go almost unnoticed.

"Pop quiz," Paul said as we walked along. "Let's see how

much you were paying attention in the assembly." He ran a hand down my back and up again.

I blushed then felt a thrill as I realized nobody could see it. This mask thing was pretty cool.

"Why do we wear masks on Samhain?"

I grinned. Too easy. "To hide from the spirits of the dead, because this is the one night of the year they can come out and terrorize magickind. Lucky us."

"That's correct." Paul shook his head. "Seems I didn't do a good enough job distracting you yesterday."

I blushed harder, remembering the way he'd traced his fingers over my hand and up and down my forearm, each touch sending tingles over my body. "Oh, I wouldn't say that."

He laughed as we stepped through the doors into Vatticut Hall. It was the oldest structure on campus and only used for special occasions, like dances and graduation. Tonight the building resembled a medieval castle even more than usual. Blue and silver silk streamers had been strung in between the ornate tapestries and heraldic banners that decorated the outer corridors. Torches hung beside the banners, creating a flickering, romantic ambiance. Of course the grandeur out here was nothing compared to the grand ballroom.

Long wooden tables set with crystal plates and goblets were spread across the hall among glistening ice sculptures of magical creatures like unicorns, dragons, and even our school mascot, the hydra. In each corner of the room stood four trees enchanted by the school's fairy gardeners to grow out of the floors. With trunks the size of industrial stovepipes, they stood tall enough that their branches covered the ceiling, creating a dark, leafy canopy. Beneath it, thousands of free-floating orbs of light shone in various colors as they flitted here and there, creating an aurora borealis effect. Every now and again, one would shoot across the room, leaving behind a trail of glittering light and a smell like fresh roses.

Paul and I joined Selene and Justin at a table across the room. Justin shared Selene's views on the anti-objectification of sirens, but neither of them seemed much concerned with politics tonight. They both looked stunning in their masquerade getups, she in pale blue silk and he in a white-on-white suit. They exuded that hypnotic sensuality specific to sirens. Still, I knew Selene and Justin were just friends and nothing more.

Selene took care of the introductions, and we sat down to wait for the feast to begin.

Eating in a mask was tricky, but I managed okay. We spent most of the feast playing a "guess who's behind the mask" game. Mask wearing during Samhain was pretty serious business for magickind, which meant nobody had taken theirs off. It was surprisingly hard to figure out who was who.

"That's Katarina," Selene said, pointing to a girl in a pink gown with a matching pink Columbina mask encrusted around the edges with sparkling pink and red jewels. A long pink feather rose up from one side of it.

"How do you know?" I asked.

"See how it looks like a cat?"

I took in the angular slant of the eye holes and the feline shape of the nose and nodded.

"She *always* wears a mask like that. Can't stand not to be recognized. It's her signature. You know, *Kat*-arina."

"That's original," Paul said.

I grinned at the derision in his voice. "That's Katarina. About as original as a Salvador Dalí print."

"About as pretty as one, too," said Paul.

Yeah, this could be love.

I shifted my gaze from Katarina to the person beside her. Eli wore a black cloak over a white dress shirt that he'd unbuttoned far enough I could see the edge of his tattoo on the left side of his chest. Vivid memories of the night before popped up in my mind. A white mask covered the left side of Eli's face. He looked like a sexy, teenage version of the Phantom of the Opera. He turned his head in my direction and our eyes locked for a moment. I glanced away first, certain that he knew it was me. My mask did little to disguise my red hair.

The teachers were harder to figure out. Probably because we didn't spend as much time thinking and looking at them as we did our classmates.

"I think that's Mr. Ankil," I said, pointing to the front of the hall where the teachers' tables were set beneath the dais.

"Which one?" asked Paul.

"In the purple mask with the gold trim."

"Why do you think so?" said Selene.

"Look under the table. He's wearing jeans and sandals."

Selene dropped her gaze. "That's him, all right. But who's that in the Medico della Peste?" She pointed to a man walking across the front of the hall wearing a long black cape over a white shirt and black pants.

"The what?" I asked.

"The plague doctor," said Paul. "That's what the masks with the long beaks are called."

"Oh." I looked at the man again. He walked with a slight hitch in his gait that I recognized at once. "That's Mr. Culpepper."

Thankfully, nobody asked how I knew.

When the feast ended, the tables and chairs disappeared, clearing the floor for dancing.

Even though it was a formal masked ball, the dancing was typical of any American high school, lots of jumping around and grinding while a band played cover songs of popular ordinary music from atop the dais. Paul liked to dance, and we spent five straight songs out there. He paid me constant attention, touching my waist, my shoulders, my hips.

But after a while, I began to feel like I was wearing railroad spikes on my feet instead of high heels, and I had to sit down at one of the small round tables in the back of the ballroom.

"Want something to drink?" Paul said, trailing his fingers along my neck.

I closed my eyes to better savor the feeling. "Sure. Anything cold will do."

Then I watched him walk off as I scooted farther underneath the table so no one could see me kick off my shoes. I breathed a sigh of relief and leaned back, awash with contentment. Not only because of my feet, but because I was having such a good time. The bad stuff about Nightmares, Keepers, and murderers seemed very far away.

At least until I spotted Eli walking toward me, his mask dangling from his fingers. I shot up and shoved my feet into my shoes as he stopped beside the table. The relaxed feeling vanished, butterflies taking its place.

"Hey," he said, sitting down.

"Hey." I debated leaving my mask in place then decided if he was brave enough not to wear one on Samhain then so was I. I pulled it off and set it on the table.

He stared at me a moment without speaking, his bright blue eyes unnerving. I dropped my gaze only to catch sight of the edge of his tattoo again. The number of butterflies in my stomach seemed to grow exponentially.

Annoyed with myself, I forced my eyes upward again before he caught me staring. "What do you want?"

He blinked at my harsh tone. "I've been thinking about the dream last night. Do you think it means something?"

"No idea."

His eyes narrowed, eyebrows slanting closer together. "What's *with* you? I thought you wanted to catch the killer, too."

I shook my head. "Catching him was never my job. I'm just supposed to report the stuff I see in your dreams, which I did. The rest is on the senate."

Eli thumped the table with his hand. "How can you say that? That dream was different from the others. Don't even try to tell me you weren't scared by it."

I gritted my teeth, unable to keep the flood of images from my mind. The Minotaur with the iron ring in its nose. The black phoenix. All that blood and screaming. "Look, I don't want to talk about this right now, okay?"

"No, it's not okay. Not if you're gonna keep avoiding me."

I glowered at him. "What difference does it make?"

"We're supposed to be a team."

"Right. A team."

"What is your deal? Are you ever *not* sarcastic?"

Oh no he didn't. I started to stand up, but Eli grabbed my wrist, pulling me back down. It surprised me how quickly he moved, a definite reminder of how physically daunting he could be. As if I needed a reminder.

I stared at him, frozen in place. His hand was so large his fingers easily encircled my wrist. My skin burned where he touched me, but not in a bad way. Oh, no. Just the opposite. Getting a grip on myself, I pulled my hand away. He slowly let go, but there was something reluctant about it.

"I'm not leaving until you tell me what your problem is," he said.

I wracked my brain for a safe, acceptable reason. "Fine. Your *girlfriend* is spreading rumors that I try to seduce you during our dream-sessions." It was the first complaint to come to mind and the only one I felt comfortable talking about.

"What?" His face reddened. I couldn't tell if it was from anger or embarrassment. Maybe both. "Man, I can't believe her sometimes. I'll get her to stop."

"Good."

"She doesn't like us spending time together. She's jealous."

"Please, like I'm stupid enough to believe that excuse."

"It's not stupid. It's true."

It was on the tip of my tongue to ask him what he meant, but I caught a flash of pale pink across the ballroom, heading this way. "I think it's time for you to go."

He drummed his fingers on the table, a scowl on his face. "Why? You afraid your *date* is going to see us and get mad or something?"

"No, but yours is."

Eli looked over his shoulder. "Crap." He stood but didn't leave. "We still need to talk about the dream. What if that Minotaur represents the killer's next victim?"

The same thought had occurred to me. "You're right. But seriously, if you don't go Katarina's gonna make a scene in a *big* way." She was close enough now that I could see the thin, furious line of her mouth beneath her mask.

"I'll deal with Kat," said Eli. "She won't bother you, and she won't be spreading any more rumors. I can't stand that crap."

He sounded a bit disgusted, and I couldn't resist asking,

"Why are you dating her? Do you even have anything in common?"

A puzzled expression crossed Eli's face. "I don't know. I'm just *really* attracted to her. I can't seem to think straight around her. We don't do much talking anyways."

Yuck.

"Might want to think about that," I said. I realized it must be hard dating a siren, especially one like Katarina who regularly abused her natural abilities. I didn't think Eli had any idea that the compulsive attraction he felt for her could be mostly siren magic. Then it occurred to me that this might be one of the chinks in The Will spell that Marrow had mentioned. Sirens weren't able to lure people to their deaths or anything, but they still excelled at seduction, which I imagined could be equally harmful.

I supposed there were some things so fundamental to a creature's nature that no spell could ever control it completely. Maybe that meant Katarina and I had something in common. I shuddered at the thought.

"See you around." Eli slid on his mask and hurried off, intercepting Katarina in the nick of time.

Paul returned with drinks a moment later and handed me a goblet of apple cider.

"Thanks." I drank it down in three swallows.

"You okay?" Paul asked. "Was that guy bothering you?"

"No." I stood up. "I'm fine. Ready to dance some more?" I'd caught sight of Eli and Katarina heading out to the floor, and the last thing I wanted was to sit here and watch them.

"If you are."

"I am." My feet gave a loud protest that *they* weren't, but I ignored them.

Another hour slipped by. The fervor in the grand ball-room grew as the clock drew closer to midnight. Selene warned me that when midnight arrived, the whole place would descend into pandemonium as everybody celebrated the official start of Samhain. She hadn't been exaggerating. I felt like one of those crazy people in New York City, waiting for the ball to drop for the New Year. Only those people weren't in ball gowns and masks.

The gowns were okay, but the masks were starting to freak me out. The plague doctor ones were bad enough, but the full-faced ones with the long pointy chins and tall pointy horns were worse. Every time I spotted one, my thoughts turned to the Minotaur, and the gruesome memory of its head being ripped from its body.

After a while, I began to feel light-headed. "I need to sit down," I said into Paul's ear. He nodded and escorted me off the dance floor to the tables in the back. I sat down and removed my mask, uncaring about any risks from ghost attack. The air felt cool on my face.

"Are you all right?" Paul asked, rubbing my shoulders.

"Just a bit dizzy."

"I'll bring you something more to drink."

I closed my eyes when he left and didn't open them again until he returned with more cider and a goblet of water.

"Will you be all right by yourself for a few minutes?" said Paul.

"Sure. What's up?"

He looked nervous. "I think Senator Kelly's here. She's supposed to be writing me a recommendation, and I want to ask her about it."

I smiled. "Go for it. I'll be fine."

Paul smiled back then bent toward me, pulling off his own mask as he did so. He kissed me. It was short and soft, hardly more than a brush of the lips, but it sent ripples of heat bubbling through my body like lava down the side of a volcano. I leaned into him, wanting more, but he pulled away and left. I closed my eyes again, savoring the tingly feel that lingered for minutes afterward.

I sat there through several songs, drinking the water and cider. Then I stood and headed for the bathroom. Careful not to smear my eye makeup, I splashed water on my face.

Through the mirror, I saw the bathroom door open behind me. A girl in a pink mask strolled inside, flanked by another girl in green taffeta—Katarina and Carla. I tried to ignore them, but Katarina stepped right behind me and poked me in the back. Hard.

"Hey," I shouted, spinning around.

Katarina pulled off her mask and sneered at me. For the first time ever, she looked less than beautiful. More like scary. "What were you doing with my boyfriend?"

I poked her back, jamming my forefinger into her shoulder. "Why don't you ask him?"

"Don't touch me," Katarina hissed.

"You started it." My hands clenched into fists at my

side, and I resisted the urge to slap her. I could do it, no question, already seeing it in my imagination. And I was just as sure she wouldn't be able to do much more than that finger poke to me. It was a heady thought, the surety of such power.

"What were you talking about?" she demanded, hands on hips.

I moved toward the door. "None of your business. If Eli wanted you to know, he'd have told you."

"Come on, Kat," Carla said. "Don't let her get to you. It was probably something stupid and you're freaking out for nothing."

"Yep," I said in my most sarcastic tone. "There's *nothing* to worry about at all. Nothing going on between *me* and *your* boyfriend."

Katarina raised her hand and tried to swipe at me like a cat. An invisible force held her back. "Owww!" She stamped her foot in frustration. I expected her to descend into full-on tantrum any second, hair pulling and all. "It's not fair. If I could just—"

"What? Do this?" I reached out and shoved her hard enough she tipped backward in her high-heeled shoes and fell into Carla.

"You *bitch*," Katarina huffed, righting herself.

Beside her, Carla pulled the bracelet off her wrist. The glamour on the bracelet fell away to reveal her wand.

"What do you think you can do with that?" I said.

A flush spread across Carla's neck, and I laughed.

The door to the bathroom swung open, and a person

in one of those plague doctor masks came in. At first I thought it was a man, given the suit and cape outfit and short hair, but then a familiar female voice said, "What's going on here?"

The blood drained from my face. It *couldn't* be her.

My mother pulled off her mask and fixed a hawk-eyed glare at the three of us. "Well?" she said.

"We were . . . um . . . just leaving," said Katarina, wiping back strands of brown hair that had fallen into her eyes when I shoved her.

"Yeah," seconded Carla, and the two of them squeezed past Moira toward the door.

"Me, too," I added, trying to follow after them.

Mom grabbed my arm. "Wait just a minute."

I turned and faced her, the power trip I'd been riding officially over.

"Were you *fighting* with those girls?"

"Uh, no, of course not. I mean . . . The Will won't let us do that."

She gave me a look that told me she wasn't buying it.

I decided to employ my usual tactic: an offense is the best defense. "What are you doing here, Mom?"

"Checking to see you're all right."

"I don't mean in the bathroom. I mean *here* at the *dance*." I waved with both hands.

"Oh . . . I'm chaperoning."

"Yeah, right. Since when do they let someone like you chaperone?"

Moira's skin went from tan to red. "What's that sup-posed to mean?" She sighed. "Never mind." She slid her mask back over her face. "You'd better stay out of trouble. And put your mask on. It's almost midnight." She swung around, her cape flaring dramatically behind her as she disappeared through the door.

I gaped after her. Unease churned in the pit of my stomach, and I marched out of the bathroom, determined to demand answers.

She had disappeared into the crowd of masked people. I stood there for a couple of minutes, trying to distinguish one person from another. Then finally, I saw someone in a plague doctor mask and cape disappear through one of the doors on the other side of the ballroom. I pushed and stumbled my way through the crowd after her, feeling claustrophobic in the crush of people. I really hoped it was my mother I was following and not someone else wearing the same mask.

The door led into one of the less-used corridors on the backside of Vatticut. It was empty, but there were only two ways to go—to the right toward the front entrance or to the left into the tunnels. My gut told me left, and I hurried as fast as I could down the slope.

The farther in I went, the more I considered giving up the pursuit. Coming this way was a bad idea. It was dark down here. It was Samhain. That was enough to scare a braver soul than me. But then I heard footsteps ahead and curiosity spurred me onward. The sound of my own footsteps striking the stone floor was so loud the person was bound to hear it.

I hiked up the hem of my dress so I could kick off my shoes. I froze halfway through the motion, startled by the thump of heavier footsteps approaching behind me. I spun around, my heart leaping into my throat. I raised my hand, ready to cast a dazing spell, but stopped when I saw who it was. Eli. Once again, he wasn't wearing his mask.

"What are you doing?" I said, half-annoyed, half-relieved by his presence.

He came to a halt mere inches from me. "Following you."

"*Why?*"

"It looked like you were onto something, and it's not safe to be running around down here alone."

"Do you have to be so *nosy*?" I looked back the way I'd been heading. "She's probably long gone now."

He stepped beside me, close enough I felt my dress move around my legs. "You're following somebody? Is it about the dream?"

"No. Now go away. This—" The words died on my lips as the sound of someone screaming echoed down the tunnel toward us.

Eli and I glanced at each other, then we both broke into a run toward the sound. I kicked off my shoes as I went, worried I'd break an ankle sprinting on the uneven surface. Eli raced ahead of me, but I didn't mind. I was glad not to be alone. The screaming continued, growing louder and more agonized by the second, filling me with terror. Images from the dream last night blazed in my brain. The scream was so high-pitched, so inhuman, surely it had to be some kind of creature, like a Minotaur.

As we came around a corner into a small chamber at the intersection of several tunnels, we spotted the source of those screams. It was a man.

He was on fire.

∼ 14 ∼

Dead End

For a few terrible seconds, I stood there, motionless, unable to think.

The person fell to his knees, writhing on the floor in a horror-movie parody of stop, drop, and roll.

"Do something!" Eli shouted, pulling off his coat and trying to get close enough to slap at the flames. But they were too high and strong.

I could only stare. This couldn't be happening.

"*Do something!*" Eli shouted again. "Put it out! Magic up some water already."

I blinked, my brain finally breaking through the terror. I raised my shaking hand, and said, "Hydro-rhe."

Faint, blue sparks shot sluggishly out of my fingertips, the magic weak and insubstantial. What little water the spell produced only made the flames hiss and smoke.

What was wrong with me? This spell was simple. *It should be easy.*

"Hydro-rhe!" I said, louder and harder this time. Faint

streaks again. More hissing. The man's screams were growing softer, his thrashing slower.

"Hydro-rhe! Hydro-rhe! Hydro-rhe!" Tears blurred my vision. I couldn't do it. I was just a pathetic excuse for magickind, incapable of a simple water spell. "Hydro-rhe . . . Hydro-rhe." I fell to my knees saying it over and over again.

Eli knelt beside me and placed a hand on my arm. "Come on, Dusty. You can do this."

A surge of power stirred inside me at his touch, like the kind I felt when I first entered someone's dream. *"Hydro-rhe!"* I screamed, reaching out with both hands.

Brilliant blue sparks flew out from my fingertips and transformed into a shower of water as strong as a burst fire hydrant, putting the flames out in seconds.

It didn't matter.

"Oh, God, Dusty. Don't look." Eli moved in front of me, shielding me with his body, but it was too late. I saw enough. I saw *everything*.

I even knew who it was—*had been*.

"It's . . . it's . . ." I stuttered as my brain processed the sight of jeans and sandals, charred black.

"Mr. Ankil," said Eli. "His hand is gone. Just like Rosemary."

I scooted away, turned, and vomited. Eli stooped over me, holding my hair back from my face, his hands as gentle as my dad's had been when I'd been sick as a kid.

"It's all right," he whispered, stroking my back.

By the time I finished, I heard the sound of more footsteps and someone calling my name. I looked up and saw Paul coming toward us down the main tunnel.

"Someone said they'd seen you . . ." The words died on his lips as he spotted Ankil's body. He covered his nose and mouth to block out the stench. "What's going on?"

Eli pointed at him. "Go get help."

Paul hesitated a moment then took off at a run. I stayed where I was on the floor, not trusting my shaky legs to hold me up. Eli remained standing over me as if keeping guard. His eyes darted around the room, his body tense like he expected something to attack us.

When Paul finally returned, a bunch of people came with him, including Sheriff Brackenberry, Lady Elaine, and Mr. Marrow. I struggled to get up. Eli took me by the arm and helped me, still scanning the room. He didn't let go as I swayed on my feet, but wrapped his arm around my shoulders. I leaned into his chest, grateful for the solid feel of him. I'd never felt more tired or sick in my whole life.

Across from us Lady Elaine knelt beside Ankil's body then placed her hands on the charred skin of the arm with the missing hand. Her eyes rolled back in her head as she went into some kind of deep trance.

Paul came over and gave Eli a hard look before fixing his gaze on me. "Are you all right? I was worried when I couldn't find you. Let me help." He reached for my arm.

Eli pushed him off. "I've got her."

Paul glowered, his hands curling into fists, but before

he could do anything, Marrow and Brackenberry came over to us.

"What happened?" the sheriff asked. He was wearing a blue suit and pink waistcoat, his mask pushed up on top of his head.

"He was already on fire when we got here," Eli said, his arm tightening around me. "We tried to put it out, but it was too late."

I shook my head, unable to hold back tears. "It was my fault. I couldn't do it."

Paul wedged himself between me and Eli. From the corner of my eye I saw the dangerous look on Eli's face. He raised one hand as if he meant to shove Paul off, but then he stepped back.

Paul slid his arm around me, and for a moment I wished it was still Eli, if only because he understood. He'd been there, too.

"It's not your fault," Paul said, kissing the top of my head.

Eli made a sound like a growl. "Of course it isn't."

"Did you see who did it?" asked Brackenberry.

Eli forced his arms to his sides, his muscles flexed and veins popping out. "No."

Marrow looked between Eli and me, his expression stormy. "But why did you come down here? It's too dangerous for students."

Eli glanced at me, uncertain.

"I . . . uh . . ." My frantic mind searched for an explanation that didn't involve my mother. I thought I'd been following her, but she couldn't have done this. She wouldn't.

"Dusty?" Marrow said.

I forced my eyes to his. "I . . . was following someone I thought looked suspicious, like maybe from a dream. Someone wearing one of those plague doctor masks."

"I see," said Brackenberry. He gazed around at the various tunnel openings. "They could be anywhere by now."

"Can I take Dusty home, Mr. Marrow?" asked Paul. "She's been through enough."

Marrow glanced at the sheriff. "Is that all right with you?"

Brackenberry nodded, but he pointed at Eli. "As long as this one stays for a bit to answer questions."

"Because that's going to make such a difference," Eli muttered.

"Come on," Paul said, prodding me forward.

I let him guide me along without protest. I wanted nothing more than to get away from that terrible burnt smell clogging the corridor. I had a feeling a part of me might go on smelling it forever.

More people began to file into the corridor as we walked, several werewolf police and a couple of Magi Senators. I wondered what all of them were doing here. Magi and police didn't normally attend high school dances. They must've suspected something would happen. Not that it had done any good.

My mother appeared in the corridor. I was afraid to look at her, but I couldn't turn away. My eyes took in the sight of her outfit, the same suit and cape she'd been wearing before, the same mask now hung from her side. If she'd been down in this tunnel, if she'd been the one to murder Mr. Ankil, there was no evidence of it on her person that I could tell. But then, her magic wouldn't leave evidence.

I pulled my gaze away from her, close to vomiting again.

"Are you all right, Destiny?" Moira stepped in front of us, blocking the way.

"I'm fine."

Her brow furrowed. "You don't look it. What have you been doing? What did I tell you about not getting involved in this? It's *dangerous*."

Oh yeah? What have you been doing, Mom?

"I'm sorry, Ms. Everhart," said Paul, "but I'm supposed to get her back to her dorm."

"The hell you are," said Moira, her eyes sparkling with outrage. "You take her to the infirmary. Look at her feet. She can barely walk."

A flush colored Paul's cheeks, and we both glanced down. My feet were covered in filth and no small amount of blood. For a moment I worried that it wasn't my blood but Mr. Ankil's. Then I realized how sore the soles of my feet were and guessed I'd cut them on the rough floor.

"And she's in shock," Moira said.

For once Mom and I agreed on something. Everything felt numb, even my brain.

"I'll take her there now." Paul stooped and picked me up.

"Don't." I tried to wriggle free, but he tightened his grip.

"Be careful," said Moira. "And don't fight, Destiny. For once in your life, please don't be difficult."

I didn't say anything, but I stopped struggling. I was so sleepy and disoriented. The world spun around me, and I closed my eyes as Paul strode off, carrying me in his arms like a child. I rested my head against his shoulder and told myself the moment I could hear him breathing hard I would insist he put me down.

But he didn't breathe hard, not once. When we arrived in the infirmary, the duty nurse directed Paul to one of the patient rooms. The moment my head touched the pillow the nurse cast a sleeping spell. I felt the magic pool over me like warm, soothing water. It dragged me under in a moment, and I went with it, wishing the oblivion it brought would last forever.

～ 15 ～

Warrant

B ut it didn't last forever.

When I woke, it wasn't even morning yet. My eyes felt like iron weights in my skull as I forced them open and looked around. Darkness filled the single window beside the infirmary bed I lay in, and the light in the corridor beyond my room was dim. I could see a nurse's station through the door, but it was empty for the moment.

If only my room were empty, too. But no such luck. My mother sat in the chair beneath the window. For a second I didn't think she knew I was awake, and I closed my eyes.

"Don't bother," Mom said. "I know you're awake, because I woke you."

I opened my eyes and shot her a glare. My head pounded. "What do you want?"

Moira stood and approached the bed. "Keep your voice down. I don't want the duty nurse to hear us."

I pursed my lips. "Of course not. Because I'm supposed to still be asleep, aren't I?"

Mom folded her arms. "You will be again once I've said what I need to say." .

I clamped my mouth shut, holding back a smartass remark. I wanted her to get on with it and leave me alone already. Horrible, vivid images of Mr. Ankil's death crowded my mind. I tried to force them away, but it was impossible. Only the sleeping spell would be able to do that.

"I'm only going to tell you this once, Destiny," Moira said, leaning over me as if to emphasize how serious she was. "You are to stay as far away from these murders as humanly, magically, entirely possible." She waved a finger back and forth in front of my face. "No more tailing suspicious people, no more investigating, no more anything besides your dream-seer duties. I would even have you stop doing that if I had any say in it. Do I make myself clear?"

I sat up, anger and fear pulsing through my body, blood rushing in my ears. I didn't trust her reasons for ordering me out of it. *As if she can order me.* Ignoring a sudden wave of dizziness, I said, "What were you doing at the dance, Mom?"

"I told you. It's my business, not yours."

I shook my head, the motion sending bright starbursts across my vision. "Then you can forget it. You can't stop me from investigating."

Moira exhaled, the sound a hiss. "Do you have any idea how dangerous the situation is? The killer's not do-ing this for the fun of it. And what he's after is—" She broke off as if realizing she was about to spill something important.

I took a deep breath and tried to make my voice civil. "No, I don't know what the killer is after, because no one will tell me anything. But maybe if I *did* know, I'd have an easier time keeping out of harm's way."

Moira frowned, her eyes thoughtful.

Sensing she was about to cave, I said in my softest, most desperate voice, "What is the Keeper spell guarding, Mom?"

Several seconds passed while Moira continued to stare at me. Then she glanced out the door as if to check that we were still alone. She turned back to me. "The spell is guarding the most powerful magical object in existence. A sword, which I'm sure you've heard of. In ordinary folklore, it's known as Excalibur, although that's not its true name."

Say what? She had to be pulling my leg. "Very funny, Mom."

"I'm not joking. I would *never* joke about something so important."

I could tell she meant it. My fingers clenched around the bedsheet. I was dimly aware that I was no longer wearing my ball gown but a green infirmary robe. "I thought the Arthur legend was an *actual* myth?"

Mom shook her head. "That is what the Magi want you to believe, but in truth, it's nothing but an elaborate work of propaganda. The story has been twisted and turned into legend to hide the truth of real events and people."

I considered the idea. Hiding truth behind stories was a familiar concept with magickind. The Tinkerbell version of fairies was nothing more than a good PR campaign. Far from being cutesy and harmless, fairies were fearsome, capable of reducing an ordinary into a pile of gooey mush in a matter of seconds—if they wanted to and if The Will wasn't keeping them in check. It was a sobering thought, and I found myself glad a Nightmare's magic was so rare.

I cleared my throat. "So Arthur and Merlin were real people?"

Moira knelt, resting her arms on the side of the bed. "No. Those are fictional characters *based* on real people."

I looked her in the eye, my mind running through all the movies and books about King Arthur. The influence of that myth was everywhere, even on campus, depicted in statues and artwork. "Then what's the true story?" I asked.

Moira waved the question off. "No time for that now. The important thing for you to know is that the sword is the power source for The Will."

I gulped, a tremor of fear rippling through me. The power source of a magical spell was essentially the spell itself, the heart of it. "Are you saying the killer is trying to break The Will?" It was suddenly hard to breathe, as if someone had punched me in the chest.

"Either that or he's trying to gain control over it. The sword is what makes The Will possible. Whoever controls the sword controls The Will. They will wield the same level of power. Power they can use over anyone and every-one. However they choose."

I thought about Rosemary, lying dead in the cemetery, her body bruised and mutilated, and of Mr. Ankil, his body a ruin of burned flesh. There was no doubt the killer would use it to do even more evil.

Mom stood, a triumphant look in her eyes. "So, now that you understand the danger, stay out of it."

I opened my mouth to argue, but Moira spun around at the sound of someone entering the room. The duty nurse's eyes registered surprise, but before she could react, my mother pointed her hand and said, "Amnes-somni."

The nurse's face went slack. She stood there, motionless and senseless. I didn't recognize the spell, but I had no doubt it was an illegal one.

"What are you *doing*?" I said.

Moira turned back and pointed her hand at me. I was asleep again before she finished uttering the spell.

When I woke next, it was to the feel of warm light on my face. In less than a heartbeat, all the details of the night before came rushing into my mind.

Mr. Ankil.

Dead.

Another victim. Another death my useless dream-seer powers had been unable to prevent.

And a killer, determined to conquer The Will.

I heard the sound of ruffling paper and slid my eyes

open, glancing around for the source. When I saw Eli sitting in a chair next to me with a magazine in his hands, I closed them again. I tried to remain perfectly still, willing myself unconscious. I wasn't ready to face anybody, least of all him.

"You can stop pretending," Eli said. "I can see your eyes moving behind your eyelids."

I peered over at him. "It's not called Rapid Eye Movement for nothing."

He smiled. "You must be feeling better if you're being snotty already."

I wasn't feeling better, worse actually, but I didn't say anything, hoping to avoid the topic of feelings at all costs.

"What are you doing here?" I asked. He was wearing regular clothes again, but he didn't appear as if he'd slept much.

Eli set down the magazine on the table in between the chair and the hospital bed. "I wanted to make sure you're okay."

I blinked in surprise at the sincerity in his words. For the first time ever he didn't look menacing or dangerous. Instead he looked like I felt—scared, exhausted, and guilt-ridden.

I sat up and stretched, realizing too late that I was braless beneath the infirmary robe. I wrapped my arms around my chest and looked around, hoping he didn't notice my blush. "I'm feeling a little better. But what's been happening?"

Eli grimaced. "Not much. They haven't caught the killer or anything."

I swallowed, resisting the urge to be sick. My throat ached, and my tummy felt hollow. Of course they hadn't found him. Someone powerful and crazy enough to go after The Will spell wasn't going to be caught easily. "Has Paul been by?" I said, searching for an easier topic.

"He was here, but his uncle came and made him leave." Eli glanced at the door. "Selene should be back soon. She's getting something to drink."

"Oh. Does she . . . know what happened?"

Eli scowled. "She's not supposed to. The sheriff and those guys are telling people Ankil's death was an accident caused by a lighting spell backfiring on him due to the 'instability of magic during Samhain' or some nonsense," he said, finger-quoting. "You and I are supposed to play along. But Selene cornered me and *made* me tell her the truth."

I smiled at the exasperation in his voice. "Yeah, Selene can be forceful when she wants to be."

"No kidding. Are *all* your friends like that?"

I dropped my eyes, not wanting to look at him. "She's my *only* true friend. Here at least."

When Eli didn't respond, I fixed my gaze on the door, hoping Selene would get back soon. I wasn't surprised Ankil's death was being played off as an accident, but it felt wrong. He deserved better.

"I'm sorry," Eli said, his voice throaty with emotion.

I looked at him. "What for?"

"Everything. Especially for not making more of an effort to work as a team." He stood up and started pacing. "I was just so *pissed,* you know? About leaving my old life. Coming here to this strange place. And I hate feeling like the only kid on the short bus." He stopped midstride and faced me. "I blamed you at first, but that's stupid and doesn't matter. I know it's not your fault. And now I can't help thinking that maybe if we'd been friends from the start, we would've been more focused on the dreams. Then maybe we could've done something to save Mr. Ankil."

I stared at him, stunned speechless. Tears welled around my eyes, and I fought to hold them back. "It's not your fault. I wasn't exactly waving the friend flag your way. I've been avoiding you because the dream-seer stuff scares me. And I understand why you blamed me. I felt the same way when I first came here. Only I was pissed at my mom for being a Nightmare."

He opened his mouth to say something more, but Selene arrived in the doorway.

"Hey you," she said, beaming at me. "How you feeling?"

"Better." I kept glancing warily at Eli as he returned to the chair.

Selene gave me a look that told me she knew I was lying. She sat down on the side of the bed and handed me the glass of water she'd brought in with her. "You aren't responsible for what happened," she said matter-of-factly. "I just want to make that clear right up front."

Eli smacked his hands against the arms of his chair,

making Selene and I both jump. "Of course she's not. But what's the good of having these dreams if we can't save anybody?"

"But it's not that simple, Eli," I said, feeling the urge to defend us. "There was no way we could have known that the Minotaur symbolized Mr. Ankil."

"What are you talking about?" asked Selene, brow furrowed in confusion.

Eli filled her in about the Minotaur getting beheaded by the black phoenix.

"Wait," Selene said when he finished. "The Minotaur had a *ring* in its nose? And then Ankil's hand was missing?"

I nodded, knowing exactly where she was going. I'd already come to the same conclusion.

"Then the senate must've known he was in danger."

"How do you figure?" said Eli.

"Because he was a Keeper," I answered, setting down the glass of water that I'd finished in three swallows.

"A what?"

I hesitated, unsure if I should trust him. I wasn't supposed to know about the Keepers myself. But I *had* to tell him. He was as much a part of this as I was.

A stricken expression spread across his face as he listened. "So all this time the killer's been targeting specific people?" he said as I finished.

Selene and I both nodded.

Eli turned his icy blue eyes on me. He swallowed. "I really wish you'd told me sooner, but I'm glad to know now."

As our eyes locked something seemed to click between us, and I felt my resentment toward him slipping away.

"So if the senate knew Ankil was a Keeper," said Selene, "why didn't they keep a better guard on him? And why did he go down into the tunnels in the first place?"

Nobody answered for a moment.

Then Eli said, "Maybe he was bait."

Selene and I both looked at him, horrified by the idea.

"Well, if that's true," said Selene, "they did a bang-up job of it—he died and they still didn't catch the guy."

"Just goes to show how dangerous and clever the killer is," said Eli.

Selene looked sick. "No wonder Ankil was so nervous lately."

"Yeah, I noticed that, too," said Eli. He ran a hand through his hair. "But it only started a couple of days ago. You'd think he would've been nervous as soon as Rosemary died."

I bit my lip, an idea occurring to me. "He must've been a *new* Keeper. Think about it. The senate probably decided to change the Keepers after Rosemary died to hide their identities. And Rosemary was so young, too. I heard Lady Elaine say that the spell had become more of a rite of passage than something to take seriously. So if the other Keepers were just as young and inexperienced, they would've had to change them."

"Rite of passage my foot." Selene scowled. "They shouldn't have been messing around with illegal black magic in the first place."

Eli leaned toward me. "So what's this Keeper spell guarding?"

I sucked in a breath, once again shocked by the enormity of the situation. "You won't believe it," I said, glancing between the two of them. Then I recapped what my mom had told me about the Arthur legend and how Excalibur was now The Will's power source.

"You're right, I don't believe it," said Selene, rubbing her temples.

"Well, I could believe anything with this crazy magic stuff," said Eli, his voice wry.

Selene turned a fierce gaze on him. "Do you know what would happen if The Will stopped working? Total chaos."

Eli scoffed. "Why do you think so? Isn't that like saying if the United States legalized drugs, everybody would turn into crackheads? Don't know about you, but I wouldn't do it just because it was legal."

Selene snorted. "*Drugs* are nothing like *magic*."

"She's right," I said. "Drugs mostly hurt the person doing them. Magic can hurt everybody."

"Especially when we're talking about the predatory magickind out there," said Selene, hugging herself. "Don't forget, the only reason why a lot of the demons and such don't hurt people is because The Will doesn't let them."

Eli held up his hands, his arm muscles flexing. "I get it. No Will is bad."

I shook my head. "It might be worse than that. My

mom said the killer wouldn't necessarily want to break The Will but control it."

"You mean so he could control us?" said Eli, raising a single eyebrow. "Like how I'm forced to fall asleep for our sessions?"

"Yep."

Selene shuddered. "That's horrible. Who knows what we might be forced to do."

Silence descended around us as we considered the frightening prospect.

Selene exhaled loudly. "Well, at least we know there's still one person holding the Keeper spell together."

I frowned. "How do you figure?"

"The senate always does things by threes at a minimum. And since Rosemary was naturekind and Ankil witchkind—"

"—the third must be *darkkind*," I said, making the connection.

"Right."

"But why?" said Eli.

"Because that's the way it's done," Selene answered. "The senate is divided into three parties, one for each kind. There's a lot of distrust between the kinds, enough that it's a sure bet if a fairy and a psychic were a part of the spell, a darkkind was, too. They would insist on keeping things equal."

"Makes sense," said Eli. "But can we be sure there are only three?"

"We can't. There could be more, but there are at *least* three," said Selene.

Eli looked at her, his expression hard. "Then someone else is going to die, too." He turned that gaze on me. "Unless we stop it."

Nobody spoke. I kept picturing Mr. Ankil with his big, flamboyant personality. The way he always acted like one of the students. He was so cool and so *young*.

And now he was gone.

Selene broke the silence first. "You're right. We've got to do something."

I shook my head, images of Mr. Ankil's death in my mind and that terrible smell thick in my nose.

"Come on, Dusty," said Eli. "You and I can do this. We've got the dreams to help, and I know loads about detective stuff. We've got to *try*."

I thought about my mother's insistence that I stay out of it, but I hadn't actually promised her. Still, we were just a couple of kids up against something huge and terrible, a person clever enough to lure Mr. Ankil down into the tunnels right beneath the senate's nose.

But Eli was right. If I didn't try, the guilt would be unbearable. I had to. *We* had to. Together. With my friends.

It was the best thought I'd had in days.

∼ 16 ∼

Task Force

We met in one of the computer rooms in the basement of the library later that night. Room 013. Pretty much everybody avoided the place—it was rumored to be haunted. But ghosts weren't the problem so much as a really rampant case of animation. The entire room seemed affected by it, even the furniture. The computers had particularly vile personalities, the kind that would wait until you'd gotten halfway through writing that essay without saving it before deciding to shut off.

Only the most desperate sought refuge here, but Eli insisted we needed a base of operations where we could work without interruption. The dorm Selene and I shared would've been ideal, but no boys were allowed. So room 013 it was.

Eli was in full take-charge mode by the time Selene and I arrived. He was sitting at the teacher's station in front of the computer that was linked into the overhead projection screen he'd switched on. The screen depicted one of his suspect graphs. I pulled out the one I'd started from my backpack and handed it to him.

"Okay," he said, examining it. "Fill us in on how you got this far." His focus on this whole investigation thing was a bit scary, but also encouraging in the way it built my confidence about our chances of success. Eli was like a professional.

I launched into a summary about everything that had happened since Melanie gave me Rosemary's diary. Well, *almost* everything. The stuff about Nightmares, and what we were capable of, I kept to myself.

"So where do we go from here?" said Selene, sitting down on top of one of the desks. The chair beside the desk squeaked its wheels in protest and then rammed into her dangling legs. "Ouch." She yanked her knees up before it hit her again.

"Think you might want to sit on the chair instead," I said, trying not to laugh.

Selene scowled at me and stood. The chair, which had been rolling back and forth like a bull getting ready to charge, stopped and swung its seat toward her, inviting her to sit. She did so, looking doubtful.

"Right," said Eli. "From here we identify all the possible suspects, then try to eliminate them one by one."

He indicated the suspect graph where he'd added my entries of F and Culpepper. Frank Rizzo was already on his graph along with a few others, but Eli had put lines through most of them and the word *alibi* in the Opportunity column.

"Dusty," he said, "you say you were following someone in one of those long-beaked masks. Let's start there. The person might've been involved or witnessed something."

"If they saw something, wouldn't they have told the cops already?" said Selene.

Eli shook his head. "Not if they're afraid. Lots of witnesses don't come forward if they think it's dangerous."

"Oh, that makes sense." Selene sounded impressed by Eli's knowledge.

He went on. "Who do we know was wearing one of those?"

"Culpepper was," said Selene, "but he's already on the list."

Eli nodded and typed a note next to the line with Culpepper's name. "It just means he's still a likely candidate. I saw Coach Fritz wearing one, too." He added the coach's name, although it took him three tries to do it. The computer kept deleting the letters as soon as he entered them. "Okay, who else?"

I swallowed hard, debating whether or not to answer. But I knew I had to. I owed it to Mr. Ankil. "My mother."

Selene and Eli both looked at me in surprise.

I began to fidget with my hair, twisting the red curls around my fingers. "It's true. I ran into her in the bathroom."

"What was she doing at the dance?" asked Selene as the chair gave a little buck beneath her. She grabbed the arms then kicked its wheels with the heel of her combat boot. "Stop that." The chair squeaked indignantly, but stayed still.

"I don't know. She wouldn't say."

"Hmmm," said Eli, writing her name down.

His lack of response made me nervous.

"Who else?"

We ended up adding another half-dozen names, including Bronson Babbit, a junior werewolf, and Lance Rathbone. Once we had everybody we could think of listed, we went through and eliminated the most unlikely.

"I know it wasn't Lance," said Eli. "I was near him right before I followed you down into the tunnels, so there's no way he could've gotten there before us. Besides, he wouldn't do something like that."

"I wouldn't be so sure," said Selene darkly.

Eli scoffed. "Just because he can be a creep sometimes doesn't mean he's going around killing people."

"You got the creep part right." Her chair squeaked again, as if in agreement. She gave one of the arms a pat.

"Hey, focus here," I said, and snapped my fingers in an attempt to head off an argument. "Doesn't matter. Eli's right. He couldn't have gotten down there before us."

Eli put a line through Lance's name.

By the time we finished, only Coach Fritz, Culpepper, Frank Rizzo, and my mother were left.

"Okay," Eli said. "Let's talk motive. Why would any of these people want to break the Keeper spell?"

"Crazy, power-hungry psychos?" said Selene. "I mean, aside from Dusty's mom."

Eli shook his head. "Not solid enough."

"Okay, try this," I said. "Since Culpepper and Rizzo are both predatory demons, The Will affects them more. You could argue they're more oppressed by its restrictions."

"Better," said Eli. He typed "DK" followed by a question mark in the Motive column.

"But what about Coach Fritz?" asked Selene, tilting her head. "He's a fairy."

"That one's easy," said Eli. "He hates humans."

This wasn't exactly news. Fritz was a fairy of the Werra tribe, a group of warrior fairies, definitely one of the most violent. And the coach didn't exactly censor his feelings about ordinaries. On more than one occasion, I'd heard him complain about how magickind were required to blend in with those "useless ants" or "demon fodder." If there were a magickind equivalent to the KKK, Fritz might well have been the Grand Dragon.

"What does hating humans have to do with The Will?" asked Selene.

"Well, he could use it to make them do things. Or punish them," said Eli, striding back and forth in front of the blackboard. "I'm an ordinary, and it definitely works on me."

I shivered at the idea of a weapon like that in the hands of a guy like Fritz. He wouldn't have to build concentration camps to kill people, he could just order them to jump in a lake and drown themselves.

"Put him at the top of the list," said Selene.

"Okay. But what about Ms. Everhart?" Eli glanced at me. "She doesn't have any motive that you know of, does she?"

I shook my head. None that I knew of, other than her overall contempt for the government and rules in general. My mother, the anarchist.

"I don't think she's a good suspect," said Selene. "Rosemary was seeing a guy so it couldn't be her."

"True," said Eli, "but we can't ignore the possibility there's more than one person involved in these killings."

A chill went through me at the idea. I couldn't believe it hadn't occurred to me before. With something this big, there was bound to be more than one person involved.

"Maybe," said Selene, pursing her lips.

Eli looked at me again, his expression apologetic. "And doesn't she have a reputation for breaking the law? Lance told me she's able to get around The Will whenever she wants."

"Sooner or later you're going to learn *not* to listen to Lance," said Selene, huffing. "He's a big fat liar. This is Dusty's *mother* you're talking about. She doesn't break laws. She just bends them occasionally."

"Oh, I understand all about bending rules, but we can't just dismiss her out of hand."

Selene scowled at him, her manner as tough as always, but I couldn't help noticing the way she fidgeted whenever Eli turned that piercing gaze of his on her. At least I wasn't the only person he could intimidate with just a look.

I knew I should say something, but I didn't. My mother

was a likely candidate for being involved simply based on what she was able to do, but I didn't want to encourage Eli and Selene in the idea. If it came to investigating my mother for murder, I would do it alone.

"I think the others are our best bet," Selene said. "They all have *F* in their names."

"You're right," Eli conceded. "We'll focus on them." He examined the list for a couple of seconds. "This is a good start."

"What next?" I asked.

He smiled, his face beaming with excitement. "We start investigating, check out offices, dorm rooms, houses, everything."

"You mean we *snoop*," I said.

"That's right."

Selene frowned. "But what exactly are we looking for?"

"That's easy," I said. "Rosemary's ring."

We started with Coach Fritz. My bet was still on Culpepper, but Eli and Selene agreed we needed to proceed with caution concerning him, given what happened last time. They were probably right. Besides, Coach Fritz should be easy.

Monday's gym class was combative magic training again, which meant Fritz would be completely focused on teaching. The plan was for Eli to sneak into his office during class and take a look. I would've liked to have gone, too, but since Eli was already sitting on the bench, he was in the best position for getting in and out unnoticed. Plus, he had experience with this sort of thing.

Selene and I exchanged a grin when we walked into the gymnasium and saw the game field packed full of barricades, climbing towers, and shelters. The sheer amount of structures indicated we were playing elimination today and not capture the flag or king of the hill. That was good. Selene and I could find a place to hole up and keep an eye on the coach, making sure the coast remained clear for Eli. Defending a structure was a common tactic in elimination so none of our classmates would notice our lack of true participation in the game.

Neither of us considered the idea of getting tagged out right away. Our performance was being graded, after all, and it was too close to midterms to purposely earn a low mark.

"All right, grunts," Coach Fritz said, calling us to attention. He had a narrow, lean face and wavy auburn hair. His large eyes were as green and sparkly as emeralds, and even though he was old, he still looked fit. I supposed Rosemary might've been attracted to him in that hot-for-teacher kind of way. *Gross.*

Fritz pointed to the game field. "You know the drill. Last man standing wins. You've got one minute for the starting bell."

The class rushed en masse onto the field. With everyone in matching black protective gear, we must've looked like a swarm of beetles. The suits covered all the vital parts, including head, torso, and legs. Although the strength of the spells was heavily dampened inside the game field, they could still do a lot of damage if not for the protection charms imbedded in the suits. They were made out of some kind of flexible plastic/rubber and fit like wet suits. The suit's secondary purpose was to let you know when you were out. If an opponent hit you with a critical spell, the kind that would've incapacitated you in the real word, it lit up and ordered you off the game field.

"There," Selene said, pointing at one of the barricades. It was shaped like a triangle, but only one of the three sides was connected, leaving two person-sized holes in the corners. It was perfect for a two-man defense and gave us a clear view of Coach Fritz.

Selene and I dashed inside and took up position at each entrance. My heart began to pound in anticipation, bringing me fully awake for the first time all day. I'd stayed up half the night on the phone with Paul. He thought what we were doing was a good idea, but he'd cautioned me about how nasty Fritz could be when crossed. It made me worried for Eli—he was taking the biggest risk by far.

The buzzer rang, and the game field exploded with the sounds and sights of spells flying out from wands and fingertips, colliding with barricades and people. I watched Lance take someone out with his signature move, a dazing-jab combo. He was a regular fixture in the winner's circle. For a second I thought he spotted me, but he wheeled around in pursuit of his next victim.

I turned my attention back to Fritz in time to see Eli slip off the bench behind him and head for the coach's office door. He walked without any particular stealth at all, moving as confidently as if he had every right to do what he was doing. I had to admire his brazenness. He disappeared inside the office a moment later, and I breathed a sigh of relief. First hurdle down.

"Did you set the timer?" I asked Selene over my shoulder.

"Yeah," she shouted. Then I heard her cast the jab jinx followed by the sound of someone cursing.

"Nice one," I said.

She didn't answer, but I didn't have time to make sure she was okay as an opponent came running toward me, wand up.

"Ceno-crani," I shouted, arm raised. The befuddlement jinx hit my attacker, and he swerved sideways, crashing headfirst into another barricade. I followed up with a daze that sent the person reeling backward, his suit lighting up. *One down.* There was no denying I was getting better at using magic. I hadn't set anybody's hair on fire in weeks.

Two more kills later, I asked Selene, "How long?"

"Seven minutes."

Halfway. Eli had sworn he'd be fifteen minutes, no longer. I glanced at Coach Fritz, making sure I could still see him. His gaze was fixed on the game field like always, but I could tell he wasn't paying nearly the amount of attention to the game he usually did.

And that was odd. Fritz *loved* fighting in all its forms. Rumor had it he was once an up-and-coming gladiator himself before he got caught taking a payoff to throw a fight and received a lifelong ban. As coach of the Arkwell gladiator team, he was always on the lookout for talent in his classes, kids good enough to turn pro and allow him to live vicariously.

Not today though. He seemed distracted. He kept checking his watch and looking around as if he couldn't wait for class to end.

A spell struck the barricade beside my head, and I leaped backward, almost falling. I straightened up in time to hear my attacker let off a jab jinx. I blocked it with a shield spell. It was a risky move. Shield spells took a lot of effort to conjure and usually couldn't withstand more than one or two hits. The jinx struck the shield and rebounded. The girl let out a squeal of surprise as her own spell struck her in the chest. She fell back, suit aglow. I grinned at my luck.

A few minutes later, Selene's watch started beeping, warning us that fifteen minutes had come and gone. I glanced at Coach Fritz. He was standing in the same place he had been, but one of the assistant coaches was crossing the room toward him.

"Uh-oh," I said.

"Crap," said Selene.

The assistant coach and Fritz exchanged a couple of words, ones I guessed were along the lines of "You've got a phone call," or "The principal needs to see you," or a hundred other things that might prompt Fritz to visit his office.

I looked behind them and saw the door opening. Eli peered out.

Selene screamed, making me jump. I turned in time to see her go down, suit lit from a critical hit. Lance appeared in the entrance. I cast a dazing curse at him but missed.

"Looks like it's gonna be three to one," he said.

He raised his wand, but before he could attack, I did the snatch-and-smack. A startled look crossed his face as his wand struck his helmet. I followed up with a jab. This time I didn't miss.

"Two for two," I shouted at him, gleeful as the lights on his suit turned on.

Then I remembered Eli, and I turned back to see Coach Fritz striding toward his office. Eli wasn't in sight, and I knew he was still in there.

Frantic, I burst out from my hiding place, ran toward the perimeter of the game field, and cast the stumbler curse. "Caso."

The magic flew from my fingers, passed through the safety spell surrounding the game field, and crashed right into Fritz's back. It hit him hard enough to lift him off his feet and fling him forward. I gaped, honestly surprised it had worked at all. His face smacked against the gym floor with a loud crack like wood breaking.

The alarms began to blare as the game field went into emergency lockdown thanks to my rogue spell. All around me, people were dropping to the floor as safety spells pushed them down. Wands were ripped out of the hands of wizards and witches as the fingers of other kinds were forced into tight fists, arms pinioned to sides. Something tugged at me like an insistent toddler, and I realized I was the only one left standing. I hit the deck, but judging from the murmurs I heard around me I was too late to escape notice.

And judging from the way Coach Fritz was still lying facedown on the gym floor, I was in the worst trouble of my life.

17

Parental Units

You knocked him *unconscious*. They've taken him to the infirmary. They're talking about moving him to *Vejovis*."

My mother had been doing the low, ominous, not-yelling thing at me for the past five minutes. I'd been doing a good job ignoring most of it, but the mention of the magickind hospital turned my insides into Jell-O.

"That can't be! There's no *way* he's hurt that bad. It was just a stumbler." I was horrified by what I'd done. Guilt tightened like an iron clamp around my chest.

Moira stopped her frantic pacing and turned her gaze on me, nostrils flaring. "It wasn't the spell so much as the nosedive into the floor. What were you thinking?"

"It was an accident?"

Moira stared at me, eyes hard and all-knowing. "I don't think there's a single soul alive who'd believe that one. Why don't you tell me what really happened?"

I resisted the urge to spill my guts. I felt bad about hurting Coach Fritz, but I hadn't attacked a teacher to save Eli's neck only to turn around and rat on him. This might be just my mother scolding me, but we were in the principal's office, which meant Dr. Hendershaw could come in any second—or might be listening through the door.

"Well?" said Moira.

I decided it was time for a subject change. "Please tell me you're exaggerating about the Vejovis thing."

Mom folded her arms. "Probably. Not that it matters. This is assault we're talking about, Destiny. Do you know how serious that is?"

"Expulsion serious?"

"Permanent criminal record serious. This could haunt you forever."

"Well, you would know," I said. I hoped I sounded less terrified than I felt.

Mom ignored the comment. "Unless, that is, you have a good reason for what you did. If you say it was because of the dream-seer stuff, they might let you off the hook."

I shook my head. There was nothing I could say that wouldn't involve telling them what Eli had been doing. As it stood now, he'd gotten out of the office unseen. Hopefully, he'd found something in there that would make this all worthwhile.

"You are so *stubborn*," said Moira.

I flashed my most patronizing smile. "Just like you, Mom."

The glare she fixed on me was so hot I expected flames

to shoot from her eyes. At least she didn't tell me how proud she was this time. Progress.

"I *will* get to the bottom of this," she said. "You're going to be seeing lots of me from here on out."

I frowned, not liking the surety I detected in her voice. "Why?"

It was Moira's turn to smile. "I'm your new psionics teacher."

"*What?* You're Mr. Ankil's replacement?" The idea made my stomach somersault for all kinds of reasons—not the least of which was how utterly uncool it was to have your mom for one of your teachers.

"That's right."

"You're not exactly liked around here, Mom, so why would the administration suddenly want to hire you?" I was worried there might be a pattern here, given the whole chaperoning bit.

Moira hesitated a moment before answering. "They didn't have a choice. I'm here at the behest of the Magi Senate."

I laughed out loud.

My mother scowled. "I'm serious."

"What about your practice?"

She tapped her foot. "I'm going on sabbatical."

"Typical. Always running out, aren't you?"

Mom didn't say anything, just marched to the door without a word. Seemed I'd hit a nerve.

I wondered if she'd been telling the truth. Given my

suspicions about her, I decided it wasn't good either way. Ulterior motive was my mother's middle name.

Dr. Hendershaw came in a few minutes later and slammed the book she was carrying down on the desk. The computer gave a little frightened squeak. "Two weeks of detention and a month of Saturday school."

I squeaked, too, sitting up straighter in my chair. I knew my punishment was going to be bad, but how was I ever going to get anything done with that much detention? And Saturday school? Shoot me now, please.

"That's what I would give you," said Hendershaw, "if I had my way."

I blinked, not understanding.

"As it is, the senate has insisted you receive no *obvious* punishment in order to protect you from repercussions. The official story being spread among the students is that Coach Fritz tripped over his shoelaces and that the emergency lockdown sequence went off due to a coincidental malfunction in the programming." She paused long enough to take a deep breath. "Consider yourself lucky that you are a dream-seer."

I knew better than to say anything.

"However. Since I cannot give you a conventional punishment, I have decided on an *unconventional* one."

Uh-oh.

Hendershaw pointed a short, pudgy finger at me. "Next Saturday night, while the rest of the student body is asleep or at a minimum confined to their dormitories for curfew, *you* will report to Ms. Hardwick."

"Ms. Hardwick the head janitor? Ms. Hardwick the hag?" I fought back the urge to smile. There weren't many schools where you could say something like that about a staff member and not get in trouble for it. It was true, after all.

An evil grin spread across Dr. Hendershaw's face, her toady eyes gleeful behind her glasses. "Precisely."

I shifted in my seat and braced for the worst. "What am I going to be doing?"

"Toilets."

I groaned, catching her drift at once.

Hendershaw's grin widened. "Oh, yes, I think that will do perfectly. You will be cleaning all the toilets in this building, the gymnasium, and every other building the students don't have access to in the middle of the night. That way no one will *see* you being punished, but you will receive the full benefit nonetheless. Oh, and you will of course be prohibited from using magic to complete the task."

Shocker.

Hoping for a light at the end of the tunnel, I asked, "Is there some kind of time limit? Because there's no way I can do that much cleaning in one night by hand."

"You'll start at midnight and work until dawn as Ms. Hardwick prefers not to venture out in sunlight. You will continue with this Saturday duty until you have managed to clean all the toilets. So there'll be no reason to slack off."

I gritted my teeth. "Isn't there some kind of child labor law against this sort of thing?"

"Oh, I think not. Not *here*."

"Right." I crossed my arms and leaned back, doing my best not to say anything snotty—well, snotti*er*.

"I think that's quite enough attitude from you." Hendershaw pointed a finger at me again. "Consider this your warning, Miss Everhart. You are on permanent academic probation. If you put so much as a toe out of line, if you so much as back talk a single teacher, including your own *mother*, I will give you *all* the punishment you so rightly deserve regardless of the senate's wishes. Are we clear?"

"Oh, yeah. Crystal."

"Good. Now get out of my office."

I stood and bolted for the door. It seemed at least half of Hendershaw's anger wasn't because of me at all, but rather at my mother. I was just an easier target. I guess this meant my mother hadn't been lying about being appointed to the teaching post by the senate.

I hurried past the secretary and into the hallway beyond. To my surprise, and unexpected delight, Paul was waiting for me. He greeted me with a quick kiss that left me thinking of blissful possibilities.

"Are you okay?"

I nodded, meaning it. With him here, that was.

"Come on." Paul took my hand as we started walking. "Tell me what's going on? I heard you hit Coach Fritz with a stumbler spell."

So much for the shoelace story.

"How'd you manage it?"

I debated for a moment the wisdom of telling this boy I hardly knew the truth about me and Nightmares. But he was a halfkind, too. If anybody wouldn't judge me for being different, it was him. Or maybe I was just a sucker for cute boys who liked to hold my hand and kiss me in public places.

So I told him what Marrow had told me. He didn't say anything when I finished. I held my breath, counting the beat of our footsteps as we walked along. We'd opted to take the tunnels to avoid the crappy November weather outside.

I hadn't wanted to come down here ever again after what happened to Mr. Ankil, but it wasn't so bad with Paul beside me. That was until I'd been confronted with his silence. Our footsteps were too loud. The rush of the canal water running parallel to the walking path sounded eerie, like the moan of a tortured ghost.

"So," I said, unable to stand it any longer, "you think I'm a freak, don't you?"

Paul stopped and faced me. He cupped my chin with his hands. "You're kidding, right?"

I shook my head as much as his hold on my face would allow. His grip was firm but not hard. He bent his head toward mine. When he kissed me, the dark dreariness of the tunnels disappeared in an onslaught of tingly heat that rushed through my body from head to toe. My mind emptied as physical sensation took over. I'd heard the expression "getting lost in a kiss" before, but I never knew what that meant until now.

It was by far the longest kiss we'd shared and still it didn't last long enough. I sighed as he pulled away.

"No," he said, and for a moment I had no idea what he was talking about. My brain had come unhinged from reality. "I don't think you're a freak."

"Oh. Well, that's good."

"Besides," he said as we started walking again. "I'm sure you've heard what *I* am by now."

I flinched at the bitterness in his voice. "Halfkind."

"That's right." He looked over at me. "Who told you?"

"Selene."

"I figured. Her mom works as a secretary in my uncle's office. Bit of a gossipmonger."

I felt I ought to say something in defense of my best friend's mother, but since I didn't know Mrs. Rivers, I decided not to. I knew better than anybody how different from our parents we could be. *And how alike, sometimes.*

"They call me a *mule*," Paul said. "Like I'm too stubborn to learn magic. Or too dumb." He touched a finger to his brow and in a self-mocking voice said, "Or maybe I'm too smelly. Real mules stink, right?"

I let out a fake laugh. I knew he was trying to make light of it, but there was no disguising the resentment I sensed in his words.

Paul shrugged. "It's all good. I may not be able to do magic, but I can do things with a computer most magic-kind couldn't imagine."

"That's right, Mr. MIT bound."

"*Hopefully* MIT bound."

"I have faith." I squeezed his hand. "And I don't care that you can't do magic."

He squeezed back. "I know."

We walked on for a few minutes in silence.

"Okay," Paul said sometime later and in a voice considerably brighter. "I'd really like to help you with your investigation—be more involved. That is, if your partners don't mind."

I glanced up at him and saw a playful smile on his face. "I don't know," I said, teasing back. "We're doing so well on our own *obviously*. What makes you think you'll be much help?"

Paul tilted his head. "Well, my uncle *is* a magistrate, and I have easy access to his house."

"So?"

"So . . . I also happen to be pretty good at snooping, too, *and* at hacking into personal computer files. Maybe I can find something useful."

I stopped walking. "Hack Magistrate Kirkwood's computer?"

Paul turned toward me. He let go of my hand only to take hold of my shoulders. He began to rub my arms up and down. "Sure, why not?"

It was hard to stay focused with him touching me like that. "Uh, maybe because he'd be really pissed if he found out?"

Paul grinned, but there wasn't any humor in it. "Just so happens that pissing him off is one of my favorite pastimes."

"Oh, yeah, how come?"

"Because he hates me." He said it in the same joking voice, but I detected that bitterness again.

I put my hand on his chest. "Why do you think that?"

"It's true. I'm a mule, you see, an utter disgrace to the family name. Honestly, I'm surprised they even let me use it."

I didn't laugh at his feeble attempt at humor this time. I was thinking about the fall he'd taken down the stairs that put him in the hospital. But the idea that Paul's uncle hated him enough to give him a little accidental push was absurd. "Well, in that case, what do you think you can find out?"

"Hmmm, well, I'd like to say the identity of the third Keeper, but I doubt it. The separate kinds make a habit of hiding that sort of stuff from one another. I imagine the only people who know are the person himself and maybe a few of the darkkind senators. I'd bet even Consul Vanholt doesn't know."

I sighed. It would've been useful information. "Okay, so what else then?"

"I might be able to find out the details of the Keeper spell, the mechanics of how it works."

"Sweet. I mean, I guess that's a good enough reason to include you in the investigation."

He pulled me into a hug. "I'm sure you won't regret it." Then he pushed me away from him just enough so that he could look down at my face. "But is there anything else I should look for?"

I chewed on my bottom lip for a minute, mulling it over. There *was* something else, but I didn't know if I was ready to go down that path.

Paul's fingers tightened around my shoulders. "What's wrong?"

I shook my head.

"Come on, Dusty. You can tell me. I won't judge." He dipped his head toward mine and kissed me again. I closed my eyes, feeling the same rush of physical sensation, making my mind fuzzy. When he broke the kiss this time, I kept my eyes closed for a moment, light-headed.

I looked at him. "Think you can figure out what my mother is doing for the senate? I want to know why she was at the dance and why they're giving her Mr. Ankil's job."

"No problem. But why do you sound so suspicious?"

I took a deep breath. "Because when I went into the tunnels that night I thought *she* was the person I was following. And since she's a Nightmare beyond the control of The Will . . ."

". . . you think she's involved."

I nodded.

Paul frowned and pulled me against his chest, his arms a comforting pressure around me. "What exactly do you want *me* to do?"

"Prove she's not the killer."

18

Secret Identities

Y ou invited your boyfriend to help us investigate?" Eli sat up from his slouched position on the chair in his dorm room.

"What's the big deal?" I said, trying not to squirm. Then I remembered I had no reason to be intimidated by Eli Booker. We were friends now. Sort of. "Paul is Magistrate Kirkwood's nephew. He can give us insider information on what the senate is doing."

Eli drummed his fingers against the arms of the chair. "I don't know, Dusty. I just don't really like the guy much."

I rolled my eyes. "Why? Did *Lance* say something bad about him?"

"Well, yeah, but that's not why. Not entirely."

"Oh, puh-leeze. You don't even know Paul. All you know is what Lance told you. And Lance doesn't like him for the plain and simple fact that Paul's a halfkind. Or a *mule,* as I'm sure Lance put it."

Eli shook his head. "I don't care about that. There's just something about him that rubs me the wrong way."

I huffed. "Geez, Eli, I figured you'd be more sympathetic considering you two have the I-can't-do-magic problem in common." Oops, I'd done it again. Let my mouth run away with me.

He bristled. "I don't give a crap about doing magic. That's beside the point."

I closed my eyes, took a deep breath. I opened my eyes. "I'm sorry. It's just that I like Paul a lot, and I don't appreciate you insulting him."

"You mean like you insult Katarina?"

"That's different."

His infuriating eyebrow rose up. "Yeah? How so?"

Paul's not an evil, manipulating, stuck-up twit. Fortunately I kept that one to myself. "Can we not fight about this? I've already told him what we're doing so it's too late anyway."

Eli looked mutinous for a moment, then exhaled. "All right, no fighting. But don't be surprised if I bring Kat to our next meeting."

"You *wouldn't.*"

Eli crossed his arms, muscles bulging, then grinned. "Okay, you're right. I wouldn't. But only because she's too much of a distraction."

Oh there *is a good reason.* An unpleasant knot tightened in my stomach.

"Although Katarina *could* actually be useful," said Eli, scratching his cheek.

"How do you figure?"

"She's pretty smart. She's got a good idea of why Mr. Ankil was a Minotaur in the dream."

I didn't say anything, trying to ignore the inappropriate sense of betrayal I felt knowing he'd shared the details of our dream-sessions with his girlfriend. They were *his* dreams, after all. Besides, it wasn't as if I didn't tell Paul. We were even, really.

"Kat thinks it's because he was a Taurus. You know, his sign, the head of a bull."

I nodded, supposing it made sense. "How does she know Ankil was a Taurus?"

Eli ran a hand through his black hair, looking embarrassed. "She's *really* into astrology."

"Totally not surprised. But whatever." I plopped down on the sofa, tired of standing with my butt leaning against the desk. "So did you find anything useful in Fritz's office?"

Eli stood and walked over to me. "Unfortunately, no."

"There was nothing?" I said, gazing up at him and trying not to squirm from sudden nervousness at his close proximity.

He hooked his thumbs through the belt loops on his jeans and nodded. "And I was pretty thorough about it, too. If he's got the rings, he's not keeping them there."

I grimaced, looking away from him. I hadn't really figured we would strike a home run the first at bat, but it was a little disheartening to know I'd assaulted a teacher, exposed the nature of my Nightmare abilities, and earned a heinous detention all for nothing.

"Thanks by the way," Eli said. He reached out and stroked the top of my head. "You really saved my neck."

Well, maybe not *completely* for nothing. I glanced up at

him, warmth climbing my neck. Patting my head wasn't exactly intimate, but it felt that way. "Don't mention it."

He smiled, dazzling me. I smiled weakly back at him, trying to hide my embarrassment at the tremble that went through my body. I'd hoped now that I had a boyfriend—one I certainly enjoyed kissing and hugging and looking at—that my attraction to Eli would somehow vanish. But apparently not. *Stupid teenage hormones.*

"Hurry up and go to sleep already," I said. "I wanna get this freak show on the road."

Eli yawned and sat next to me. Then he lay down and swung his legs over my lap, pinning me.

"Hey." I shoved his legs off and stood up.

Chuckling, Eli said, "Don't forget that we've got to focus my dreams on the investigation."

I scowled at him, flustered rather than angry. "I won't. Trust me, I'm sick of ice fishing and football." I leaned over and poked him in the chest. "You have no imagination."

He seized my hand and squeezed it. "That's what I've got you for," he said, grinning. Then his face grew slack and his grip loosened as he fell asleep.

We were in the tunnels again. Me and Eli. I heard the scream, smelled the smoke and that bitter, nauseating stench of something on fire that shouldn't be. Something that was never meant to burn.

Not this. Not again. It was bad enough I couldn't escape

what happened with Ankil in my own dreams and nightmares. I refused to experience it again in someone else's. Closing my eyes, I thought about warm sun, soft sand, and sparkling water. The Hawaii of my imagination.

A warm breeze caressed my face, and I opened my eyes. Eli and I were standing on a deserted beach. He marched over to me, looking furious.

"Whoa, Nelly," I said, backing up.

"Why did you do that?" Eli stopped a safe distance away and gestured at the tropical landscape. For some reason he was shirtless, his scorpion tattoo exactly how I remembered it, and I forced my eyes away from his chest. "We were right where we wanted to be already."

"I couldn't . . . I mean . . . I can't . . . it's too soon. I'm sorry."

Eli's expression softened. "I don't want to see it again, either. But, Dusty, we can't just sit around here." He waved again.

"I know. It was just an automatic reaction. Give me a minute to fix it, okay?"

"Sure."

I closed my eyes and concentrated. Going back to the tunnels was out of the question. I wasn't ready for that. But I thought I could handle the scene with Rosemary. Her death had been less violent and scary. Far less recent.

I pictured the scene as I remembered it from Eli's dream, the cops in uniform, the cemetery at night. I envisioned Rosemary lying beside the headstone, not as she'd been in the dream, but as I'd seen her in real life that brief moment after her mother broke the shield.

"Wow," Eli said. "It's just like I remember."

I opened my eyes and saw he was only partially right. Somehow I'd managed to combine his dream with the real thing, overlaying them like two pieces of stained glass.

Eli approached Rosemary's body with the caution of a true cop. He knelt beside her, taking a good, long look. I left him to it while I scavenged for clues. I examined the face of each police officer, hoping for recognition, maybe an indicator of who was behind all this.

After a while Eli stood and came over to me, shaking his head. "I've got nothing."

"Me too."

"This is so frustrating." He looked around. "I mean, here we are, right here. Just two hours too late. If we could only hit the rewind button or something."

I thought about it a moment. "What if we *can*?"

He swung back to me. "Huh?"

"What if *I* can?"

"You think it's possible?"

Here we're like gods, I remembered my mother saying. If so, then I could control not just the where, but the *when*. "I don't know, but I'll give it a try."

"All right."

"Don't get excited or anything. Probably won't work."

He grinned. "You know what your problem is, Dusty? You don't give yourself enough credit."

I ignored the comment and the warm fluttering in my stomach. I closed my eyes again and concentrated harder than I ever had before in my life. I had no idea what to do besides follow my instinct. Surely I had to have some.

For a while, nothing happened, and I was close to giving up when I remembered Lady Elaine telling me that all dreams are symbolic. *Symbolic . . . symbols. What kind of symbol represents time?*

A clock.

No sooner had I thought it than I pictured it, a huge grandfather clock with a serene face covered in big roman numerals. The hands were pointed at the two, around the time when the werewolf cops had brought me to Coleville. I imagined the second hand moving *backward*. I expected it to obey the command easily, but instead I felt resistance almost at once, a sort of foot planting in my imagination as the hand refused to move. It pushed back against me, wanting to go forward.

No. Go back. I pushed and pushed, straining against it, willing it to obey. There was a loud, piercing crack like lightning striking a rooftop. My eyes flashed open as Eli let out a gasp.

"What's going on?"

Around us the world of the dream had gone from something substantial to a swirl of color and blurred images like I usually saw when first entering a dream. For a moment I thought I was being pushed out, only it couldn't be that with Eli seeing it, too.

"I think I'm going to be sick," he said, shutting his eyes. But the swirling soon began to slow and the images to grow clearer.

"Eli," I whispered. "It *worked*."

We were still in the cemetery, but the police were nowhere in sight. A living, upright Rosemary stood only a few paces in front of us.

She wasn't alone.

I held my breath, my gaze focused on the person with her. He was nothing more than a dark blur in the shape of a man. A shadow man. *F*. It had to be.

Beside me, Eli stepped forward.

"Don't," I said. This wasn't like a normal dream, not even one of the prophetic ones. The world here felt tenuous, as flimsy as a spider's web. One wrong move and the whole thing would unravel.

Eli held still, and we both watched and listened.

"I can't tell you that," Rosemary was saying to the shadow man. "Not unless you tell me why you need to know."

The shadow man stepped closer to her, first taking her by the shoulders then raising his hands to cup her face. "Because," he said in a voice made of silk. "I love you, Rose. I *need* this from you. You love me, too. You *want* to give it to me. Give it to me *now*."

I watched Rosemary's expression slowly go from alert to dazed, like someone slipping into a trance. There was some kind of magic going on here. I was sure of it.

"Now," the shadow man said, "tell me who the other Keepers are."

"I . . ." Rosemary's wavering voice matched her dazed expression. "I don't know any of them. Just me." She raised her hand. The diamonds on her Keeper ring flashed in the moonlight. "Isn't it beautiful?"

"Yes, beautiful. Just as you are. Now tell me where they're keeping the sword."

"Here at Arkwell."

"*Where* exactly?" The shadow man's image seemed to shudder.

Rosemary shook her head.

"Where? Tell me, my love." He gripped her shoulders again. "*Now.*"

Huge tears filled Rosemary's eyes. "I don't know. They never told me. They don't want anyone to find it."

"Tell *me.*" He started to shake her.

"I don't know. I don't know. I don't know."

The shadow man let go of her, uttering a sound of frustration. Rosemary slumped to the ground, whimpering. I stared at her, shocked by the realization that her tears were from guilt at having disappointed this horrible man. The man who had been using her, manipulating her with some evil, black magic.

"Look, Dusty." Eli spoke so softly that I almost thought I imagined it.

I pulled my gaze off Rosemary and saw that another shadow man had joined the first. This one looked smaller, more diminished, and yet I could tell at once he was in charge by the way the first shadow man deferred to him.

"She doesn't know," the first said. "I've tried my best."

The second nodded. "Yes, I know. It's all right. We will discover the others in time. Now stand her up. We need to finish this quickly."

The first hesitated. "Do we have to? Isn't there some other way?"

"No. I've already explained to you the nature of the spell. It must be done. It is the *only* way for you to get what you want. And for me."

The first hesitated a moment longer, then he stooped and grabbed Rosemary by her arms, dragging her to her feet. He held her there as the other stepped behind her. A chain rope made from some shiny metal hung from his hand, glistening with an iridescent hue like fish scales in sunlight. He wrapped it around her throat. Rosemary began to scream.

Eli took a step forward as if to intervene.

"Don't," I said, fighting the same urge. This was just a dream, nothing but shadow and vapor. But there was something I could do that *would* make a difference—I needed to see beyond those blank faces.

Like I'd done on the clock, I concentrated on the shadow men, focusing all the strength of my imagination, of my magic. I pictured noses, mouths, and eyes. I willed them to come into focus.

"What are you doing?" Eli hissed, pressing his hands to his temple.

I was vaguely aware that the dream world around us was trembling as if from an earthquake. I pushed harder. Sweat broke out on my skin. My whole body began to ache, but I could tell it was working. I could see the faint outline of the shadow men's faces. In a moment, I would know who they were.

Both of those shadowed faces turned toward me in eerie unison. Their unseen eyes bored into me as they stood frozen in place.

I heard Eli's quick intake of breath.

"It's just a dream. They can't hurt us," I said. But they definitely knew we were there. And they didn't like it.

The second shadow man's form began to change shape. The vague outline of a person gave way to something solid. Something sleek and shining, as black as onyx and with eyes as bright as the moon. It took a moment for me to realize what it was. When I did, a jolt of fear surged through me as if from a lightning strike.

The black phoenix let out a shriek that was both beautiful and terrible at the same time. It made me want to fall down on my face before it, prostrate and willing to give myself up as its prey.

It swooped down at us. Even though I knew this was a dream and not real, I dove to the right on instinct while Eli dashed left. *Time to leave.* I closed my eyes and pulled back from the dream, willing my consciousness to rejoin my body.

I couldn't. Something blocked the way.

Terror seized my heart like a clenched fist. Eli was across the cemetery, far away. "I can't get out."

"*What?*"

"I'm trapped. You need to kick me out."

He started to run toward me, but the phoenix made another pass at us. I hit the ground as the loud *whish-whish-whish* of massive wings beat in the air. I heard the clack of a sharp beak snapping. The bird shrieked again in its deadly musical voice.

I focused on changing the dream, trying to imagine the glass box my mother had used on Bethany, but I was too panicked to concentrate.

Something blocked out the moonlight above me, and I covered my head with my arms. Air swept across my body, followed by a hot sear of pain as the phoenix's talons sliced my right arm from shoulder to wrist.

I screamed. The pain was so real. It was impossible. This couldn't be a dream. Not with pain like that. Blood soaked my hair. What would happen if I died in here?

"Dusty!" Eli shouted, drawing nearer. "Grab my hand!"

I pushed myself up and dashed toward him. We collided like opponents in a football game. The dream world exploded around me in a shower of light and pain, but I welcomed it as my consciousness rejoined my body where it belonged.

I leaped backward off Eli, landing on my feet, ready to keep running if the phoenix had managed to follow us out somehow. I looked around at the dorm room, convinced it was here. But we were alone, and I breathed a sigh of relief.

Eli's eyes flicked open, and he looked at me with a stunned expression. "Well," he said in a dry, sarcastic voice. "That was fun."

I couldn't help it; I started laughing. The reaction was involuntary and borderline hysterical. "We should try it again sometime," I said between guffaws.

Eli's expression hardened. "I don't think so, Dusty."

I wiped away a stray tear, finally getting control of myself. "Why not?"

He stood and came over, taking hold of my wrist with one hand. "Look at your arm."

I glanced down. The sleeve on my right arm was torn. The skin beneath glowed red from three long wicked scratches.

They were the exact width of a bird's talons.

ᗗ 19 ᗕ

Exchange

I woke late the next day and contemplated blowing off classes. My head ached, and my arm was throbbing, despite the makeshift bandage Eli had made for me. Worst of all, I felt like I hadn't slept a wink. When I left Eli's last night even my bones were tired. I barely made it back to my dorm room and had passed out without entering a dream journal.

Crap.

I sat up, moaned once, then did a double take when I saw the time.

Crap, crap, crap.

I jumped out of bed and raced into the living quarters.

"Where's the fire?" said Selene. She was already dressed and ready, looking perfectly refreshed.

I scowled. "I didn't do my dream journal. And why didn't you wake me up?"

"I did, but you must've gone back to sleep. We had a conversation and everything. Mostly surly grunts on your part. Don't you remember?"

No, I didn't remember, but that wasn't surprising—Selene had told me on more than one occasion that I talked in my sleep. I switched on the eTab, opened a dream journal, and started typing. Two words into it, I decided to do some serious editing. For one thing, I didn't have time to put in all the details. For another, there was no telling how Lady Elaine would react if she knew I'd been physically hurt in a dream. She might not insist I stop dreamwalking with Eli, but I wasn't willing to take that chance. After seeing what happened to Rosemary, I wanted to find her killer now more than ever.

Two killers, I thought, remembering the shadow men. So Eli had been right in his hunch. And they were both men. Maybe my mother wasn't involved after all.

You can't be sure, a dark, cynical voice said in my head. *The first was likely male, but you didn't see either of them. Not even their voices were distinctly male.*

That was true, but I chose to ignore it. The *impression* had been male.

Ten minutes later, I followed Selene down to the cafeteria. Silence descended when I walked in, as everyone turned to look at me. It was the first time they'd seen me since I attacked Coach Fritz. The silence was even worse than my first day here. Then the stares had been mostly curious. Today it was open animosity.

"Come on," Selene said over her shoulder. "Ignore them."

I trudged after her, doing my best to keep my head up. I glanced at Eli's table. To my surprise, he smiled at me. It seemed our newfound friendship held even in a public arena. I smiled back, grateful for the support, although I couldn't help but notice how tired and pale he looked this morning, as if he hadn't slept in weeks. I'd noticed him looking drained after one of our dream-sessions before, but never this bad. Beside Eli, Katarina glowered at me, but she was easy to ignore.

The day went from bad to worse. Everywhere I turned, people were whispering about me in voices loud enough to overhear. I caught snippets like "She tried to *kill* Coach Fritz. . . ." and "I heard she found Mr. Ankil. Maybe his death wasn't an accident. . . ." and "You can't trust a Nightmare. . . ."

Selene regularly defended me, of course, and I'd even caught Eli telling off a senior boy for saying stuff about me. The guy stood nearly a foot shorter than Eli and looked terrified. I appreciated their help, but it failed to keep those words from doing damage. Barely an hour into the day, I felt as if my spirit had been flayed alive.

I did my best to ignore the comments, and focused on figuring out the clues in last night's dream. I'd learned some important things. The sword was somewhere on campus. Assuming, of course, that the conversation between Rosemary and the shadow man had been literal and not symbolic—as I suspected it was. Actually, I'd begun to think the entire dream had been literal. There was no denying the welts on my arm were real. Maybe that meant the black phoenix was real, too, a shape-changer or something.

The last ten minutes of history, Mr. Marrow gave us free time to do some extra studying for midterm exams next week. I took advantage of the opportunity to pull out my eTab and do some Internet/e-net searching. I kept it hidden under the desk. Marrow might be supportive of my endeavor to find the killer, but I didn't think it extended to wasting class time on nonschool work.

I typed in the search box: Who is the black phoenix?

The e-net results were more or less the same as they had been the last time I tried to find out about phoenixes, lots of links to sites concerning the birds as a species, detailing their magical properties, and the countless numbers of foolish magickind who'd gone hunting them.

When I flipped over to the Internet results, I received a shock from the very first entry—*The Black Phoenix Will Rise Again.*

Surely, it had to be coincidence. Only, at this point, I didn't *believe* in coincidences. I clicked on the link and was immediately greeted by a log-in box. I blinked, experiencing déjà vu. I clicked on the register as a new user button and started entering the necessary information. When another message popped up asking me to identify the name of my initiator, I realized why this seemed so familiar. I'd tried to access this website before when I'd been researching Keeper spells. I glanced at the name and saw Reckthaworlde.com.

Definitely not a coincidence.

I stared at the screen, contemplating some way to get in.

"Excuse me, Dusty."

I winced and glanced up at Mr. Marrow. "Yes?"

"I believe you should be studying now."

"Right." I put the eTab to sleep and stowed it in my bag. I forced my eyes on my textbook, but my mind remained fixated on getting into the website.

The solution to the problem presented itself less than twenty minutes later when I spotted Paul standing in the hallway outside of the cafeteria before lunch. Paul Kirkwood, computer genius.

I beamed at him. "I'm so glad to see you." I gave him a hug, feeling totally unselfconscious about it.

"Same here." He wrapped his arms around me and kissed the top of my head.

I pulled back from him but stayed close enough that he could hear me whisper, "I need a favor."

He twined his fingers with mine. "Whatever you want."

Tough opening to resist—there was so much I wanted from him. But I kept it simple. "I need you to hack into a website for me. That is, if you think you can."

He laughed. "Sweetheart, if it's got an IP, I can hack it."

"Huh?"

"Forget it. What site?"

I pulled a piece of paper out of my backpack and wrote down the address before handing it over.

"What's it about?" Paul said, reading the address.

"No idea. You've got to have special permission to log on, but I think there are some answers in there about what's been going on."

Paul raised his eyes to mine. "What exactly do you

want me to look for? I mean, a website can have a lot of info on it."

I glanced around, making sure no one was close enough to overhear. "Anything about a black phoenix."

"As in the bird you keep seeing in Eli's dreams?"

"Yeah, only I think it's a person. Like some kind of shape-shifter."

His eyes widened. "Weird. Well, I'll take a look and let you know what I find."

My stomach rumbled. With everything going on, I hadn't been able to eat much for breakfast. "Excuse me," I said, rubbing my tummy.

Paul smiled. "I don't mean to keep you from lunch, but I wanted to give you this." He handed me an envelope from his coat pocket.

"What is it?"

"Some stuff about your mother."

My stomach dropped. "Is it bad?"

He tucked his hands into his pockets, looking nervous. "Not sure. Maybe. Depends on what you make of it. Just don't open it where anybody else can see, okay? My uncle would really kill me for this one if he found out."

"I won't," I said, finding it hard to speak.

Paul kissed me. "See you later."

I walked into the cafeteria, clutching the envelope tight enough to crumple it. I ignored Selene's questioning look as I joined her at our usual table. Hunching over, I opened the envelope, pulled out the paper inside, and began to read. It was an e-mail addressed to Magistrate Kirkwood from Consul Vanholt. There was nothing in the subject line and the content was brief:

The Nightmare must be involved. We should bring her in but keep a close eye on her. She can't be trusted, but I'm sure she's the key to solving this.

I read it three times, trying not to jump to conclusions. My mother wasn't mentioned specifically, after all, and the overall meaning was pretty vague. Still, it didn't exactly give me a warm fuzzy. Not when I considered how few Nightmares there were in Chickery.

"Aren't you going to eat?" asked Selene.

I nodded even though the idea of food made me want to throw up. I tucked the e-mail back in the envelope and hid it inside my psionics textbook. I went through the motion of getting food and pretending to eat it, but I didn't manage more than a couple of bites.

After ten minutes of silence, Selene broke down and said, "Do you want to talk about it?"

I marveled at how long she resisted asking. Selene was my hero in that way, the epitome of self-control.

I shook my head. "I've got to go, actually. I want to get to psionics early."

Selene narrowed her eyes. "You going to talk to your mom?"

"Something like that. I'll see you later, okay?"

"Be careful. She'll be mad if she catches you snooping."

I grimaced. Leave it to Selene to guess my real purpose

for leaving early. During the lunch hour, I figured there was a good chance my mom wouldn't be in the classroom. There was also a good chance she'd left her purse in there, too. She had a chronic habit of doing that. Sort of defeated the purpose of carrying a purse, in my opinion, but that was my mother for you.

I'd been hearing rumors about the new psionics teacher all day, most of them surprisingly positive, like how cool and fun she was, and how pretty, of course.

When I arrived at the classroom, I stopped outside the door and listened for noise inside. I didn't hear anything, so I went in. The room looked the same as always. This was the first time I'd been in here since the dance, and the sight of what remained of Mr. Ankil hit me like a sudden plunge into icy water. The sadness was almost unbearable for a moment.

With a huge effort, I bottled up the sorrow and focused on the task at hand. I spotted a leopard print purse on top of the teacher's desk and made a beeline for it.

I was halfway done riffling through the obscene amount of contents—lipstick, travel-sized hairspray, toothbrush, wallet, and so on—when I heard footsteps outside the door. The lunch bell hadn't rung yet, and I panicked—it had to be my mother. Shoving the emery board I'd been holding back into the purse, I yanked the zipper closed and raced to the closet.

I stepped inside, wedging myself in between the items and pulling the door shut. Something was groping my butt, and I glanced over my shoulder to see a head-and-hand dummy. Thank goodness it was just bad positioning and not because of animation. When I looked back, I realized the door hadn't closed all the way. I reached for the handle then stopped. Through the small slit, I watched my mother enter the room with Mr. Culpepper trailing behind her. My curiosity did a wild leap inside my chest at the sight of them together.

As they approached the desk, Moira said, "Do you have it with you?"

Culpepper pulled a handkerchief out of his back pocket and wiped his brow. "If you've got the payment."

"You're *sure* it will do all you claim?"

"Cut from the same stone as mine, in a manner of speaking. But if it don't work you can return it for a full refund."

"What a comfort." Moira opened the purse, pulled out some money, and gave it to Culpepper.

He handed her a brown paper package the size of a small jewelry box. "What're you planning on using it for?"

Moira smirked at him. "Do you ask that question of all your clients?"

"Nope. Most of the time it's obvious."

"Well then, I think the same can be assumed here. And if I'm not mistaken, this concludes our business."

Culpepper grunted then stalked out the door in his slight, shuffling gait.

Moira slid the box into her purse then cut her eyes to the closet. I stepped back from the crack in the door, my pulse quickening. There was no way she could've seen me. Not unless she had X-ray vision.

"You can come out now, Destiny," my mother said.

I froze, dumbstruck.

She waved. "Come on. I know you're in the closet."

Wishing I knew an invisibility spell, I pushed the door open and stepped out. "Hey, Mom."

"Don't 'Hey, Mom' me." Moira put her hands on her hips. "What are you doing in there?"

"Looking for a broom?"

"Ha, ha, ha. Why are you here?" She tapped the toe of one boot.

"Um, class is starting?"

"Try again."

I hesitated, knowing I was on shaky ground, and not just because she was my mother. No, I understood that if I asked what I wanted to, what I *needed* to, I might do irreparable damage to our relationship. I wasn't entirely sure I was cool with that. True, it wasn't much of a relationship, but she was still my mother.

Who may be a killer.

"What were you doing with Mr. Culpepper?" I said, stalling, although I wanted to know the answer to this, too.

Mom raised her hand and began examining her fingernails. "Not your concern, and also not pertinent to why you're here so early."

"All right, I want to know what you're doing for the senate."

She dropped her hands, casting me a snide look. "And that's why you were hiding in my closet? I don't think so.

Stop avoiding the subject, Destiny. I'm wise to your little 'ask a lot of questions to avoid the truth' game."

I glared at her, not appreciating her smug attitude that she knew me so well. Truth was she didn't know me at all. Two weeks a summer and the occasional phone call or e-mail didn't cut it. Not by a long shot. "I want to know what you were doing at the dance."

Moira sighed, angrily. "What's this sudden obsession with my activities? You've never cared before."

I never cared? *Give me a break.* "Fine. You want the truth? My sudden *obsession* is that you're the reason I was down in the tunnels when Mr. Ankil was killed. I was following *you.* So you either had to have seen something or *done* something. And I know what you can do, how The Will doesn't matter to people like us."

Her nostrils flared. "Just what are you insinuating?"

"Oh, come off it, Mom. I know the truth about Nightmares."

A flush spread up Moira's neck, but she didn't respond, merely stood there, staring at me as if I were some new and ghastly species of bug. One she'd like to squish under the sole of her high-heeled, black leather boots.

The lunch bell rang. The realization that we weren't going to be alone for much longer spurred me onward. I *had* to know the truth. "Did you do it, Mom?"

Her gaze turned fiery. "I can't *believe* you would ask me that. What kind of a *daughter* are you?"

Her words hurt, cutting me in deep, sensitive places. Tears flooded my eyes. All the emotions I'd been bottling up for the last few days exploded outward. "Me? Me? What kind of *mother* are you? You're no mother at all, that's what. You left me and Dad when I was just a baby. You didn't care about me, not when I was a plain old human. When you thought I was just your *mule* offspring from a marriage you'd rather forget. Oh, no, you didn't care about me until I got magic. So don't you dare criticize me as a *daughter* when you've been such a crappy *mother*."

By the time I finished my tirade, I was panting. I hadn't gotten this worked up over my mother's exit from my life in years. I'd long since learned to ignore the resentment, the hurt like a canker sore around my heart. But I couldn't ignore it right now, staring her in the face.

Moira's eyes remained fixed on mine, her expression masked. If she'd been moved by my outburst, it didn't show. Her lack of response bothered me even more, especially considering the torrential downpour on my face. Someone so cold was capable of anything.

I threw my hands up in exasperation. "Say *something*."

"Fine. How's this?" she said through gritted teeth. "You only think you followed me down into that tunnel, Destiny. And even if it was me, that's hardly reason enough to believe me capable of murder."

I threw up my hands. "Oh, yeah? I've got more reasons than that. Even the senate thinks you can't be trusted."

"Don't be absurd."

"You don't believe me?" I yanked open my backpack and pulled out the envelope with the consul's e-mail. "Take a look at this."

My mother snatched the envelope from my hand, ripped out the paper inside, and read the e-mail. Then she looked at me, her expression darkening. "Where did you get this?"

Uh-oh. *Stupid, stupid me.* I paled at my blunder. "It's a secret. And it doesn't matter, anyway."

Moira pursed her lips.

People were starting to file into the room, and I quickly wiped away my tears with my shirtsleeve. Unfortunately, there was no hiding the telltale puffiness in my cheeks.

"I want that back," I said.

"I don't think so."

"It's *mine.*"

Mom shook her head, and from the stubborn look on her face I knew it was no good, not unless I wanted to fight her for it. Somehow, I didn't think tackling my mother/teacher would go over very well. Not to mention the total mortification I'd face when I lost.

"I suggest you don't push me about it," she said in a steely voice. "Not considering how *violent* you believe me to be. Now go sit down. And don't you dare speak to me again."

I swallowed, unsure if I felt guilty or relieved. I also wasn't sure if she meant don't speak to her again today or *ever.* In the end, I decided I didn't care.

~ 20 ~

The Tomb

By Friday, I understood my mom meant what she'd said about never speaking to her again. She hadn't even looked at me during any of my psionics classes. I told myself it didn't bother me, although it was tough not being able to ask questions. Especially when I came to accept that she *was* a pretty good teacher. There wasn't much point in raising my hand, though. Not when the person with the power to acknowledge it was pretending I didn't exist. I'd gone from a bug to a nonentity.

Worst of all, I still didn't know if she was innocent or not. She never actually said that she hadn't been in the tunnel. She might've blown a lid at my accusation, but I couldn't tell if it was righteous anger, guilt, or just plain good acting.

Then there was the exchange with Culpepper. I showed up early to class twice more, hoping to rummage through her purse again, but she stopped leaving her stuff unattended. The next step would be to search her home, but I didn't know if she'd moved into one of the faculty town houses on campus now that she was a teacher or if she was still in her apartment on Waterfront Lane. It was rather depressing not knowing where my mother was living, but given the current state of our relationship, not that surprising, either.

I meant to ask Paul what he thought about my mother's behavior, but every time I saw him or spoke to him on the phone, we ended up talking about other things—things that made me feel all tingly inside and more than a little eager for our next date.

I wanted to confide in Selene, but I was afraid of her reaction. What if she told me to go to the sheriff? I definitely wasn't ready to take my suspicions about my mother that far without solid proof.

It was my mother I was thinking about when I left the dorm room at midnight on Friday, headed for Eli's. I opened the door, stepped out, and collided with someone that shouldn't have been there. I shrieked and leaped backward.

"You're late," the someone said in a familiar voice.

I let out a huge exhale as I recognized Bethany Grey. "Um, okay. And you care because . . . ?"

She grimaced. "Heaven help me, you are *so* much like your mother. We're finally going to begin our dream training session tonight. I would've preferred to have done this much sooner, but seeing how you skipped the last few sessions . . ."

"It's not my fault I was sick." *Conveniently,* I silently added. In truth, I blew off the first one because it seemed like a waste of time after all I'd learned from my mother. And the second had been scheduled a couple days after I found out the truth about Nightmares from Mr. Marrow, and I didn't think I could face the possibility of learning any more unpleasant facts. "And I'm *nothing* like my mom, thank you very much."

Bethany huffed then turned on one thick, bulky heel of her Dr. Martens boots and headed down the hallway toward the exit. I followed after her. She wore all black clothes like me and had her hair pulled back in a severe bun. Her resemblance to a gorilla was more striking than ever in that getup.

"How come I didn't know we were doing this tonight?" I asked as we descended the stairs into the tunnels.

"Last-minute decision. Lady Elaine had some concerns over the apparent lack of progress in your dream journals."

"Like she's got any business complaining about lack of progress," I muttered, although I suspected the truth was that Lady Elaine sprung it on me so I couldn't ditch again.

Bethany marched along, ignoring me.

As usual, Eli was still awake when we arrived. To my horror, Lance was up, too.

"Well, here she comes," Lance said when I came through the door. "Quick, Eli, better run and hide before she curses us."

"Leave her alone," said Eli.

"I quite agree," added Bethany, following me in.

Both boys startled at the sudden appearance of this strange, oversized woman in their dorm room.

"What are *you* doing here?" Lance said with his mouth hung open like a hooked fish. His fingers, which had been twirling a joker card, stilled mid-flip.

Bethany fixed a glare on him. "Not your concern, Mr. Rathbone."

"But . . . you're Bethany Grey, right?"

She gave him a mock bow. "So glad to know you've heard of me."

Lance gulped. "Yeah, you work for Consul Vanholt. Sort of his personal . . . something or other."

"Yes, that's right, but no time to dwell on specifics. Off to bed with you." Bethany shooed at Lance like a dog, and to my surprise, he obeyed, disappearing into the bedroom without a word.

Now it was me looking like the hooked fish. I'd never known Lance to be obedient to anybody. I stared at Bethany, feeling more curious about her than I ever had before. "*What* exactly do you do for the consul?"

She waved the question off and turned to Eli. "On to the sofa, young man, and hurry up." She snapped her fingers. "We don't have all night."

He narrowed his eyes at her. "Why are you here?"

I stifled a groan at Eli's antagonistic attitude and jumped in between him and Bethany. "It's okay," I said, thumping his shoulder. "She's a Nightmare, too. She's going to teach me some things, so we're both going to enter your dream."

Eli frowned, eyeing the woman who stood nearly as tall as he did, which was saying something. "You're not actually going to *sit* on me, are you?"

I hid a giggle even though I sympathized with his worry. Bethany would crush him.

She scowled. "Don't be ridiculous. A Nightmare doesn't have to sit on your chest to enter your dream. That is merely the most effective position for creating a strong connection between dreamer and Nightmare. But only a single touch is necessary for entry. There are even some Nightmares powerful enough to enter your dreams from a distance."

"There are?" I said.

Bethany glanced at me, frowning. "Didn't you know?"

I shook my head.

"Not surprised. I'm sure Moira failed to teach you anything useful."

"You're probably right." Seemed there were a few things Bethany could teach me after all.

"Humph," Bethany said, although she sounded mollified.

Eli sat on the sofa, and we waited for him to fall asleep. Then Bethany and I moved into position on either side of him and entered the dream.

I was in the tunnels again and had to fight back panic. I managed it, but only because there wasn't any sign of somebody on fire. Actually, there wasn't any sign of anybody period, not even Eli.

I took off at a run, trying to find him. The tunnel curved around then ended at the threshold of a vast underground chamber. Lit torches hung at intervals around its circumference. The purple haze of the flames told me it was Everlasting Fire, created by a difficult spell that few magickind could perform.

In the center of the chamber, Eli stood next to what looked like a raised altar with a long, rectangular box set on top of it that seemed to be made of some pale crystal. Facets of it twinkled in the light of the purple flames.

Eli spotted me and shouted from across the room, "What is this place?"

"No idea," I hollered back.

Bethany emerged from the tunnel next to me and the two of us headed into the chamber.

"You've never been here before?" I asked Eli when I reached the raised altar.

"Nope." He was staring fixedly at the box, which was indeed made from some kind of crystal.

I stared, too, taking in the engravings on its side like the kind you might find on a tomb. Then it clicked. It *was* a tomb. I could just make out the form of a body inside it.

I put my hand on the side of it, surprised to find the surface warm. My gaze focused on the engravings, which depicted some ancient, magickind battle. The people carried wands and staffs along with swords, shields, and bows. I'd seen such images before in my history textbook, but none of them came close to capturing the visceral detail here.

Although the figures were posed in different combative postures, they were all bent toward the middle like two armies converging on a battlefield. The three figures in the center were larger and more intricate than the others, two men and a woman. One of the men lay on the ground, clutching at the sword sticking out of his chest. The other stood with his back to the woman who was covering his eyes with her hands. The man looked like he was in the process of falling down. The woman's expression was impossible to see clearly on the crystal surface, but I thought there was something both sad and victorious about her posture.

My gaze drifted up from the woman's face to the sky, where a huge bird hovered over the people's heads, wings outstretched. Like hearing the opening notes of a familiar song on the radio, recognition hummed inside me at the sight of it.

"Eli," I said, pointing. "Do you see what I see?"

"Oh, yeah. It's the black phoenix."

"How can you tell?" said Bethany, approaching the tomb for a closer look.

"Because we've seen it." A humorless smile curled one side of Eli's lips. "A lot."

I scrutinized Bethany's face, trying to read her expression. "Do *you* know what it is? Or *who* it is?"

Bethany met my eyes. "Nobody's told you?"

I flipped my hair back behind my shoulder. "Well, no, but we haven't exactly asked."

"Hmmm, I suppose if the senate wanted you to know, someone would've told you before now."

"Oh, that's *great*." Eli waved his hands through the air. "Because leaving the people with the ability to stop these murders clueless about everything makes *so* much sense."

"I'm not supposed to talk about it," said Bethany. "The subject is restricted."

I motioned to the vast chamber. "I'm pretty sure nobody can hear us inside a dream."

"You're mistaken."

My eyes widened in surprise. "Seriously? Somebody can spy on us here?"

"Only another Nightmare, but yes. They can even influence the dream if they're powerful enough. But don't worry, your mother *isn't*."

I frowned, uncertain if she was being honest or just spiteful. "If my mom can't listen in then there's no problem with you telling us the truth. I mean, there's no risk of being overheard since you and I are the only other Nightmares around."

"Besides," added Eli. "We already know what the killer is after, so what's the harm in learning the truth about the phoenix?"

A smug expression rose on Bethany's face. "You couldn't possibly know what the killer is after."

"Wanna bet?" said Eli, equally smug. "It's the power source for The Will spell. Excalibur."

Bethany looked like she'd just swallowed something sour. "Who told you? Was it Moira?" She turned her glare on me.

"Um, yes," I said, taking a gamble with the truth.

"So she told you about the sword and not the identity of the black phoenix? How typical."

"I know, right? I mean, I'm sure she had her reasons, but I'm equally sure they're in *her* best interest and not the senate's."

Bethany nodded, vigorously. I stifled a smile, pleased that my mother's bad reputation was working in my favor for once.

Bethany took a step closer to the tomb and traced a finger over the phoenix's outline. I shivered, remembering the eerie, hypnotic sound of the bird's cry.

"Only one black phoenix has ever existed," Bethany said. "The familiar of the greatest and most feared magic-kind ever to be. A wizard who has been called by many names throughout history. His last title was the Red War-lock. But in ordinary folklore, he's known as Merlin."

Eli chuckled. "Merlin? Are you kidding me?"

"What's so funny?" asked Bethany.

"It's just hard to take the idea seriously when you've grown up seeing Merlin as this crazy old wizard who's always tripping over his beard in cartoons. Hard to picture that guy having a familiar as fierce as the black phoenix we've seen."

I sympathized with Eli's point, but it was no different than the Tinkerbell version of fairies. If Merlin had been so great and fearsome, then the Magi would've softened his image on purpose to make people forget how danger-ous the real man had been.

Only the "had been" wasn't right, if I understood the implications of what Bethany said. I asked, "But if the Red Warlock has a phoenix for a familiar does that mean he's immortal?"

"Yes," said Bethany. "Through his bond with the bird, he has died and been reborn many times. Some say his existence predates the ancient Egyptians."

"Oh-kay." I paused, trying to digest the information. "So in other words, the Red Warlock, *Merlin,* could still be alive today even though the Arthur legend is like a thousand years old."

Bethany wagged a finger at me. "Not *could* be alive. There's never been any doubt he lives. What has been in doubt is whether or not he's currently awake and wandering around Arkwell's campus."

I blinked. "What do you mean *awake*?"

Bethany grimaced. "Don't you know the story ordinaries tell about what happened to Merlin?"

"Uh, no."

"I do," said Eli. "There're lots of different versions, but most say he was imprisoned in some kind of magical tomb by a witch named Niviane or some such."

I gaped at him, surprised by the depth of his knowledge on the subject.

"What?" he said, shrugging. "I have sort of a thing for mythology and folklore."

Yeah, that might be even cuter than the cop stuff.

Bethany turned a pointed gaze at me. "Nimue was her real name. And she wasn't a witch, but a *Nightmare*."

I swayed on my feet. Nimue was my mother's maiden name. There was too much coincidence here, too many threads that seemed interwoven in a deliberate pattern.

Bethany said, "Nimue imprisoned the Red Warlock in a *dream*. That's what you're seeing depicted here." She pointed at the tomb and the woman standing behind the man. "And until a couple of weeks ago, when you first saw the black phoenix in Eli's dream, we believed him still imprisoned."

"Well, is he or isn't he?" Eli stooped toward the engraving once more.

Bethany sighed. "Nobody can say for sure. The Red Warlock's tomb isn't in America but somewhere in Britain. The senate has asked the Magi Parliament over there to confirm whether or not his body is still inside but they either don't know or are unwilling to tell us for some reason."

"Nice," said Eli. He pointed at the second man on the tomb, the one with the sword sticking out of his chest. "Who's this guy supposed to be then?"

"King Arthur," said Bethany.

Eli opened his mouth to say something, but I cut him off. "The senate thinks it's the Red Warlock behind the murders, don't they?"

"Most likely, given the regular appearance of the black phoenix in Eli's dreams." Bethany paused. "Or it *could* be someone trying to free him from the tomb by using the sword. Impossible to know for sure. There aren't any recorded pictures of the actual man. Some say he cursed his own image a long time ago to prevent his likeness being recorded. He could be anybody. Young or old, there's no telling. But it's certain that if the Red Warlock has escaped he will come after Excalibur."

"Why?" asked Eli, straightening up.

"Because it belongs to him. Always has."

"But wait," said Eli. "If Merlin was entombed in Britain why is his sword in America?"

Bethany shifted her weight from one foot to the other. "The Magi governments decided a long time ago it was best to keep as much distance between the sword and wizard as possible. So it was brought to the States and hidden away somewhere around here in case the Red Warlock ever escaped."

"You mean like he might've done now," said Eli.

"Precisely."

I wanted to know more about the true history of the sword, but something more pressing occurred to me. "Do you think *this* is Merlin's tomb?" I bent close to the crystal surface, cupping the sides of my face with my hands as I tried to see into it.

"I don't know," said Bethany.

"Let's find out." Eli put his hands on top of the tomb's lid and pushed. He strained so hard he groaned, but it wouldn't budge.

"I think you need some kind of key to open it." Bethany pointed at a round hole just above the phoenix's head. She was probably right, except I saw two similar holes on each end as well, and none of them looked like normal keyholes.

"No, we don't," said Eli. "This is a dream. Come on, Dusty, force it open."

I shook my head. If Merlin was in there, I didn't want to risk freeing the black phoenix. I was learning not to believe that everything in dreams wasn't real.

"You truly think she's strong enough to open it when you weren't?" asked Bethany, her tone sarcastic.

"She can *dream* it open," said Eli, "or whatever it is she does to change the stuff in here. She's done it before."

Bethany turned her fierce gaze on me. "You've been *manipulating* the content of his dreams?"

I fidgeted beneath her admonishing look. "Um, yeah, a little bit. I thought that was normal for Nightmares."

Eli snorted his disagreement on my definition of little, but thankfully he didn't elaborate.

"Is that bad?" I asked, guessing the answer already as I remembered how worn-out Eli had appeared the morning after I'd forced his dream to show us Rosemary's death. Not to mention the furious way Bethany had reacted when my mom had done the same to hers. At the time I figured it was just Bethany's animosity toward all things Moira.

"*Very*," Bethany said, nostrils flaring. "It's dangerous to manipulate dreams. The more you do the more fictus you drain from your victim. Of course, if you'd come to your dream training sessions with me, you would know that." She pointed a finger at Eli. "She can trap you in your own dream forever if she's not careful."

My chest went tight at this news, making it hard to breathe. I remembered what Mr. Marrow had told me about how Nightmares had earned their bad reputation by sucking people's souls out through their dreams, condemning them to a fate worse than death. Now it seemed I'd almost done the same to Eli without even knowing it.

"Well, she didn't trap me last time, and we did a lot more than open a tomb," said Eli. "Come on, Dusty. It's fine—I'm fine."

Bethany shook her head at him then looked at me. "I can't believe your mother didn't warn you of the dangers involved. She knows better, never mind how much manipulating she does herself."

I didn't reply, my heart sinking. Not just from the fear of what I might have done to Eli, but from the knowledge that my mother had lied to me on purpose. She'd *encouraged* me to manipulate his dreams.

Had she wanted me to hurt him? There was only one reason I could think of why she would do that—if she was working for the killer. The person behind the killings stood to lose the most from what Eli and I might predict in the dreams. But if Eli wasn't around to do the dreaming . . .

Yes, her involvement made a lot of sense. Maybe her attempt to get me to run away with her that day was just a ploy to keep me from identifying the killer. Except there'd only been *two* killers in the dream, one of them F and the other—who? The Red Warlock? The person *had* transformed into the black phoenix. Did that mean my mother was innocent or merely that the dream wasn't as literal as I suspected? Maybe there were three killers.

I closed my eyes and willed my head to stop pounding. There were just too many questions. Too much information I didn't have.

"What's wrong, Dusty?" Eli said, his voice soft.

I opened my eyes and shivered. "I'm just thinking."

"It's all right." Bethany patted my arm. I looked up at her. She was smiling down at me with something like sympathy on her face, but I detected a note of smugness, too. "You're not the first person your mother has tricked into doing something dangerous. She's the one who taught *me* how to manipulate dreams. Only I wasn't so lucky as you seem to have been."

"How do you mean?" I whispered.

Bethany took a moment to answer. "My dreamer didn't survive. And it was all Moira's fault."

~ 21 ~

Hags and Candy

I met up with Paul the following afternoon. We went for a walk in the tunnels, finally stopping in an alcove I'd never been in before, one far out of the way. With our feet hanging over the edge of the pool, a reservoir that fed into the canal system, I filled him in on my latest suspicions about my mother.

"What are you going to do?" Paul said.

I sighed. "I don't know. Do *you* think she's involved?"

"I think a lot of people are capable of things you'd never believe."

I swallowed, disliking the certainty in his voice. "Sounds like you're speaking from experience."

He nodded, not meeting my eyes. "Most people think my uncle is a great man, a good and wise leader, but they have no idea the horrible things he's done."

"Like what?"

A bitter smile twisted Paul's lips. "Put his nephew in the hospital. More than once."

I covered my mouth as I let out an involuntary gasp.

"So you didn't break your cheekbone falling down the stairs?"

"No, just the wrist and the sprained ankle." He traced a finger over his cheek where only the barest hint of bruising remained. "This was from his fist, which made me lose my balance and *then* stumble down the stairs."

"But how is that possible? I thought The Will keeps magickind from doing physical violence?"

"It's supposed to, but it doesn't always. The spell's probably focused more on magical violence than the physical. Either that or my uncle's paying one of the Will-Workers to allow him to get away with stuff."

"Chinks," I said, thinking about Mr. Marrow. I grabbed Paul's hand and squeezed it. "I'm so sorry. Have you told anybody?"

He laughed. "Who'd believe me? Or care, for that matter."

"But what about your mother?"

He shook his head. "Haven't seen her in years. She moved to Costa Rica when I was three and hasn't been back since."

"That's terrible. And to think I'm mad at *my* mother."

Paul wove his fingers through mine. "Please don't tell anyone, Dusty. I've never shared the truth before."

"I won't. But I still think you should. He needs to be stopped."

He smiled. "There's not much point now. I've got less than a year to go before I can move out and start my own life."

I rested my head on his shoulder. "Right. Then you'll be free."

He leaned his head on mine. "You have no idea."

We didn't speak for a couple of moments, just sat staring at the water. We'd come down here for some privacy, but I was surprised to find the small chamber so warm and comfortable. Given better subject matter, it might even have been a little romantic.

"Well," Paul said sometime later. "We've decided how I'm going to handle my problem but not yours. What are you going to do about your mother?"

I sighed, straightening up. "First, I suppose I should tell Eli and Selene about everything. Then maybe we could do some snooping. If I find certain proof she's involved, I'll go to Sheriff Brackenberry."

"Sounds reasonable."

I glanced up at him. "Speaking of which, our next meeting is tomorrow if you'd still like to come."

"Sure."

I tried not to grin. It occurred to me that I must suffer from some form of schizophrenia, given how quickly my mood had gone from utterly depressed to happy. "Hey, I almost forgot. Were you able to hack into that website?"

He grimaced. "Not yet, but I'm still trying. It's got a lot of security on it. I've got a sniffer in place though, so it's just a matter of time. I'll let you know as soon as I do."

"Oh," I said, wondering what the heck a sniffer was. "Sounds like a lot of work."

He beamed at me. "Yeah, but I like it."

We stayed down there for another half hour. We talked a little about the tomb in Eli's dream, speculating whose it might be. For all her insistence that she was so much better than my mother at everything, I hadn't learned any new tricks from Bethany. All we'd done was explore the tunnels surrounding the main chamber. Most of them only led to more tunnels. Except for one, which rose steadily upward for a long time, only to dead-end in front of a locked door so small it must've been designed for midgets or maybe overly large trash trolls.

After a while the discussion gave way to kissing then touching. His fingers left trails of tingly heat behind as he touched my arms, face, the sides of my breasts. My fingers did their own dance over his skin, enjoying the hardness of a body so different from my own. I was as eager to touch him as to be touched.

He moved closer to me, leaning me backward as he deepened the kiss until my head rested on the hard floor of the tunnel. It was uncomfortable, but I didn't mind. I was too consumed with wanting to be close to him. And I knew he felt the same. Our interaction came naturally, without thought or awkwardness.

But as he moved on top of me, his weight pressing my backbone into the harsh ground, I came back to my senses and realized what I was doing. I pulled back from the kiss and gently pushed him away. I liked him a lot, but I wasn't sure I was ready to go further. He resisted for a long, tense moment then moved off me. We sat up, both panting.

"Sorry," I said, glancing at my watch. "But if I don't get

some sleep, I'll never make it through my detention tonight."

"'S okay," he said. His lips were red from kissing and his
cheeks flushed. I'd never been more attracted to him. If
we'd been making out like that somewhere else, someplace
with a comfortable surface, I wasn't so sure I would've
stopped him.

He stood and offered me his hand. "You want to be
careful of Ms. Hardwick. Hags can be deceptively nasty."

"So I've heard," I said. And just like that, gloom drove
all my happy thoughts away.

Trying to fall asleep at five o'clock on a Saturday was almost impossible. The girls in the dorm room next door
liked to play their music full blast. Rather than lull me to
sleep, the steady thump of the bass only made my head
ache. By the time I did fall asleep, it seemed my alarm
sounded a moment later. I slapped it off, feeling groggy
and wishing I had some way out of this.

Dr. Hendershaw had sent me instructions to meet Ms.
Hardwick in the foyer of Riker Hall. I dressed quickly
and got down there with five minutes to spare. I waved at
Frank and Igor when they turned their eyeless stares
at me.

"Detention, boys," I said. This seemed to satisfy them,
and they turned their gazes back toward the front door.

Ms. Hardwick showed up ten minutes after midnight,
appearing from the entrance to the tunnels. She ignored

the knights completely and shouted in a sickly sweet voice, "Come on, girl. The night's half gone already."

I hurried toward her, relieved to see she wasn't the horrible, misshapen old woman I'd expected. Instead she looked like someone's little old grandmother in her pea green housedress and gray hair in an untidy bun. She was short and plump with chubby cheeks and small dark eyes that would've looked at home on a ferret.

Then she smiled and shattered the illusion completely. Her mouth contained far too many teeth. They were tiny and looked sharp enough to cut through raw meat in a single bite. I realized with a sickening feeling that this was probably exactly what they were designed to do.

"Um, are you Ms. Hardwick?" I asked.

"Yes, dear. Hurry. Right this way."

Hardwick headed down the sloping path into the tunnels. It took every ounce of bravery I possessed to follow behind her. She scurried along down the corridor far too fast for someone who appeared so old. Definitely creepy, like how eerily fast spiders move. I kept glancing over at her as we walked, taking note of all the other things wrong with her appearance, like the greenish tinge to her skin.

"So, they tell me *you* are the one who put Fritz in the hospital," Ms. Hardwick said.

"Um, yes, I did—but I didn't do it on purpose or anything."

"That's all right, my dear. You can be honest with me. I daresay Fritz deserved it, the horrible little fairy."

"Mmmm," I said, unsure of what to make of this. She was acting like we were kindred spirits or something. I knew that Nightmares were often mistaken for hags in folklore, but we were very, very different creatures. A hag, free of The Will's control, would make human flesh a regular meal, the younger the better. Nightmares only fed on dreams.

And souls, sometimes.

"So how *is* your mother?" said Hardwick, surprising me yet again. "I understand she's teaching here now. Shame I haven't bumped into her yet."

"Uh-huh." We were walking so fast, I was finding it hard to speak without panting. It would've been easier to jog, but I didn't want to get outpaced by an old hag.

Ms. Hardwick didn't seem to mind me not holding up my end of the conversation as she prattled on. "And you're the new dream-seer, so they say. Surprising, but then maybe fitting, too."

I wanted to ask her what she meant, but she never gave me a chance as she chattered on. In no time at all, we were climbing the slope from the tunnels into Jefferson Tower. Any ideas I'd had at getting a chance to catch my breath were short-lived as Ms. Hardwick marched to the staircase and headed up.

"We'll start at the top and work our way down," she announced.

"Great." I'd meant the response to sound sarcastic, but it came out so soft and breathless, she probably mistook it for agreement.

We reached the restrooms on the top floor at last, and I slumped against the nearest stall, panting.

"Tsk, tsk," said Hardwick. "You children just don't spend enough time focused on your health these days. Too much entertainment, I daresay."

I would've rolled my eyes, but it wasn't worth the effort.

"I suppose I will summon the cleaning supplies for you then." Hardwick walked over to the nearest wall and traced a rectangle with her finger while she muttered an incantation. A moment later, a cupboard door appeared in the wall. She pulled it open, revealing several shelves of cleaning supplies—everything a girl could want for getting the job done. Awesome.

"There you are," said Hardwick, clapping her hands. "Let's get to it, lots of bathrooms to go."

Sighing, I selected a pair of rubber gloves, a toilet brush, bleach cleaning spray, and a handful of rags. Then I bent to work. Ms. Hardwick conjured a chair out of thin air and sat down, watching me with her ferret eyes. I did my best to ignore her.

When I finished the last stall, I straightened up, stretched the crick out of my back, and said, "Done."

Hardwick flashed her too big smile and stood up. "Are you sure?"

"Yeah, of course. I've cleaned my fair share of toilets before." Maybe not public ones, but I was trying not to think about that so much.

Hardwick entered the first stall, bent her head toward

the toilet, and sniffed long and deep like a starving person over a pot of stew. I stuffed the heel of my hand into my mouth, trying not to gag. For a moment I was certain she would start licking it.

Hardwick stepped out of the stall, letting out a contented sigh. "I don't think so, my dear. I can still smell the foulness. You're going to have to scrub harder with that brush of yours."

"You're kidding, right?"

Hardwick flashed her teeth and said in that same falsely sweet voice, "Do I look like I'm kidding?"

"Uh, no." I glanced down the row of stalls. "I guess I'll do it again then."

Three attempts later, Hardwick pronounced the work satisfactory, and we moved on to the men's. My hands felt raw already despite the gloves, and my muscles felt tense and achy. It was going to be a long night.

And so it went, stall after stall, floor after floor. If I'd disliked Dr. Hendershaw before, I despised her now. Talk about cruel and unusual punishment.

By the time we reached the second floor, I was ready to throw myself in front of a bus rather than clean another toilet. I opened the door to the men's and was greeted by the biggest mess I'd ever seen in my life.

"Oh, screw this," I said, taking in the three inches of water on the floor, the clogged sinks with the taps turned on full blast, and from the looks of it all ten toilets and urinals overflowed.

"My, my, what a mess. I wonder what happened in here?" Ms. Hardwick said, wading inside.

I had a pretty good guess as I spotted a joker playing card floating in the puddle of muck, "3–2" written on it in big black letters. Lance Rathbone. I could've killed him.

"Not to fret." Hardwick pulled out a cell phone from the front pocket of her housedress and flipped it open. The cell chirped in a perfect imitation of R2D2 as she dialed.

"Hello?" she said a moment later. "It's Emma. I'm in Jefferson Tower. We've got a problem on the second floor . . . uh-huh . . . looks that way . . . yes, we'll wait. Oh and why don't you bring my package along with you? . . . Yes, I know it's early, but it's been a long week. You know I'm good for it . . . of course . . . good-bye."

She stowed the cell away again, turned off the faucets, and we stepped out. Then she conjured two chairs for us, and we sat down. "It'll be just a few moments then."

Grateful as I was for a break, I wanted to get done with this already. "Can't you just magic the mess away?"

"Afraid not. All the bathrooms at Arkwell have antimagic spells on them, which block everything save glamours and the simple cleaning spells *I* employ, which aren't nearly enough for that mess."

I raised my eyebrows. "Why's it blocked?"

Hardwick began to pick at something in her teeth. "To prevent students from playing pranks, for one thing. And there's the issue of animation of course. The administration likes to keep the liveliness in the bathrooms down to a minimum."

"Nothing worse than a talking toilet," I muttered.

Hardwick nodded. "But unfortunately the spells don't prevent a highly motivated student from disrupting things the manual way."

That was Lance, all right, highly motivated to make my life difficult. I wondered how he knew about my detention.

It seemed Mr. Culpepper was highly motivated to make my life difficult, too, seeing how he took nearly a half hour to arrive. A strange clicking sound preceded his appearance down the corridor. Mr. Culpepper was leading a leashed dog beside him. No, not a dog—a hellhound. As it grew closer, I saw the hairs of its black coat were more like scales than fur, hard and slick as armor. Its eyes shone like flashlights. I'd heard rumors that Culpepper had a hellhound, but I'd never seen it before. Not surprising, since hellhounds were nocturnal—and extremely volatile.

"Why on earth did you bring *that* mangy thing along?" Ms. Hardwick said.

The hound growled as if it had understood the insult. The sound made the hairs on the back of my neck stand up.

Culpepper grunted. "Somebody's out there killing folk, if you haven't noticed."

Hardwick snickered. "And you think they might come after you? My goodness, Faust, you're getting more paranoid every day."

Culpepper glared at her. Then he looked at me and glared some more. "What's *she* doing here?"

"Detention. Did you bring my package?"

"Yeah, but what about *her*?"

Hardwick waved, dismissively. "Never mind that. Hand it over, if you please."

Culpepper grunted again as he set the toolbox he was carrying with him on the floor. He bent over it and pulled out a brown paper package the size of a pencil box, which he handed to Ms. Hardwick.

He stood up again. "Gonna check things out." Then he turned and entered the bathroom, taking the hellhound with him.

I sucked in a relieved breath—the hound had been watching me with its eerie eyes like it was hoping I might make a run for it so it could give chase.

Hardwick ripped into the paper surrounding the box with her long, thick fingernails and yanked the lid off to reveal a stockpile of candy bars. "Would you like one?" she said, pulling out a Baby Ruth.

Under normal circumstances, I would've jumped at the chance to indulge in a piece of contraband candy, but something about the way Hardwick was looking at it, like a dog drooling for table scraps, decided me against it. "No, thanks."

Hardwick shrugged and tore in—literally—gobbling down the Baby Ruth in a matter of seconds. Next she started in on a Mr. Goodbar, then a Butterfinger followed by a Clark Bar, and so on. I was beginning to notice a disturbing theme to the names of these candy bars and had to rein in my imagination before it started picturing what *other* edible things a hag might eat that would produce that same chomp-chomp-chomp sound.

To take my mind off the sick feeling in my stomach, I thought about Culpepper. It seemed a safe bet he was running some kind of black market here at Arkwell, apparently one that provided the faculty with banned substances like chocolate. But I knew my mother didn't have a sugar problem. So what had he given her? Sugary contraband wasn't very serious, but what if he dealt in harder stuff? Like maybe black magic items. The little I knew about black magic was enough for me to suspect you could do any number of horrible, vile things with it.

Culpepper and his hellhound emerged a few minutes later, long enough for Culpepper to pull out a couple of tools. It struck me as a bit odd that he hadn't tied the hound up in the restroom so he could have both hands free. He must not want the animal out of his sight. What was he so nervous about?

I checked his fingers for rings when he emerged again to get even more tools, but he wasn't wearing any. It was a stupid idea anyway. For one thing, I seriously doubted anybody would've made Mr. Culpepper the third Keeper. For another, it was highly unlikely I would recognize a Keeper ring if I saw one, besides Rosemary's. There was no reason to believe the rings looked the same. Even if they did, surely the person wearing it would be smart enough to disguise it with a glamour.

When Culpepper went back into the bathroom again, I noticed that the contents in the toolbox had shifted to reveal a set of keys. Not just any set, but the mega-ultra-open-every-door-on-campus set. At least a hundred keys hung from the big silver loop. I thought it likely that *one* of them would open the door into the crypt Culpepper had disappeared into that night.

I spent the next couple of minutes contemplating how to steal the keys without getting caught. Fortunately, I'd worn my Chickery High School hoodie, which had a huge front pocket. Unfortunately, I was certain Ms. Hardwick wasn't distracted enough with her candy bars not to notice me pilfering Culpepper's toolbox.

When Mr. Culpepper came out of the bathroom for the third time, he looked like someone had given him a swirly. Droplets of water fell from his wet hair and shirt, and he was angry enough that I could see the tips of his horns showing through the glamour and the hint of an electric green glow in his eyes.

"This is going to take the rest of the night to fix, *stupid idiot sons of* . . . No point in hanging around here if you've got other things to do. I'll let you know when I'm done, Emma. It's gonna need a good cleaning." He turned around, muttering swear words as he went back inside.

"Well, that's a shame," said Hardwick, wiping her mouth with the back of her sleeve. The gesture didn't help. The chocolate smears remained around her lips, looking like dried blood. "I suppose you'd best call it a night, my dear. We can pick this up again next week."

"Oh, okay." I stood, not sure if I should consider myself lucky or not. On the one hand, I was so tired my eyeballs were twitching, but on the other, I hadn't made it through one building in an entire night. Detention was going to last forever at this rate.

Then I remembered the keys, just sitting there, begging to be picked up. Acting on impulse, I flicked my wrist toward the box of candy bars perched on Hardwick's lap, giving it a little push with my magic. It went flying down the corridor, spewing its contents like a burst piñata. Hardwick startled so badly she tumbled sideways out of her chair.

Whoops.

I tried not to laugh as I rushed over to help, feigning concern. "Are you all right?" I put a hand on her wrist and pulled. Hardwick's skin beneath my fingers felt as slick and slimy as a snake's.

"Oh, I'm fine. We must have a poltergeist in here."

Glad to find she wasn't the brightest hag in the monster book, I grabbed the keys out of the toolbox as she scurried away to retrieve her precious chocolate.

"Um, do you want some help, Ms. Hardwick?"

She waved at me. "Not at all. You run along now."

Don't have to tell me twice. "Okay. See you."

I turned and trotted down the corridor to the stairs with both hands inside my front pocket, holding the keys so they wouldn't jangle. Spending the night cleaning toilets with a chocolate-crazed hag might not have been fun, but it was totally worth it. I was certain that all the answers were waiting inside that crypt.

Somehow, I just *knew* it.

⁓ 22 ⁓

The Crypt

Paul and I spent the morning traipsing around Coleville in search of the crypt. I was only slightly worried about bumping into Culpepper—he was probably still asleep after the late night he had. It took us two hours to find it. Paul wanted to check the keys right then, but I thought we might be pushing it. When Culpepper did wake up, he was bound to be suspicious about his missing keys.

So we waited and brought the keys to Room 013 that afternoon to work out a plan for breaking in with the others.

"Wow," Selene said when we were all gathered together. "That's a *lot* of keys. Did you guys figure out which one it is?"

"No, but it shouldn't take too long to try them all," I said.

"I don't know," said Eli. "With that many, it could take all night."

"Let me see them," said Selene. She was sitting in the

same chair that had given her such grief last time. It seemed to have developed an attachment to her. The moment she walked into the room it had chased her around until she'd given up and sat on it. She hadn't moved since.

I set the key ring down on the desk in front of her. She started shuffling through them one by one, finally stopping on a small skeleton key with a weird greenish color to it. She ran a finger along its edge then looked up at me. "This is the one."

"How do you know?" Eli stepped up next to me for a better look, brushing his upper arm against my shoulder.

"It's a moonwort key." Selene slid it off the ring and handed it to me. It wasn't made out of metal but rather some soft, flexible material.

"Um, color me crazy," I said, "but doesn't a key have to be kind of rigid in order to trigger a lock?"

"Not if it's moonwort," Paul said, joining us around the table. "May I see it?" I handed it to him, and he nodded. "Selene's right. Moonwort."

"Okay, somebody explain already," said Eli, rapping his knuckles on the table.

"Moonwort is a type of plant that will open almost any lock when made into a key," said Selene. "It's completely illegal."

"My turn, please." Eli gestured at Paul, who handed him the key. "Huh. If you're right, then this little thing is a private detective's dream tool."

"So we sneak into the crypt and look for Rosemary's ring or one that might've been Ankil's, right?" Selene said.

Paul cast me a significant glance. I still hadn't told them about my mother. Sighing, I said, "Well, not *only* the rings." Then I told them my suspicions about my mom and the truth about Nightmares. It got easier as I went along, mostly because nobody went screaming from the room at the news or started looking at me like I'd turned into a giant spider.

Selene was the first to speak afterward. "I'll help you figure out whatever it is your mom got from Culpepper, but I don't believe for a second she's the killer."

Her words made me feel better at once. I knew that for Selene, my mother's innocence was the same as mine. Right or not, her loyalty meant a lot. And no matter my resentment to my mother, I didn't want her to be the killer.

Paul cleared his throat. "What makes you so certain?"

"Because I just know," Selene said, staring up at him from under her baseball cap. "Why would she do it?"

"Does it matter?" said Paul. "She's the only one we know for sure *could* have done it."

Selene glowered. "Just because someone has the *power* to do something doesn't mean they will. Sometimes people choose to be good even when they don't have to."

"Yeah, and sometimes they don't."

"Hold on, guys," Eli said, a reproach in his voice. "Don't forget, Dusty's mom isn't the only Nightmare around. Bethany Grey could have done it. And after what Lance told me, I think she's a better candidate."

"What did he tell you?" I asked.

"That she's some kind of hit man or assassin for Consul Vanholt."

Selene rolled her eyes. "That's just a rumor. Contrary to what Lance says, he doesn't know half as much about the goings-on in the senate as he claims. His dad absolutely refuses to let him in on anything. If Senator Rathbone gets his way, Lance will stay as far away from politics as possible. Trust me. I know."

Eli looked ready to argue, but I cut him off. "Rumor or not, she is *capable* of doing it, so we can put Bethany Grey down on the list, right?"

"Right," Eli said.

Selene folded her arms, pouting. "Right. At least she's a better option than Dusty's mom."

Eli nodded, although I couldn't tell if it was in agreement or if he was just pacifying her. "Now we need a plan for getting in and out without getting caught."

"And fast," I said. "We've got to get those keys back to Culpepper."

"No problem," said Selene. She removed the plastic barrette from the end of her braid and placed it on the desk in front of her. She concentrated on it, muttering an incantation. A moment later the glamour charm had transformed the barrette into a nearly perfect reproduction of the moonwort key. She picked it up and slid it onto the key ring. "There, that should buy us some time. I'll just drop this in the lost and found."

"Smart," said Eli. "That's one problem down."

Unfortunately, the next problem wasn't so easy. Even

though Mr. Ankil's death had been reported as an accident, security on campus had still been heightened afterward. The dorm room curfew was set at nine as usual, but nobody was supposed to be outdoors or in the tunnels after sunset without permission.

Since the Suits of Armor were the primary enforcers of the curfew, and they didn't do actual floor checks, we decided the best solution was to simply find somewhere to hide in Coleville and wait for it to get late enough to break in. After my week of tailing Culpepper, I knew he kept pretty regular daytime hours. It was possible that the werewolf policemen might patrol the cemetery at night, but that was a risk we would have to take.

Yeah, this would've been a *great* plan if it were June or maybe even September. November, however, meant cold and more cold. The four of us took up positions in various hiding spots around the entrance to the crypt. Fortunately, the trees and bushes were still in full bloom, thanks to the magic of the fairy gardeners, which gave us extra coverage. Unfortunately, the foliage didn't improve the temperature any. By the time the sun went down, my fingers had turned to icicles.

We'd agreed to hold out until midnight in the hope that Culpepper would've turned in for the evening. But by a quarter to eleven I made an executive decision and stood up from my hiding place behind a gravestone.

"What are you doing?" Eli hissed at me from across the way. I could barely make him out, dressed all in black as he was.

"I'm done waiting." I walked up to the crypt, pulling the moonwort key out of my pocket. Selene, Eli, and Paul joined me a second later, and I slid the key into the hole. The key vibrated for a moment, like some machine kicking on. Then I heard a soft *click,* and the door swung open of its own accord. A wave of hot air swept out from the doorway, stunning me with welcoming warmth. I stepped in automatically, thinking about nothing other than defrosting my appendages.

"Hold up, Dusty," Eli said. "You don't know what's in there."

Too late. I was already four steps inside the crypt, which was dark and gloomy despite the warmth, when suddenly the floor disappeared beneath my feet.

I choked on a scream as I went tumbling down a narrow flight of stone steps. Ten bumps later, I came sliding to a stop in an underground chamber. I sat up and groaned, assessing the damage. Aside from some scrapes and inevitable bruises, nothing felt broken. Lucky again, I supposed.

"Are you okay?" asked Eli, racing down the steps toward me. He was the only one of us who owned a flashlight, which he now held pointed in my eyes.

"Fine, but you're blinding me."

"Sorry."

Paul appeared, bumping Eli out of the way to get to me. Eli glowered at him as Paul grabbed my arms, lifting me to my feet. "You might want to be more careful next time."

"You think?"

"Here're the torches," Selene said, rummaging in her backpack. She lit one with a simple fire spell and handed it to Paul. She did the same for me and finally one for herself.

"You sure you're okay?" asked Eli. He touched my arm, a concerned look on his face.

I nodded, distracted by the sight of the crypt. We were in some kind of huge storeroom. Dozens of freestanding shelves filled the place, packed with all kinds of stuff. The one nearest to me held crate-sized boxes of candy—Twizzlers, Pixy Stix, Sprees, not to mention all the candy bars Hardwick had gone so bananas for.

"I think it's safe to say he's got some kind of side business going on," said Paul.

"Either that or he's preparing for nuclear fallout," said Eli.

"Or," I said, walking over to another shelf that had caught my eye, "he's thinking of starting World War Three." This shelf held crates with ominous labels like "C4" and "TNT." Beside them were countless rifles and handguns hung from racks set next to other crates full of various types of bullets.

"Yikes," said Eli, coming over to me. "Didn't you say this guy was an ex-Marine? 'Cause I'm not seeing the ex part so much. He could kill everybody with all this stuff."

"Um, guys?" said Selene, a hint of panic in her voice. "I think we've got even more to worry about."

I turned to face her, but she'd disappeared down another aisle. When I found her, I understood her worry at once. This aisle was full of black magic items.

There were individually wrapped boxes of shrunken heads, jars of severed hands floating in liquid, and rows of crudely made dolls with no faces. Other jars contained dead scorpions and spiders, snake fangs, live maggots, rat tails, even one labeled "eye of newt." I would've laughed at the irony, but I was too grossed out. Some of the stuff I didn't recognize at all, but from the rank, decaying smells lingering in the place, I could tell it was all bad.

"Wow," said Eli, covering his nose. "What the hell is this guy into?"

"Look, there's moonwort." Paul pointed down the row.

I shook my head. "This is creepy, but it's not what we're looking for. We should spread out, see if he's got an office or something."

Everybody agreed to the plan, and I made a left at the nearest aisle and walked all the way until I reached the edge of the chamber. I made my way around the perimeter and in moments had come across a door. I undid the dead bolt and swung it open, fully expecting to find another storeroom beyond it.

It opened into a tunnel. I looked right and left trying to determine where it went, but the tunnel disappeared into blackness a few feet from the doorway. The air was much cooler and damper out here than in the storeroom and held the distinctive, slimy odor of canal water. The tunnel must connect to the main ones on campus. Well, there was one mystery solved. Culpepper must've used this as his exit the night he came up behind me in the cemetery.

I stepped back into the storeroom and moved on. After a while, I came to a desk set in a small nook between two rows of shelves. More evil-looking items cluttered the desk, so much so that I was afraid to touch anything for fear of bumping into what looked like the severed hand of a werewolf being used as a Post-it notes holder or the skull that held an assortment of pens and pencils sticking out from its eye sockets and nose hole.

"Need a hand?" Eli said from behind me. I jumped, knocking over a pile of paper on the edge of the desk.

"Crap." I stooped and started picking them up.

Eli squatted down to help and said in a low voice, "I didn't get a chance to tell you earlier, but I think Selene's right. Your mom doesn't give me the impression that she would do something like this."

I snorted. "You just think she's hot."

He grinned. "Yeah, well, so does everybody. But there's more to it than that." He paused. "She reminds me a lot of you, actually, like the way you play soccer, so fierce and tough, but honest."

I blushed, my heart rate increasing. "I never knew you saw me play."

He shrugged, looking embarrassed. "It's sort of hard not to notice you. But the point is, I know someone like you would never get caught up in something as bad as this."

"You don't know that for sure. I mean, look at what I did to Katarina in that dream." It was the first time either of us had mentioned it. For whatever reason, Eli had pretended it never happened, and I was grateful for that. But it had happened. There was no denying it, much as I wanted to.

He touched my arm, his hand warm through my jacket. "That was different—you didn't know what would happen. Besides, we've all done things we're not proud of."

"Well, I really hope you're right about my mom," I said, "but it's like Paul says, people are capable of anything."

Eli grimaced, letting go of me. "Doesn't surprise me *Paul* was the one to say that to you. Have you noticed how he sort of eggs you on about your mom being guilty? Giving you that e-mail. Doesn't it bug you that he's so ready to pin it on her? There's something not right about it."

I stood up, suddenly angry. "Don't start in on him again, okay? I mean, geez, I haven't said anything bad about Katarina in at least twenty-four hours."

"It's not about that, it's just—" He broke off, and I turned to see Paul coming toward us.

"Find something?" he asked, his gaze shifting between Eli and me.

I motioned toward the desk. "I was just getting ready to check the drawers."

"Here," said Eli. "I'll do it." With way more bravery than I possessed, he started pulling open drawers. Thankfully, they contained the kind of stuff you expected to find in a desk, like a stapler and tape dispenser. The largest drawer on the left held hanging file folders. The first one was labeled "Ankil."

"Jackpot," said Eli, pulling out Mr. Ankil's file. He pushed aside the junk on the desk and flipped the file open, rummaging through the contents.

"What is it?" I asked, peering around him.

"Looks like he's keeping tabs on people. Here are vital statistics, family background, and I'm guessing this is a record of purchases."

I looked at the paper he was indicating and saw a list of dates, items, and prices. The dates were pretty regular, one every couple of days. Beside nearly all of them Culpepper had written the word *pot*.

"Do you think that means ordinary pot?" I said. "Like marijuana?"

"Well, he always did strike me as a bit of a hippie," said Eli.

"But why would Culpepper keep all this?"

Eli turned to the next page. "Blackmail maybe?"

Paul squatted in front of the drawer and started shuffling through files. "Everybody's in here." He paused. "Even my uncle."

"What about my mom?" I asked.

Paul pulled out a file labeled Everhart and handed it to me before returning his attention to his uncle's. His eyes flew across the page.

I opened the file to discover it wasn't *only* about my

mother. Culpepper had written a note on one of the pages about me taking the ledger and using spells on him. I shuffled to the page where he kept track of purchases. There was only one listed for my mother, dated last Monday with the words *moonwort key* written beside it.

"Looks like your mom wanted to do a little breaking and entering herself," said Eli.

I bit my lip. "Yeah, but where?"

He didn't answer, but stooped, examining more files. A moment later he said, "Check it out, guys. There's a file on Rosemary." Eli set it on the desk and began flipping through the pages. I leaned in close to him to see. The first page held vital statistics and the second a list of purchases for Pixy Stix. The contents further in nearly made my heart stop from shock. A photograph of Rosemary's smiling face stared up at me. Someone had drawn a heart around her in red ink.

Eli picked it up. "I don't believe it."

There were more photos beneath the first, covered in more hearts.

"*Faustus*," I said, still stunned by disbelief. "Culpepper's first name is Faustus. Do you think this means he's the F from Rosemary's diary?"

"Looks that way," said Paul.

Before anyone could speculate further, Selene darted around the corner, running toward us with a look of alarm on her face. She slid to a stop, waving her hand and muttering the anti-fire spell. All our torches went out, even Eli's flashlight.

"Someone's coming," she whispered.

I heard a familiar clicking noise in the distance, the sound of claws hitting stone. Culpepper was here, and he'd brought his hellhound with him. By the faint flicker of torchlight shining through the shelves, I could tell he was near the entrance and moving this way.

"Where are they, George?" Culpepper's voice boomed throughout the chamber.

The hound whined in answer.

He named his hellhound George? Seriously?

"Come on out! I know you're in here," said Culpepper. "Got this place bewitched to let me know when people break in. You didn't really think you'd get away with taking my keys, did you?"

I looked around, trying to figure a way out of this. Then I remembered the door leading into the tunnels. "Follow me," I whispered, taking hold of Selene's hand.

The light from Culpepper's torch was just enough that I managed to navigate the aisle without running into anything. By some miracle, I'd left the door unlatched. But that didn't keep it from making a loud creak as I pushed it open. George the hellhound started barking in response.

"Get them!" Culpepper screamed, which was followed by the distinctive sound of a leash unsnapping.

The four of us hustled through the door, and Eli managed to slam it closed in time to keep the hound from following us out. The creature struck the door so hard Eli almost fell down. Paul jumped forward, adding his body weight to Eli's.

"Quick. Somebody seal the door," said Paul.

Selene performed the barricade spell while I relit our torches.

"We better hurry," said Selene. "That spell won't last long."

"Which way?" I said.

Beside me, Paul glanced left, then right several times, his face tense with worry and indecision. "This way," he finally said and took off to the left. Selene and I followed after him, but Eli remained in place.

"Hang on, guys," he said. "I think this is the way we should go."

Selene and I stopped and looked back at him, but Paul kept walking.

"Why do you think so?" I asked.

"There's something familiar about it." He shook his head. "I'm having déjà vu."

"A tunnel is familiar?" asked Selene, incredulous. "Don't they all kind of look the same?"

Eli shook his head, his body tense. "There's a draft this way, too."

"Hold on, Paul," I called.

Paul stopped and turned around, his eyes narrowed, but still worried. "Why?"

I didn't answer, as I walked back to Eli, trying to detect the draft. I didn't sense anything different, but I was struck by my own sense of déjà vu.

"The dream," I said, a wave of dizziness washing over me. "It reminds me of your dream Friday night."

Paul rejoined us. "We don't have time for this. It's that way. Trust me."

"No, it isn't," said Eli, his voice hard and his expression dangerous.

The loud rattle of the door behind us shut everybody up for a moment. Culpepper and his hellhound would be breaking through any second.

Eli turned and started walking.

I didn't know what to do. Paul did seem to know his way around the tunnels, but I couldn't deny the strong pull I felt to go the opposite way. It wasn't just déjà vu. It was more like gravity. And I realized I couldn't walk away.

I glanced at Paul. "I'm sorry, but we're going this way."

He looked upset, but there was no time to worry about it. I turned and jogged down the tunnel beside Eli. The sense of being pulled grew stronger the farther we went, almost to the point that I felt as if I was riding one of those moving walkways they have at airports.

We traveled a long time before reaching a midget-sized door on the right side of the tunnel. It was so small and inconspicuously made, I didn't think we would've seen it if it weren't already open.

We came to a stop. There wasn't a doorknob, just a tiny keyhole with a small key sticking out from it. A moonwort key.

"Are we going in there?" asked Selene.

"Yes," said Eli. "We have to."

He was right. It wasn't just mere coincidence that had

brought us here, but something more. *Dream-seer,* I thought. Was this what it truly meant to be one, that things happened by fate instead of chance?

Even though a part of me didn't want to see what was beyond that door, there was no turning back. But nothing in the world could've prepared me for what happened on the other side.

~ 23 ~

The Keepers

Just like in Eli's dream, the other side of the door revealed a cramped tunnel leading steeply downward. It twisted and coiled like a snake as we walked along it, moving slower now than before. Eli had removed the moonwort key and shut the door behind us, giving us another layer of safety from Culpepper and George the hellhound.

Within moments, we heard the sounds of a struggle somewhere ahead. Somebody was fighting, casting combative spells and curses the same you'd hear in gym class or the gladiator games. What wasn't the same were the loud bangs and vibrations of unrestrained magic crashing into stone. My heart thudded against my rib cage as we picked up the pace. There was a loud *boom* followed by silence.

At last, the tunnel led us to a chamber, the same chamber from Eli's dream with the tomb sitting at its center on a raised platform. Not everything was the same as the dream, but close. Everlasting Fire burned in the sconces, bathing the chamber in an eerie purple light, but centuries of dirt covered the tomb, obscuring the crystal and engravings. And also like the dream, Bethany Grey was there.

So was my mother.

I stopped, shocked by the scene before me. Bethany was lying beside the tomb with her belly against the ground and her arms and legs bent backward behind her, wrists and ankles tied together with silvery rope made of magic. It looked as if my mother had used the binding curse on her. Bethany was whimpering as blood flowed from what remained of the ring finger of her right hand.

Above Bethany, my mother had pushed the lid off the tomb and climbed inside. She now sat crouched in a position I knew all too well—a Nightmare feeding. *What the—?*

Eli sprinted into the chamber toward Bethany, outdistancing the rest of us. He knelt beside her and grabbed at the silver rope.

"Don't!" I shouted, but it was too late. There was a sizzling sound like water striking hot grease, and Eli jerked his hand away, swearing. Blisters popped up on his skin where he'd touched the rope.

Selene cast the counter-spell, and the ropes fell away. Bethany let out a groan as her limbs returned to normal position. Selene bent down and helped her sit up while Eli ripped off a piece of his shirt and wrapped it around the bleeding stump where her ring finger used to be.

"What happened?" Eli said.

Bethany took a shuddering breath. "Moira found out

I'm the third Keeper and attacked me. She took the ring to open the tomb."

I wondered how Bethany could be the third Keeper and still be alive, but I didn't get a chance to ask.

"You've got to go after her, Dusty," Bethany said.

"What?"

"Your mother. She's going for the sword. You need to stop her."

"Where is it?" I glanced up at the tomb, not understanding. There was no doubt my mother was dream-feeding, but I didn't see how that was possible. It was a tomb for goodness sake, a place for dead people. And dead people didn't dream.

I stood and walked to the side of the tomb, taking note of the three Keeper rings that had been placed inside those small round holes that Bethany had said were locks. The one on the left I recognized as Rosemary's. The one on the right I guessed had been Ankil's. The one in the middle was smeared with Bethany's blood.

I peered over the side of the tomb, unsure what to expect as dread pounded inside my skull. It couldn't be the Red Warlock's tomb, not if that one was supposed to be in Britain. A woman lay inside it, and from the looks of her she was far from dead. She appeared not much older than my mother, although it was hard to say for sure. There was something ageless about her face. Her body seemed frail like an elderly person's, but no wrinkles or age spots marred her skin. Yet, she had to be old. Even magickind didn't wear dresses like that anymore. She looked like a medieval princess, Sleeping Beauty waiting for her prince.

Then it dawned on me how familiar her face was. It was *my* face, only different, like an intentional variation. I glanced at my mother, perched above the woman. It was Moira's face, too. The same nose and mouth, same tilt to the eyes.

Then I understood. This woman was my ancestor. "This is— "

"Nimue," Bethany said from behind me. "She's the fourth Keeper. The sword is hidden somewhere inside her dream. You've got to find it."

I turned to look at Bethany, shivering with fear. She wanted me to go in *there*? Face my mother inside a *dream*? "Why can't you go after her?"

"I won't stand a chance against her right now. But you might. You're her daughter. She won't hurt you."

I shook my head.

"You've got to go now. If she gets the sword first, there'll be no stopping her."

I couldn't believe it; I didn't want to believe it—my mother, a villain. Then I remembered the horrible sound of Mr. Ankil's screams as he burned to death. Only someone truly evil could've done something like that.

People are capable of anything, I heard Paul say. I glanced at him now, standing a few feet from the tomb and watching me with anxious eyes, waiting for me to play the hero and save the day. But I couldn't do it. Not me. Not against her.

In the end, it was the gruesome sight of Bethany's severed finger that swayed me. Here was physical proof of the lengths my mother would go to. Gritting my teeth, I climbed into the tomb and positioned my body around Nimue's legs. Then I glanced at my friends, watching me from below.

"Go get help," I said. I wanted to say something brave, like *Don't worry* or *I'll be fine,* but lying didn't seem like a good idea at the moment. I closed my eyes, pressed my hands against Nimue's leg, and entered the dream.

It was unlike any I'd been in before. The scene was as solid and realistic as any of Eli's, but everything was washed out, like a photograph faded over time. I was standing in the middle of a vast field of tall grass. The stalks around me were wilted as if from a rainless summer under a hot sun. They brushed against my legs and arms, stirred by a faint breeze. I winced as welts rose on my skin where they touched me despite my clothes. I tried to jump up and fly above the grass, but something held me in place.

Yes, this was definitely unlike any dream I'd been in before. No bending the laws of physics, it seemed. I wasn't a god in here. I was just me. A teenage girl as scared and helpless as a rat in a maze.

Go back, Dusty, a voice whispered in my mind. *Don't do this. You're too weak.* The worst part was I knew I *could* go back. Slipping out would be as easy as taking a breath. All my instincts were screaming at me to leave.

Ignoring the urge, I stayed put and looked around, wondering what to do next. There was no sign of Nimue. The sword could be anywhere. As far as I knew this dream world could go on forever, as endless as outer space.

A few feet in front of me, I saw a patch of crumpled grass and guessed it was the place where my mother had arrived. A clear trail extended out from it, heading toward the sun sinking behind a forest in the distance. Bracing myself for pain, I leaped toward the crumpled grass. Now instead of leaving welts, the stalks sliced into me like razors. I screamed, then immediately wished I hadn't as something else screamed back in answer. Something not human.

A flock of birds alighted into the sky from the forest and soared toward me. The screams became screeches as they drew closer. Only they weren't birds, but *bats*. Ones with fat-cheeked human faces like babies. I wanted to run away as I saw their needle-like teeth, but fear of the grass held me in place. I ducked, covering my head with my arms as the bats swooped down at me. Claws clutched at my clothes and yanked my hair. I swatted at them blindly, knocking one aside only to have another sink its teeth into my hand. Pain lit up my arm, making me woozy.

Desperate, I tried to think of some way out of this. The easiest thing would be to leave the dream completely. But what would I tell my friends if I came back without even trying? No, I had to think, had to fight.

I couldn't bend reality here like in a normal dream, no imagining a giant paddle to swat them with, but I didn't know about using magic. Magic *was* my reality. Quickly deciding that fire was the best weapon, I grabbed a handful of the tall grass and yanked it out, ignoring the sting as it sliced my hand. Then I muttered the fire incantation, feeling no hope that it would work.

The tips of the grass burst into flames. I didn't question it, but stood up and started waving my makeshift torch in the air. The bats shrieked away from the fire, only to swerve and try again. Over and over they came down at me, but I drove them off, feeling a perverse pleasure whenever one of them let out a shriek as the fire singed them.

When the last of the bats gave up, I watched them disappear into the sky. I threw what remained of the grass to the ground, shaky with exhaustion. The fire spell had drained my energy. There was something wrong with the fictus in this dream. As if there weren't any here at all.

At least I wasn't as afraid as before. Surviving a bat attack had a way of bolstering bravery. I took off at a slow jog, following my mother's path through the grass. I couldn't imagine how much it must've hurt her to come through here first, but I appreciated how much easier she'd made it for me.

After a while, I entered the forest filled with trees the width of houses. My fear began to grow again with every step as I heard the sound of things moving through the brush and rustling the branches overhead, but after walking for what felt like an hour nothing attacked me.

When I came around a bend in the trail, I realized why. A dead animal that looked like a combination of a wolf and a scorpion was lying across the path. I carefully stepped around it, making sure not to disturb the brush for fear of alerting other beasts to my presence the way I had the bats. I passed another half dozen of those dead wolf things with their curved tails like a scorpion's stinger and pincers on their front feet instead of paws and was again thoroughly glad my mother had come in before me.

Eventually, the path began to slope downward, and I caught glimpses of water through the massive trees. Distracted, I didn't notice when the trail abruptly ended in a drop-off to a rocky beach below. I slid over the side, yelping in surprise and renewed pain as dirt coated the cuts on my legs and arms.

I stood up, brushed myself off, and approached the water's edge. The lake was small enough that I could see the shore on the other side, but the water in between was murky and eerily still. I knew I had to go *in* that water. It was the only way to go other than out of the dream or back up the bank into the forest. The idea of jumping in filled me with terror. *Anything* could be in there. Slimy, slithering things that might grab hold of me and pull me down.

If that happens, just leave. But after my run-in with the black phoenix, I knew better than to trust in an exit.

A scuttling sound echoed in the woods above me, and I dove in. I had no idea how to kill one of those wolf-scorpion things, and I wasn't keen on figuring it out. The water was so cold I almost fainted from the shock, but the sight of dark shapes moving toward me was all it took to drive off the dizziness. I dove downward toward a faint light in the distance. The dark shapes swooped closer, and I swam harder and faster, wishing I could transform into a fish.

When I reached the source of the light, I saw it was some kind of dome on the bottom of the lake. My mother stood just inside it, dripping wet but no longer submerged. In the center of the dome, a sword stuck up hilt first out of the lake bed. The sword was the light source. Even from outside the dome, I could see the magic pulsating from it.

I swam to the dome's edge, passing through it as if it were made of air instead of something solid enough to hold back water. I plopped to the ground with a wet thud, startling my mother who turned around, poised to strike. Shock, then anger crossed her face at the sight of me.

"What are you doing? Where's Bethany?"

I wiped water off my face. "We set her free."

"You did *what*?" Her eyes flashed.

I pushed myself up to my feet. "I can't let you do this, Mom."

I realized how unprepared I was for this moment. Sadness and pity squeezed my chest, and I held back a sob. Until now I'd always been secretly proud of my mother, of her fierce independence, her reputation as being someone unafraid to do her own thing no matter what people thought. But not anymore. Now I saw a desperate, power-hungry woman. A murderer.

"The sword *must* be destroyed," Moira said.

I took a step forward. "No. I won't let you."

"I don't have time for this right now." She turned toward the sword once more.

I raised my hand and pointed. "Hypno-soma."

Nothing happened.

My mother turned back, outrage on her face. "What the hell?"

I tried again. Still nothing.

My mother cast her own dazing curse to the same effect. It wasn't like how The Will absorbed magic, but as if there weren't any magic at all, like we were in some kind of magic-free zone. Mom and I came to the same conclusion at the same time, and we both sprinted for the sword. She reached it first, but I crashed into her, knocking her to the ground.

My mother was more experienced at fighting than me, but she wasn't stronger or faster. Neither of us played by any rules. We pulled hair and bit and kicked and scratched. I saw a nasty-looking wound on Moira's side that looked as if something had taken a bite out of her, probably one of those wolf-scorpion things. I tried my hardest to grab hold of it.

She caught onto this strategy at once, and before I knew it she managed to get behind me, pin her arms around my neck, and cut off my ability to breathe. I clawed at her, but she wouldn't budge.

"Stop fighting me, Destiny," Moira said. "You've got to

trust me. I'm your mother. I don't want to hurt you, but the sword has to be destroyed."

Panic was a living thing inside me, a demon that had possessed me, making me thrash and kick.

Through my hazy vision, I saw something approach the dome. My mother's grip loosened as she saw it, too, and I was able to take a full breath. Then we both gaped in surprise as Bethany Grey emerged from the water beyond.

Moira whispered in my ear with a note of panic in her voice, "You've got to help me, Destiny. Beth's the villain here, not me."

I bit back my automatic denial of this lie and nodded. Bethany had been looking intently at me, sending me a silent message—she was here to help. Together we could overcome.

Moira let go of me, not once disbelieving my nod of agreement. As soon as I was free, I turned on her, Bethany jumping to help me. Mom was no match for the two of us, and when we finally managed to pin her down, Bethany was heavy enough to keep her there.

"Get the sword. I'll hold her until you're out," Bethany said.

I fought back guilt at the sight of my mother struggling to break free. "Don't hurt her," I said.

Bethany bobbed her head, her face pinched with effort.

I approached the sword cautiously, both afraid and mesmerized by it. The hilt looked made of bone, and strange rune marks ran down the blade. I wrapped my hands around the hilt, and raw energy shot through me so hard it almost knocked me over. But I held on and yanked upward.

Resistance. Something held the sword in place. I squatted down and pulled with everything I had. Finally, slowly, the sword began to move. When it at last came free of its earthen sheath, I saw why it had been so difficult to remove. A woman was clawing her way out of the lake bed from the place where the sword had been, like a zombie emerging from a grave.

Only she wasn't some monster, but Nimue, her face ageless and familiar. Our gazes locked on each other, and I could sense her appraisal. A moment later she nodded, and the last of the resistance on the sword vanished.

"Go," Nimue whispered.

I shut my eyes, but I had no idea how to bring the sword out of the dream. I'd only done such a thing once before with the Milky Way, but that had been unintentional. Still, there was nothing else to do but try. Holding the sword tightly, I *imagined* myself bringing it out.

Nothing happened. I couldn't leave the dream at all, sword or no. I looked around, fighting back alarm.

"You must take it beyond the dome," Nimue said, and her voice was like a soothing balm on my nerves. "But don't let him have it. *Never* let him have it."

I watched her slowly sinking back into the lake bed. Then casting one last glance at Bethany and my mother, I dashed for the dome's edge and plunged through it into the cold, dark water. It seemed all the creatures out there were waiting for me, unspeakable things with red eyes and forked tongues. I closed my eyes and tried again, willing myself and the sword out of the dream.

For a terrible moment, nothing happened. The creatures closed in. Something hard and scaly brushed against my leg. Then with a jolt, my consciousness rejoined my body. I opened my eyes and saw the sword was still in my hands.

I stood up, my limbs trembling both from the terror of Nimue's dream and grief over my mother, but also from joy at my victory.

Something was wrong.

Eli and Selene were lying on the floor a few feet away from the tomb in the same position as we'd found Bethany, wrists and ankles bound with silver rope. They were gagged as well with more silver rope. Paul stood over them.

My brain couldn't make sense of it. "What are you doing?"

Paul looked at me, but before he could answer a familiar voice spoke from my left. "Anything I ask him to. Anything at all."

I jerked my head in the direction of the voice and saw Mr. Marrow standing there, looking at the sword in my hand with something more than curiosity. He walked over, a broad smile on his face. "Well done, Dusty. You've far exceeded my expectations. Now, hand over my sword."

His sword? I blinked at him.

Then I remembered what Bethany had said about how

the Red Warlock could be anybody. Was it possible? Could it have been Marrow all along?

That was when I noticed it. There, perched on the end of the tomb and staring at me with the same look of satisfaction as its master, was the real black phoenix. It was even more fierce and terrible than it had been in Eli's dreams.

~ 24 ~

The Red Warlock

B ut that means you're . . . you're . . ." I couldn't say it out loud. The words wouldn't come.

"Merlin is the name you're looking for, I believe. Although it's the wrong name," said Marrow.

"But it *can't* be you."

"Oh, but it is. I warned you, didn't I? That the killer was clever enough to use you without you knowing it."

I gritted my teeth. "You didn't use me."

A sneer twisted Marrow's features. "Are you so sure? I'm the one who told your mother what the Keeper spell was guarding. I'm the one who planted in her mind the idea of telling you as a way to scare you off. But I knew your reaction would be just the opposite. A rebellious nature is so easily predictable."

I opened my mouth to argue, but I couldn't, as a sickening feeling rose up in the pit of my stomach. Beside me, the black phoenix crooned, as if to mock me.

"I *needed* you to know about the sword, you see," Marrow continued. "You're the dream-seer. I needed you to find the location of this tomb for me. You've done well. I'm grateful. Now give me my sword."

I shook my head, but it was pointless. Marrow raised his wizard's staff toward me, free of its cane glamour, and with one casual flick, he ripped the sword from my hands. He heaved a sigh as he grasped the hilt. The look on his face was like someone welcoming home a lover. He dropped his cane, seized the sword with both hands, and waved it over his head in a circle. A shower of magic rained out from the tip and sprayed downward around him, obscuring him from sight for a moment.

When the magic cleared, he no longer wore his usual suit but a crimson cloak over a pair of loose-fitting black pants and undershirt. His face was changed as well. He looked younger, his skin less careworn and wrinkled. Yet he was older, too, ageless like Nimue. It seemed his transformation was complete. The teacher I'd known was gone, an ancient, evil wizard in his place. For there was no denying he was evil. He'd murdered those people. It took all the courage I possessed not to run away screaming.

"Is it done then?" asked Paul. He sounded both relieved and anxious. I looked at him, my chest seizing from a literal heartache. I couldn't believe he was involved. It seemed impossible. He'd even tried to stop us from coming this way. Why?

Marrow turned his gaze to Paul, eyes assessing. "See for yourself." With a flick of the sword, he sent his staff flying across the room into Paul's outstretched hands. "Give it a try on the girl."

Before I knew what Marrow meant, Paul turned toward Selene, pointed the staff, and said, "Ana-acro."

Selene's body rose into the air, hoisted by the silver rope around her wrists. She shrieked in pain, limbs straining. I gaped at Paul's sudden ability to do magic.

Jumping off the tomb, I shouted the counter-spell. The magic surged out from my fingers, but Marrow deflected it with a spell from the sword. No, not deflected. He *absorbed* it into the sword like The Will always did.

Whoever controls the sword, controls The Will, my mom had said. The Will didn't work on Nightmares, yet the sword did. I couldn't understand it.

"There's no point in trying to attack," Marrow said. "Your spell casting has certainly improved, but it's no match for me. And I wouldn't try running away, either. Phoenixes fly very fast, you know." The bird crooned as if in emphasis, the sound as beautiful and deadly as it had been in the dream.

Paul lowered a now-whimpering Selene back to the ground, breaking the spell. Beside her, Eli looked fit to kill.

I stared at Paul, the truth clawing at my insides. "You're the F from Rosemary's diary, aren't you? It was never Culpepper."

He nodded. "Paul *Foster* Kirkwood. I've no idea why Rose fixated on my middle name, but it did its job in hiding my identity."

"How *could* you?"

He flinched before his expression hardened. "You don't

understand what it's like to be so powerless. To be *hated* by your own family. Your own *mother*."

"But you killed them. Rosemary and Mr. Ankil."

"I didn't . . . kill . . . only . . . helped."

"*Why?*" I choked on the emotions raging through me at his betrayal. He'd used me as he had Rosemary. None of the things we'd shared had been real.

"Leave him be," Marrow said. "Paul did what he had to do to be free."

I glowered at Marrow. "Free from *what?*"

"It was only The Will preventing him from using magic. But the spell, at least as you knew it, is no more, due in no small amount to Paul. This sword has the ability to absorb magic and to hold it like a reservoir, making it possible for The Will to work on magickind. But the spell wasn't intended for them. I created it as a weapon against the ordinaries who persecuted us. A thousand years ago magickind were far fewer in number and most of us lived in isolation, easily overpowered by the sheer number of ordinaries. The spell gave me control over the mind and will of mankind, forcing them into submission where they belonged. Where they would be now if the Magi had never stolen the sword and spell from me."

I gaped at his lunacy. It was like listening to the magical reincarnation of Hitler. "What does this have to do with Paul?"

Marrow pointed the sword downward, resting the tip of the blade on the floor. "The only reason Paul couldn't do magic is because the Magi and their Will-Workers manipulated my spell to prevent *halfkinds* from using their powers at all. Most of them, anyway."

I scoffed. "Why would they do that?"

Marrow straightened up to his full height. He seemed so much taller and imposing now. "Because they feared halfkinds above all others. *I* am halfkind, the first one ever born. Half-wizard and half-demon but more powerful than either. That's the way it works, usually. The Magi don't approve of anyone more powerful than they are, so they enforced sterility through the spell as a way to stop the kinds from interbreeding. Not anymore though. Now *I* control The Will. And you've helped set so many free, Dusty. You should be proud."

I wasn't. Choked by guilt, I understood the full weight of what I'd done. All that magic no longer in check. But I hadn't done it on purpose. I didn't know what I was doing.

You didn't think, that nasty voice whispered in my head. *You never stop to think.*

Marrow's gaze shifted from me to the tomb, and I turned to see that Bethany Grey had returned from the dream. For a moment my heart leaped, convinced that here was the answer to getting out of this. Together we might be able to overcome the Red Warlock.

She smiled at Marrow, her face shining in triumph.

"Well done, Bethany," he said.

"But . . . ," I stammered. "You're working for *him*?"

Bethany's grin widened.

"Then my mother . . ."

"Was trying to destroy the sword before I could get to it," Bethany said, stepping down.

"But your finger . . ."

"Cut it off myself. Self-maiming is the only way to survive the breaking of a Keeper spell, don't you know."

I shivered, but my disgust at her actions quickly turned to anger. "You *tricked* me."

"No," said Marrow, clucking his tongue. "You tricked yourself. Paul told me how easily you suspected your mother once I told you the truth about your kind. And of course, my encouragement of her only helped. She's also been doing her own search to find me, but her actions only made her look more suspicious. Still, she almost succeeded in getting the sword first. She might have if she had shared what she found out. But she didn't. I suppose you can blame it on her distrust of everyone. Even you."

I shook my head, wanting to deny it.

Marrow looked at Bethany. "Where is Moira now?"

"Dead," Bethany replied.

A terrible pressure seized my lungs, and I swayed on my feet, unable to breathe. It couldn't be true. It couldn't. Then I realized my mother was no longer sitting upright in the dream-feeding position, but had slumped forward, lying as still as someone . . . someone . . . dead.

An anguished cry escaped my throat, the sound a pale, pitiful reflection of the despair raging inside me. "You killed her. You killed her! *I'll kill you.*" I bounded toward Bethany.

Marrow's dazing spell struck me in the back, and I fell forward, hitting the ground. I lay there for a moment, my body seized with pain. I'd never been hit so hard before, never felt magic so powerful. Was this how all spells would be now that Marrow controlled The Will?

When the pain eased, I rolled over and saw Bethany standing over me, holding out her uninjured hand. "There's no reason to be so upset. You're better off without her."

How many times had I told myself that very thing, when I was younger, resenting her absence in my life? Hundreds. But it wasn't true. It never had been. I shook my head as I sat up and curled into a ball, arms wrapped around my knees. Guilt at my betrayal scorched like acid poured over my heart.

Marrow knelt in front of me. Then he said in a kind, soothing voice, "I understand your anger, Dusty. I understand your hurt and loss. You've a right to them, no doubt. But you must accept that hurt and loss are a consequence of war. And this *is* war, Dusty. You just didn't know it. But now it's time to choose your side."

I fought back the urge to cry. I couldn't give in to my emotions now. I'd failed my mom, but there was still Eli and Selene to think about. It was my fault they were here. I had to find a way to get them out, and I couldn't do that while overcome by grief.

Marrow continued. "The Magi must be stopped. Magickind needs to be free, and those that choose to follow me *will* be freed." He adjusted his grip on the sword as if preparing to use it. "We shouldn't have to disguise ourselves with glamour. Shouldn't be forced to blend in with the ordinary world, adopting their crude ways of life, like using electricity and natural gas to run our homes. Magic can do those things for us. Ordinary technologies are a nuisance, all those cell phones and televisions. And some of them are even *dangerous*. Take the Internet, for example. Did you know Paul has created a website that allows me to recruit for my very own army? Hundreds of oppressed magickind, organized and ready to fight with a mere click of a button."

I shivered at the implications. With social networking sites he could coordinate wide-scale attacks with ease. *I've got to do something.* Not just for Eli and Selene, but for everybody.

With adrenaline pumping through my system, a focus came over my mind. I needed to find a way out of this. "How did the Magi steal your spell in the first place?"

I didn't expect Marrow to answer, but he said at once, "I fell in love with the wrong woman, and she betrayed me." He stood and approached the tomb, forgetting about me for a moment. He lifted my mother's body out of the tomb with his magic and tossed her over the side, out of sight. I bit my tongue, holding back a cry.

Marrow peered into the tomb. "But she wasn't just any woman, my Nimue. She was my dream-seer, and I hers."

Comprehension struck me. "You and she were—"

"The same as you and Eli, yes. Dream-seers have a special bond, you know. One that far exceeds anything physical." He reached into the tomb and stroked Nimue's cheek.

"Uh-huh. Right. So her betrayal makes *perfect* sense then."

"She had her reasons. And she made her choice." Marrow withdrew his hand and then raised Excalibur over his head, holding it like a stake with the blade pointed at Nimue. He drove it downward into her body with one fierce stroke.

I screamed, but the sound was drowned out by another scream, one so loud it shook the walls of the chamber, raining down bits of rock on top of us. Magic fueled that scream, giving it weight and power. Marrow hadn't only killed Nimue; he'd broken whatever spell had enabled her to live so long, trapped in a dream of her own making.

The silence afterward rang almost as loudly as the scream. Blood rushed in my ears as deafening as a storm-swept river. I didn't want to die, too.

Marrow walked back to me, holding the sword casually as if he hadn't just used it to kill. Blood dripped from the tip, leaving red splotches on the ground.

"Don't be upset, Dusty," he said. "Nimue was a prisoner, but I've given her rest at last. It's more than she deserved after her betrayal, I assure you."

Even though I was more afraid than I'd ever been in my life, I still couldn't keep my mouth from running away with me. "Rest. Revenge. Same difference, right?"

Marrow smiled at me with something like affection. I recoiled from the look, disgust churning in my belly. "You remind me of her in many ways. Same feisty spirit, same talent as a dream-seer. Perhaps that's why I've always been so fond of you. I hope you will consider joining me. You and Eli. There's nothing more valuable than a dreamseer pair. I can give you everything and anything you want. Just ask Paul. His greatest desire was to do magic. And now he can."

I shook my head, still hearing the sound of Nimue's death cry echoing in my mind. His pitch about freeing magickind from oppression would've been more effective if he wasn't going around murdering innocent people. "No. Not *ever*."

Marrow sighed. "I can't say I didn't expect this reaction. You inherited Nimue's bull-headedness as well." He motioned at Paul. "Make her change her mind."

Paul shook his head, his face going pale. "I . . . I can't. Not on her."

Marrow pointed the bloodstained sword at him. "You *will* do it or I will take back what I have given you."

"Wait," I said, trying to delay again. "First tell me how you did it. I know what happened with Rosemary, but what about Mr. Ankil? How did you get him down in that tunnel with all the senate watching out for him?"

Marrow looked at me, a smug smile on his lips. "More easily than you could imagine. Paul, you see, was never as powerless as his uncle believed. He is half-siren, able to manipulate and seduce despite The Will. A useful talent under the right circumstances. The more desperate or lonely the person targeted, the more effective the power. Arturo Ankil was an easy mark, unable to resist when Paul lured him out of the dance right under the nose of his guard."

I swallowed, disgusted at the image that rose in my mind. I didn't want to look at Paul, but I couldn't stop myself. His eyes were fixed on the floor, his face now red. A muscle ticked in his jaw.

"But don't be too quick to judge poor Arturo," said Marrow. "Not until we see how *you* fare against the same power." He waved Paul forward.

I tried to stand and run away, but Marrow held me in place with his magic. I steeled myself as Paul approached and knelt before me, setting Marrow's staff on the ground beside us. When he raised his hands to my face I jerked away.

"Don't fight, Dusty," Paul whispered. "Please don't fight. He'll *kill* you."

"What do you care?" Hatred and pity warred inside me. "You lied to me. You *forced* me to like you. It was just magic. *Fake.*"

"No, it wasn't, I swear. Everything was real between us."

I shook my head, refusing to believe him.

"Enough," Marrow said. "Get on with it. Now."

I cut my eyes to Marrow, glaring at him as hatred scorched my insides. "Why don't you just use that stupid sword and The Will spell to make me do what you want? Why bother with siren magic?"

"Explain it to her," Marrow said to Paul.

Paul exhaled. "For the oath's magic to work you must choose to say it, not be forced. I'm not going to make you say the oath. I'm supposed to make you *want* to say it."

Paul cupped my face with his hands, and I heard him whisper, "Why didn't you listen and go the other way like I wanted?" Before I could respond his eyes locked on mine and something strange happened. The disgust vanished, an attraction far more powerful than any I'd ever felt before rising in its place. I had a wild urge to kiss him and run my fingers through his hair. I knew it wasn't real, that it wasn't *me,* but I couldn't fight off the feeling. It was like being swept under by a wave so strong I couldn't tell which way was up or down.

He began to speak in a low, velvety voice. "Join us, Dusty. Swear allegiance to Marrow and you and I can be together forever. It's what I want. It's what you want, too, isn't it?"

I felt myself nodding.

"Yes, that's right," Paul murmured. "Now all you have to do is speak the oath. It's a simple spell, really. I'll say it first, and you repeat after me. All right?"

"All right."

" 'On't, 'usty."

The strange words barely registered in my ears, which seemed stuffed with cotton.

" 'On't oo it."

Were these the words I was supposed to be repeating? I closed my eyes, and my mind cleared a bit.

"Look at me, Dusty," Paul said, squeezing my face.

" *'On't!'* " that other voice said again, and I realized it was Eli, trying to speak through the gag.

"Be quiet," Marrow said, and Eli cried out in pain.

"No," I said, but my voice was weak.

"Open your eyes and look at me," said Paul.

I shook my head, but it was no good. My eyes opened of their own accord as my will gave way to his. I didn't mind. My head ached, and I tasted the blood in my mouth from where it had run from my nose. It was easier not to fight.

"Okay," I said. "I'll do it."

Paul opened his mouth to continue, but his eyes wavered on my face. The shift in his vision was just enough for his hold on me to ease.

"Wait," I said, pushing against his magic. "Eli will, too."

"Hold on, Paul," said Marrow, taking a step toward us.

Paul let go of me, and the spell broke completely.

"What did you say, Dusty?" Marrow said.

I struggled to my feet, an idea forming in my mind. "I'll go through with it, swear whatever oath you want, but first let me convince Eli to do it with me. I need him."

Eli was shaking his head, his eyes wide with horror at my words.

Marrow frowned. "What makes you think you can?"

"You said yourself that dream-seers share a special bond. It's the same with me and Eli. I can do it."

"We'll see," said Marrow. He motioned at Paul. "Bring Eli here."

Paul approached Eli and muttered the counter-spell to release him from the binding curse. The silver ropes fell away, and Eli let out a relieved groan. Paul hauled Eli to his feet and steered him toward me.

"What are you doing, Dusty?" Eli said as Paul forced him to a stop in front of me.

I shook my head at him, just slightly, trying to tell him with my eyes to play along. I glanced at Bethany, who stood leaning against the tomb, looking bored. I fixed her position in my mind then took a step toward Eli, putting myself in line between him and Marrow.

"Do you remember the first time you found out what I was? You know, that night at your house when you kicked me out of your dream, and then you knocked me off your bed, and I tried to get away but couldn't?"

Eli blinked, frowning. "Yeah?"

I nodded, encouragingly. "Well, this is going to be just like *that*." I threw my hand toward him. "*Hypno-soma!*"

The spell shot from my fingers, struck Eli, and rebounded. I ducked, and the magic soared past me right into Marrow. He stumbled backward, the sword going slack in his hand.

I aimed a spell at Paul, but Eli punched him in the face first, then kicked him in the stomach, knocking him over. Eli jumped on top of him, fists swinging.

I spun around, going for Bethany. She cast a jab curse at me, but I blocked then countered. She ducked sideways, avoiding my spell. Before either of us could cast another one, a strange noise echoed around the room. The piercing howl of a dog. No, not a dog. A hellhound.

I glanced to my right and saw George charging us,

fangs bared and eyes glowing. Marrow, who had only now recovered, flung a spell at the animal, but George jumped over it easily.

Bethany cast a spell at the hound, but before it reached George, a magic shield popped up around him, and the spell bounced off, streaking upward and striking the ceiling. Huge chunks of rock broke free and fell down on us. One struck me behind the ear, making me see stars.

I blinked them away in time to see George drawing close. I fell down as I tried to avoid him, but the hellhound leaped past me, going for Marrow who had been knocked over by the falling rock. But before George reached him, the black phoenix swooped down. It collided with the hound and sent him careening sideways, yelping.

Someone cried out in alarm, and as I got back to my feet, I saw it was Culpepper. He was in full demon mode, green eyes aglow and horns exposed. He aimed a spell at the phoenix, only to have it countered by Bethany. At the same time, Marrow struck Culpepper with a curse I didn't recognize, but it lifted Culpepper off his feet, spun him like a top, and flung him halfway across the room.

I bashed Marrow in the knee with my foot. His eyes widened in surprise, and he went down, striking the floor with a satisfying smack. I dove for Excalibur still in Marrow's hands, but one of Bethany's spells hit me. Gashes appeared on my arms and down my side where the magic struck, slicing through clothes and skin. I screamed and turned on her.

"Come on, little girl," Bethany taunted. "Give it a try."

Boom!

A spell struck the ceiling above Bethany, raining down more rocks on top of her, enough that she disappeared beneath them. I had no idea where the spell came from, but then a voice I would've recognized anywhere said, "You never did know when to shut up, Beth."

My mother stood up from behind the tomb.

"*Mom!*" Relief and joy filled me near to bursting, making me feel weightless.

Moira pointed a hand at me and uttered a spell. I backed up, bracing for the attack, but the magic hit Marrow instead.

"Get behind the tomb, Destiny," Moira said as she aimed another spell at Marrow.

I took an automatic step toward her then remembered Selene. I pointed at her. "Ou-agra." The silver ropes fell away at once, and she bounded to her feet.

"Watch out, Eli!" Selene shouted, and she let fly a befuddlement jinx. I glanced over my shoulder to see the spell strike Paul. He swayed on his feet, and Eli punched him again, sending him reeling.

A shriek echoed above us, and I looked up to see the black phoenix diving toward me. Before I could react, Selene cast a jab jinx at it. The phoenix screeched as the spell grazed its side, the sound more angry than hurt. It veered toward Selene and crashed into her so hard she flew backward, head striking the floor.

"Fligere!" I said, letting off my own jab. This one hit the

phoenix in the back. It lurched sideways off Selene and then flew up into the air and away from us.

I raced over to Selene and dropped to my knees beside her. She was unconscious. Three deep, bleeding cuts ran down one side of her face from forehead to chin.

"Stay down, Dusty!"

I looked up in time to see Eli launch a rock into the air, aimed at the black phoenix, which was swooping down toward Selene and me. The rock struck the bird at the base of its left wing. It let out an outraged screech and then spun away, now flying erratically.

Eli sprinted toward me. He picked Selene up and threw her over his shoulder. Then he and I dashed toward the tomb where my mom was keeping Marrow on the defensive. He stood with Excalibur in front of him, deflecting and absorbing each spell.

Eli set Selene down at the base of the tomb, shielding her from most of the danger. I glanced around, on the lookout for the black phoenix.

A few feet away, Bethany had managed to free herself from the rocks. Blood ran down the side of her face from a cut on her forehead. She charged us, arm flung out as she cast another one of those cutting curses at me. Eli jumped in front of the spell, pushing me out of the way. I stumbled sideways, just barely staying on my feet. The spell struck Eli full force. Gashes appeared on his chest through his shredded clothes. The spell knocked him backward, and his head struck the side of a rock as he fell.

I cast a shield spell, deflecting Bethany's second attack. I needed to stop her before she took us all out. Behind me, my mother was still casting at Marrow. She had to be exhausted.

I raised my hand to throw the binding spell at Bethany, only to have Culpepper beat me to it. Silver ropes wrapped around Bethany from head to toe, and she toppled sideways. Culpepper came running toward us, limping badly on one leg and flinging spells up into the air at the black phoenix, which was trying to get at us. I could tell he was exhausted, too.

I grabbed Eli's arm and dragged him as near to the base of the tomb as I could. To my relief, he was still conscious, although dazed. Hoping Culpepper could manage against the phoenix, I turned and joined my mother. Side-by-side we took on Marrow.

Although we were keeping him occupied, I understood at once that it was hopeless. There seemed no way to get around the sword's ability to absorb spells. I even tried flinging rocks at him just like we learned in psionics, but Marrow repulsed them easily.

I tried to puzzle out how the sword could absorb a Nightmare's magic but The Will couldn't. Maybe it was the difference between a spell set to run on autopilot and one being actively controlled by a wizard, like the difference between playing a live opponent in a video game instead of the computer. The Will couldn't deflect Nightmares because it couldn't intuit magic based on imagination. But Marrow could. He could see, hear, and imagine himself.

With this realization, I edged my way around the tomb. If I could sneak behind Marrow, or at least far enough that he couldn't deflect both me and my mother at the same time, I might be able to disarm him.

As I moved, I saw Excalibur begin to glow. First a faint purple light emanating from the runes on the blade, then the blade itself until it looked like a torch lit with Everlasting Fire. A slow smile stretched across Marrow's face, and he started to laugh.

The sword's a reservoir, he had said. And a reservoir could only hold so much before it overflowed.

I felt the tremor of the power building a second before it unleashed in a brilliant explosion of magic that pulsed outward like a nuclear bomb. The tomb shattered as the spell hit it, and I was thrown backward so hard I collided with the wall. I fell to the ground, dazed and paralyzed by pain.

I heard the sound of footsteps approaching a moment later. It was Marrow, still laughing. He was the only one standing, the only one unaffected by the sword's explosion.

He peered down at me. "It was a valiant try, but there is nothing more powerful than this sword. Took me more than a lifetime to find it, you know, and even longer to learn the secret to make it obey my command."

He knelt beside me and sighed. "You should have joined me when you had the chance. But my gratitude remains nonetheless. I will let you live, Dusty Everhart. For now. But not Eli, I'm afraid. If you won't be *my* dream-seer then you will be no one's."

He turned away, holding the sword downward like a stake again. I saw Eli lying in the rubble nearby, and I knew what Marrow intended. But I didn't have the strength to cast another spell. I felt as if every bone in my body had been broken, and my muscle and sinew vaporized.

Try, Dusty. You've got to try.

I managed to push myself up on one elbow. A thousand images danced in my head, pictures of all the people Marrow had killed, all the people he *would* kill. Rosemary, Ankil, Nimue, Moira, Selene, Eli, Rosemary, Ankil . . . *Ankil . . . the snatch-and-smack.*

It was moronically simple, effortless. I remembered Ankil explaining how The Will couldn't anticipate the move if you did it fast enough and didn't try to hold on. You just had to use the laws of physics within the spell. Maybe even the most powerful magickind of all time wouldn't be able to anticipate it, either.

I reached out and snatched the sword from Marrow's hand with my magic in one quick motion, then let go. As it started to fall, I smacked the hilt downward with all the energy I had left.

The blade struck Marrow in the chest, sinking straight through him. He gasped, staggering on his feet. He turned his eyes to me, shock on his face. Then he started to laugh. And he kept on laughing even as his knees buckled and he fell forward, driving the blade even further into his body.

I turned away from the sight, sickened. I couldn't believe it. I'd killed Marrow. The Red Warlock was dead. It was over.

My relief vanished a moment later as a loud, angry cry echoed above me. I'd forgotten about the black phoenix. It was a fatal mistake. I slumped in defeat, helpless to defend myself. There was nothing left inside me to fight with.

The black phoenix flew toward me only to veer away at the last second. I turned my head in mild surprise, wondering if it was playing some kind of game with me. Then I heard something crackle. I looked over to where Marrow had fallen. His body burst into flames, quickly turning to ash.

The black phoenix swooped down, mouth open, and swallowed the flames and ash whole. Then the bird vanished, leaving behind only the scorched outline of a body on the floor with a sword lying in its center.

I stared at it for several long moments. Then everything went black.

Something moved in the rubble, drawing near. I didn't know what it was. I wasn't sure I cared. I was too tired, too hurt.

A hand touched my forehead, fingers gentle. "You all right?" *Eli.* Voice low and rough from exhaustion. "Please tell me you're all right. Please, Dusty."

I nodded.

He exhaled, his breath a caress against my face. He leaned over me and pulled me into his arms, his body a comforting weight against my own. I was alive. We both were.

Then he kissed me. His lips were impossibly soft against mine, and hot enough to warm my skin. The kiss was short but tender, filled with relief. *Finally, a good dream,* I thought before drifting back to sleep once more, still cradled in his arms.

~ 25 ~

Nightmare Investigations

Arkwell's infirmary had never been so full. Or so Nurse Philpot kept saying every time she walked past my room. By some ironic twist of fate, I'd ended up in the same room they put me in the night Mr. Ankil died, giving me full view of the nurse's station and ample opportunity to eavesdrop. Which I did—often.

I'd been stuck in here for two days, under constant observation even though most of my injuries from the showdown with the Red Warlock were already fading. I guessed maybe they were worried I would go insane or something after the ordeal. But I was doing okay. I'd survived, after all. That was something to be happy about.

My only visitor, besides Sheriff Brackenberry, who'd come to record my account of what happened, was Dr. Hendershaw. I was still sore at her for my toilet duty. She thanked me for my bravery and expressed the school's gratitude and all of that. I asked her if this meant my detention was canceled, but she said it wasn't. Yeah, there was gratitude for you.

I kept asking every nurse who stopped by for updates on Selene, Eli, and my mother. They reassured me they were fine and recovering quickly, but no one was willing to say when I would be allowed to see them. I wanted to desperately, if for different reasons. My memories after the fight with Marrow were fuzzy to say the least. I had no recollection of the police arriving, although I knew Culpepper was the one to fetch them. And I couldn't remember how I'd gotten from the cavern to the infirmary, either.

But I did remember Eli kissing me. I just didn't know if it was real or not. Or how I felt about it.

Finally, I had another visitor, one I wasn't disappointed to see. Lady Elaine looked far older and frailer than the last time we'd met. She came in and sat on the edge of my bed.

"I'm so sorry," she said in a resigned voice. "I take full responsibility for what happened. I failed to recognize Marrow for what he was." She took a deep breath then cleared her throat, the sound like broken glass. "I should have been suspicious when he offered to help analyze your dream journal entries. And even *more* suspicious when he suggested Bethany would make a good Keeper for the darkkind ring. But I was fooled by his charm and intellect."

"It's all right," I said, uncomfortable with her confession. "He fooled everybody, didn't he? And he's like thousands of years old. He's had a lot of time to get good at hoodwinking people."

Lady Elaine smiled. "True, but I'm not exactly inexperienced myself. Nevertheless, I thank you for being understanding. And for defeating him, of course. It's quite remarkable, you know."

I shook my head, thinking about Mr. Ankil and what he'd told me about the arrogance of witchkind. I'd decided this was the only explanation for how I'd overcome Marrow. Because he was cocky. "I just got lucky," I said.

Lady Elaine patted my hand. "Sometimes that's all you need. Now, is there anything I can do for you?"

"I want to see my friends. And my mom."

"Yes, I'm sure you do. The nurse told me they're planning to discharge you tomorrow. You'll be able to visit them then."

"So they're not here in the infirmary?" Out of habit, I glanced at the door, hoping I might catch one of them walking by.

Lady Elaine glanced at the door, too, then shook her head. "Selene and Eli left a short while ago. They wanted to see you, but weren't allowed. Your mother is still here."

I swallowed. My guilt over what I'd done to her had only gotten worse in the long hours I'd been forced to lie in this bed. "Is she all right?"

"She's fine. Just very weak."

"Oh. Has she asked to see me?"

Lady Elaine hesitated, looking uncomfortable. "I don't know."

"Okay." I wanted her to leave so I could have a good cry, but she didn't seem to be in any hurry. Deciding to make the most of it, I asked, "So what happens now? What did they do with the sword?"

Lady Elaine brushed a piece of lint off the blanket, not meeting my eyes. "It will be destroyed."

"So no more Will?"

She nodded. "It seems when you killed Marrow the spell broke completely. It was so old and so complicated no one knows how to rebuild it from scratch, I'm afraid."

"But Marrow isn't actually dead, is he?" I kept thinking about the way he'd laughed with that sword sticking out of his body, as if he found death nothing but an amusing detour.

Lady Elaine glanced up at me, grimacing. "Probably not. But there's no way to be certain. So far there's been no sign of him. I expect there won't be any for some time to come. We did identify the website, however, but haven't been successful getting into it yet. Did you know that the name of it, Reckthaworlde, is an anagram for the Red Warlock?"

"I'm not surprised. It seems like the kind of thing . . . *Paul* . . . would do." Saying his name was hard. Thinking about him was even harder. I was doing my best not to.

"Mmmm," Lady Elaine said. "Paul has asked to see you. If you want, I will take you to where he's being held, once you're discharged."

I shook my head. My feelings about Paul were a giant tangled mess inside me. I didn't know what had been real about him and what hadn't. But I kept seeing his bruised face and wondering if the abuse, at least, had been real. I couldn't help thinking it was, and that it had played its part in sending him down Marrow's twisted path. Not that it excused the vile things he'd done.

"I don't want to see him," I said. "Ever."

Lady Elaine sighed. "I'm afraid you will have to face him sooner or later. During the trial, at the very least."

I swallowed. It was time for a subject change. "So what will happen now that people are allowed to do magic at will?"

She considered the question a moment. "Too early to say. So far, nothing seems to have changed. There's been no mass revolt or taking up of old prejudices. Things are different now than when The Will was first imposed. Attitudes have changed. Perhaps it will be all right. And I'm sure the senate will come up with other ways of keeping folks in check. There are all those Will-Workers in need of a job, after all."

I didn't reply, my thoughts on Eli. He had believed that people wouldn't suddenly become monsters just because they could. Maybe he was right. "So did the senate publically acknowledge that The Will's no more?"

"Yes. I don't believe they had a choice." An amused smile rose to Lady Elaine's face. "They've been surprisingly open about everything. They even sent representatives to explain matters to the students here during an assembly yesterday. They told them all about the Red Warlock and how you and your friends defeated him."

I gulped, uncertain how I felt about everybody knowing I'd killed a person. A part of me wished *I* didn't know it. I'd already had one nightmare about it. "Why would the senate do that?"

"Damage control. Marrow may be gone for now, but he has his followers. I imagine they feel the truth will help flush them out, in case any of them are students."

"Makes sense, I guess. Given Paul." I shivered from the idea and tried to push it from my mind.

Lady Elaine left a few minutes later, and I drifted off, not waking again until the next morning when the nurse arrived to dismiss me.

"You can visit your mother before you go if you'd like. She's in room twelve down the hall," said Nurse Philpot.

I thanked her as she left. I stayed in the room another couple of minutes, trying to muster the courage to face my mother while I changed out of the hospital gown into a pair of jeans and a shirt someone had fetched from my dorm room. Mom must hate me. Still, I had to see with my own eyes that she was okay, and I needed to say I was sorry, even if it didn't matter.

My mother was lying in the bed when I came through the door. Huge bruises rimmed her cheekbones, and she'd lost weight, making her look almost old. Though still beautiful.

"Hi, Mom," I said when she looked up at me. She didn't speak for at least a minute, and I stood there, wondering what to do. Saying I'm sorry didn't seem enough. "Are you feeling okay?"

"Better," said Moira.

"Oh, well, you look great."

She narrowed her bright eyes at me. "You never were much good at lying. I suppose that's one trait you didn't inherit from me."

I tried on a smile, but it felt weak around the edges. "I think that one's Dad's. But all the good ones are yours, right? Like the stubbornness and independence."

My mother returned the smile, shattering the tension between us. She held out her arms, and I ran forward, hugging her so hard she groaned.

"I'm so sorry, Mom," I whispered against her shoulder.

"It's all right." She stroked my hair. "It's my fault, too. I should've told you what I was doing. I should've been around more. You had no reason to trust me."

I pulled back and looked up at her. "That's not true. You were around, I just didn't pay attention."

Moira chuckled. "Your generous nature is *also* from your father. Speaking of which, you need to call him as soon as you can. I'm sure he's worried. But he has no idea what's been happening, and I suggest you don't tell him. If he finds out the kind of danger you've been in lately he'll kidnap you to Siberia."

"I promise I won't," I said, laughing.

"Good." She hugged me and whispered, "It was never about magic, Dusty. I've always loved you. Always. I just let my own selfishness, *childishness,* get in the way. But not anymore."

I nodded, tears stinging my eyes. It was the first time she'd ever called me Dusty. "I love you, too, Mom."

There was more to say, more healing that needed to

take place, but I knew this was the start of it. And I was glad.

I said good-bye a few minutes later and stepped back into the hallway. I turned to leave, but I noticed that the room beside my mother's was occupied. Mr. Culpepper was lying in the bed, with George the hellhound curled into a ball at his feet. I imagined the nursing staff was thrilled about that one.

I stopped in the doorway, staring in at him. He stared back, his expression inscrutable.

"Can I come in?" I asked, even as a part of me wondered what the hell I was doing.

"Okay," Culpepper said.

George raised his head and looked at me with his glowing eyes. But he didn't growl, which I took as a good sign.

"Are you doing okay?"

Culpepper grunted. "Been better. What do you want?"

I shoved my hands into my front pockets. "To, uh, say I'm sorry. For everything. And to thank you for helping us out."

He grunted again.

"But why did you help us?" The question had been bugging me for a while now. It seemed that a demon like Culpepper would stand to gain a lot more with Marrow in power than the Magi.

George made a strange, whining noise, and Culpepper patted him. "You mean why didn't I volunteer for that

~ 360 ~

lunatic's army?" He looked up at me. "Oh, yes, I was there. I heard him saying those things to you about putting ordinaries in their place and whatnot. But I don't believe in it. Not at all."

"Why not?"

"It's like they teach you in the military. Power has to be kept in check. You've got to have rules and guidelines for things to work proper. Otherwise people get hurt that don't need to."

I stared at him, my brow furrowed in confusion. "Okay, but what about your magic? I thought Metus feed off fear and stuff."

Culpepper's expression turned stony. "We do. But there's plenty of fear enough for me coming off you high school kids every day. Worries about tests and boyfriends, break-outs and squabbles with friends. I don't need nothing more."

I wasn't sure how I felt about this, but I couldn't help seeing him in a new light. "Well, I'm glad you're all right. I promise not to bother you again."

Culpepper tilted his head at me. "Does this mean you're not going to tell everybody about my business?"

I frowned, not having thought about the warehouse at all. "Um, sure. I mean, you're not planning on blowing up the school or anything, right?"

"Nope. And I don't sell the explosives, neither. I just like to be prepared in case Arkwell's ever attacked."

I decided his paranoia was a good thing, considering

that nobody knew when or if Marrow was coming back. "Well, okay, but I might hit you up for a candy bar or two every now and again," I said, grinning.

He rubbed the stubble on his chin. "Don't usually sell to students." He paused. "But I suppose I can make an exception for you."

The grin slid from my face as I remembered the files in his storeroom. "What about Rosemary?"

Culpepper shifted his gaze to the window, looking as if I'd slapped him. "She was an exception, too. Always so nice to me she was. So sad when she left that way." He faced me again, moisture in his eyes. "I'm glad you stopped her killer."

Unsure what to say, I nodded. When I left a moment later, I couldn't help thinking how strange it was that Culpepper turned out to be one of the good guys. I'd misjudged a lot of people it seemed. I vowed to work on that. I needed to stop jumping to conclusions and give people a chance no matter what. Who knew, maybe even Ms. Hardwick would turn out to be okay.

I checked the clock over the nurse's station as I passed and saw it was noon, which meant Selene and Eli were probably at lunch. Nurse Philpot had told me I was excused from classes for the rest of the week, but I wanted to see them.

When I walked into the cafeteria, everybody fell silent. I froze. I hadn't expected this kind of reception. I spotted Selene sitting at our usual table. Even from a distance, I could see the line of stitches running down one side of her face from the worst of the cuts the black phoenix had made. To my surprise, Eli was sitting with her.

I never knew who started it, but someone clapped, slowly at first and then with more enthusiasm. An embarrassed flush came over me as most everybody joined in. Next thing I knew Melanie Remillard was there, giving me a huge hug. She cried so hard she left wet marks on my shirt.

The applause didn't last long, but more than a few people told me how glad they were that I'd stopped the Red Warlock.

When I finally reached the table, Selene stood up and hugged me. "Don't feel weird," she said. "Everybody's been congratulating me and Eli, too."

"Oh, well, that's good."

As she let go, I said, "Are you okay?" The stitches weren't large, but the sight of them made my skin prickle with alarm. I wasn't used to her looking anything besides perfect. She was still beautiful, but different now.

Selene raised a hand to her face and touched the red puffy skin beneath one stitch. She smiled. "I'm fine. The doctor says it might leave a scar, but I'm okay with that." Her easy acceptance of it surprised me.

Before I could question her further, Eli pulled me in for a hug, enveloping me with his arms and dwarfing me with his body. "We did it," he whispered against my ear. His breath made me shiver. He took his time letting go, and I knew in that moment the kiss hadn't been a dream. He cared about me; we were something more than friends. *Dream-seers.*

I wanted to be happy about it, but I was afraid to read too much into it. Thoughts of Paul kept crowding my mind, provoking that ache in my heart.

As he stepped away from me, I saw Lance watching us from across the cafeteria. No, that wasn't right. He was watching Selene, not me, his gaze locked onto her like a missile-targeting system. He looked pissed off, but somehow I didn't get the impression the anger was directed at her.

Across from Lance, Katarina was watching us, too. Her face looked red from crying.

"You hungry?" said Eli. "I can go through the line for you."

"Um, okay." I wasn't in the mood to eat, but I wanted to talk to Selene alone.

I sat down as Eli left and said, "So what's the deal?"

"They broke up, or are on a break or something," said Selene.

I blinked, surprised she'd known exactly what I was referring to. It was a testament to how well she knew me. "Why?"

"Because of what Paul did to you. I think Eli was worried Katarina was manipulating him."

"Do you think she was?" I'd suspected it before, but I didn't want to offend Selene by assuming all sirens acted that way.

"Not like Paul was." Selene's expression darkened. "Most sirens can't help themselves when it comes to manipulating. It's our nature. And it's expected, too, you know? That's why I keep saying we've got to change the system and stop treating sirens like sex objects." She slapped the table in emphasis.

I grinned at her enthusiasm and the underlying confidence I sensed behind it. That surety hadn't been there before. I was thankful for the distraction from thinking about Paul. Only, I couldn't help feeling a bit sorry for Katarina. Selene was right. She hadn't done anything like what Paul had done, and I thought her feelings for Eli were probably genuine. She had no reason to use him, after all.

Eli returned a moment later with my tray.

"Thanks," I said.

"No problem."

We ate in silence for a couple of moments.

After a while, Eli leaned across the table toward me and said, "You know. There's really something to this dream-seer stuff. I was thinking we should start our own private investigation service. We could take on student clients for now and maybe teachers and staff later. I bet between the dreams and our natural investigative instincts, we could do a lot of good."

I frowned at him. "We can't just point the dreams at whatever mystery we're trying to solve and figure it out."

"Sure we can."

"*Hel-lo*? Remember the stuff Bethany said about manipulating dreams and trapping people?"

"She lied. Or exaggerated greatly, to be more accurate."

"How do you know?"

"He asked Lady Elaine about it," said Selene, patting her lips with a napkin.

Eli nodded. "She came to see me in the hospital. Apparently, we're *supposed* to do that kind of thing. Lady Elaine thinks Bethany just told you that because she wanted you to keep suspecting your mom and not her. That, and she didn't want us spying on what Marrow was up to, like we did when the phoenix attacked us."

I chewed on my bottom lip, thinking it over. "But if she only exaggerated, then there's still a risk, right?"

Eli waved a dismissive hand. "Not enough to worry about. We'll be careful."

I didn't answer.

"Oh, come on, Dusty," said Eli, his blue eyes fixed on my face in a way that made me want to squirm. "Together, we're unstoppable. Besides, what else have we got to dream about now that we found the killer?"

I began to fiddle with my hair, dropping my gaze off Eli. "Nothing, I guess." *Well, not until the Red Warlock comes back.*

"If you two are starting a detective agency, I want in," said Selene, adjusting her ball cap.

"Well, duh," said Eli, beaming at her.

"And we're going to need a name," Selene said. "Something good and catchy."

"You're right." Eli scratched his chin. "How about the Arkwell Detective Agency. The A.D.A."

Selene wrinkled her nose. "Sounds too much like a chemical or something."

"What about Booker and Associates?"

I rolled my eyes. "It's not all about you, you know?"

Eli grinned. "Says who?"

"I think we should call it Selene Investigations."

"No, Nightmare Investigations."

"Dreamer Investigations."

"The Dream Team."

"How about Magic Eyes? You know, like private eyes, only for magic."

"Corny much?"

On and on it went, everybody arguing and trying to one-up the other. But it was all in good fun. After a while, I realized I was even *having* fun. Despite the terror we'd faced down in the tunnels, death and blood and all things horrible, we were okay. Funny how having friends beside you could do that. With friends, you could survive just about anything.

Exclusive:
Mindee Arnett retells the pivotal first scene of
The Nightmare Affair from Eli's point of view

Prelude to a Nightmare

Eli Booker didn't know he was dreaming.

In fact, he might never have realized it if the girl with the red hair hadn't appeared in the graveyard. At first she was just an odd flash of color out of the corner of his eye, something he would've ignored if his senses weren't already so keyed up from the presence of a murder victim not ten feet from where he stood.

He turned his head, his jaw slackening as he realized it was a girl, just a teenager wearing all black like some kind of ninja-wannabe assassin. A ping of recognition struck him, but he couldn't quite bring a name to match the face. She was pretty, even though her goth-girl-gone-funeral wardrobe made her fair skin look washed out. But there was something off about her, too, the way she moved, as if she wasn't quite present. A ghost maybe.

No, that couldn't be right. Ghosts weren't real.

Eli blinked, shaking off his confusion. Then he fixed a glare at her. *What's she doing at a crime scene?*

He paused as a new and alarming thought occurred to him: *What am I doing at a crime scene?*

Eli pulled his gaze away from the girl, a sensation of vertigo sweeping over him, as if the ground had tipped forward. He thrust his hands in front of his body, bracing against air. The feeling passed a moment later, and when it did, he realized the redhead wasn't the only one sporting a strange outfit. *What the hell?* Why was he wearing one of his dad's suits? The hideous orange and blue necktie brought an automatic gag to his throat. He grabbed it, about to rip it off, but froze as the redhead began to move. She glided forward in that ghost-like way until she reached the body of the dead girl splayed among the crumbling, ancient headstones.

As she knelt beside the body, Eli opened his mouth to tell her to stop. She would destroy the evidence. Only, why did he care? He wasn't a cop. His father was. *Then why am I wearing his clothes?*

The answer came at once like a blast of wind on a cold day: *I'm dreaming.*

Once he realized it, all the wrongness of the scene struck him. The half dozen police officers standing nearby were wearing outdated uniforms; his dad's department had replaced the pale blue shirts with black ones months ago. And one of the officers was Bernie Mahanoy, only he'd transferred to another department last year.

Even stranger, Eli had no recollection of how he'd gotten here or even where here was. The cemetery was like something out of a gothic horror movie, the giant, ivy-covered mausoleums of the sort that might house a dozen zombies, easily.

Thank goodness I'm armed. One headshot should . . .

Eli shook his head. That was the wrong thought. A dream thought. He was dreaming. He glanced back at the redhead. If this was his dream, then what was she doing here? And why did she feel so wrong? Almost . . . like an intruder.

Tension spread though his body as he walked nearer to the redhead. The shift in position brought the dead body into partial view. The victim was another teenage girl, this one blonde and completely unfamiliar to Eli. Puffy, dark strangulation marks rimmed the girl's throat, and her right hand had been cut off at the wrist, the hand itself missing. *Taken like a trophy.* This time the thought didn't feel wrong at all. Just the opposite. Somehow that bothered him even more than the rest of it.

The redhead at last stood up and turned around, moving so quickly that for a second, Eli thought she might break into a run. A stricken expression marred her face, her full, pink lips drawn into a tight line, and her pale eyes hooded.

That was until her gaze landed on him, and her mouth expanded into a horrified "O." She stumbled to the right, swerving to avoid him. Eli gaped, surprised and more than a little offended by her response—pretty girls normally didn't react that way to him. Did he have horns growing out of his head or something? Volcanic-worthy pimples on his face?

Before he could check, she was walking past him fast enough to stir the air between them. On impulse, he reached out and grabbed her arm.

She jerked to a stop, and as her head turned toward him, her expression even more horrified than before, Eli felt the ground pitch forward again, this time giving way completely. His vision went black, and his body dropped into sudden free fall.

He woke with a start, his heart in his throat and his lungs seizing as he struggled to draw a breath. *That was one helluva night . . .*

The thought died inside his brain as he realized the reason he couldn't breathe had nothing at all to do with fear, and everything to do with the girl sitting on his chest. He had the feeling she'd been touching his forehead a moment before, but now she had her fingers pressed against her temples as if to still her pounding head.

At the sight of her, Eli didn't think, just reacted—placing his hands on her arms and shoving. She toppled backward right off the bed, letting out a pathetic little yelp as she hit the floor.

Eli winced. *Stupid.* What had he been thinking, hitting a girl?

Yeah, but she broke into your house, and was sitting on top of you! a voice argued in his head.

Ignoring it, Eli swung back the covers and stood up, barely aware that he was wearing only red boxers. Cool air from the open second-story window across the way licked at his chest. He bent over the girl, who was struggling to catch her breath. He grasped her by the arms, picked her up, and set her on her feet. He had half a foot on her easily, and she seemed to weigh hardly anything at all.

Before he had even let go of her, she pointed a hand at him and said, "Aphairein!"

Something invisible bumped against his ribcage. It didn't hurt, but he sensed the thing rebound and slam into the girl as hard as a lineman on the football field. As she stumbled backward, Eli tightened his grip on her shoulders, meaning to keep her upright, but the force of it was so strong he lost his balance and they both fell. His hard, large body was squashed against her much softer—and very feminine—one.

A flush heated his skin. He must've fantasized about some hot girl breaking into his bedroom in the middle of the night a hundred times, but somehow, he never imagined it going quite like this.

"Get off," she said, pushing against him. Then she spoke that strange, nonsensical word again and that invisible something bumped against him once more.

Eli rolled off her and stood up, his bewilderment and embarrassment provoking his temper. He pointed down at her, finding his voice at last. "Who the hell are you?"

The girl, whose hair he now realized was a bright shade of red, leaped to her feet, the movement bringing her closer to the window and in full display of the moonlight.

Eli sucked in a breath, half choking, as recognition struck him. It was the girl from his dream. *Dusty Everhart*, the name finally came to him. She'd gone to his school up until last year. He'd heard she transferred to that shady private school, Arkwell Academy. He'd seen her dozens of times over the years—mostly because she was the kind of girl you couldn't help but *see*—but it was always at a distance. Their paths had never crossed before until tonight.

"I know *you*," he said. "What are you doing here? And what's wrong with your eyes? They're . . . *glowing?*" A thrill, half of fear, half of wonderment, slid over his spine, making his muscles tense. Her eyes looked as bright as lamplights or two pieces of shining crystal. "What kind of *freak* are you?"

Dusty flinched, and Eli realized too late that he'd spoken that last part aloud—*you idiot.*

The panicked expression on her face flashed to anger. "At least I'm not the freak dreaming about dead girls."

He gaped. "How do you know that?"

She blinked, and then her gaze flashed to his bedroom door just as he heard the distinctive pound of footsteps beyond it. Great, his dad was coming, and he had a girl in his room. *Won't that be fun to explain.*

But as he looked back, Dusty jumped up onto the window ledge and climbed out, disappearing. Alarmed, Eli charged over and leaned out the second-story window. Below, he watched as Dusty reached the ground then stepped away from the drainpipe she'd used as an escape ladder. She peered up at him.

And stuck out her tongue.

Eli almost laughed. The gesture was somehow both feisty and adorable—maybe even a little sexy, too. Only nothing in the last five minutes had made any sense whatsoever, and all he could do was stare after her as she raced down the sidewalk, disappearing around the nearest corner.

He heard the door to his bedroom swing open a second later.

"What's going on?" his father shouted. "Was there somebody in here?"

Eli turned around, his eyebrows raising at the sight of his dad in his blue bathrobe, Marvin the Martian boxer shorts, and .40 S&W, police-standard handgun in the ready position. "Uh . . ." Eli sputtered as his brain tried to form a coherent thought.

His dad ignored him and strode over to the window, peering out. "Did somebody break in?"

Eli opened his mouth to finally answer, but froze at the sound of the doorbell.

His dad, looking more than a little crazy with his black, silver streaked hair standing up in weird places and a scowl on his face, brushed past him toward the door. "Stay here," he said over his shoulder.

"The hell I will," Eli muttered, taking off after him. He paused just long enough to slip on the pair of jeans he'd left discarded on the floor when he'd gone to bed hours before.

But by the time Eli climbed down the stairs and reached the front door, his father had already opened it to the sight of four large men wearing dark suits. *FBI*, was Eli's immediate thought, and when the nearest man reached inside his jacket and withdrew a badge, he believed he was right. Except . . .

"What is that supposed to be?" his dad said, gesturing at the badge. "A prop for your Halloween costume?"

The man made a noise that sounded strangely close to a growl. "Like I said. We are the magickind police, investigating a disturbance at this house. We need you and your son to come with us for a debriefing."

Magickind? The image of Dusty pointing at him and speaking those strange, nonsensical words flashed in Eli's mind. Magic? Had that been . . . had that . . . ?

No. That's crazy.

Even if it wasn't, how could these policemen have gotten here so fast?

Simple, more magic.

Shaking his head at the thought, Eli turned and headed up the stairs.

"Where are you going, son?" the man said, that same growl in his voice.

Eli looked over his shoulder at him. "Back to bed. I'm pretty sure I'm still dreaming."

Only he wasn't dreaming, as he found out a short while later. Dusty, the dead girl in the graveyard, the magickind policemen. All of it was real. And the life he knew, the world that had once made sense, vanished forever.

Just like a dream upon waking.

Turn the page for a sneak peek at Mindee Arnett's new novel

~The~
Nightmare Dilemma

Available March 2014

～ 1 ～

Where No Nightmare Has Gone Before

The mermaid was lying on the hospital bed, looking distinctly un-mermaidish. And not just because she was in her human form. Britney Shell looked more like a zombie with her skin the color of cigar ash and ghoulish lines of black stitches across her forehead, cheeks, and neck.

I turned to face the only other person in the room, the woman who'd summoned me out of my dorm in the middle of the night to the school's infirmary for a reason I was sure I didn't want to know. Lady Elaine stood near the foot of the bed, her pale, cloudy eyes fixed on Britney. She was an old woman, and tiny, hardly bigger than a kid. But that didn't make her any less intimidating. As a chief advisor to the Magi Senate, her presence at Arkwell Academy meant trouble.

"What happened to her?" I said.

A grimace crossed Lady Elaine's thin face, turning the wrinkles into deep crevices. "We don't know. That's why you're here. To help us find out."

"Me? What can I do?"

"You're a Nightmare."

I frowned. Not because this was an insult or anything. It was true. I am a Nightmare, or at least a half one. My mom's a full Nightmare, but my dad's an ordinary human. Not that you can tell by looking at me. For the most part, Nightmares look like ordinaries, but we're magical beings who feed on human dreams.

"You want me to dream-feed on her?"

"Precisely," Lady Elaine said, clanking her teeth.

I didn't know why I was surprised. There wasn't any other reason a person as important as Lady Elaine would want someone like me here. Britney and I were friends, but given the number of magickind police officers waiting out in the hallway, I didn't think this was a bedside vigil.

I shifted my weight from one foot to the other. "How's that supposed to help? Dream-feeding doesn't heal people, right? I mean, if it does, then calling my kind Nightmares is like false advertisement."

Lady Elaine scowled. "Now's not the time for cheek, Destiny Everhart."

"It's Dusty," I mumbled, looking back at Britney. Guilt made my skin prickle. Lady Elaine was right. Now wasn't the time for smart-ass remarks, but I couldn't help it. Seeing Britney like this freaked me out, an event that never failed to make my mouth run away with me.

Lady Elaine let out an exaggerated sigh. Out of the corner of my eye, I watched her turn and sit down in a chair on the other side of the bed. Like everything else in the room, the chair was the mottled gray color of cinder blocks.

Lady Elaine's feet dangled two inches above the ground. "You're here because you might be able to identify Britney's attacker by what you see in her dream."

More confused than ever, I swung toward her. It wasn't the first time I'd been asked to identify a bad guy through someone's dream. A few months ago I discovered I was a dream-seer, that I could see the future in certain dreams. But . . .

"I thought my dream-seer skills only work in Eli's dreams."

Lady Elaine waved a hand at me. "I'm not asking you to predict the future but to read the past."

"Huh?"

She sighed again, clearly at the end of her patience. Not that this was anything new. She crossed one leg over the other, feet swinging. "Whoever attacked Britney did so less than an hour ago. And as far as we can tell, she's been in a constant dream-state ever since. If she saw the person, there's a good chance his image has left a residue on her dream."

"A residue?"

"Yes, a *magical* residue," said Lady Elaine. "She was hit by a powerful curse. One we haven't been able to identify yet. But all magic leaves traces of the person who wielded it, and only a very few magickind would be skilled enough to remove those traces."

I considered the idea, pushing back strands of my curly red hair that had escaped my haphazard ponytail. "So it's kind of like a fingerprint or DNA."

Lady Elaine gave me a blank stare.

I crossed my arms, wishing I'd worn something more substantial than a hoodie, hastily donned over my pink-and-red-striped pajamas. The mid-April rain outside tapped against the windowpane, putting a damp chill in the air. "You know, like forensic science stuff. How ordinary cops figure out who the bad guy is."

Lady Elaine's stare deepened toward incredulity.

I couldn't figure out what her deal was. Most magic-kind were junkies for ordinary pop culture. "Don't you watch TV?"

She looked taken aback by the question, but recovered quickly. "Not *those* kinds of shows."

I raised an eyebrow, wondering what kinds of shows she *did* watch.

"But I suppose your interpretation is correct," said Lady Elaine. "It is something like magical DNA."

Which made me the scientist in this scenario. What a joke.

Still, I didn't protest as I turned my gaze back to Britney. If she'd been hit by a curse, then it was my fault. I might not have done the actual cursing, but I'd played a big part in making it possible for magickind to use combative spells whenever they wanted. It used to be that such magic was prohibited by The Will, a massive spell designed to keep magickind in line. But I inadvertently helped destroy The Will a couple of months ago. At least I'd been fighting an evil warlock at the time, one with Hitlerish ideas about world domination.

Small comfort now.

And no comfort at all to Britney. She looked miserable, her expression pained even in sleep. Her eyelids quivered as her eyes pulsed back and forth beneath them.

Even though I knew I was responsible, I didn't want to dream-feed on her. What if I messed up? I might miss something important.

I cleared my throat. "Isn't there some other Nightmare better qualified?"

"No," Lady Elaine said, a pointed edge to her voice. "Well, yes, there are certainly others more qualified, but none available tonight. Someone else was supposed to be here, but they've been delayed, Bethany Grey is still imprisoned, and your mother is still out of town. Which leaves only you."

I swallowed hard, my stomach twisting into a knot. The pathetically small number of Nightmares in existence wasn't something I wanted to think about right now. This attack on Britney was just another in a string of magickind-on-magickind violence that had been happening since The Will broke. The same kind of violence responsible for my lack of Nightmare relatives.

Screwing up my courage, I said, "So you want me to figure out who she's dreaming about."

Lady Elaine gave me a tight-lipped smile. "Yes. Just observe and report."

Sounded simple enough, although in my experience nothing to do with magic was ever simple.

I drew a breath. "Okay, but tell me more first. Who found her? Where was she?"

Lady Elaine frowned. "There's no time for details. She might stop dreaming any moment, and the longer we wait the fainter the residue becomes."

"I get it, but her dreams aren't going to be all clear like Eli's. If I've any hope of spotting the person, I need to know more about what to look for."

This sounded mostly true, even to my ears, but secretly I was thinking about how if Eli were here he would demand to know more. Ever since we defeated the evil warlock, Marrow, he'd had his heart set on starting an amateur student detective agency. We'd worked one minor "case" involving a stolen necklace, but this was the first hard-core mystery. He would want to investigate. As always, thoughts of Eli made me feel both flustered and comforted at the same time, a result of our more-than-friends-but-not-really status.

"Fine." Lady Elaine stood up, her heels giving a little click as her feet touched the floor. She marched past me out the door. I heard a murmur of voices, and then she reentered the room, followed by a tall, hairy-looking man in a dark blue policeman's uniform.

Sheriff Brackenberry fixed an irritated look at me. It was the same look he'd given me when I arrived a few minutes ago and Lady Elaine had asked him to wait out in the hall. I couldn't decide if his irritation was strictly for me or just a side effect of being bossed around by a little old lady. Probably both. I smiled sheepishly back at him, trying to win him over. Not only was he the magickind sheriff, he was also head werewolf, which made him only slightly less scary than Lady Elaine.

"We need to hurry this up," said Brackenberry. "Britney here is due to be transferred to Vejovis Hospital as soon as you're done."

The knot in my stomach twisted harder. Her injuries must be pretty bad if they were sending her there. I opened my mouth to tell him no need to bother with the details, but he started speaking before I got the chance.

"She was discovered at approximately eleven forty-five P.M. by Ms. Hardwick in one of the alcoves of the tunnel between the library and Flint Hall," said Brackenberry.

I grimaced at this news. Ms. Hardwick was the school janitor and resident hag. Definitely not the kind of person I wanted to meet inside a dream. Especially one other than Eli's. With any luck, she hadn't been involved, although I wouldn't put it past her.

"There was no apparent sign of a struggle," Brackenberry went on. "But Britney was lying half in, half out of the water, which suggests she might've been trying to flee her attacker. It appears Ms. Hardwick arrived only minutes afterward, but she didn't see anyone else." Brackenberry's tone turned scornful. "Is that enough information for you?"

I gulped. "I think I can make do with it."

"Well, go on then." He shooed at me.

I bit my lip. "Would you, um, mind leaving again?" Dream-feeding was kind of personal, and the last thing I wanted was a male audience.

If I'd been a bowl of ice cream I might have melted on the spot from the hot intensity of his stare. I glanced at Lady Elaine, hoping for some support, but she looked as impatient as the sheriff.

Resigning myself to the inevitable, I walked around to the side of the bed. I was just about to climb onto it and resume the proper Nightmare position, when I remembered a mere touch would do. I closed my eyes and reached my hands toward Britney's forehead.

"What are you doing?" Lady Elaine said.

I looked over my shoulder. "Checking her temperature."

She stomped her foot. "Not like that. This is too important, Dusty. You need to be in the traditional position to get the deepest connection to her dreams."

It was my turn to scowl as I climbed onto the bed. I hadn't dream-fed on anyone besides Eli in a long while. And feeding on a girl, especially one my age, just felt weird. There was nothing sexual about dream-feeding, but the pose was a bit on the lewd side.

I swung one foot over Britney's middle. Then I squatted down onto her chest, doing my best to keep as much weight off her as I could. I wasn't that heavy, but Britney was smaller than me, and I didn't want to hurt her.

As always, the moment I was in place, instinct took over. Britney was dreaming, all right. The stuff of those dreams, the fictus, made something deep inside me burn with a terrible thirst. A thirst for magic.

Closing my eyes, I stretched my hands toward her

temple. When my skin touched hers, I felt my consciousness slip from my body and slide down, down, down into the world of Britney's dream.

A swirl of colors—a chaotic mixture of blues, purples, and greens—enveloped me like some kind of living light, warm and pulsating with energy. It lasted a long time before the chaos settled, and I found myself in a dark, damp cave. A single torch hung nearby, its light making the wet walls around it glisten and reflecting in the water from the canal that ran parallel to the walkway I stood on. To my left and right, the canal and walkway disappeared into the blackness of a long tunnel. Across from me, the canal widened into a small, circular pool, one of the many alcoves in Arkwell's tunnel system.

The clarity of my surroundings surprised me. Most dreams, aside from Eli's, were confused, disorienting things, usually in black-and-white, but this place was so real for a moment I thought I'd been transported here in the waking world.

The illusion broke almost at once. The walls began to lean inward, as if the tunnel were being drawn in on itself. The natural orange glow of the torch turned a molten red. And the water began to bubble and spurt in a rapid boil.

A scream rang out even louder than the raging water. I looked down to see Britney's head break the surface of the alcove's pool. I'd never seen her in her natural mermaid form, but I knew her skin should be pale, almost translucent, not the angry red color it was now. Blisters popped up on her skin. She was being cooked alive.

No, this wasn't real. This wasn't even a dream.

It was a nightmare.

My first instinct was to change the dream, manipulate the setting to somewhere safe and calm, but I resisted. Watch and observe, Lady Elaine had said.

It was hard, especially as Britney swam toward the edge of the pool, struggling to pull herself out of the water. I wanted to help her, but I couldn't, not here. Any physical contact with my dream-subject and I would be kicked out.

I closed my eyes, unable to watch any longer. I was about to cover my ears when everything went silent. I opened my eyes again, relieved to see the scene had shifted on its own. The tunnel had given way to a strange, small room with bright, colorful walls. I felt oddly weightless, and as strands of my red hair swam into my vision, I realized I was under water. As soon as I thought it, I became aware of the wetness and a sudden need to breathe.

Britney floated a few feet away from me in her mermaid form, her long tail a strawberry pink color that matched her hair. I focused my imagination on copying her form, and a moment later my body had transformed into a mermaid and my panic subsided.

I looked around at what I guessed was her bedroom. No furniture decorated the place, unless you counted the gigantic sea anemone growing along one side of the room that looked big enough to sleep in. But there was something personal and bedroom-ish about the trinkets set on the floor-to-ceiling shelves built into the coral walls.

Before I could examine the items, an odd, garbled,

shrieking sound drew my attention. It seemed to be coming from Britney, who had her back to me. I swam to the left to see around her. Another mermaid floated in a small opening into the room. She had the same strawberry pink-colored hair, and I guessed it was Britney's mother. They were arguing. Loudly. But in mermench.

Even though I couldn't understand them, there was no mistaking the animosity. Fury seemed to emanate from both, but when I caught a sideways glance at Britney, she looked frightened, too.

The scene changed once more, the colors melting and bleeding together before righting again. This time Britney and I stood in the middle of a forest full of dead, deteriorated trees like hundreds of brittle finger bones sticking up from the earth. A stream full of glowing green water ran sluggishly through the trees. Garbage lined its banks. A terrible chemical smell hung in the air, burning my nose. The stench of rotting fish blended in with it. Several animals moved among the trees, all of them looking as sick and listless as the water in the stream. A deer hobbled past me on three legs, scorch marks on its body.

The scene shifted again. We were back in the tunnel, but the water no longer boiled. This time Britney stood beside the alcove's pool in her human form, her hair more blond than pink, her skin fair but not covered in translucent scales. A dark figure stood a few feet down the tunnel across from her, face hidden in shadows.

The residue. I moved toward the figure, eager to see his face and leave this dream behind. But the scene shifted again, back to the underwater bedroom. The change was so abrupt, I fought back dizziness. Pinwheeling my arms through the water, I focused on Britney still caught up in the argument with her mother.

A moment later, we were back in the forest. But as with the tunnel scene, we were no longer alone. Britney was arguing with a guy, one whose face made my heartbeat double and all the air vanish from my lungs. Paul Foster Kirkwood, my ex-boyfriend. What was he doing in Britney's dream? For a moment, I thought he must be her attacker, until I remembered that Paul was in jail, awaiting trial for his involvement with Marrow's scheme to overthrow the magickind government.

I took a step toward him and realized it wasn't Paul, not exactly, but close, as if Britney had seen the real Paul but her dreaming mind had forgotten the details.

The scene shifted again, back to the tunnel. After that, the changes started happening so quickly, my vision blurred as if I were riding an ultrafast merry-go-round. I tried to close my eyes, but couldn't. I kept catching glimpses of the almost-Paul and Britney's mother, even Britney herself, crying out in pain.

Finally, when I didn't think I could stand it any longer, I reached out with my Nightmare magic and willed the dream to stop its chaotic swirl. At once, everything went still.

The scene before me was the strangest yet. It seemed to be a mash-up of the three scenes, blended into one. I stood in the tunnel again, but the walls were now made up of those spindly, dead trees. The canal water glowed the same sickly green of the stream. It wasn't boiling. In fact it wasn't moving at all, but looked as if it had been frozen in place.

Glancing around, I realized that everything was frozen, including Britney, who hung suspended mid-jump into the pool. A look of terror darkened her features. Behind her, I saw the shadowed figure again, frozen as well, but in an attack position, one arm stretched out in front of him as if he were hurling a knife at Britney's back.

I took a step toward the figure, and pictured a flashlight in my hand. It appeared there at once. I switched it on and shone it at the person. He carried a wand, held out in front of him like a gun. I raised the light to his face and let out an involuntary gasp of alarm. It wasn't Paul, as I'd expected. It wasn't even Britney's mother.

It was Eli Booker.

Mindee Arnett lives on a horse farm in Ohio with her husband, two kids, a couple of dogs, and an inappropriate number of cats. She's addicted to jumping horses and telling tales of magic and the macabre. Her short stories have appeared in various magazines, and she has a master of arts in English literature with an emphasis in creative writing. She also blogs and tweets, and is hard at work on her next novel in the Arkwell Academy series. Find her online at www.mindeearnett.com.